LIES IN
THE DARK

Liars and Vampires
Book 4

Robert J. Crane
with Lauren Harper

Lies in the Dark
Liars and Vampires, Book 4

Robert J. Crane
with Lauren Harper
Copyright © 2018 Ostiagard Press
All Rights Reserved.

1st Edition

Chapter 1

Witness me, a normal girl, ending a normal day of school.

Saying goodbye to her totally normal friend with the blue hair—bye, Xandra!—exchanging waves, promising to call later, and ducking out of the sunny, locker-lined halls into the Tampa sunshine.

The air smells faintly of magnolia blossoms and salt water—also normal. The crowd forms to get on the school buses parked outside. There's shoving, jockeying for position, boasts, shouts, laughter.

All totally normal.

And here I am, normal girl, following my mom's totally normal order to get on the bus and be home by quarter after three in the afternoon. On the dot.

But ... I'm not really normal.

Which is why instead of getting on the bus, I gave a quick glance around to make sure no one was watching totes innocuous, totes normal me—

Then, in defiance of Mom's orders, I bailed for the parking lot, where a long, black stretch limo and a driver with brilliant green eyes waited for me. The driver opened the door and I ducked inside, where the tinted windows were so dark it practically felt like night.

"Well, hello."

And there, in the shadows, waited my vampire boyfriend.

This, for me, is totally normal. At least ... lately.

Mill's hair was slightly ruffled, his blue-grey eyes tired but happy. Today he'd donned a crisp navy suit with a white shirt, and wing-tipped shoes. Sharp. A little more formal than usual, but if he was willing to go out of his way to look good for me, I'd go out of my way to appreciate it.

"Hi," I said, a little out of breath, both from the run over and the closeness to Mill.

He lifted his arm, and I immediately scooched myself across the warm leather seat to slide in.

Lockwood, our driver, closed the door behind me and made his way toward the front of the limo.

Mill smiled a sleepy smile at me when I gazed up at him and planted a cold, firm kiss on my lips. Daylight hours were when he usually slept. A tingling rush spread all the way to my fingertips.

I didn't think that would ever get old.

"How was school?" he asked.

"Fine," I said. We could have been talking about the weather and I would have been happy. As long as I got a few minutes with him, it didn't really matter.

"You got out a little later today."

"Yeah. Chemistry test was a little more difficult than I expected. Had to rush through the last three questions, but then I got caught up talking to the teacher so …" I shrugged. "Here I am. Late. Done. Yay."

The engine hummed to life as Lockwood resumed his seat in the front.

Mill was drawing little circles on my arm with his thumb, his touch cool and comforting.

"This just means we have to get you home sooner," Mill said.

"Not an issue, sir," Lockwood said from the front. "I can take a shortcut."

I sighed heavily, resting my head on Mill's shoulder. "When will this torture end?" I asked dramatically, my bottom lip pouting out. I touched his coat. Soft, well made. Probably cost more than my college tuition would.

Mill brushed my lip with the tip of his finger. "We'll take whatever time we can, right?"

"Hey, complaining about parents is a time-honored

tradition among teenagers. Gimme a minute to gripe, okay?"

"I'd rather use our time together more wisely," he said. "Instead of whine about your parents the whole time."

I raised my eyebrows. "Did you just say 'whine'?"

He looked away from me and out of the dark windows. The street beyond was barely visible, whizzing by as Lockwood drove us along. "I meant … never mind what I meant."

I stared at the side of his face. His jaw, strong and prominent, was tight. His shoulders were tense. His eyelids were heavy.

"You're crabby," I told him plainly, returning to the crook of his arm.

"Am not," he said, and then softened. "All right, maybe a little. I should be sleeping right now."

"But you'd rather be spending time with me?" I said hopefully.

"I'd rather be spending time with you, yes." He pressed a small kiss on top of my head.

"I really wish I wasn't still grounded," I said. "I probably will be for the rest of my life. I'll be lucky if I'm un-grounded before I'm in a nursing home."

"Your teeth will fall out before you're free again." Mill smirked.

I shook my head, chuckling. Ever the romantic. And so focused on dental hygiene, these vampires.

"But seriously … you know we have a security camera on the front porch? She has it all set up to her phone, ready and waiting to catch me coming home even a second late …"

"You've been dodging her just fine for weeks now," he said. "It'll all work out."

"I don't know," I said. "She's been in kind of a … mood since we got back from New York. And it's not improving."

"Oh?"

A tightness formed in my chest. "I guess she heard back from the insurance company. Finally. They're refusing to pay so far. She thinks we're going to have to sue them."

"Good luck with that," Mill said. "Insurance companies get a little touchy about arson. Especially an unsolved one."

"Urgh," I said. "I wish I could have handed the guilty parties over to the police, but they would have burned up at sunrise when the sunlight came flooding into the jail cell." Damned vampires. Except for the one who was nuzzling me now.

Speaking of, he stopped, and I raised my head. Mill was giving me a look.

"Right, sorry. Complaining. I'll stop."

He squeezed me more tightly against him, the coolness of his body helping to take some of the angry heat away.

"One day you'll be free again," he said. "And we can … hang out properly." He stiffened. "That is what they call it these days? 'Hanging out'? Or 'hooking up,' or something?"

"Um …hanging out, yes, that works. But maybe someday we can … yes, hang out properly. At night. When you won't have to worry about the sun or getting caught by my vengeful mother."

"That … would be nice," Mill said. "Maybe get some … pizza? Netflix and chill?"

I suppressed a giggle. "I don't think we're quite ready for 'Netflix and chill.' And pizza? Really? I thought that you said that—"

But whatever I had thought he had said was lost, because just then, something slammed into the limo and sent me hurtling against the side of the car as glass shattered all around me.

Chapter 2

I was upside down when the world stopped tumbling. Or maybe the world was upside down. All I could be sure of was the ringing in my ears and the pounding in my head.

Light was coming in from somewhere above me, and I could hear muffled shouts, almost as if I was at the end of a long tunnel.

I blinked, but everything was hazy.

There was a strong metallic smell in the air, and my fingertips were numb.

I realized then that they were trapped beneath me.

Cas … sie …

Who was calling me? Where was I?

What had happened?

"Cassie!"

I opened my eyes and stared straight ahead. The top of the limo was there, and it was suddenly a lot brighter inside.

"Mill?"

He leaned over me, and I felt his hands underneath me, trying to lift me. I was flat against the carpeted floor, its fuzziness tickling my ears, my head resting heavily against it.

"You're okay," he said. Light was shining around us, but Mill was crouched down, avoiding the beams. He looked pale.

"What happened?" I asked, rising to my knees.

He brushed his sleeve against his nose. His beautiful suit was ruined. "An accident, I think." The air held a slightly

ROBERT J. CRANE with LAUREN HARPER

smoky quality.

My bones turned to liquid, the blood in my veins to ice. My head just ached through it all.

"Mr. Mill!" Lockwood's shouts came through the window separating the driver from the back. "Mr. Mill, are you and Miss Cassandra all right?" He peered through a small vertical gap in the divider.

"Serves me right for not wearing a seatbelt," I said, rubbing the back of my neck.

"We're all right," Mill said. "What hit us?"

"I—" Lockwood said. "I'm not sure. But it was no traffic collision."

The tentative nature of his voice amped up my own worries, sending shivers all down my limbs.

"Mill," I said, "the sunlight."

I was looking back toward the seats where we had been seated before being flung forward, and saw that the back windows had been broken. Bright, golden sunlight was beaming down right on the spot where Mill had been.

"Oh, I've noticed," he said, keeping his head down. "Believe me." He smiled tightly, and I realized that smoky smell was not the engine on fire—

It was him, catching stray UV rays.

"This isn't good," I said with my usual talent for understatement. "Mill, don't move. I'll try and—"

BOOM.

My shoulder collided with the side of the limo, pain shooting up the side of my arm.

There was another clatter of breaking glass, the window right over my shoulder bursting into a hundred pieces.

I ducked my head, but pebbled glass rained down across my skin on my back, my neck, my shoulders like a hard shower.

Hot, bright sunlight fell upon my back, and I froze.

"Mill, move!" I said.

Mill was way ahead of me.

He had pulled his knees in, his feet just out of the reach of the beams, throwing himself against the driver's compartment of the limo. There he huddled, barely out of

8

reach of the light. Sweat slid down his forehead, making him look waxy.

"It's okay," he said. "I can stay here like this until—"

The moonroof overhead shattered, glittering pebbles of glass tumbling down into the limo. I dodged away as it fell, allowing even more brilliant light inside.

The shafts of light cornered Mill up against the back of Lockwood's seat. His knees were now pulled up to his chest, his head bent low.

"Don't … move …" I told him, my voice shaking.

"I have to cover myself," he said, his lips tight. He put his hands up, carefully avoiding a stray beam that shone right over his head as he slipped off his jacket and draped it over his head like a shawl.

My heartbeat was wild inside my ears, inside my head, against my chest. This was not good.

Someone knew that there was a vampire inside this limo.

I crawled back through the limo, scattering safety glass as I went, my hands trembling.

I checked myself; no blood. I didn't need to go back to the hospital. If anything was broken, I couldn't feel it. But the adrenaline was probably pumping too hard, too fast, for me to know if I was injured or if my body was just covering it up.

"Wait here," I said, casting a look over my shoulder as I tugged the handle.

"Yeah, sure," he said, "I'll just play sunlight Twister until you get back. No big deal."

"That's the spirit," I said, and threw my weight against the door farthest away from Mill, grasping the handle with weak hands. It popped open, and I tumbled out of the limo and onto the street.

It only took me a second to figure out where we were. Only two blocks from my house, off the main drag. The sun was hot and bright overhead, making me squint my stinging eyes up against it. Beads of sweat were already working their way down the back of my neck, either from the nervousness and exertion or … maybe just because it was Florida in May.

I turned to look at the limo. Dents covered the black metal

as if it had been pierced with bullets. Almost every window was broken. The front grill was bent inward as if we had struck a tree.

Had we been in a battle I'd somehow missed? You know, during the nuzzling? Because that was good nuzzling, but it felt like I would have noticed or heard someone shooting up my car. How long had I been unconscious?

We were right in the middle of the street. Houses on either side sat quiet, undisturbed by whatever was happening to us. There were no other cars around, no obvious reason for the severe amount of damage to the vehicle.

What. The. Hell.

I heard another cry and wheeled around. Lockwood was on the other side of the limo, shouting something intelligible. He jumped into the air and leapt over the roof, waving his hands in the air.

I saw why.

Dozens of little lights, no bigger than my knuckles, were swirling in the air around him. They were bright, flashy colors, like disembodied Christmas lights in flight. I might have probably found them beautiful if they hadn't been darting around Lockwood like a swarm of militant fireflies.

Panic flared as another group of little lights appeared around the side of the limo and came flying at me. I ducked, purely out of instinct, and they slammed into the side of the limo, knocking it aside. The crash they made was as loud as if a car had struck the limo; it physically moved across the pavement a few feet.

I stood, gaping.

"Uh, Lockwood?" I asked. "Did you fail to renew your vehicle registration with supernatural Uber or something? Cuz I'm pretty sure we're being attacked by psychotic, miniature stars."

The lights pulled themselves from the car's side panel, buzzed in the air for a second—

—then hurtled toward me.

"Oh, crud."

I tried to dive out of the way, but I was way too slow. They didn't move quite at the speed of light—which was ironic given that they were, uh, lights—but they were blazing fast and a few of them met their mark.

They hit like dulled bullets, and I went flying from the impact, sprawling on the ground.

"Ow." Pain like pin pricks covered my exposed arms where they'd struck. Little beads of blood bloomed on my arms like polka dots. Aches spread where I'd landed, and my vision swayed, head spinning.

I tried to push myself away from them, crawling on hands and knees around the other side of the limo. Each impact on my knees stung, but not nearly as much as those things had when they'd struck.

The lights followed, shimmering above my head, dancing as if taunting me. A faint tinkling sound like crystal or wind chimes seemed to resonate from them. Giving up on getting away, I swatted at the air, trying to shoo them. "Get lost, you glittery bastards! Go light up someone's roof for the holidays—seven months from now! Shoo!"

"Miss Cassandra!"

Lockwood appeared around the side of the limo, his typically pristine suit covered in small slashes. He looked like he had gotten into a fight with a paper shredder. And maybe lost.

"Lockwood!" I said, wincing as another tiny light managed to sting me, drawing more blood. "What are these things?"

He dashed across the distance to me, the glass beneath his shoes cracking as he ran.

The little lights flickered as he approached, and after some aggressive waving of his hands, he chased them off down the street a ways before they ascended into the sky, disappearing in the bright sunlight.

Lockwood returned to me, both of us panting as he helped me back to my feet.

"Okay, level with me," I said. "Is this a Florida thing I'm not familiar with? Like nuclear mosquitos, maybe?" I cringed in pain. They certainly seemed to have bitten.

Lockwood paled as he stared up into the sky after the shimmering lights.

"Mill!" I called, questions about what had hit us momentarily

11

forgotten. I whirled around and stuck my head inside one of the broken windows. "Mill, are you all right?"

"Oh, I'm fine," I heard in response, though his voice sounded muffled. "For now."

I sighed, then turned back to Lockwood. "I don't—" I started, gazing around. The limo was trashed, engine smoking. "This is just—"

Broken glass glittered in the street. Blood was now streaked up and down my arms like some kind of bizarre tattoo.

"I'm …"

Lockwood turned and walked back toward the front of the limo.

"I don't even understand," I said. "Was this Draven? Did Draven hire miniature light drones to dive bomb us?" I picked my way over the glass back toward the limo, staring at it. Holes everywhere. "Or were they like … vampire homing bullets or something?" I ran my hand over the damaged paint, the dented metal.

I looked at Lockwood. His face was slack, his bright green eyes staring at the sky. He looked sad. Or afraid.

Or maybe a little bit of both.

I felt a flash of fear. "Lockwood …? Lockwood, they almost got Mill. A little more sunlight, and your boss would have gone poof."

Nothing from him. He just stood there, staring, white as a passing cloud.

"Okay, I'm a reasonable person," I said, walking over to him. He wouldn't look at me. "All those ideas are ridiculous, right? But what I want to know about the lights is … how were they so strong? Why did it feel like they had a mind of their own?" I stopped in front of him. "And why did they leave when you went after them?"

Of course it hit me as I stood there, looking at his face. It wasn't blank, wasn't controlled, wasn't calm, wasn't …

It wasn't Lockwood.

Not the usual Lockwood, anyway.

Those lights weren't here for Mill.

Or for me.

Draven hadn't sent them.

They were here for Lockwood ... and the look on his face told me that whatever they'd come for ... he knew exactly why.

Chapter 3

"Lockwood?" I asked.

The hood of the car was smoking, the hiss penetrating the quiet calm of the surrounding neighborhood. A few birds called to each other in the trees, entirely unconcerned about our predicament. Or, apparently, the screaming nuclear bees that had been buzzing around moments before.

He finally looked down at me, worry lines prominent on his face.

"Lockwood," I asked. "What's going on?"

He cleared this throat.

"You and Master Mill need to leave," he said. "Of course, I must remain here to deal with the police. I am sure that they have been called."

I stared blankly at him. He just completely ignored my question.

"But—"

"Master Mill needs to get out of the threat of the sun," Lockwood said, a little more sternly. "Here, take my jacket. Ensure he is entirely covered before he gets out of the vehicle. But you must hurry."

Sirens had started to sing in the distance.

His eyes were clear, the uncertainty, the blank staring, gone. "You don't have much time."

With one more lingering glance over my shoulder, I ducked back into the limo for Mill.

"Come on, we have to hurry," I said as I stooped back inside. I winced as my hands found more pebbled glass. It stung. "The police are on their way."

"Fabulous," Mill said. "Think they'll give me one of those blankets they're always giving people at emergency scenes?"

"Not until you've already combusted after the ambulance attendants haul you out of here," I said, and tossed Lockwood's jacket to him. He wrapped his own around his head, buttoned his shirt all the way up, and then pulled Lockwood's jacket on, shoving his hands inside.

I shuddered. I knew that Mill didn't need to breathe, but seeing his face completely enclosed in his jacket made me take deep breaths, reminding myself that I wasn't constrained the same way. Even still, I felt a sympathetic wave of dizziness at the claustrophobic nature of his current predicament. "Ready?"

"Let's get this over with," he said.

I led him out of the limo, my hand underneath his arm and pulled him toward the sidewalk. Our shoes crunched on the glass as we walked away, and I tossed a look over my shoulder at Lockwood.

He was just standing there, staring into the distance again. Wasn't looking at us, either, he was just …

Staring. Lost in thought. And the look on his face …

He had something very serious on his mind.

"What was that about?" I asked as I started to lead him up the street, away from the accident. I tried to walk quickly, but not so quickly that we looked guilty. Who was I kidding? Mill was wearing a suit as a ski mask; there was no way he looked like anything other than a prisoner heading to the gallows, about to be hanged.

"I'm a vampire, blindfolded and being dragged along a sun-drenched Florida street at midday," Mill said, voice muffled by the suit wrapping him. "All I know is that I'm seriously questioning my decision to skip sleep for this today, and not just because I was crabby before."

I found the shade of one tree, and paused as I looked around. Where in the world was I going to take him? We were in the middle of suburbia, a well to do neighborhood with nothing but nice houses and small fenced in backyards around. There were very few trees for shade, no alleyways to hide in.

We were out in the open, and we were going to be seen.

"Order me an Uber, will you?" he asked, his voice muffled. He shifted his body toward me, jutting his hip out.

"What?" I asked, looking up at him.

"Grab my phone. It's in my pocket."

"Uh …" Until now, all we'd done was kiss a little, and I felt a little awkward sliding my hand into his pants pocket, but this wasn't the time for being bashful.

I pulled out the phone, sure that Mill could hear my heart thundering against my chest with his superior vampire hearing. "Got it."

I clicked it on and froze when I saw the time.

3:25.

I swore, loudly enough that everyone in every house down the street probably heard me.

"What?" Mill jumped, head turning inside the jacket-hood. "Are they coming back for us?"

"No, I'm ten minutes late," I said, my hand knotting in my curls in frustration. "My mom is going to kill me. Literally kill me."

Mill let out a sigh of relief … or possibly exasperation. "Probably more like figuratively. Let's deal with one issue at a time."

"Mill," I said, clicking the button to bring his phone back to life after it had timed back to black screen, "I'm covered in cuts and blood again, and I'm ten minutes late. How am I going to explain this and keep her from either literally or figuratively killing me?"

"Cassie—"

"Why does this keep happening to—"

"Cassie!"

I gulped. "Right. Uber."

I opened the app and ordered a driver that was closest. Thankfully, there was one only a few miles away.

"They should be here in five," I said. I was going to be at least twenty minutes late.

"Thank you," he said.

I looked up. The tree's branches overhead were blocking most of the sunlight, so it was likely that we were safe for a few more minutes … as long as Mill didn't let even a fraction of his skin show, and strong gusts of wind didn't shake the branches and send more light down on us.

Just down the road, I could see the limo, unmoving, steam billowing out from the hood. Lockwood had pried it open, and was staring over it.

"I wonder what sort of story he is going to come up with for the cops?" I asked as I watched him try and clear the air in front of him as he peered at the engine.

"Lockwood is pretty resourceful," Mill said. "He'll come up with something. I don't mean to keep harping on it, but I'm kinda burning here. How far away is that Uber?"

"Just a few blocks," I said.

The sirens were growing louder, and I frowned.

"What was all that about?" I asked again. "I've experienced some pretty strange stuff with all this vampire business but … nuclear bees. This is the most rational explanation I have for what happened back there." I touched my curls again. "Oh, man … is my hair going to fall out if those really were nuclear bees?"

Mill just sighed. "They were not nuclear bees. You're not going to lose your hair."

"Whew. Because that would have been super awkward to explain. Way worse than the cuts. Maybe worse than burning down the house in New York, even—"

"'Nuclear bees.'" Mill just shook his head. "Those fae sure were angry, though, weren't they?"

I froze. "… What's a fae?"

"You know," he said.

"Uh, no," I said, "I do not know. Hence my asking. And also, my worries about nuclear bees. What's a fae? Is it radioactive?"

"I doubt it," Mill said. "Fae. Creatures of faerie."

I thought for a second, trying to free associate up an explanation. "What, you mean like pixies? Little tiny people with wings and green hair?"

"Read up on it," he said, shifting beneath his hood uncomfortably. Even if he didn't need to breathe, I couldn't imagine that it was very pleasant inside that stuffy jacket. The cloth was pretty heavy, and it was not cool outside.

"Lemme get this straight," I said. "In addition to vampires … there are actually faeries? This is a real thing?"

"Uh, yeah," Mill said. "Why is that so hard to believe?"

"Next you're going to tell me there's werewolves and witches, too—"

But Mill shushed me as the Uber pulled up along the sidewalk. I opened the back door and helped him slide into the back seat without cracking his head on the roof. The driver watched us with a baffled look out of the rearview mirror. I slammed the door behind me.

"Your house first," Mill said, muffled inside the jacket.

I rolled my eyes. "We should get you home—"

But Mill rattled off my address.

I glared at his covered face.

"You're right around the corner," he said as if he had seen my expression.

The driver arched an eyebrow, shrugged, then pulled away from the sidewalk.

"That's a wicked accident back there," he said as he turned onto the road where my house was. "Did you see what happened?"

"Not really, no." I crossed my arms over my chest.

"So … are you guys like … famous or something?" the driver asked, staring at Mill in the rearview mirror again. "Trying to be all discreet?"

"Just turn here," I said, checking my phone. I was now officially seventeen minutes late getting home.

There were two missed calls from Mom within the last five minutes. A voicemail accompanied each call. I already knew what they'd say.

I looked down at my arms, where a few of the pricks from the lights were still bleeding.

Lights? Fae? That was going to be hard to digest and harder still to explain. They were going to be a dead giveaway that something had happened to me. As though Mom needed evidence of my wrongdoing at this point. Showing up late was plenty enough for a jury-less guilty conviction.

"You should get inside," Mill said. "And make sure you get bandaged up."

Mill was touchy about the sight of my blood.

"Okay." I leaned over to try and kiss his face through the jacket, but he dodged away.

"Fine," I said, my cheeks burning with embarrassment and frustration.

It was so not fine.

I got out of the car and slammed the door, with a strong surge of hurt.

The Uber driver pulled away from the curb and I watched as the car drove out of sight.

What was that all about? I could understand wanting to be discreet in front of a stranger but … what had happened between me leaving school and the accident to turn him off to me so much?

I winced as I touched one of the spots where that—I wasn't ready to call it a faerie—thing had bitten me. It was tender and enflamed, even as it started to clot.

I dug a bottle of water out of my backpack and poured it on my arms, the cool water stinging against the wounds.

I was not going to cry thinking about Mill. I was not going to let whatever that was get to me. Maybe he was worried about Lockwood. Maybe he was worried about dealing with the insurance company. Maybe I had been complaining too much.

Maybe he thought it was my fault.

I scrubbed at the dried blood on my arm, pleased that at least some of it came off with the water. But the small scrapes and welts from the lights were still there.

There was no hiding this. Not from the camera on the porch now, not from Mom in person whenever she showed up. Also … I was twenty minutes late, now.

I tossed the empty water bottle back into my bag and walked up the sidewalk the rest of the way to my house. I checked my phone. Another missed call from Mom.

I fell in the parking lot at school, skinned my knees.

No, that was lame.

We had to do some experiments during chemistry today. One kid next to me spilled their vial—true, Dillan had been an idiot and nearly burned me just yesterday—and it got on my arms. Maybe that would work.

No, they knew I had a test today. No practical element, all paper work.

The bus got delayed because of some freak accident with a limo just a few blocks from here. Like the school wouldn't contact parents for something like that. Sigh.

Who was I kidding? She and Dad wouldn't believe me even if I told them that I had been attacked by faeries and had to try and keep a vampire from bursting into flames. Especially not for that, actually. Which was sad, since it was the truth. Now I had to come up with a lie for this, too.

I braced myself as I opened the door from the garage.

And there they were, both Mom and Dad, looking just as I expected.

I was sure steam was going to start pouring out of Mom's ears any second. Her face was so red she might as well have applied blush with a paint sprayer.

Dad looked only marginally less furious, like he was more worried than angry—but still plenty angry. Either way …

This was not good.

"I'm sorry I'm late," I said, falling back into old habits. Again. Lie on the fly, that was me. Apparently always, no matter how much I wished it weren't the case. "The weirdest thing happened …"

Of course, they didn't believe me.

Chapter 4

Mom's wrath was like the end of the freaking world. I thought I'd seen the worst of her after New York when vampires burned down the old house, but no—my deviation from the straight and narrow meant I wasn't atoning properly or something—and she let loose on me the moment I'd finished spinning my lie.

Dad wasn't much better. He kept saying things like "I expected more from you," and "How can we trust you when you can't even follow simple rules?"

I was certain by the end of it that I had forgotten what Mom's normal tone of voice was. Encouragement? Support? What did those sound like? I forget.

Not that I deserved anything other than a place to sleep and food to eat at that point in my life. (Their words, not mine.) I was pondering the local freeway underpass as a viable alternative, provided the yelling stopped.

The sounds of their alternating fury and disappointment and the familiar feel of the hard, wooden bar stool where I sat while they scolded me was getting really old. I realized I'd started to avoid sitting there when I ate my breakfast in the mornings. Negative reinforcement, I guess.

Once I'd been read the Riot Act sufficiently, I was sent to my room. No argument from me; my lies had failed, I didn't really have anything else to offer, and they didn't seem to want to press the issue of where I'd been or how my arms had gotten messed up. Probably thought I'd shot a ton of heroin, given how low their opinion of me was these days.

Slamming the door once I was upstairs, I stared at the four walls around me. Even my room wasn't a source of comfort anymore. I'd surrendered my cell phone during the haranguing, just like I did every day when I got home, though they usually weren't here to witness it.

The lack of electronic entertainment meant I'd managed to read through all of the books I had gotten for Christmas, and my attempt to start journaling was not doing anything to alleviate any of my stress. Rehashing all the ways in which my life was going terribly wrong did not bring any comfort.

Imagine that.

I sighed heavily as I sank onto my bed. Weeks of Mill and Lockwood picking me up and delivering perfectly on time, ruined now because of stupid fairy lights wrecking the car. How was this my fault? Sure, I could have just not spent time with my boyfriend, but ...

It was all so unfair. I'd wanted to reform my lying ways, really I had, but vampires—and now fae folk—had kinda ruined my life in Tampa, making it impossible to tell my parents the truth about what was going on.

I sighed, so bored that I made my bed. I had taught myself how to do it like housekeeping at those fancy hotels. I figured if I was confined to such a small space, I might as well make it pretty.

Honestly, I was grateful that Mom hadn't—yet—discovered that I wasn't actually riding the bus. With my track record and her bloodhound-like nose for my misdeeds, it was probably inevitable.

I groaned and lay back on the comforter, smoothing it out again. Seemed like Mill and I were going to have to discuss how we were going to spend time together. I doubted we'd be able to sneak around in the afternoon for a while without provoking Mom's wrath, at least until the heat was off.

I wanted to serve my time, and then move on with my life. I would do it without complaint. Anything to get it over with.

Still, it burned that I couldn't have the freedom it felt like I deserved. It wasn't my fault that I couldn't tell Mom and

Dad what was really going on. They didn't understand. All of this—the punishments, the NSA-like monitoring, the relentless attempts to get me to 'shape up and fly right' (Dad's words), was not going to stop me from lying.

I had to lie. Had to. Before, in New York, it was a compulsion I indulged, one that I felt like I had no control over. There, I felt like I had to lie to protect myself.

But here, in Florida … I had made the conscious decision to lie in order to protect *them*.

Ever since Byron had showed up, I'd had to cover over almost everything in my personal life. Even after he had kidnapped my parents and I'd staked him through the heart with a piece of a broken chair, I'd still had to lie to them about what had happened. They had no idea that Byron was a vampire, or that vampires were even a real thing.

Lucky them.

I longed for the days before I'd found out the ugly truth about vampires in our world. They seemed like such simple times compared to what was going on now. The vampire lord of Tampa was still looking for me, after all. His servants had narrowly missed killing me in my hometown in New York.

I tried to imagine Mom and Dad attempting to come to grips with the actual truth of things, the state of my life at present. It always seemed to end with their heads exploding.

I rubbed my eyes with my palms, the little welts on my arms still stinging. My lie in this case? That I'd been attacked by fire ants just after getting off the bus. It was the best I could do. Mom had little sympathy, especially after Dad had pronounced them superficial and recommended irrigating and Band-Aids.

I ran my fingers over the enflamed spots. They were healing, but there was a residual burning beneath the skin, like an itch that I couldn't quite scratch.

The lights that had swarmed around us like angry hornets had reminded me of Christmas lights, bright even in the middle of the day. Pale blue and mint green, gold and rosy pink. So non-threatening in appearance, but vicious in reality. Did they bite? Did they scratch?

Whatever they'd done, they'd hurt a lot worse than fire ants.

Lockwood had looked really worried, and it was obvious he didn't want to answer my questions.

Why? What did he know about these fae?

Was Draven behind it? I blamed Draven for all my misfortunes these days. All Draven, all the time, that was the explanatory loop in my head. He'd been too quiet for too long.

There was a knock on my door, and I closed my eyes, bracing myself.

"Yes?" I called, sitting up.

The door swung inward, and I was surprised to see Dad step inside.

"Hey, kiddo," he said, a tight, short-lived smile vanishing as quickly as he'd appeared.

"Hi." I picked at a seam on my blanket. Didn't want to look him in the eye. I hoped he'd interpret it as contrition, which it sorta was. I didn't like lying to them, after all.

"Dinner will be ready in ten minutes," he said.

My throat constricted. Lecture forthcoming, I figured, since he could have just shouted that up the stairs.

"Okay," I said, crossing my toes in my socks, wishing he would just leave.

He nodded and turned to go but hesitated. Of course.

Come on, Dad. You don't want to say it, and I don't want to hear it right now.

"You know, Cass," he started, turning back around to face me. "I know you're probably numb to it by now, but … I really am disappointed."

I hung my head to avoid his gaze.

His disappointment was worse than Mom's rage. She tended to take the lead on discipline, and then Dad followed after her with pure, unfiltered disappointment. Like a surgical scalpel of quiet guilt to Mom's cudgel of anger.

Thanks, Mill, for teaching me about weapons. Because every Tampa high school girl should know a mace from a gladius.

"Your mom and I are just at a loss," he went on. "We just

don't understand why this keeps happening."

That made three of us.

"These rules that we've set up for you aren't that tough to follow, kiddo. We're starting to think that there must be something deeper going on here."

Ding ding ding. We have a winner.

He sighed, and his face softened. "Is there something going on that you want to tell us about? Are you having trouble with some friends? Your schoolwork?"

I wished it was that easy. *No, Dad, I'm just dealing with vampire attacks and now fae folk crashing my ride home. No big deal. I'm sure everyone goes through a 'fae folk attacking their boyfriend's limo phase.'*

"No," I said. Too many things that happened weren't my fault. I only wished that they could see that.

Dad nodded, and looked at me, sadness radiating from his eyes. "We just feel like … we don't know you anymore. It's starting to feel like all we ever do is fight with you."

My blanket was super interesting. Way better than looking him in the eyes. "That's about how I feel, too."

"We understand you love Uncle Mike, but I think we can all agree that you were way out of line going all the way to New York without telling us—"

"I have already apologized about this. So many times."

"—we do understand, Cassie. We aren't complete idiots. We know life's been stressful since we moved to Florida. It makes sense to us that you're having a hard time adjusting. But—"

"I'm … I'm trying, Dad," I said. "I know it doesn't look like it, but … I'm trying."

"Are you?" He looked at me with sad eyes.

"Yeah," I said. "I am. But if it's not obvious, I mean … what's the point?"

"We don't think you're a bad kid, Cass," my dad said, curiously frozen in front of my door. If he was feeling anything like I was, he probably wished he could just walk out of it rather than keep going with this terrible conversation. "We just want you to really pull yourself together and leave this part of your life behind."

What I wouldn't give to leave the vampires behind.

With a flare of unease, though, I thought of Mill, and Iona, and Lockwood. Would I really be better off without them in my life, even with the other nasties that came along with them?

"We just don't know how much more of this we can take," Dad said. "You need to understand that your choices don't just affect you. Everyone in your life has to deal with the consequences."

He didn't even understand the half of it.

"Your mom is worried sick about you all the time. She's terrified that something has happened to you that you aren't telling us." He took a long, slow breath. "She lies awake at night wondering if this is all her fault somehow."

A little, ghostly smile tugged at the corners of my lips. "She would make this about herself."

"I'm serious," Dad said. "Your mom is worried about you. *We're* worried about you."

"I'm fine," I said. So very many lies. Why even try to keep from lying when the truth was the bitterest pill of all?

By old, New York standards … I was not fine.

I had not been fine for a very, very long time.

I didn't even know what fine was anymore.

By new, Tampa standards? With a vampire boyfriend? With the truth utterly out of reach?

Pfft. All was normal in the Sunshine State.

"I guess we'll see, won't we?" Dad said. "We do love you, Cass. I love you. You know that, right? That the only reason we're doing this is because of how much we care?" He kept his distance.

"I love you too." What else was there to say?

At least that wasn't a lie.

"All right. Dinner in five minutes." He closed the door behind him.

I exhaled heavily and sank back against my blankets.

Could you drown in lies? Because that was how I should have felt. Buried in them, over my head. A liar in her element, I supposed, but …

If I was a liar … why did they still feel so …

Cold. They felt cold to me. I shivered and mussed up the blanket pulling it over me. Didn't help.

A tap at the window jolted me a second later, and I sat up, my gaze darting toward the door. The last thing I needed right now was to be caught with my vampire boyfriend at the window, hanging out on the roof in the new-fallen night. I came up with a story, just in case my dad had heard, and I darted to my feet, ready to tell Mill that he needed to go, to get out of here, that I was in sooo much trouble already.

The explanation went out the window a second later as I looked at who had tapped on my glass.

It wasn't Mill staring at me through the glass.

A pair of bright green eyes waited there instead.

Lockwood.

Chapter 5

Well, that was unexpected.

I quickly unlocked the window and pushed it open. The warm evening air rushed in, along with the familiar clean, citrusy scent that seemed to hang around Lockwood.

"Lockwood!" I said. "This is a surprise. I don't think you've ever made a house call to me before."

He had changed since the accident. He now wore a grey suit with a red pocket square. There was no evidence that he had been in a scuffle. I brushed at my bare arms, the marks from the fae attack still glaring brightly on them.

"I haven't," Lockwood replied, crouching on the roof just outside. He made it look effortless. "I am a firm believer in people's privacy. Especially yours, Miss Cassandra. I am so sorry to be disturbing you in what I am sure is a dire hour."

"It's only dire if my parents hear you," I said, listening. Dad was already down the stairs. "Come on in." I moved aside. "Is everything all right?"

Lockwood slid in as gracefully as Mill or Iona would have, then straightened his suit. "It was me," he pronounced, cheeks flushed, his eyes wide.

"What ... was you?"

"The fae," he said.

I looked him up and down. "You don't *look* a tiny nuclear bumblebee."

"No," he said, shaking his head. "I mean they were after me."

I stared at him, my brow wrinkling. "Oh," I said. That was interesting. "I was so sure it was Draven."

Lockwood shook his head. "I truly am sorry for not being more … forthcoming this afternoon. I was in a state of shock. Not to mention worried about being discovered." He looked at me, concern all over his face, his green eyes searching me. "Are you certain you're quite all right? I feel simply terrible about all this."

"I'm fine, Lockwood."

He hadn't waited for my answer, instead taking my hand in his, running his fingers up and down the welts the lights had left. "I was concerned that these would be getting worse."

"Worse?" I asked. "Worse how?"

"Faerie bites are … different."

"Bites?"

He reached into his lapel pocket and pulled out a small blue bottle. "This salve will help," he said, offering it to me. "Go on."

I unscrewed the tiny metal top, and found a white lotion that smelled like amaretto. I shook a small amount on my palm before rubbing it on one of the spots.

Instant relief. I sighed, my shoulders sagging, tension I didn't even know I'd been holding in gone just like that. I shook more onto my palm, taken in by the sweet scent and the relief it brought.

"You were home late today, weren't you?" Lockwood asked as he looked around my room.

"I was."

"I am sorry."

I shrugged. "It is what it is. I'm grounded for pretty much forever." I rubbed lotion into the last small welt on my arm. "Thank you for this."

"I'm glad I got that to you before the oozing began."

"Oozing … ?"

"It … is blue," Lockwood said. "And shimmering."

That would have been hard to explain. I stared at him. "Would those bites have killed me?"

Lockwood seemed surprised. "Certainly not. But you would have been very uncomfortable for a few weeks. Especially during the uncontrollable urination phase, I think."

"Uncontrollable … *what?*"

"No need to worry, the salve will attend to it." He wandered over to my dresser, examining my collection of perfumes, makeup, and a few knick knacks from when I was a kid. "Your room is a very accurate representation of you," he said, peering at a stack of books. "I thought you might be interested in mysteries."

"Oh, *Nancy Drew*? I read those when I was a kid. They are some of my favorites, though," I said.

He nodded. "I assumed as much." His face tightened.

"What do you mean that my room represents me?"

"It's … friendly. Warm. Unique."

"You know, unique is a word people use to describe weirdos. Losers. Just more polite."

Lockwood shook his head. "It has personality. Your personality. Your love of the color blue. Your favorite scent, lavender and vanilla. Everything I look at, I know it belongs to you."

I crossed my arms over my chest and pursed my lips. "Lockwood, what's going on? I appreciate the salve and all, but … you didn't just come here to deliver that, did you?"

He picked up a small figurine of a unicorn. The very same one that Byron had picked up when he was skulking around my room. Lockwood turned the small ceramic creature over in his hands.

"I know that your life has taken a rather dramatic turn these last few months," Lockwood said, rubbing a thumb over the unicorn's golden mane. "And you have taken everything that we have said, everything that has happened, in stride. You have trusted us. You have trusted *me*."

He replaced the unicorn where he had found it, in exactly the same position. Even the dust appeared undisturbed.

"I … I find myself in a most curious position, Lady Cassandra." He met my gaze with those striking green eyes. "I must ask you to trust me again."

My heart fluttered uneasily. "With what?"

"Perhaps you should sit down," he said, gesturing to my bed.

It was strange being asked to sit down in my own room, but I obliged.

"I am an exile from my homeland. That was the genesis of this afternoon's troubles." He kept a reasonable distance from me, speaking across the room in quiet tones. "My difficulties have … followed me over from Faerie."

I stared up at him. It was obvious how uncomfortable he was even talking about it. In all the time I had known Lockwood, I hadn't heard him talk about himself hardly at all. Dodged it handily, in fact, when asked before.

"So … what are you going to do about it?" I asked.

"I have run from it for some time," he said, "but … it seems like that this will be only the first attempt to bring me back to my home. I expect things will escalate should I remain here. Yet …" He turned away again, his shoulders slumping under his exquisite suit. "I don't know that I can face this difficulty … alone."

Oh, no.

No, no, no, no.

Not again. Not this time.

"Who … would you need to help you there?" I asked.

I wasn't an idiot. I was fully aware that by asking that question, I was tiptoeing into trouble. I was opening a door that was going to be incredibly difficult to close.

And I needed more trouble in my life like I needed more vampires.

"I need *your* help," he said, all too serious, turning to face me once more. It was clear by the look on his face that this was the reason he'd come. "And only yours. You are the only one who can help me, Lady Cassandra."

Chapter 6

Of course. Cassie Howell, the human, to the rescue of the paranormal types again. How was it that after all this time, after all the danger I had put myself into, I still managed to find myself in these situations?

I mean, it wasn't like I was competent. On the contrary, how I had managed to escape these scrapes with my life so many times was beyond me. Or rather, it was because I had made friends with two vampires and a faerie, apparently. They were the reason I was alive. It was nothing I did.

"How can I possibly help you?" I asked. "I'm human. Not as strong as a vampire, not as … whatever … as you fae folk are. What good could I possibly do for you?"

Here, he hesitated again. "You sell yourself short, I'm afraid. You possess a very specific skill that I need. One powerful enough to deal with fae."

I rolled my eyes. "Yeah, okay."

"That is the truth," Lockwood said.

I stared at him. "I'm still having a hard time believing this whole faerie world stuff. I mean, I knew you weren't human. But faeries? Magic? Is it wrong that 'angry, radioactive bees' still seems a more reasonable explanation to me?"

Lockwood nodded. "Would it help if I told you a little more about Faerie?"

I threw my hands in the air. "Sure, whatever. Have at it."

Lockwood assumed a very professor-like pose and cleared his throat. "The world of the fae is a mystical place. It is very much like your world, yet at the same time, entirely different."

"That … clears up almost nothing."

Lockwood smiled. "Almost anything that you've heard a tale about exists somewhere in the world of Faerie. It is a place beyond belief. Glowing trees. Singing flowers. Creatures of magic that you've heard tell of in bedtime stories—"

"Unicorns?" I interrupted, indicating the tiny little ceramic figure on the dresser.

Lockwood glanced at it. "Absolutely. Though real unicorns are very different than your representation there. Much more majestic and lovely."

I looked at him eagerly. "Really? How?"

He smiled slyly. "Hooves made of crystal, and a hide that shimmers like millions of tiny diamonds?"

The seven-year-old in my squealed with delight. Teenage liar Cassandra managed to keep that buttoned up, though. Because I had dignity, dammit.

Also, I'd seen vampires and the depths of their depravity. Something as light hearted and perfect as faeries and unicorns just didn't seem possible.

"This all sounds wonderful," I said, "but you've got to admit it all sounds like … well, like the aforementioned bedtime stories."

Lockwood shrugged. "You believe in vampires now, do you not?"

"Yeah, but I've actually seen those. Experienced them, gnarly teeth and all. The bad and the ugly. There isn't much good in that world, other than Mill and Iona."

Lockwood's gaze sharpened. "And you've seen me, and the little fae this afternoon."

I pursed my lips. "I did …"

"Are you telling me that you will only believe in something if you see it?"

I looked up at him. "Well … it does make it easier. Seeing is believing and all that."

"Well, then I am asking you to have faith in me." He drew himself up to his full height. "I am asking you to trust me."

It was really hard. Just when I thought that nothing about the world around me could surprise me anymore, I was faced with an entirely new world.

"Mill said something similar to me today," I murmured. "About other creatures."

Lockwood nodded. "All of our worlds are aware of one another, though they seldom come into contact with each other."

"And yet, somehow humans are totally unaware of all of them," I said. "Other than through stories and fairy tales, we think that there is nothing else to this world."

"Some humans are aware of us. You, for instance, have found a way inside the intricate web we have woven."

"Yeah, but I'm in the small minority there."

"Even still," Lockwood said. "These worlds exist, whether humans discover our secret or not."

"So, when you say *world*, do you mean like another dimension? Or are all of these faeries holed up in a tiny grotto or something somewhere in Ireland?"

Lockwood smirked. "It is, as you said, more akin to another dimension."

"And why don't you have wings?" I asked.

"Oh, I do," Lockwood said. "But you can only see them in the world of Fae. On Earth, we have glamours that allow us to look like humans."

"Figures," I said, crossing my arms. "So are like, half the people in my life mythical creatures? Or am I the only human and you're all here just for my amusement?"

Lockwood laughed. "Very few people who you pass on the street are not human. There aren't as many as you might think of my sort who wish to wander in the world of the humans. It can be … fatal."

I raised an eyebrow. "So why do you do it? Got an addiction to danger? Because that'd explain why you seem to like me."

Lockwood smirked, and for the first time, I saw something like mischief in his eyes. "I do have a soft spot for a few special creatures. I find the lives they lead interesting, and I prefer to offer my services to fight the good fight."

"Who met you first? Iona, or Mill?"

"Mr. Mill. I have worked for him for quite some time, although not exclusively. As to Miss Iona, I met her at a large vampire gathering. She looked terribly sad. It happened that she had just been turned. We … commiserated about being fish out of water. She seemed to be having the worse of the adjustment." He smiled. "And then you came along."

"I've always known that Mill and Iona rely on you. I guess I didn't realize there might be more to how you know each other than … employer/employee stuff."

Lockwood shrugged his shoulders. "It is predominantly just that. They would do fine without me."

Seeing this side of Lockwood was very bizarre. He was relaxed. Informal. Almost as if we were old friends. I had always been comfortable around him, but this was different.

But this wasn't all supposed to be question and answer hour.

He had come to me for help.

"So … what's the issue, exactly?" I asked, sitting back on my hands. "I want to know what I'm getting into before I agree to anything."

"Fair enough," he said. "Well, it would appear the Seelie court has found me, and it is causing—"

"You've already lost me," I said. "Seelie?"

"Ah," Lockwood said, bowing his head. "My apologies. Let me start even simpler. The world of Faerie is split into several types of fae, but the two most prominent are the Seelie, like myself, and the Unseelie. These two types of fae each have courts, or what you might consider a seat of rule, a kingdom. Each is ruled by a queen and her king, and there is a constant tension, a perpetual vying for power between them. Each wants control of the world of Faerie, but for very different reasons."

"Makes sense so far," I said.

"The Seelie court, or what we called the seat of the Shining Throne, and the faeries who belong to it, the Golden Ones, is made up of faeries who use light magic. The Seelie have the best relationship with the other creatures of Faerie, as well as non-faerie creatures. Humans, for example. We are helpers."

"Let me guess …" I said. "The Unseelie are pretty much the exact opposite."

Lockwood nodded. "Not all Unseelie are bad, but surely you have heard of faeries who are mischievous? Devious? Those are typically Unseelie. They use what we consider dark magic, and do not usually get along well with humans. They believe that faeries are the leaders of all creatures, and that other non-faerie creatures, especially humans, are nothing better than a form of entertainment."

"I see." I rubbed the side of my head. "This is all a lot to take in. A real crash course."

"I can understand that."

I could have probably asked him another hundred questions, but I knew that it would have led to even more questions, and I knew that we didn't have time for that right now.

Best to cut to the chase.

"So you ruffled the feathers of the … honestly, I don't remember which court is which."

"Ah, sorry," he said. "Think of it this way—Seelie is also known as the Summer Court. Unseelie is associated with Winter."

"Seelie, Summer," I said. "Unseelie, Unsummer. Okay. So … what's the issue? Why do you need me?"

"Well, I am not presently welcome among my own. The queen of the Shining Throne has banished me until I can right the wrong that led to my coming here. And that leaves me a bit spare on options."

"Which is why you are turning to a human high-school girl for help," I said. "Makes total sense."

Lockwood lost some of his composure. He ran a hand through his dark hair, his green eyes staring into the void.

"Yes—and no," he replied. "There is something else that you need to know about these faeries. True faeries, anyway, not the other fae-associated spirits and creatures, at least those of us from the Seelie. We look like you … but we cannot lie," he said.

I swallowed hard.

Uh oh.

"I think I see where this is going …" I said.

He nodded. "I need you to come with me to the Seelie court … and help me lie my way out of trouble with them."

Chapter 7

Yay. More lying.

It was strange to think that Lockwood wanted me to do the thing I had apparently become best known for. Not my curly hair, not my vivacious personality. No, no. Cassie the liar, that was going to be my place in history.

Urgh.

Upstanding, wholesome Lockwood, asking me to help him by intentionally lying.

"Hang on …" I said. "Can't faeries tell half-truths? Which are technically lies …?"

"No," he replied. "We can make a choice to omit information, but everything we say must be the truth."

"Does that apply in the human world, too?" I asked.

"It does," he said.

I wasn't really sure why, but it brought me a great sense of comfort to know that Lockwood had never once lied to me since I had met him.

"Which is why I need your help," Lockwood said. "You have a propensity for convincing lies, and I need that skill right now more than ever."

I sighed. "Lockwood, I appreciate your admiration … I think … but you totally have it wrong. All my lying has done is gotten me in trouble, especially with my parents. And look at Draven. If I hadn't started lying, he wouldn't be after me like he is."

"You have lied for noble reasons," Lockwood said. "If you

hadn't, and Draven had found out you were human—"

"Yes, yes," I sighed. "I see your point. But the thing is, Lockwood … lying is not the way out of your problems. Take my word for this, buried as I am under a forever grounding. Lying only makes things worse."

"But you just said—"

"I hate lying," I told him honestly. "I really hate it. It has ruined my life. In more ways than one."

Just then I heard footsteps on the stairs, and from the heaviness of the footfall, I knew it was Mom.

My blood turned to ice as I leapt up from the bed.

"Closet—now!" I hissed, shoving Lockwood toward the doors.

But just as I had grabbed onto his suit coat, it had disappeared from beneath my fingers.

Into thin air.

The door to my room flew open, and Mom stepped in.

The sight she must have seen. Me standing there in the middle of my room, pale as a sheet, grabbing onto nothing.

My heart was hammering against my chest as I looked up at her.

She was looking around the room. She opened the door to look behind it, then walked over to my closet and threw the doors open.

"Who were you talking to?" she asked as she got down on her hands and knees and peered underneath the bed.

I blinked a few times and then regained my composure.

"Myself, obviously," I snapped, throwing myself back onto the bed, my tone surprisingly even. "Since you took away my phone, and there's clearly no one else here."

Mom glared at me, her brow still firmly knit together. "You didn't sneak your father's iPad up here, did you? I told you—"

"Mom, come on," I said. "There's nothing to see here."

Mom's eyes narrowed even more. "Fine," she said. "Just … keep it down. And dinner is ready."

"Fine," I said. "I'll be down as soon as I wash my hands."

Mom shot me a last, skeptical look before disappearing, closing the door behind her.

I looked around the room.

"Where are you?" I whispered, feeling like a Grade A imbecile.

There was a small pop that echoed with the sound of wind chimes and I nearly jumped out of my skin. Lockwood was back, standing exactly where he had been before.

"Where the heck did you—"

"I crossed over to Faerie," he said. "Was that your mother?"

"Yeah," I said. "That's a pretty neat trick. Mind teaching that one to Mill? Might be handy if we ever want to make out here—"

"If you're not fae, you can't learn it," Lockwood said, obviously missing my joke.

"Well, a little bit of warning next time would be nice."

Lockwood shrugged. "I've done that more than once with you around, and you didn't even notice."

That comment piqued my interest, and I thought back to times when he had seemed to disappear. "I always just assumed you were … quick. Resourceful."

"I am both of those things," he said.

I looked at the back of the door that Mom had just closed.

I sighed heavily, realizing full well that I might regret what I was getting myself into. "I was going to make up this whole convenient lie about how I'm not *really* that good at lying … but obviously, that's not true." I turned to look at Lockwood. "And lying to your face after you've saved me and helped me … so many times … would be kind of insulting."

Lockwood smiled. "Well, I appreciate your candor, as well as the respect you offer me by not attempting said deceit."

"I'm serious, though," I said. "I don't deserve the kindness you've shown me. You've gone way out of your way to take care of me. You drive me around, including all the way to New York. You always look out for me, Lockwood. You …"

Now was not the time to get overly emotional.

But damn. I owed him.

Certainly enough to do the thing that I apparently did best on his behalf.

I let a small sigh. "All right. What do you want me to do?"

"Come with me," Lockwood replied simply. "To Faerie. Come to the Seelie court and help me explain my side of the story."

"Which is what, exactly?" I asked. "Your side of the story, I mean. And why do you need a liar?"

"I will explain everything once we get there," he said. "I'm not exactly welcome at the court at the moment. I may need your expertise to help me get an audience with the queen."

"But aren't they going to know that I'm lying?" I asked. "I thought faeries were really smart. I mean … you're smart."

Lockwood's cheeks flushed. "We are intelligent creatures, yes, but if they think that you are fae, they won't have reason to question your honesty. The lie will stand as truth, and my troubles … will be at an end." He got a far off look in his eye, and I squirmed, because I suspected he was imagining me lying him out of trouble. I didn't have the heart to tell him that when Cassie starts lying, that's when the trouble usually *starts*.

I chewed the inside of my lip. "One problem. I'm *not* a faerie."

"That's part of the lie," he said.

"Aren't they going to be able to figure out that I'm not a faerie?"

Lockwood shook his head. "If anyone can pull it off, you can."

"This is crazy," I said. "You know that, right?"

"We have been through crazier things together, have we not?" he asked.

Yeah, and they weren't exactly the most happy, happy, fun times, were they? No. They definitely were not. This, I kept to myself.

But through them all, Lockwood had never backed down, never voiced a complaint, never failed to help me.

Everything seemed to be pointing to the same fact; I owed Lockwood. Like, a lot by now.

"Okay," I said. "Let's do it—"

Before I had even gotten the words out of my mouth, Lockwood had reached across the distance, grasped onto my outstretched hand, pulling me toward him.

In one full swoop, he scooped me into his arms, causing

me to gasp audibly in surprise, and then with a soft *pop*, and a flash of brilliantly green light, we had left my room …

And were standing in a place that was straight out of a fantasy novel.

Chapter 8

As a kid, I loved fairy tales. I loved the idea of knights in shining armor, fierce dragons, and worlds beyond my imagination. But that was the thing: they were always in my imagination.

"I kinda thought I'd have more time," I breathed, looking around. "... didn't mean ... right this minute ..."

We were standing on what looked like a dirt path, surrounded by trees. But the trees were wild, strange looking. The bark was as smooth as glass, and came in varying shades of blue. The leaves fluttered in a gentle breeze and glittered as the light touched them.

Which was strange, because there didn't seem to be an actual source of light. Everywhere I looked, through the trees, up the path, the landscape faded into a green mist that obscured the view. The air was warm but not unpleasantly humid. There was a delightful scent in the air, something like honeysuckle and roses.

I now understood why the air around Lockwood smelled so nice all the time.

"This ..." I stammered, my mind reeling, "this is Faerie?"

"It is," Lockwood said, smiling gently.

And that was when I got a good look at him for the first time.

He'd ... changed. His hair, normally as dark as night, was now a dark, silvery blue, like slate. It was longer, too, hanging around his ears—which, I realized, were now pointed. He still had that dignified air, but there was something wilder about him now.

He turned his gaze to me, and I was relieved to see that his eyes were still the same shade of bright green.

His clothes had changed, too. He was wearing a grey tunic that hung to his thighs, a long-sleeved, white cotton shirt beneath it, and a thick leather belt with tiny pouches around his waist. His boots, also leather, stretched all the way up to his knees, and he was wearing what looked like black breeches beneath his tunic.

But the most magnificent thing were the wings protruding from his back. They were sheer, shimmering, and glowing faintly, little bits of faerie dust falling from the tips as they fluttered gently. They were blue, like his hair, and reminded me of a dragon's wings. They reached over his head and almost all the way to the ground below him.

"Wow …" I said. I had a strong desire to touch them, to feel their silky texture beneath my fingers.

His wings shimmered and flexed.

"It must feel good to stretch them," I said. "Are they constrained back …" I really didn't know what to call it. "Back home?"

"I just haven't used them in some time," he said.

"Even though you use a glamour and we can't see them, can people still bump into them?"

"No," Lockwood replied, shaking his head. His blue hair ruffled as he did.

"Man, Xandra would be super jealous of the shade of your hair," I said, pointing at his head. "That's the sort of color you see only in pictures."

"Hence why I glamour my hair," he said. "Well?" he asked. "What do you think?"

I looked around again. The wind rustled through my own hair, ruffling my curls. A faint tinkling sound, like an unearthly wind chime, floated through the air. I didn't recognize any of the flowers along the path, as beautiful as they all were.

"Everything feels familiar …" I said, turning all around in place, afraid that if I moved off the path I might get lost immediately. "It's like a long forgotten dream. I mean, there are trees here, and they are very different, but I … recognize them. And flowers, and wind. But it's all … different."

Lockwood smiled, his wings waving gently, no faster than a heartbeat.

"That's a good way to describe it," he said. "But there are a lot of things here that would intentionally try and trick you. While we are here, I need you to follow my every instruction, all right? And never wander away from me. It could be … detrimental. If any of the creatures here knew that you were human …"

There was a bright flash in his eyes. "Right, yes. We need to give you a glamour as well."

"What? Why?" I asked.

"The faeries here won't believe you're one of them without wings."

My heart skipped a beat. Wings? Of my own?

"Now, they won't work like real wings. They will flutter and move like mine, but they won't actually be able to support you. So let's avoid situations that call for flying, shall we?" He raised a knowing eyebrow.

What a bummer. "Sure. It's cool. Who wants to fly anyway?"

"Sorry," he chuckled. "All right, what sort of wings do you want?"

"You're letting me choose?"

He shrugged. "Why not? Seems appropriate."

"What are my choices?" I asked.

"Any color you can think of, and pick a winged creature. I can recreate their style wings for you."

"A butterfly, for sure," I said. "Monarch. Those were my favorite butterflies back home in New York. And color …"

I looked around. There were so many lovely flowers around, growing wildly at my feet.

"Oh, I like that one," I said, kneeling down and pointing to a small, five-petalled flower. It was a pale blue-green, like the Gulf of Mexico, with a glowing white center.

Lockwood stepped behind me as I stood back up.

I was about to ask him if it was going to hurt at all when I saw a flash of brilliant white light over my shoulder.

"There we are," he said.

I blinked. I hadn't felt a thing.

I looked over my shoulder and gasped.

There they were. Wings! A shimmering teal that looked just like a monarch's.

A memory of wearing wings just like this as a child rushed back to me, when I was older than seven, getting dressed for Halloween. I had wanted to be a fairy after I had fallen in love with a little pair at the store that you wore like a backpack. I had worn them every day for months afterward, until Dad had run over them with the lawnmower when I had forgotten them outside one afternoon.

"They're the same color as your eyes," Lockwood said softly.

"They're … amazing," I said, looking back and forth over my shoulders to get a better glimpse of them. They shimmered, fluttering without any effort on my part. "Was that … magic?"

Lockwood nodded. "Indeed. I just applied a glamour to you. Anyone who looks at you won't be the wiser. Would you like to take a look at yourself?"

"With my wings? Uh, yeah."

He gestured a little farther up the path, and I followed after him. He turned off the path and walked into the tree line. Despite its beauty, the forest felt … forbidding somehow.

Lockwood didn't go far. Just inside the trees, there was a small brook that bubbled along merrily, the sound of rushing water both familiar and comforting. Some of it flowed off into a little pool to the side nearest us.

"Go ahead, take a look," Lockwood said, gesturing to it.

I leaned over the side and stared down at my reflection, and gasped.

"Whoa." I had to touch my face to make sure I was actually looking at myself. My hair had changed color and grown. It was now the same shade of blue-green as my wings, and so long that it was tied into two loose braids that hung over my shoulders, small strands of ivy woven into them. My face was flawlessly smooth, showing no evidence of the car accident that afternoon.

I was also wearing a long, flowing, sleeveless dress, adorned with what looked like real flowers. It was sheer, but a long slip in solid green beneath it provided modesty. It seemed to change color as I moved, shifting to different yellows and golds and greens.

I looked down at my hands and arms, but I could still see the still fading marks from the faerie bites, along with the ratty T-shirt I had been wearing back in my room.

When I looked back into the water's reflection, the skin on my arms was unmarked, the dress back in place.

"Your reflection shows your flawless self, because in Faerie, that is what is visible to others."

"So what I see in the water there," I said, pointing to it, "is what you see right now?"

"Yes. Your hair is changed because of the glamour I put on you, but even without the glamour, the reflection would still show you the very best version of yourself." His smile faded. "We may not be able to lie, but lies remain in this world, nonetheless."

"Wow …" and then my heart sank a little. "Would it, for instance, show my mom without the extra stress weight she's put on since New York? Or without the bags under her eyes?"

Lockwood nodded.

"Neato," I said. "I oughta get a mirror made here for her for Christmas. Those suckers would sell like crazy, actually. I wouldn't need student loans …"

Lockwood shook his head, amusement dancing in his eyes. "It wouldn't work quite like that. The illusion only remains in Faerie. Cross the boundary …" He shrugged.

"You'd look normal in the reflection," I said, looking down at myself. "Oh, well. I guess I'll stick to crushing student loan debt like everyone else." Even this news couldn't bring me down, though. My heart was full to bursting with excitement. This whole experience—it was surreal. I still wasn't convinced I wasn't dreaming.

But then I froze. Dad. Mom. Dinner.

"Lockwood! I have to get back right now!" I said,

scrambling back to the path. "My parents, they're going to—"

"Easy, Miss Cassandra, it's all right," he said soothingly, catching me up. "Time passes differently here."

"Differently? How?"

"Faster than back on Earth. Now, if we hurry, we should be able to complete our mission and return before they ever know you were gone. Hopefully just a moment or two after we left."

"I better not get in trouble …" I said. "If I do, it's on you."

He arched an eyebrow at me. "You seem to be quite capable of getting in trouble without my help, in ways that I couldn't imagine," he said, looking around the forest. "And I can imagine quite a lot."

"You may have a point there, good sir," I conceded.

"All right, let's get going," Lockwood said. "I don't want to be caught out in the open like this. This way."

He started back down the path, in the opposite direction from the stream. We hadn't walked far before another, smaller path broke away into the trees.

"I don't know why …" I said. "but I keep feeling really uneasy about these trees."

"That makes sense," Lockwood said. "The trees know the truth about you. You had best hope that they don't share your secret."

"The trees are … sentient?"

"Magical, more like," Lockwood said. "The trees hear everything, see everything. If you can befriend them, they are your greatest ally in Faerie. If you anger them … well … you very may well get lost in these trees for all eternity."

"That's sort the vibe I was getting, yeah," I said. "Note to self: don't anger the foliage. It's cool, guys. I only eat Earthly vegetables."

The path was winding, and the trees grew more dense as we walked. They angled over the path, boughs dangling as though to tickle my face.

"You know, you might have given me the chance to pick better walking shoes if we weren't taking the limo," I told him, nearly falling on my face after tripping on a root that I swore hadn't been there a moment earlier. Maybe the vegetation was already taking exception to me. They knew of the legendary Broccoli-Eating Cassandra, scourge of the Tampa farmers' market scene, and were reacting accordingly.

Ahead of me, Lockwood shrugged his shoulders, moving effortlessly through the trees. Clearly, he hadn't offended the local flora.

"Where are we going, anyways?" I asked. "The Summer Court?"

"The court, yes, but indirectly. We will have to undertake a journey to arrive there, for my passage is barred in Seelie." He drew a deep breath, seemingly undeterred. "And we are going to need to find some clever weapons."

I reflexively checked my bun for the stakes I often stored there, then remembered I had left them on my bedside table.

"Stakes won't work here," Lockwood said, reading my mind.

"Right. Not vampires."

"And you can't bring metal here across the dimensions," he said.

"Wait," I said, "so the old tale that faeries are weak to iron is actually real?"

Lockwood nodded. "It absorbs magic. Since iron is not found in Faerie, and it is a metal that humans have found produces quality tools, it conflicts with our natures and hence can harm us."

"So it just, what … disappears if you try and bring it here?"

"There are spells in place between the barriers of our worlds that prevents it from coming across, yes. A very complicated and delicate array of spells that could very well be broken if humans tried hard enough."

"Really?"

Lockwood glanced over his shoulder. "Yes. Why do you think we are so very keen to keep our world hidden?"

The idea of faeries being vulnerable to metal surprised me. Magic seemed so much more powerful than anything humans could use, but if their magic could be canceled out with iron …

Well, at least I knew how to protect myself from faeries back home.

"Wait a second—" I said, hurrying to catch up to Lockwood. "You drive a car. Isn't it made from steel?"

"Steel, being an alloy of iron, is not instantly fatal to us," Lockwood said. "All the same, I tend to lean toward higher-end vehicles for their aluminum bodies."

"This is fascinating …" I said. "All this time I wondered what you were. One of the fae." I shook my head. "I never would have guessed."

He smiled. "That's the point, is it not?"

We walked in silence for a moment, the bright trees swaying in the gentle breeze. The weather was utterly perfect. In Florida, I would have been swarmed with mosquitos, but here, there was no sign of insects. Which made it even more perfect.

"Would you have told me you were a faerie if we hadn't been attacked by them today?" I asked. "I mean, I saw that you have silver blood in New York. But would you have just … told me eventually?"

Lockwood was quiet, his eyes fixed ahead as we walked.

I didn't want to press too much, but part of me really wanted to know the truth. And I knew he couldn't lie.

"No," he said, to my surprise. "Not unless it was necessary. It would have been … safer for you that way."

Or maybe safer for him.

I didn't know if Lockwood just didn't trust me, or he really believed he was protecting me. Either way, his confession hurt me more than I wanted to admit.

The trees seemed endless. I wasn't sure how long we walked, but it felt like a long time after Lockwood's admission. The leaves crackled against each other, and I looked into the gorgeous sky, trying to spot it between the boughs. It shone like a reflection off of water, almost surreal.

Caught up in my own thoughts, I was surprised when I was suddenly yanked to one side. Losing my balance, I fell hard, my knees colliding painfully with the ground.

"What the—"

But Lockwood's hand clamped tightly over my mouth, stifling my voice.

"Shh!"

We had ducked behind some bush with tiny, twirling branches, and Lockwood was crouched beside me.

What were we listening for?

Lockwood was peering over the bush, and I could see the tension in his shoulders.

He removed his hand from my mouth, but placed a finger over his own to tell me to remain silent. I nodded, and he resumed his gaze over the top of the bush.

I pushed myself up a little to peer over the top as well, then quickly sank back down so as not to be seen.

What the … ?

I chanced a glance again, if only to be sure of what I had seen.

Three men—no, not men, creatures—stood by what looked like an intricately carved wooden gate leading to … nowhere that I could tell. Enormous and grotesque, they walked on two legs, but their feet were cloven hooves. Great two-headed axes rested on their shoulders, and their heads looked like those of a feral pig's, curved tusks and all.

My heart felt like it stopped beating altogether.

I would have rather faced seventy-five thirsty vampires head on than these … whatever they were.

"D'you hear that?" said a wheezy, gravelly voice.

With horror, I realized it was one of the pig creatures.

He had heard us.

Chapter 9

"We really don't have time for this," Lockwood murmured beside me.

Of course he wasn't surprised by the appearance of those things. But he definitely could have warned me that there were creatures in these woods aside from pretty, sparkly unicorns.

"What *are* those things?" I hissed from my place on the ground.

I felt more vulnerable than I cared to be. No weapons, no way to defend myself. And Lockwood looked none too pleased that they were standing in our way.

"We call them avara," he said, keeping behind the bush. "Based on a word that means *greedy* in Latin."

"Greedy?" I asked. "What does that have to do with anything?"

Lockwood's gaze lingered on the creatures for a moment before glancing back to me. "Believe it or not, they used to be human."

"I thought you said that very few people knew about faeries and other mythical creatures … ?"

"I did," he said, jaw tight as he stared over the foliage at them, "but you aren't the first of your kind to visit the land of the fae – only the first in quite some time. Whether they were lured here or they accidentally found a border, is unclear, but their desire for wealth or power or love drove them mad, causing them to wander the forests for a very long time …"

I heard one of the avara snort angrily.

"Their greed twisted them into swine. Remember how I told you that Faerie shows your true self?"

"So pigs are a symbol for greed here, too, huh?"

"For humans, yes." He breathed quietly. "I see something quite different than you."

"What are we going to do?" I asked.

"We will have to make a deal with them, I'm afraid." He looked no more pleased about this than I was at even stepping out to face them.

"Great," I said. "What could go wrong, striking a deal with people so greedy that they've morphed into pigs?"

"Indeed," Lockwood said, his tone spiked with annoyance. "Just stay close to me. Still, their greed is a sort of binding upon their action. They won't attack if we're willing to give them what they want. And, Cassandra?"

"Yeah?"

His gaze was stern.

"Don't say anything."

"Why—"

"Just trust me."

And he stood, stepping out from behind the bush.

I scrambled to my feet and held my chin high like I imagined a faerie would. I don't know what faerie, because Lockwood sure didn't act that way, but maybe some highly pretentious faerie would.

"Who's this?" one of the avara snuffled.

"Good evening, gentlemen," Lockwood said, bowing fluidly.

I tried to mimic the action, but I probably looked like a broken mannequin.

"What do you want?" the second asked, his axe whooshing through the air in a clearly threatening practice swing. He aimed it right at Lockwood's chest.

I had to give Lockwood props for not flinching, because my mouth had gone dry.

"We seek passage through your gate," Lockwood said.

The avara all towered over Lockwood and me. They stood

in place, neither advancing nor taking so much as a single step back.

"I wish to bargain in good faith with you, toll collectors," Lockwood said. I had a feeling that the only thing that made them toll collectors was the fact they were blocking the gate with weapons. "Out of respect for your clearly superior negotiating position, I will cut right to the chase," Lockwood said. "I wish negotiate safe passage through the gate."

The avara laughed stupidly, their large bellies jiggling. I guess they were getting what they wanted here. "Only if we are the one to name the price," one of them said.

Lockwood's jaw worked as he considered. Hopefully he'd be able to outwit them, because I didn't know what we even had that could be used for trade.

"What about some mitoar horn?" Lockwood asked. "I can provide you the highest quality."

"No."

"Then perhaps an ounce of gold?" Lockwood asked. "Straight from Earth."

The avara shook his head, his fingers curling menacingly around the haft of his huge axe.

"Might I suggest a—"

"A lock of your hair," the avara said. And then he nodded at me. "And hers."

Lockwood blinked. I guess he hadn't expected that request.

Lockwood frowned. "What of some sleep tonic, eh? I have some right here in my—"

"Your hair!" the avara snarled, taking a step toward Lockwood, prodding him in the chest with the haft of the axe. "Or you don't get past."

My heart was hammering against my chest, but I didn't let my anxiety show on my face. A lock of hair didn't seem like a big deal to me, but Lockwood was clearly reluctant. Was hair some kind of currency in fae? If so, the contents of my shower drain could have made me a very rich woman here.

"All right," Lockwood said, clearly angry but resigned and holding his hands up in defense. "You bargain hard. I will offer you a lock of my hair, as much as you'd like, *if* you leave her out of the deal," he said, gesturing to me.

The avara all looked about at one another. One nodded, another shrugged. The one who had been speaking glared at Lockwood, his beady black eyes bulging.

"Fine. But we will choose the length."

He walked over to Lockwood, lifted up a handful of his hair, and before I could even flinch, he produced a knife from his belt and sliced it through the air, parting the fistful of hair from Lockwood's head.

The hair shimmered a bright yellow before returning to its silvery dark blue color.

"There, a fair price," Lockwood said with a note of bitterness. "May we pass unharmed now?"

"You may," the avara said, inspecting the hair closely, grinning. He was missing several teeth, and the ones that were left appeared to be rotting. If his breath was anything to go by, he was.

Lockwood reached over and grabbed my hand, and we walked between the avara.

I did everything I could to keep my eyes glued to Lockwood's back. I could feel their eyes on me, combing over me, and it took all of my courage not to snatch at the back of Lockwood's tunic. Something about the avara made me skin crawl like little lice were running over it.

Lockwood touched the gate, which I could see this close was carved to look like a large tree, and immediately, it swung inward.

There was nothing but the forest on the other side.

Lockwood stepped through, and when he did, I did reach out and grab him, afraid of being separated.

But we hadn't moved. Our surroundings had not changed.

I wheeled around, to find that the avara had disappeared.

"What—"

Lockwood had closed the gate behind himself, sliding a large, shimmering metal lock home behind it with an echoing crash.

"Thank you for listening to me," Lockwood said. "About not speaking."

"What in the world was all that about?" I asked. "Why did you want me to stay quiet?"

"Avara have developed a sort of magic of their own from long residence in this world." He sighed. "When you make a deal with them, you are bound to fulfill it, no matter what, otherwise it costs you your life. One way or another." He touched his hand to his neck.

"Scary," I said. "How does that work?"

"The person they make a deal with is linked to them, magically, until the debt is paid." He sighed. "They could even trace you through the barrier to Earth, in theory. Without doubt, they could track the person across Faerie to fulfill a bargain."

"Magical bindings?" I asked. "Sounds worse than Mom's stories about contract breaches."

"Indeed," he said, "which is why it pays to be very, very careful in bargaining with an avara. You may end up losing more than you expect, especially if you negotiate in bad faith." He absently pulled at the ends of his hair.

"Okay," I said, "but one thing I don't get—why did they want our hair?"

Lockwood smiled mirthlessly. "Faerie hair is incredibly magical. Any piece of us is, really, but our hair is obviously the most easily parted with. It is used in various potions and salves, and it has transmutation powers."

I stared at him. "Your hair can turn stuff into … like, other stuff? Like gold?"

"Among other things, if done properly," he said. "I will … as they say on Earth, 'catch hell' for this bargain from the Seelie court, if they find out about it." His eyes were grim as he looked at me. "In their eyes, it is better to kill the avara than to honor their deals. And I tend to agree with that, but we are not in a position to fight right now. I suppose that is what happens when the Seelie revoke all your privileges."

"That's why you don't have any weapons?" I asked.

"I used to be one of the most decorated faeries in the court …" Lockwood said sadly. "Absent my privileges, to carry a weapon in Faerie now would be a death sentence were I caught."

"Oh. That sucks." I paused for another thought, feeling that what I'd just said was probably woefully inadequate, as far as consolations went. "Why didn't you want them to have my hair?"

"For the same reason I didn't want you to speak. I didn't want them to know you're human. If they had cut your hair, they would have seen that it was not as it seemed, and that you were wearing a glamour. That would then tip them off to the fact that you aren't a faerie, and we can't have them running to the Unseelie to tattle on us." His expression darkened. "Furthermore, leaving them with your hair could have ... consequences."

"Uhh ..." That didn't sound good. "What kind of consequences?"

"Well," Lockwood said, his lip curling, "they could give it to the Unseelie, who could easily use it to cast all manner of magic upon you, even at great distance. If we were very fortunate, it would be merely the mischievous kind." He turned quite serious. "It would be best not to consider anything beyond that."

I shuddered. None of that sounded good. "I didn't realize hair was so magical."

"It is a part of us," Lockwood said. Then he sighed. "What is done is done. At least you are safe still."

"Where do we go from here?" I asked, deciding it was time to change the subject.

"We are now in Seelie territory, so we must travel even more carefully." Although the words were cautious, I could see him brighten at the thought of being closer to home.

"What happens if we run into another faerie?" I asked.

"Let me do the talking, and hope that they don't recognize me." Here he gave me a smile of great reassurance.

But I was not reassured. "And if they do recognize you?"

Lockwood hesitated. "Then ... we hope they have pity on us and let us through anyway."

"What are the chances of that?"

He frowned. "I hope they're better than what I have been told."

Oh, wonderful. It sounded to me like we may as well have been walking straight into Draven's penthouse with sheets over our heads pretending to be ghosts.

"Lead the way," I said, resigned.

This part of the forest looked exactly like the other, and it was easy to see how someone could get lost in its depths. A hazy green mist was prominent in every direction, and I kept glancing over my shoulder for more avara. The idea that my hair would be valuable for some crazy dark magic faerie was … unnerving at best.

My feet ached more and more the farther we walked. Every snapping twig made me start as though someone were shooting at us. The shoes I was wearing were definitely not made for traipsing through the woods. I could feel every pebble as it pressed into the soles of my feet.

"Have Mill or Iona ever been to Faerie?" I asked.

"No," Lockwood said. "Vampires cannot come here."

"Why not?"

"They are undead creatures, and as such, cannot step into a world of such potent magic without perishing." He looked somber. "And for the same reason, stakes from our trees work particularly well against vampires. They are imbued with the magic of Faerie."

I frowned. "How do they work better?" It was unclear to me how you could do better than poking a vampire in the heart and watching them turn to black slag.

"The wood is stronger, sharper, more resilient against breakage," Lockwood said, "and sometimes it can cause the vampire to combust upon impact."

"Oh man, I need some of those," I said, and an image of Draven with a shiny, blue stake through his chest bursting into flames danced across my thoughts.

"I doubt it possible we could arrange to bring a few back with us …" he said. "To assault a tree at this juncture would be to call all of my countrymen down upon us."

"Well, let's not do that, then." I looked around, feeling a chill breeze raise goose bumps on the back of my neck. "Are vampires and faeries on good terms with one another?"

Lockwood shrugged. "Seelie tend to get along with vampires better, as the Unseelie think they are meant to rule all worlds, but vampires don't like too many faeries in their territory."

"Yeah, vampires are funny about their territory," I said.

Lockwood nodded. "Yes. That said, we have been known to help each other from time to time. You see, unlike werewolves, vampires and faeries can live in harmony together. Neither one needs the other, nor do they fight over the same resources."

"Has a faerie ever been turned into a vampire?" I asked.

Lockwood glanced over his shoulder at me. "You certainly are full of questions, aren't you?"

"You expected me to not be?" I asked. "Have you met me?"

"Yes," he said. "And I appreciate your curiosity. It is one of your more interesting attributes."

Up ahead, the pale, warm light all around seemed to be growing brighter.

"Is there a sun in this world?" I asked. "Because all this light—"

"It's just the magic," he said. "But yes, outside of the forest, you can see that we actually have two suns. And three moons."

"Three?"

He nodded.

"And the forest does end at some point?" I asked, "Because my feet feel like they're about to fall off."

"Where did you think we were heading?" Lockwood asked as we crested the hill we had been climbing.

As I stepped up beside him, my mouth fell open. I looked out over a city, every building made from mossy grey stone. A great, thick wall surrounded the town, and snow blanketed the mountains in the background. It was like something out of medieval days, but it shimmered with hints of magic. It had a strange aura about it.

Lockwood sighed, his whole body stiff. "Welcome to Stormbreak, a city of the Unseelie." A shadow crossed his face. "This ... is Winter territory."

Chapter 10

The Unseelie city was breathtaking, like something out of a fairy tale. The breeze blew over it, and I caught sweet smells of baking bread and flowers, none of the stink I would have expected from a city of old, without indoor plumbing.

Lockwood just stood there with his hands on his hips, shaking his head.

"What's the matter?" I asked. I couldn't pull my eyes away from Stormbreak. The longer I looked, the more detail I noticed. The roofs were made of a shimmering, opaque tile, almost like the inside of an abalone shell. Multi-colored smoke drifted out of the chimneys, and I half expected a dragon to suddenly appear over the wall.

"We are lost," he said.

My heart skipped a beat. "Lost? What do you mean?"

Lockwood glared at the tree closest to him. "I intended to take us along the road to Mercyhill, one of the largest Seelie cities. Apparently my friends have forgone their loyalty and led us here instead."

"I thought you said the gate would lead us to Seelie land."

"It should have," he said, face tightening. "Plainly, though, it has not."

He ran his fingers through his slate-blue hair.

I didn't like Lockwood's unease. He was all I had to keep me safe here.

"So we came out the wrong side or something?" I asked.

"The treachery is two-parted," Lockwood said. "The gate

was the first. The second being that the trees tricked us."

My eyes narrowed. Tricked us?

"Did whatever happened with you … affect how the trees treat you?" I asked.

Lockwood was staring out over the hilltops at the city. His whole bearing was repelled, as though he wanted to turn and run. It was obvious he had no desire to go into Stormbreak.

Yet he didn't run.

For me, it was easy to be entranced by the whole scene. It was as if my eyes could see nothing else, and my mind could think of nothing else but the walled city below, so different from anything I'd ever seen on Earth. Nothing like New York, upstate or the city, nothing like Tampa.

I looked at the tallest tower, what looked to be part of a castle behind the wall, and the scene … flickered. Like a horror movie. And when it did, I saw everything bathed in a black fog, almost like a very dense shadow. The buildings were in ruins, and an unearthly screech sounded in the distance.

I shook my head.

The city had gone back to normal.

"Don't look long," Lockwood said. "Unseelie magic at work. It makes you see what you want to see. Or what you don't want to."

I forced my eyes to focus on Lockwood, though there was an itch in my mind to look back, as if I might miss something miraculous if I didn't.

My own mind working against me was frightening.

"Can you even get into an Unseelie city?" I asked after realizing he wasn't going to answer my previous question.

He nodded, though reluctantly. "We can, but we are going to have to glamour ourselves."

"Again? Can you put a glamour over glamour?"

"I can," Lockwood said with quiet unease, "but it is going to make the first weaker. One glamour alone is stronger than five piled on top of one another."

"Of course it is," I said. "Because nothing can just be easy."

"Relax, Cassandra," he said. "This city is on the border of

Seelie and Unseelie territory. We aren't far. We will cross through it and be in the land of my people."

"Well good, then let's go—" And I started down the hill.

He put a hand on my shoulder, stopping me. "It isn't quite that simple."

Lockwood in Faerie was very different from the Lockwood on Earth. I had never seen him so uptight, and his stress was contagious. Where was his confidence, his calm? I needed it, especially in a place where *magic actually existed.*

"Nothing ever is." I waited for an explanation. It wasn't forthcoming, and after a minute my annoyance built to the point where I said, "Okay, this is me, done."

"Beg pardon?"

"You're a clam, Lockwood," I said. "This is the last in a long line of times you haven't been forthcoming. Start spilling, or I'm going to march down there and … I don't even know, buy a loaf of magical bread with my hair—"

"That would be incredibly ill-advised," he snapped, then he looked sheepishly at me. "But … I am sorry. You are correct. My lack of candor has not been fair to you."

I folded my arms. "No, it has not."

"This was something that I never wanted to drag you into," he said. "I would have preferred you never found out about me, or what was happening here."

"Well, you're good then, because I still haven't a clue what's going on," I said, crossing my arms. "Now … please. Give me something. An idea of our course. A fuller explanation of what's happening. Anything, honestly."

He looked pointedly at me, the green of his eyes reminding me of poison ivy. After a long moment, he spoke. "There was a murder."

I blanched, my heart beating faster. "A … murder?" I asked. That seemed very of our world and out of place in a land of shimmering, magical smoke and stone towers. Somehow I had a hard time imagining a CSI Faerie. A lump formed in my throat as I stared at him.

A thought occurred, stirring my stomach a little. He was in trouble with the Seelie court. He needed me to lie to get him out of trouble.

He had always been very mysterious … very secretive …

"Lockwood?" I asked, knowing that I wouldn't be able to rest until I asked, " … did you kill someone?"

"No," he said, shaking his head. "No, good heavens, no. It wasn't me."

I sighed with relief, the ache in my stomach loosening. He couldn't lie. He wasn't the murderer. "Whew. Yay." He didn't look grossly insulted, either, so I plowed on. "Who did?"

"I—"

Lockwood was suddenly beside me, his hand over my mouth.

"It isn't safe to talk about it here," he whispered. "And someone is nearby."

I pried his fingers from my mouth and ducked out from underneath him.

"You don't have to do that," I whispered back. "You could have just told me to shut up"

"Cassandra …" he said slowly. "You *must* understand … Faerie is full of magic. Everywhere. It twists and changes the way you perceive things. It can alter time, appearances, and even your location. You cannot … absolutely *must not* … underestimate it. Do you understand?"

If I hadn't been so annoyed at him, I would have been frightened by his words, but I didn't like that he was treating me like a child.

"Fine," I grumbled.

"Good," he said briskly, apparently not in the mood to coddle me. "We need to keep moving. I don't want to be caught outside when it gets dark."

"Great …" I said. My feet were throbbing, and my leg muscles were begging me to sit down. "So what's the plan? Go through Stormbreak?"

"Yes," he said, "… but we still need some protection."

"I can help."

I wheeled at the sound of a tinkling voice from behind us.

A tall, slim woman stood there. Hair the color of molten gold spilled over her shoulders and swirled around her as if suspended in water. She wore a golden silk gown that split at the hip, revealing long, slender legs beneath. Her face was thin, her jaw narrow, her eyes were also golden … and her pupils were slitted like a cat's.

Lockwood forced himself in front of me, an arm wrapped around me protectively.

The woman had wings on her back, and they were fluttering madly, like a butterfly preparing for flight. She was standing like a little child or a cartoon character, her knees together, her shoulders hunched forward, a slim, golden-nailed finger on her bottom lip, her eyes as wide as a doe's.

But the smirk on her face was … mischievous.

"Well, isn't she a pretty little thing?" the woman twittered. "Such lovely wings … such innocent looking eyes."

Innocent eyes?

Me?

"Get away from us," Lockwood growled.

His wings fluttered, brushing the skin on my arms as gently as a feather. They were soft, warm, and a pleasant tingle was left in its wake.

"Oh, don't be that way," the woman said, her voice reminding me of wind chimes, clear and lovely. "I just want to help."

"What's the matter?" I whispered.

"Unseelie," Lockwood said. "She's a tyls."

"A what?"

"A Tylwyth Teg," he said. "They are the sorts of faeries that humans are more likely to encounter … and they are often despised because of how they seduce men."

The tyls giggled, sounding like a set of bells, and fluttered her eyelashes at us. "Me, seduce? Noooo."

Lockwood yanked me away from where we had been standing. I looked back.

The spot where we had been standing was encircled by small, round white stones of varying sizes, wild and ancient looking.

"Fairy circles …" I mumbled. "I've read about these on—" and then bit off the word *Earth*. After all, I was supposed to be a faerie.

Lockwood nodded in her direction. "It's her kind that

leaves them behind, very commonly here. Very seldom *elsewhere*." He gave me a look of significance.

"It sounded like the two of you were in trouble," the golden haired girl said, her eyes wide, "so I put it down to protect you."

"We don't need your protection," Lockwood said. "Now begone."

"I can help you," she said, her voice as smooth as velvet.

"No," Lockwood said flatly, and he grabbed onto my hand and started dragging me along the path up toward Stormbreak.

"Wait!"

She flew, actually *flew*, and landed right in front of us on the path, her face sad, her eyes wide.

"Get out of the way," Lockwood said angrily. "I'm warning you."

"You have no weapons," she said. "But I can take you to a shop where no questions will be asked. You can get whatever you need—"

"I am not going to listen to you," Lockwood said. "Every word you say drips with lies, Unseelie—"

"No, please!" She grabbed the front of Lockwood's tunic, serious now. "Please! I need your help, too."

"Ah, now there might be the real truth," Lockwood said. "You don't care to help us. You just want something yourself."

"Well, doesn't everyone?" the woman said, crossing her legs in midair as if she were seated instead of floating on whispering wings. "I help you, and you help me. We both win. What's so wrong with that?"

"You are Unseelie," Lockwood said. "Therein lies all the wrong."

"An Unseelie who has been ostracized by the Unseelie court …" the woman said, her wings sagging as she landed on the ground once more.

That sounded awfully familiar. I looked sideways at Lockwood, but he didn't react.

She resumed her child-like stance, clasping her hands together as if in prayer, and bowed her head. "I have experienced some … events that have caused me trouble with the Unseelie court. Misunderstandings from me trying to protect those I care about. And in doing so, others have been hurt, or don't understand …" The girl sighed heavily. "And so now I wander, cast out of the Winter Court."

She floated back to the ground and stamped her foot, very much like a little girl, her bottom lip protruding.

"It's not safe for me in Unseelie territory right now. I need help getting to neutral territory. And you need to cross into Seelie territory. Well, I happen to know the way, and you can help me cross safely into the neutral territory on your way." She brightened. "We both win."

Lockwood shook his head. "No. Absolutely not. I don't care a feather whether you make it to neutral territory or not. Your problems with your court are your own."

"You don't understand," she said, flushing bright scarlet. "No one does. But I had to do what I did. I had to keep the secrets I did."

Listening to her, it suddenly felt like I'd been struck upside the back of the head with a baseball bat.

This faerie … she just said everything that I had ever thought myself about my own situation with the vampires.

"Lockwood …" I said, reaching out and putting my hand on his shoulder, "…maybe we should help her."

"What?" He looked back at me, green eyes burning emerald with emotion. "No. Absolutely not."

"But she can't lie," I said. "She's telling us the truth about what she's going through."

"She may not be able to lie directly," Lockwood said, "but she is very likely leaving out crucial information. For instance, maybe she's being followed. Or that her wickedness was so great that she caused unrest in the court."

I looked at her. She was staring at me with immense, round eyes. Her pupils were large, her golden irises nearly engulfed by the blackness, beautiful and mysterious. I could see why men would be seduced by creatures like her.

"What's your name?" I asked.

"Cassandra, no—" Lockwood said.

"Orianna," she said. "Please," and she switched to a tone

of begging, her hands clasped tightly together. She was trembling, her narrow shoulders hunched. "I have no other hope. They will find me soon, and I can't get through to neutral territory on my own."

"Why don't you just go to the gate and back out into the rest of Faerie?" I asked.

Her eyes narrowed. "To the wilds? And be eaten alive? You jest."

I glanced at Lockwood. "What?"

"I thought that would be obvious," he said. "It goes down to why I was trying to keep you quiet on our travel. It isn't safe for us faeries out there, is it? Especially ones who have been ostracized."

"No armor, no weapons, no wands …" Orianna said quietly. "To have been cast out … truly cast out … No one who hasn't gone through it can understand how utterly defenseless you feel."

Wands? Before I could ask about them, Orianna continued.

"But I can get you into the town," she said. "If we go in together, we will be safer. They don't look as closely at parties. The castouts seldom band together. There's much more margin to preying on one another—if they survive even long enough to manage that."

"You are leading us into a trap," Lockwood said.

"No, I'm not," she scowled. "Why won't anyone believe me?"

"Because you're Unseelie," Lockwood said, as though that settled it.

"I believe you," I said.

Both she and Lockwood looked at me in surprise. But I did.

"I know how it feels to live the way you are …" I told her. "Always running from those who don't believe you. Having to keep secrets in order to protect yourself because no one will understand."

Orianna was standing before me, and she took my hands in hers, squeezing them tightly. Her eyes were brimming with tears. "You … you understand?"

I nodded.

Lockwood was standing behind her, pinching the bridge of his nose.

"Lockwood … I am helping you," I said. "The very least we can do is help her, too. She's clearly in a rough situation … one that we are very familiar with."

Lockwood studied my face, and I could see him pleading in his own way. He did not want to have anything to do with her. And normally, I would trust him and understand. Especially here in Faerie, where I was the stranger who knew nothing.

But I could understand her … and faeries couldn't lie, by Lockwood's own admission. Maybe she wasn't telling us the full truth, but … I could see it in her eyes. She did need help.

"And if she can get us into the town, isn't that better that not?" I asked.

Orianna nodded her head. "You won't be able to get through alone. You know that."

Lockwood crossed his arms over his chest.

"And I promise that I won't betray you." This she said with utter, wide-eyed sincerity.

"That's no lie," I said, and looked at Lockwood. He did not meet my eyes as he nodded, so very slightly, waving his own flag of surrender.

Chapter 11

"You'll need some convincing glamours," Orianna said, her hair swirling around her as if it had a life of its own. "Come to think of it, so will I ..."

Lockwood sighed heavily and snapped his fingers. His hair withdrew back into his scalp right before my eyes, and he was entirely bald. His eyebrows darkened, and his eyes were suddenly red.

I flinched away from him. With the scowl on his face, he looked downright evil.

"Lockwood?" I asked, looking down at myself.

"Don't worry, yours is not as ... terrible," he said.

Orianna looked different, too. Her wings were grey now, like smoke. Her hair and eyes were the same shade, and her pupils appeared more normal.

"But her face is the same," I said, a little dubiously.

"Aww," Orianna said sadly, frowning at Lockwood. "You aren't going to change my features?"

"Must I?" Lockwood asked.

She nodded. "If you don't, I'll be recognized."

He rolled his eyes and snapped his fingers once more.

Her jaw widened, her nose grew, and her eyelashes turned white. She turned to me for confirmation.

"Better," I said. Orianna beamed.

We started on the slow path down to the city, the multi-colored smoke wafting out of the chimneys growing nearer with every step we took. Lockwood eyed it all warily, the stone towers getting taller as we drew closer.

"You need to be careful in Stormbreak," Lockwood said, as Orianna outpaced us slightly.

"How so?" I asked.

He gave me a pointed look. "Try not to adopt any more strays, for one thing. Even ones with pitiable stories. Sweet lies, every one of them."

I rolled my eyes. "She's not lying, Lockwood. And she's not a dog."

The city loomed ever closer, and Orianna kept hurrying ahead of us like … uh, well, a dog, then rushing back to greet us once more. In spite of Lockwood's worries, though, she seemed harmless enough. Maybe a little over excited about, well … everything. So again, like a dog.

"So the baldness, the evil stare … is that what Unseelie look like?" I asked.

"Largely, yes." Lockwood glowered, and I had to keep reminding myself that it was really him, not some stranger. He pulled up the sleeve of his shirt, and just on the underside of his wrist was a symbol. An intricate, incredibly detailed snowflake resided there, like a tattoo in silvery ink. "This is also different. Seelie have a star, instead."

"But you knew she was an Unseelie before you even looked at her wrist," I said, nodding at Orianna, fluttering about a hundred feet ahead of us.

"Because of the fact that she was all gold," Lockwood said. "Tyls are all that way. And they are all Unseelie."

Orianna appeared again, zipping out of the air next to us. "Okay, let me do the talking. They'll check you at the gate."

Lockwood frowned. "If they suspect us to be Unseelie, why shouldn't I say anything?"

"Are you a fool?" She laughed out loud. "Haven't you heard?"

"Heard what?" Lockwood asked, though I could see his face had paled.

"The attacks? The hidden spell work?"

Lockwood shook his head.

"The duel?"

She threw her head back and laughed again. "Where have

you been, Seelie? The world has fallen apart while you were away."

Was this something to do with what happened to Lockwood? Did this have to do with the murder he had mentioned?

"You can't get into Stormbreak unless you have reason, especially if you aren't a resident," she said. "It's contested territory at this point."

"So it's a dangerous town?" I asked.

Orianna's eyes sparkled at my question. "Very. Why do you think I want to be out of here so badly?"

Goosebumps appeared on my arms, and I was glad she couldn't see them under the glamour.

"Contested?" Lockwood asked. "Why … the only reason that would happen is if …"

Orianna nodded. I noticed her toes were just scraping the ground as she hovered with her wings.

"What?" I asked.

Orianna flashed a look at me. "What, are you from the reaches?" She flicked her gaze at Lockwood. "Where have the two of you been hiding, to be so ignorant of current affairs?"

"The only reason that Stormbreak would be contested," Lockwood said, ignoring her question, probably wisely, "is if the armies of Summer and Winter were in some clash around here." He seemed pained to say it. "And since it is Unseelie territory … that suggests that Summer has come this way."

Orianna nodded. "That's right."

We were nearing the gate, and the air was becoming considerably cooler. There was a stronger wind, and the bright light had dulled to a cloudy sort of haze overhead. There were two other faeries standing guard, both of whom had silver-tipped lances in their hands.

The city suddenly flickered before my eyes, that dark mist appearing, ethereal screams cracking out in the night. I tensed, and Lockwood caught my arm. "What is it?" he asked.

I shook my head as I looked up into his concerned eyes. There was no way I was going to discuss it in front of

Orianna. I might have believed her about being in a tough spot, but this was some grade A weirdness, and I had a suspicion it had something to do with me being human. Something I definitely didn't want Orianna to know about.

The world flickered around me again, another scream echoing, and I squinted my eyes shut, hoping it would pass. A slow ache spread out from my temples in a rolling wave of pain.

"Good afternoon, gentlemen," Orianna cooed. I opened my eyes to find her nearly bending herself in half in a sort of bow before the guards at Stormbreak's wall.

"Arms!" one of the faeries barked.

It took me a second to realize they didn't mean weapons, and I was a little slow to imitate Orianna and Lockwood as they revealed the underside of their wrists.

My heart hammered against my chest. I couldn't see a thing on my wrist except a scrape from the limo attack, and I hoped that Lockwood's glamour was going to hold up.

They checked Lockwood, staring at his tattoo for a very long moment before nodding to let him through. Then they turned to Orianna, giving her a careful once over before allowing her to walk under the archway into the city.

My turn.

The faerie grabbed my wrist and pulled me toward him. He examined it like my dad looking at a vintage baseball card, running a finger over the flesh. I held in a hard gulp as he stared, stared, *stared* at nothing but my wounded arm, the hundred nettle-stings of the little faeries just sitting there in front of his eyes, beneath at glamour that I *hoped* he could see, but that I couldn't.

His thumb lingered longer over my wrist than it had with the others. He raised his eyes to mine, glaring at me.

"You may pass," he said, finally.

I hurried after the other two.

"Phew," Orianna said, grinning. "Lucky they didn't decide to peel our glamours off. Or try to, at least."

"How?" Lockwood asked.

"Something that the Unseelie have designed," she said. "Some hostile kind of magic. Painful, really."

Lockwood sucked in his breath. "You should have informed us of this before we walked blindly into a trap."

Orianna shrugged. "I assumed you knew. Next time I'll assume you're ignorant."

"Always a safe bet in my case," I muttered. Orianna chuckled.

Despite those rainbow smoke trails reaching skyward, the city smelled of regular burning wood. It also had the scent of cold snow, and something else, what I assumed was the smell of magic. It was a heady sort of aroma, like a potent, herbal perfume.

The city flickered again, and we were surrounded in darkness.

I gasped and latched onto Lockwood's arm.

"What's the matter?" he asked as everything flickered back to light, to normal.

"Nothing," I said, loosening my grip. "Just ... it was nothing."

Orianna arched a perfectly shaped eyebrow. "We need to turn here."

We took a corner down a street with glass windows, shops lining it. The faeries that passed by us varied in size and color. Their wings were all shimmering and opaque, and they spoke in hushed tones, not looking in my eyes as we passed them.

I shivered as I followed Lockwood and Orianna down the street. Maybe I could buy a sweater or something wherever we were going. It was a sad moment for this New Yorker. Clearly Florida was getting to me.

Orianna turned into a narrow alleyway, then slipped inside a door with a wooden sign out front adorned with a crown. Lockwood paused outside, extending a hand to me, and waited for me to enter before he followed, protectively, just behind.

The inside of the shop was humid, probably because of the cauldron in the corner, roiling and frothing with a strange blue, glowing substance. It smelled strangely like vanilla and cinnamon. I forced myself to not inhale deeply, though I really wanted to.

Every corner of the shop was packed with stuff. Boxes and crates, old books, cabinets with rusted swords and daggers. There was a cage in the corner with a brightly colored bird with two heads, one blue and feathered, the other black and bald with glowing red eyes.

"Talon!" Orianna cried, rushing through the tiny openings between the shelves.

Lockwood hung back with me near the door.

"Well, she wasn't wrong about finding supplies …" he said, looking around. "I could easily find an amulet for you, and maybe a sword. I'd really like to find some—"

"Come on, you two, up here," Orianna said from somewhere in the depths of the shop.

"Just …" Lockwood was looking into my eyes with great significance, his green ones bright and shining.

"Stay quiet, I know," I said.

The man behind the counter was less of a man, more of an animal. He had the head of an eagle, but the torso, arms, and legs of a man. A big, burly sort of lumberjack. He watched us cautiously as we approached.

"—but she won't leave. Not after the raids again last night."

"Raids?" Lockwood cut in, examining the glass cabinet in front of Talon. It was loaded with chunks of crystals, mirrors, and a mask that swirled like it was made of mercury.

"Seelie," Talon said, clacking his beak and taking in Lockwood and me with fierce attention. "They've been getting closer to the castle each time. If they end up taking the city, it's going to start a war in earnest."

"How long have these raids been happening?" Lockwood asked.

"Where've you been?" Talon asked. "Been years now. But it's gone and got serious these last months."

Lockwood's face paled. "I've been away too long, it would seem."

"Everyone's getting tired of it," Talon said. "What do we care about the murder of some Seelie? As far as I am concerned, it doesn't affect us in the least. The sooner they realize this, the sooner they'll leave us be."

"Surely the Unseelie will retaliate?" Lockwood asked.

Talon shook his head. "At what benefit?"

"Justice, of course. Strike for strike." Lockwood said it was the most normal thing in the world.

Talon smirked. "Sound like one of them Seelie, there, friend. You best be careful saying things like that too loud these days. Lucky for you I don't talk to guards." He turned his penetrating gaze and amber eyes back on Orianna. "What can I get for you?"

"Whatever he needs," Orianna said, inclining her head toward Lockwood.

"Ah, yes," Lockwood said, "we could use …"

Lockwood started reeling off a list of things he wanted. I lost interest quickly, and my eyes started to wander. There was a set of armor on one wall, with a hole right through the chest. A bandolier with a set of seven bells, from small to large, so dusty it couldn't have been used for years. And a box full of what looked like chocolate bars, but there was nothing in the world that would make me try one.

I wandered over to a bird cage while Lockwood bartered with Talon, Orianna standing there, grinning from ear to ear, so pleased with herself. The two-headed bird peered curiously out at me, both of its heads turning to stare at me with one eye each.

It opened its beak and let loose a trilling song, surprisingly gentle and soothing. I wondered if it was a wild sort of bird in Faerie, or if they were like dogs over here, and domesticated. The cage suggested otherwise.

My vision flickered once more, fragmented, moving back and forth from what I was seeing and the other.

The bird in the cage was suddenly nothing more than charred feathers and bones, with black, empty eye sockets, its song gone.

I put my hand over my face, shielding my eyes until the song returned, along with the light.

"Cassandra, are you all right?" Lockwood had appeared. His hand landed on my shoulder.

"Fine," I said. The bird was back to normal, feathers of red and orange. No bones.

"Come with me," Lockwood said. "I've purchased you some things. Orianna is just wrapping up now."

I followed him out of the shop, the environment around me back to normal, but my heart was beating uncomfortably. I wiped my palms on my jeans as we stepped out back into the cold, mountain air.

"All right," he said, pulling some things from the sack I hadn't noticed he was carrying. "These should help protect you. You can't put them on here, though, because they will ruin your glamours. Once we are out of town and I can remake your glamour, I will incorporate your new items."

"Fine with me," I said, wrapping my arms around myself. Damn you, Florida, for making me susceptible to cold. Or maybe it wasn't Florida at all, but these strange visions. "Lockwood? Did you get me something to keep me warm?"

"Oh, I am so very sorry," he said, and with a twirl of his finger, it was as if I had stepped out into a perfect afternoon in Florida, warm but not uncomfortably so.

"Thank you …" I whispered, the chattering of my teeth slowing. I brushed my hands against my arms to find they were still bare. Maybe he'd created a glamour to keep me warm, or some other spell.

"I also have a sword for you," he said, "and an amulet for spell resistance, and—"

I held out a hand to shush him. The two guards who were had been at the gates, the ones who had checked our Unseelie marks, had just walked past the alleyway. Their heads were moving, sweeping the street. As if they were looking for someone. Tucked into the shadows as we were, they hadn't noticed us.

"Lockwood …" I said, tugging on his sleeve.

"What is it?" he asked, his ramble about his purchases broken.

"Those guards from the gate," I pointed at the mouth of the alley. "They just went past, looking for something." I looked up at him. "I think they know we're not Unseelie."

He frowned. "How could they?"

The guards reappeared, staring straight into the shadows where we stood. In spite of that, their eyes locked on

Lockwood and me.

"You there!" one of the guards called.

"Oh," Lockwood said.

"What's the—" Orianna had just appeared outside of the shop, a bulging bag in her hands, and her face fell. "Oh, dear."

Lockwood grabbed onto my arm and turned the opposite direction up the alley, away from the guards. He surged into motion, dragging me along at high speed as I tried to keep up.

We were running from the law.

My feet, already aching and tired, were suddenly pounding against the cobblestone street, the adrenaline making me forget all of my pain. I clutched Lockwood's hand tightly, my palms growing sweaty once more, threatening to slip out of his grasp. He did not let me go, though.

We ran, the shouts of the guards echoing against the stone as we tore through the city, knocking other faeries out of the way. Orianna was flying ahead of us.

My heart clenched as I panted. Lockwood would have been able to get away by flying if he hadn't been stuck dragging me along.

The world flickered again, and I shrieked, pinching my eyes shut, trusting Lockwood that I wouldn't run into anything.

We were out of the gates when I opened them again, the wild world of Faerie ahead, trees and mountains and river banks.

"Was that the faerie with the glamour?" one of the other guards on duty asked as we ran past, not stopping.

"Get them!" the other said, leaping to their feet. Maybe they'd been on break. If so, it was over now, and they were hustling to pursue us.

Lockwood must have had enough, because suddenly I was in his arms, and we were in the air, off the ground and flying higher, and higher, and higher.

I gasped and shut my eyes tightly.

"Um, we're flying," I said, trying to keep my low-key panic from busting into a higher key. "We are officially off the ground and flying, which is not normal for me, absent a plane."

Lockwood was frowning, the strain of carrying me while he flew showing on his tight face. "They must have been able to detect you were wearing more than one glamour …" he said, glancing back over his shoulder. "Remember how I said that two were weaker than one?"

"How?"

"I don't know, it seems that additional measures have been taken since I was last here …"

"You don't think they suspect I'm human, do you?" I asked.

He shook his head. "No. They probably think you are one of the Seelie who raided the city last night."

"That does not sound like the sort of thing I want to be while here," I said.

"Indeed," he said, his muscles straining as he carried me toward a river below. "I don't imagine they would look kindly upon you should we be caught."

"Let's not be caught, then," I said.

"I assure you, I am endeavoring to make that so," Lockwood said. Now his voice was straining, too.

Orianna flashed into view ahead of us, coming in for a landing on the bank of the river. A simple, wooden bridge stretched hundreds of feet over it. The sound of it raging below was like distant thunder. The other side was distant, shrouded in a thick mist, and much darker.

"Why aren't we crossing?" I said over the roar of the water. I looked behind me. The guards had stopped a short distance away. "Wait, they aren't following anymore …"

"They don't care enough to put their own lives in danger," Orianna murmured. "Going this way is practically a death sentence."

"What … is out here?" I asked.

"Neutral territory," Lockwood said heavily. He glanced over his shoulder at the guards and Stormbreak again. "And it's twilight. Wonderful. I was hoping we could at least stay the night there …"

"The witching hour …" Orianna said, just as darkly. She laughed, then it cut off abruptly as a more sober look came over her. The nerves were just radiating off these two faeries. Two people who knew this land, and knew what we were in for on the other side of this bridge.

And something told me that it wasn't going to be a tea party and a nice nap waiting for us.

Chapter 12

Neutral territory was strange.

I mean, everything in Faerie was weird. I wasn't entirely sure that I wasn't dreaming. Or hallucinating. Either was likely, given the amount of stress I had been under in my life as of late. Or maybe I was spending too long on Netflix.

Neutral territory, though, crossed from weird to eerie. Everything looked perfect on the outside … but something just didn't … feel right.

I couldn't put my finger on it as we walked through the trees, the fallen leaves crunching beneath our feet, Orianna humming quietly. It was beautiful, it really was. The swirling, glowing green mist had returned, surrounding us, but never really there. It just screamed … magic.

Lockwood had removed his glamour, thankfully. Baldness didn't suit him. Neither did the red eyes. Orianna was back to her golden self, grinning mischievously as she hovered in the air behind us.

"Why don't we fly again?" she asked after we had crossed the bridge. Lockwood had muttered something mystical-mumbo-jumbo-y about why we couldn't fly over the river. Something about the water. "We could cover a lot more ground that way."

"I hurt my wings," I said flatly. I didn't need Lockwood attempting to make something up for me … especially since he couldn't technically make anything up anyway.

Orianna's eyes widened. "How did you do that?"

"You don't even want to know," I said.

Lockwood looked at me with mingled frustration and gratitude.

"Besides, we should try to keep a low profile," Lockwood said. "There are sure to be others here. And if we can be as cautious as possible …"

Orianna clicked her tongue in annoyance, floating on her back as if swimming, her arms crossed over her chest. "Caution is slow. Caution is boring."

"You prefer death?" I asked, getting grouchy.

"Why are you still with us, anyway?" Lockwood glared at her over his shoulder. It was strangely amusing to see him so flustered. I still wasn't sure how I felt about Orianna, but we had agreed to help her, and I meant to keep my word … in this case. Something about breaking a promise here bothered me. Maybe it was the fact that I was already marching toward telling a massive lie in service of Lockwood. Adding broken promises on top of that? Yuck. "I thought you said that you just wanted to get to the neutral territory."

"Do you think I'm stupid?" Orianna asked. "It's dangerous here! Only a fool would travel through neutral territory alone." Her eyes flittered around, as though someone were going to come leaping out at us at any second. "Maybe I'll join a caravan or something if we come across one. Tag along with faeries who aren't injured or exiled." She gave me a pointed look.

"I'd advise keeping your opinions to yourself. Last I checked, the only sort of protection that you had was a pair of pretty eyes and the power to lure children away from their mothers." Lockwood's hands were balled into fists.

Orianna stopped in mid-flight, staring daggers at Lockwood's back. "And all you have is some flimsy sword and a bag of charms. Not much for a mighty Seelie warrior, is it?"

Lockwood had pulled the sword that he carried at his hip from his sheath, whirled around and pointed it right at Orianna's breastbone faster than I could follow.

I could see the rapid rise and fall of his chest, but his hand was steady as he held the blade. The gaze in his eyes could have melted steel.

"Don't push me, tyls. I can end you with one word."

Her eyes narrowed, and a wicked grin spread over her face. She folded her arms and laid them down on top of the blade as if it were made from plastic, leaning on it. "Go ahead, then."

The tension was thick as a summer night in Florida as I stood there, staring between the two, unsure what to do.

Silver blood was beginning to drip from the blade where Orianna's arms pressed into the metal, hitting the ground below with a soft splatter. I was half surprised that it wasn't gold.

Lockwood gritted his teeth, and then lowered the sword from underneath her arms, drawing it back toward himself.

She took up her balance as he removed it and snickered low in her chest. "That's what I thought."

Lockwood didn't look as he turned and started back up the path, each step turning up dust as he stepped lightly, but with surprising fury.

I fell into step beside him as he pulled a cloth from his pocket and began wiping down the blade.

"I … uh …" I started.

"Don't worry yourself," Lockwood said under his breath. "It's fine."

It definitely didn't look fine. A power play had just occurred, Orianna testing Lockwood's resolve and finding him...weak? Well, maybe not weak, but definitely a little too compassionate to just strike her down out of caprice. That she had the measure of him this quickly maybe should have worried me, but that was a distant concern next to the awkward tension now filling the air around us.

"Where are we heading now?" I asked, hoping to break the very uncomfortable silence that seemed to be getting louder and louder with every step. He may not want to talk to her, but I didn't want him tuning me out, too.

"Still on track for the Seelie court," he said. "Hopefully with one less companion, soon."

Orianna shrugged as I glanced at her.

"You know where you're going, right?" I asked him. "This

isn't like the gate?" I looked around. The forest seemed just as normal as it had the last time something had gone awry. "The trees aren't, uh … betraying us again?"

"No," he said. "We're quite fine now that we're out of Winter's territory. We are going to have to find a place to stay for the night, though," and he stared up through the trees. "While I no longer fear betrayal from the woods themselves, we don't want to be caught out here where it's dark."

"Why not?" I asked.

"Beasties," Orianna chortled.

I looked at Lockwood for confirmation.

His refusal to reply was as good as a yes.

The trees had begun to thin, and the green light became more golden, deeper, darker. We followed a curve in the dirt path, as it wended its way to a clearing, at the edge of which stood a building that resembled a farm house. A great expanse of open fields stretched into the distance. A building made of stone, almost like a little castle, was nestled in the middle, smoke billowing from its copper-colored chimney. A whinnying sound, something like a horse, but higher and hauntingly beautiful, echoed across the plain.

"We'll stop here." Lockwood started to trudge through the field, each row of crops evenly spaced. Strange pink and green plants were growing there, their leaves transparent like stained glass. I was careful not to tread on any as I followed.

The earth smelled sweet, like cinnamon, and my feet churned up fresh folds of it as we walked. Orianna floated along behind us, eyes darting around in all directions. Her demeanor had changed, all amusement gone. Her wings twitched nervously as she looked about, as though expecting attack to come from above at any moment.

Who might be doing it? Well, that I had no idea about.

It certainly seemed quiet. Not uncomfortably so, but the tension in Stormbreak had been heavy, and the unease and apprehension that both Lockwood and Orianna had felt as we crossed into the neutral territory was enough to keep me on my guard. I'd been expecting calamity any second the first hour or two we'd walked, but with every hour that passed, I started to wonder what they had been so worried about.

Dimly, I still hoped I wouldn't find out. If it was worse than the avara, after all …

Lockwood's hand was suddenly around my arm, halting my steps.

"What is it—"

A figure was flying through the air toward us, wings blue against the reddening sky overhead.

I jumped behind Lockwood as the figure struck the ground a short distance away. I saw a great flash of yellow light, and heard the sound of metal swooshing through the air.

"Who are you?" It was a deep voice, clear and demanding.

I peered over Lockwood's shoulder. A tall male faerie stood before us, his short blue hair as bright as a turquoise, his skin reminiscent of a glass of electric green soda. He had four ears. Behind him, his wings trembled angrily, like a cat whose tail is twitching in protest.

"We are friends," Lockwood said, holding his hands up, revealing empty hands. Not that that mattered much, since I had seen Lockwood do magic with his bare hands.

Lockwood stood up straight, and then threw his left hand behind his back, curled into a fist. He must have made some sort of sign in the front that I couldn't see, because the opposing faerie's eyes grew wide.

"A paladin?"

"I used to be," Lockwood said, a tightness in his voice.

"What is a Seelie doing traveling with an Unseelie?" the faerie asked. A curved blade that looked like it was made of yellow sparks shimmered over his head, swinging back and forth menacingly.

"We're helping her out of some trouble," I said.

Lockwood and the farmer glanced at me. I couldn't tell whether Lockwood was mad at me for speaking out of turn. His face was as neutral as the territory.

"Another Seelie?" the faerie asked.

"She's my charge," Lockwood said. "I've been tasked with getting her to the court unharmed."

A lie, but not. Oh, it was sneaky, all right. No doubt Mill had told Lockwood to protect me. And he was in charge of protecting me so we could reach the court. But he had managed to leave out the most important fact: that I was human.

"I've certainly seen my share of odd partnerings this side of the territories," the faerie said, relaxing slightly as he stood upright. "I suppose a tyls is harmless enough since there are no young ones here."

"I don't prey on the young," Orianna muttered under her breath. "That's such a vicious slander about tyls." Everyone ignored her but me.

"We seek some food and a bed for the night. A place to rest," Lockwood said. "We have coin and will pay."

"I suppose that could work," the faerie replied, his four ears moving. Was that excitement? Or did he hear something? "As long as you don't mind sleeping in the barn with the unicorns."

My heart skipped a beat. Unicorns? UNICORNS?!

"We are not particular," Lockwood said.

"Speak for yourself," I said, "I'm all about the unicorns." This time he gave me a non-neutral look. So I shut up.

"And I can pay you in either charms," Lockwood continued, "or with gold."

"Gold, you say?" the faerie asked. "From Earth?"

Lockwood nodded.

"You didn't tell me that you had gold," Orianna said.

"What do *you* need gold for?" I asked, taking her in with a glance. "You're practically made of it.'

Orianna stuck her tongue out at me. I flinched away from her as I realized it was forked.

"While the gold is tempting, the charms are of more value to me," the faerie said. "We need all the protection we can get out here." His decision seemed to be made. "Follow me." He beckoned.

The sword hovering over his head turned and headed back toward the house, leading the way. But it didn't disappear.

"Things must truly be grave if you are turning down gold," Lockwood said, effortlessly following the faerie back through the fields without stepping on … well, anything.

The faerie nodded. "You heard about the Seelie raids over

the river? Well, they passed through here just a few weeks ago. It's a wonder that any of our crops survived."

I glanced back over my shoulder. Just weeks ago? Everything looked calm. The crops were healthy, or at least they looked like they were.

We drew closer to the stone tower, our little procession following the green faerie. His sword still hung in the air above us, crackling and popping like electricity.

"I'll take you to the barn," he said, "see you settled, and then I will come and fetch you some food."

"Wait, you were serious? We have to sleep in the barn?" Orianna asked, her wings shivering.

"You expect me to allow strangers into my home? In these times?" the faerie asked, his black eyes narrowing. He shook his head, the sword overhead trembling. "Be grateful that I am letting you anywhere near us."

Orianna snorted. "Such charity."

"Thank you," Lockwood said. "We are grateful for your help."

"I'd expect nothing akin to it from the Unseelie," the faerie said, darting an unkind look at Orianna.

All my visions of unicorns living in the forest, in the wild, were shattered at the sight of the barn. It was the first thing I'd seen in Faerie that was totally unremarkable. I wondered if it was possible for a unicorn to really live in such a shabby place.

"I'll be back with some dinner," the faerie said, leaving us as we reached the wooden door. He pushed it slightly open, then wandered off, wings flittering.

"Is he Seelie? Or Unseelie?" I asked after he was gone.

"Neither," Lockwood replied. "He is a silva. Related to us, but a different kind of fae entirely. They are often skilled with organic matter, and as such, they set up farms like this where they are normally undisturbed by our … disputes."

Orianna had wandered away, peering closely at anything she could. Now she was looking into a trough, making a face. She reminded me a little of a nosy child, getting into stuff she wasn't supposed to.

"I am concerned, though …" Lockwood said.

I tore my eyes off Orianna's inspection of a hay bale, her lips curled in a sneer. "Why?" I asked.

"Nothing," he said. "Come, let's see our accommodations for the night. I'm sorry it isn't more like Mill's condo, or even your own home."

Mill … With a dart of guilt, I realized I had hardly thought of him at all since coming to Faerie. I wondered if he knew where I was, or if he even knew I was gone? Was this what it felt like for him, living for such a long time? I didn't know how long, exactly, but time was definitely passing here.

"Am I going to get older here?" I asked.

Lockwood hesitated, his hand on the barn door. "What do you mean?"

"Being here for as long as we are. Am I actually … aging?"

Lockwood's brow furrowed as he searched my face. "No. The magic of Faerie will preserve your youth, but …"

"But what?"

"You might experience some … uncomfortable symptoms when we return to Earth."

"Like?" I didn't love the sound of any of that.

"Nothing severe," Lockwood said. "A little fatigue. Some cold symptoms, maybe. Nothing horrible."

"Oh, is that all?" I kept a wary eye on Orianna, who walking around the barn, eyeing it—and us—with a distaste that bordered on how I felt about physical education classes.

"Whatever consequences come, I promise that I will give you something to ease the symptoms, all right?" Lockwood looked at me with those shining eyes. "Let us not worry about it before the hour comes 'round. That is still some days away, at best."

"And we'll get back at the same time we left?" I asked.

Lockwood hesitated.

"We won't, will we?" I asked. "That's what you said earlier."

"It will just be a few moments later," he said. "Ten minutes, at most."

I rolled my eyes, my hands pressed against either side of my face. "Dinner was supposed to be in five," I mumbled through my fingers. "I'm going to get caught for sneaking out for sure." And it wasn't like he could just drop everything and take me home now.

"If we had arrived in Seelie as I had planned," Lockwood said, "then we would likely be at the court by now, pleading my case. Unfortunately …" Here, once more, he evinced obvious regret.

"Which has something to do with that murder, right?" I asked. What was done was done; if I was going to catch hell for sneaking out, there wasn't much I could do about it now other than hurry and finish this and hope I could get home before too many minutes ticked away in the human world.

Lockwood paled. "Yes."

"Why aren't you telling me what really happened?" I asked, turning back to him. Maybe if I could get him to spill some details, I could pay attention to that rather than my accursed and impending forever grounding. "Just get it all out there. Trust me, holding in the truth always hurts, it never helps."

"Because—"

But then Orianna was back, staring at us.

"Are you not going in?" she asked. "We really don't want to be out here when it gets dark."

"Dark is still an hour or so off," Lockwood said.

"Oh, well, my apologies, great *paladin* …" her eyes flashed dangerously. "If you ever really were one."

He glared, and then pushed the door all the way open.

Even though I was frustrated, my heart still beat faster at the idea of seeing a real unicorn.

The inside of the barn was similar to a stable. Eight stalls waited all in a line, straw covering the stone floor, but only the very last was occupied.

My heart nearly burst within me as I gazed at the creature that was there.

Just like Lockwood had described them, the unicorn had a coat that glittered like it was made of millions of tiny diamonds, and its hooves were perfectly clear and cut like crystal. Its horn was silver, and its eyes, large and deep, were staring straight at me.

My breath caught in my throat, and I could only stare back at it. I reached my hand out toward it, and began walking slowly over to it. Unicorns were supposed to like girls, right?

And then the world flickered.

The unicorn was there, but it was lying on its side, its hide torn open, golden blood pooling on the floor beneath it. The other stalls were filled with seven other unicorns, all slain, their corpses stretched out over the floor, the blood all gathering together. An eerie glow, like fire, lit the night sky, and the barn was dark. Everything was so dark.

I gasped for breath, clutching my chest as my heart thudded against my ribcage. A cold fear rushed through my veins as I stumbled and fell onto the hard, stone floor. I caught myself on my hands, and I shrieked as I lifted them in front of my face, golden unicorn blood drenching my palms.

I scrambled to my feet, trying to get my balance. The second I had it, I rushed outside, each thudding step like a hammer beat through my whole body. I burst back out into the cool air …

… And froze.

The fields were ablaze with black flames, licking up the side of the stone tower, lashing upward toward the sky from the fields, everything turned to ash.

Screams rent the air, and there was a group of figures across the field, at least a dozen, wearing armor as white as snow, marching in a regimented fashion, all wielding shining silver swords.

I blinked.

And the peaceful farm returned.

"Cassandra …"

I looked up, and Lockwood was standing beside me, his arms outstretched toward me. Orianna wasn't far behind, cowering near the door to the barn. The look she was giving me …

My breath was coming in quick bursts, and I looked around for some sign of what I'd seen. Anything to suggest it was real.

What the hell was happening to me?

"Cassandra … ?" Lockwood asked. "What's the matter?"

I lifted my hands to my face again. No blood, golden or otherwise.

But still … I couldn't shake the feeling that it was on my hands, like a stain that wouldn't leave. I shook my head, looking over the peaceful farm, all trace of what I'd seen gone from my eyes … but not from within me. "We can't stay here."

Chapter 13

"What do you mean, we can't stay here?" Lockwood asked.

I was trying to calm myself down. Forcing myself to take slow, deep breaths. There were no flames, no blood, no marching fae. Things were peaceful.

"What's the matter?" The faerie farmer had returned, arms laden with food. He approached slowly, suspicion creasing his features.

"I … not sure," Lockwood said, and he bent low to speak in my ear. "What happened?"

"I …" I started. "I don't know how to describe it. But something isn't right here … we have to leave."

Lockwood straightened up. "I am sorry for the trouble, friend, but we are going to have to leave."

"Leave?" Orianna asked. "We just got here, and already you want to leave? This close to dark?"

Lockwood held up his hand to stop her. "I will give you both the gold and the charms I promised for the trouble, if you wouldn't mind still giving us the food, and perhaps a tent?"

The faerie looked confused. "I … suppose."

"Thank you," Lockwood said. "I truly am sorry for the inconvenience."

The faerie nodded his head. "None at all. You better get going if you want to find a safe haven before dark."

Lockwood passed him a small, crystal vial and the bag that he had purchased in Stormbreak. The faerie snapped his fingers, and a green bundle appeared in his hands, binding up the food, which he passed to Lockwood.

And then we were off. I didn't even look back in the barn at the unicorn. I was too afraid that somehow, whatever was happening to me would end up hurting the creature, turning it into that twisted vision I'd seen with my waking eyes. I couldn't bear to be responsible for that.

Orianna was fuming as we moved farther and farther from the stone tower and the barn, but the farther we moved away, the calmer my heart became.

"This is just perfect. What happened that we had to leave the only safe place for leagues around?" Orianna asked.

"Not now, tyls," Lockwood said. "Let us find a safe place first."

"Is your friend cracking up?" Orianna asked, peering at me with those huge eyes.

"Enough," Lockwood said.

Silence fell as the darkness began to creep in. Lockwood swirled his finger in the air and a small orange flame appeared just over his palm, flickering warmly in the shadows pressing in on us.

We came to the edge of the woods again, and passed beneath the cover of the trees. Immediately, we were blanketed in complete darkness, the orange flame the only light against the dying of the sky.

"I hope you're happy," Orianna said. "We're probably going to get eaten by the avara. Or maybe the haryns. And you know what those nasty little—"

Lockwood dropped the bundles in his arms and rounded on Orianna. "I would kindly ask that you shut your mouth for a moment while I secure the area, yes?"

Her mouth hung open as she glared at Lockwood for a moment before she snapped it shut.

"Fine!"

Lockwood laid the tiny flame down on the forest floor, and it doubled in size almost immediately, waving and swaying gently. It revealed that we were standing in a small clearing, perfectly round. Lockwood slowly walked around the perimeter of it, and as he touched the air with his fingers, it rippled as if he had touched the surface of a still pond, expanding ever outwards as he moved on.

I sat down on the ground, exhaustion falling over me. I didn't even realize how tired I was until I had a chance to sit. Now it was washing over me like a drowning tide.

The image of the unicorns kept popping up in my mind, unbidden. I squeezed my eyes shut, trying as hard as I could to push the images out, wanting to think of anything but them.

"Why don't you go and try and find some water?" Lockwood asked, handing a large bowl to Orianna.

"Couldn't you just conjure it?" she asked, looking at the bowl, then the darkness, with clear unease.

"I've just spent my energy protecting us," he said. "There's a small stream a short walk from here."

"If you set up protection charms, won't I get lost?" she asked.

"You won't, since you already know the location. You'll be able to see it. No one else will."

Orianna glared, but took the bowl and floated out of the circle. As soon as she broke the tree line, she disappeared entirely.

"Here," Lockwood said, kneeling beside me. He placed the bundle of food the faerie had given him into my arms, and smiled gently at me. "Would you mind seeing what he's given us to eat while I set up the tent?"

I nodded glumly and pulled open the bag.

"This … is all food from Earth," I said, a little surprised.

Lockwood smiled as he started to pull the sticks and fabric of the tent apart. "I wondered."

"How?" I asked, my fingers grazing over the food in disbelief.

"It isn't really food from Earth. It's part of that faerie's magic. They can give you certain types of plants that will appear to be your favorite foods. And when you eat them, they will seem to be just that." He peered over my shoulder. "What do you see?"

"Some apples, tea, and berries."

"I see some of my favorite fruits that I ate as a boy here in

Faerie," Lockwood said, pulling one of the apples from the sack. He bit down into it, the juice trickling down his chin. "Mm. But you see an apple, yes?"

"Strange," I said.

Lockwood finished chewing and stared hard at me. "No … what was strange was what happened to you at the farm."

I looked down at my hands.

"What did you see, Cassandra?"

"I don't know, it's hard to explain. It's like …" I sighed. "It's like I am seeing an alternate version of Faerie. A dark side of it. Like the opposite. It's frightening. That unicorn … it was dead. There were a lot of them dead. The fields were burning, and there were soldiers in white armor—"

Lockwood's face drew tighter as he listened.

"It happened back at Stormbreak, too. The first time I saw it. Except there was a dark mist all over the city. And then in the shop—"

"You better appreciate the work it took me to get this water!"

Orianna's voice filled the clearing as she suddenly reappeared, the bowl in her hands sloshing as water spilled over the sides.

Lockwood took the bowl from her hands. "There's barely anything left."

"Well, then you go get some yourself," she said, crossing her arms over her chest. "I'm not going back out there to be eaten by greedy, hungry pigs. Have you seen their snouts? They can probably smell someone as tasty as me from miles away."

Lockwood's jaw clenched, but he took the bowl and disappeared through the trees.

Orianna smirked, tossing her swirling hair. There was no doubt she knew how much she annoyed him—and reveled in it.

"You look pleased," I said, in no mood to let her prima donna her way through Lockwood's last nerve.

Orianna crossed her legs and sat down in front of me, hovering just above the ground. She squinted her eyes and stared at me. "You're strange, even for a Seelie," she said after a long pause.

I raised an eyebrow, a little rattle of nerves tickling the back of my neck. "Am I?"

"You don't seem to care much that you can't fly. That would drive me insane."

"I prefer walking," I said, trying to keep calm and lie on, as my version of the slogan went. "It's good to stretch my legs."

She made a face that suggested she might have downed a lemon by accident. "You're joking, right?"

I sighed, shaking my head.

"What's bothering your friend, hmm?" Orianna jerked her head toward Lockwood. "He seems a rather surly individual."

"Um … you?" I asked. "You are bothering him. I thought that was your intention."

"Okay, yes." Orianna rolled her eyes. "But it's more than just me, come now. I might be a nuisance, but he's burning with some glorious purpose, isn't he?"

I looked down. Sharing details of Lockwood's quest—most of which I didn't even know—with Orianna? Sounded like a bad idea. "I suppose he is," was as much as I was willing to admit.

Orianna gasped with delight. "You don't know, do you?" She giggled excitedly. "Oh, isn't this a surprise?"

"Don't be ridiculous," I snapped, staring at her. Angry and defensive. Not an effective posture for denial. But I was too deep in now to back off it. "Of course I know."

She giggled again, reminiscent of a chorus of bells. "You're a young Seelie, aren't you? Haven't quite mastered the art of deception yet?"

It was like a slap in the face. Me? Not good at lying?

Oh, hell no, she did not just throw down on my only marketable skill.

Lockwood reappeared, a very full bowl of water levitating behind him.

"What's the matter?" Lockwood asked, stopping and staring from Orianna to me. He turned his gaze on Orianna. "What did you say?"

"Nothing that she didn't already know," Orianna trilled, grinning innocently up at him.

She was right. It wasn't anything I didn't already know.

Still … being stuck here, in Faerie, on this quest with Lockwood, who I really didn't know that much about …

It stung anyway.

Chapter 14

The tent that Lockwood had procured from the faerie turned out to be a great surprise. I followed Lockwood inside, only to find that he was nowhere to be found. I could hear him, but it wasn't very big, and there was nowhere for him to hide.

"Where are you?"

"It's the magic, Cassandra."

"Please, she hasn't ever been in a tent before?" Orianna's voice rang through the air, as if she were sitting right beside me. "How old is she?"

"Ignore her. You are in your own tent, but we are all occupying the same space."

"But—"

"*Magic*, Cassandra."

I sighed, but soon forgot the other two. There was a soft, squishy feather mattress waiting for my bedraggled, exhausted self, along with blankets that would have kept a polar bear warm. As soon as I lay down in it, I fell into a deep sleep.

The next morning, I woke feeling more rested than I had in months, and I had a sneaky suspicion that Lockwood—or magic—or both—had something to do with it.

I polished off the berries from the night before in silence, my stomach still rumbling uncomfortably. Was it possible that back on Earth, it was still the night before?

I shook my head. Nope. Didn't want to expend the energy

it would require to wrap my head around that. Physics was never one of my favorite subjects.

"Good morning, sleepy head," Lockwood said as I lumbered out of the tent.

Orianna and Lockwood were already awake, Orianna hovering above the small orange flames that still burned as brightly as the night before, Lockwood standing on the edge of the clearing, staring out into the pale woods beyond. Their gazes did not meet.

At all.

I had a feeling some words had been exchanged.

"What's the plan for today?" I asked, trying not to reignite whatever conflict was between them. I'd seen enough of that yesterday anyway.

My teeth were mossy as I ran my tongue over them. A toothbrush would have been a great—

A small bundle appeared in my hands, and Lockwood looked meaningfully at it.

I peeled back the cloth and found a small tube of toothpaste and a toothbrush, along with a small hairbrush.

I smiled at him gratefully. "Thank you …" I mouthed, and I slipped back into the tent to clean up.

Refreshed and happier, I returned to them a few minutes later. Orianna took no notice of me, still hovering and staring up at the sky, presumably pointedly avoiding looking at Lockwood.

"We are still at least two days from the border of Seelie," Lockwood said. "It would be best for us to get moving as soon as we can."

With a blink of my eye, the tent was collapsed, the fire put out, and there was no evidence in the grass that we had been there at all.

I shook my head. I wasn't sure I was ever going to get used to Lockwood openly using magic. Had he used it like this in front of me on Earth without my even realizing it? Probably.

"Shall we?" Lockwood asked. "We need to find one of the main roads."

"No," Orianna protested. "We need to stay off the main roads."

Lockwood glared at her. "It is the fastest way to Seelie."

"You don't know how bad it is now," Orianna said. "What sort of corruption has been—"

"You're one to talk of corruption, Unseelie," Lockwood said darkly. "We take the main roads and you'll have a better chance of finding a caravan to latch onto. Like the snifflefrim worm you are."

Her fists were firmly planted at her side. "You would do well to heed my words, Seelie. It will be to your detriment that you won't humble yourself and take advice from me."

"Maybe we should listen to her …" I said. I really couldn't explain why, but something was telling me that she wasn't lying or being actively deceptive in that moment. Call it liar's intuition.

Lockwood shook his head. "No. Cassandra, I understand your heart is in the right place, but I still know these parts better than her," he said, with a pointed look at Orianna. "We will take the main roads. But we will glamour you. It's safer for us all if we do."

Orianna reddened. "You are going to regret that decision. I promise you."

I groaned. The last thing that we needed was any more difficulty.

I still worried about the flicker I had been seeing. I was unsure what it was or what was causing it. Was it something that might happen in the future? Or was it something that *would* happen? It didn't make any sense. But since Orianna never gave Lockwood and me more than a moment to speak, it was likely I wouldn't understand what was happening for some time—because hell if I was going to give away that I was experiencing magical acid trips to Orianna, in spite of how innocent and/or helpful she might have appeared to me. Her finding out I was a human suffering bizarre hallucinations was trouble we definitely didn't need.

With a sick feeling in the pit of my stomach, I followed Lockwood back through the trees, grateful that he knew the way. I would have gotten hopelessly lost in these woods, especially if they were intentionally trying to confuse us.

I kept glancing over my shoulder at Orianna, who was

refusing to walk at all, it seemed. Her wings were moving so fast they were nothing more than golden blurs, and they hummed like a hummingbird's. She just buzzed along behind us, staring at the ground like a bloodhound or a pouting child, the sound of her wings like white noise.

What was her plan? It wasn't like Lockwood and I could really offer her anything. She certainly had enough to say about Lockwood's choices. Was it because she was Unseelie that she was so obstinate?

Though Lockwood, to be sure, wasn't all that much better, at least as it related to Orianna. He seemed to tolerate her for my sake. He always seemed about a half second from violently exploding and telling her to leave, which I was … mixed on. In spite of my initial pity, Orianna had been enough of a pain in the butt by now that if we weren't in a dangerous spot, I'd have gladly told her to take her leave. As it was, I didn't want to leave her high and dry.

The image of Orianna leaning on Lockwood's blade flashed across my mind, and I wondered with a jolt of fear if he actually could overpower her. Did Unseelie have some sort of hidden powers? Did she? Was that why Lockwood was so wary of her?

I rolled my eyes and nearly tripped over a protruding root in the ground.

Maybe I had been too eager to allow her to come with us. But could we really have stopped her? She could have easily tagged along with us, and then it could have ended in a fight. If she had somehow taken down Lockwood … what would have happened to me?

I shuddered.

"What's the matter, little Seelie?" Orianna patted me on the head.

I ducked away from her, waving her hand away.

"Nothing," I lied.

"Hmph," Orianna said.

"Here we are," Lockwood said, taking a step up.

And I realized what he meant. We had found our way to a great cobblestone street, but unlike any I'd ever seen on Earth. The stones were all exactly the same size and were white with a sheen like a pearl. The road was bordered with a long stretch of stone like a sidewalk, but there were no weeds poking up through cracks or pieces of gum scattered on top. It was so perfect and so clean it might have been finished just a moment before.

Yet something told me that these roads were older than me by ten times. Maybe even more. And the strangest thing was that it was entirely deserted. There was no sound of anyone in the distance, and our footsteps echoed off of the trees as we walked.

"This really is the stupidest thing that you've suggested this far," Orianna said, hovering just off of the road. Her arms were crossed, and her eyebrows were knit together in one angry line. Her cranky disposition made her golden aura glow with a darker sheen.

"I already told you. You don't have to follow us," Lockwood said, already starting up the road.

"And I already told *you*, it's stupid to travel alone. So I'm stuck with stupid either way."

"I'd really rather you chose the other form of stupid, then," Lockwood said. "The solo form, where you can inflict your charming personality only upon yourself."

"Can we just … not fight for a little while?" I asked. "Please?"

Lockwood's eyes were narrow as he glared at Orianna. Without another word, he turned and started up the deserted road.

I huffed, but continued on after him.

My feet were sore from the day before, and I nearly asked Lockwood to conjure me up some comfortable boots or something. But I couldn't say anything remotely human-like with Orianna around.

So I had to suffer in silence.

As we walked, I wondered what sort of creatures traversed this road that made it so necessarily large. Four or five horses could have easily walked down it, side by side. Were there creatures this large in Faerie? Giant unicorns, maybe? Perfectly healthy, non-bleeding-in-vision ones?

Yeah … I didn't really want to know the answer to that

question.

"Come on, Seelie, aren't your wings better by now?" Orianna moaned. "We could go much faster if we flew!"

"Are you mad?" Lockwood asked. "We are sure to be spotted if we were to fly. The whole point of walking is to stay out of sight."

Orianna trilled with laughter. "You really did something naughty, didn't you?"

Lockwood ignored her, but I wondered the same thing. I knew that Lockwood was using that as an excuse because of me, since I obviously didn't have real wings, but since he couldn't lie …

Lockwood suddenly stopped. His gaze was intent, pointed at something off in the distance, through the trees.

I followed his eyes and my heart sank.

There was a place that looked like it had once been a perfectly lovely little fairy tale cottage. The thatched roof was scorched and blackened. Half of the stone wall had been knocked down, the stones like pebbles at this distance, rolled all over the earth before it. The garden out front was trampled and mangled, no sign of crops within, only upturned earth and carbon scoring close to the building.

"This war is touching all corners …" Lockwood murmured.

A house so remote, so far removed, that was destroyed like this?

Orianna fluttered over to us. She crossed her legs in midair and shrugged. "They were probably hiding an Unseelie. They destroyed the house for good measure."

Lockwood's face was murderous. "And what if they were hiding a Seelie? It is far more likely that is the work of Winter."

I flicked my glance between the two of them. There was no way to tell, I suspected.

"Whatever happened … it shouldn't have," I said. Somehow, it was sadder to wonder what had happened to the owners than to know. An untold story that we would probably never know the ending to.

"Come on. It's not wise to linger in places of Winter

magic," Lockwood sneered.

"Summer magic can be just as deadly," Orianna spat.

Lockwood was silent for some time after that, his hands in the pockets of his tunic. I could see the tension in his shoulders and posture of his body.

Orianna had taken up humming again, apparently unperturbed by what we had seen. Maybe she had seen so much that she was just desensitized. Or maybe she really didn't care.

"I wonder who lived in that house," I murmured. "If they had kids. Or if they lived there alone … ?"

"War doesn't care who gets hurt," Lockwood said. "As long as victory is achieved, the winners will write it all off as collateral damage."

My stomach tied itself in knots. A lump formed in my throat. He said that with too much conviction to have been a simple bystander …

Suddenly, before I could react, I was yanked to the side, off the road and back into the trees.

Lockwood's hand was clamped over my mouth, and he was shooshing in my ear.

My heartbeat pounded in my chest, and the hair on the back of my neck stood up.

He must have grabbed Orianna, too, because I blinked and she was there beside me, golden hair tangled up in the branches of a large bush. Through the leaves, I could see the clear sky overhead.

My heart skipped a beat as a half a dozen faeries flew over us, all wearing the same white armor that I had seen at the farm the day before, when the whole world had wavered. Their wings made but a whisper, and they flew with great speed.

"Patrols …" Lockwood said after they had passed. He helped me to my feet, where I dusted off the knees of my jeans, and winced as I touched a small prickle on the back of my arm where a branch had gotten me. When I pulled my finger away, there was blood on it.

I quickly hid my hand behind my back. Red blood would be a dead giveaway to Orianna that I wasn't, in fact, a real faerie.

"Patrols for what?" I asked.

"All this war nonsense," Orianna said.

Lockwood's eyes blazed. "It would seem to make sense to try and keep the enemy out of your lands."

"This isn't their lands," Orianna laughed. "Or it wasn't. They're not even here for anything as noble as conquest, either. Probably just looking for anyone they can string up—"

"I'm done listening to you." Lockwood grabbed my wrist and pulled me to the road once more as we resumed our walking.

Orianna floated back over to us, her eyes fiery.

"I see that you still took the time to hide me, too," she said. "Summer soldiers … I'm sure they would have enjoyed finding me here."

"They would have searched the area had they found you," Lockwood said. "I couldn't very well risk being spotted."

I was staring up into the sky once more.

"Why are you afraid of your own people?" Orianna asked, a genuine curiosity oozing out.

"I'm ensuring that we get to Seelie as quickly and as safely as possible," Lockwood said. "Being forced to stop and answer questions from some junior officer looking to his regulation book would slow us down."

There was a movement just above the tree line, but it moved so fast that I couldn't be sure I actually saw it.

"Shouldn't a paladin be able to waltz right into the court?" Orianna asked. "Oh, that's right!" She snapped her fingers. "You aren't one anymore!"

I squinted, and was sure that I could see a patch of white there. Was it a cloud? Why wasn't it moving? Why hadn't I seen any clouds in Faerie?

"It is none of your business why I am choosing to—"

"Um … guys?" I said, pointing up at the tree. "What's that?"

Lockwood and Orianna both looked up, and at the same time, the thing revealed itself to be three more of the white-clad patrol Seelie. They stood up on the branches of the tree, as effortlessly as birds, staring down at the three of us.

"Good morning, there, friends," called one of the patrols. In spite of what he said, he did not sound ... friendly.

Lockwood tensed again. "Good morning," he called back.

"You folks all right?" one of the others, a skinny male with green wings and hair, asked. "Awfully strange to see Seelie walking along the roads instead of flying."

"I've been injured," I called, knowing very well that Lockwood would not be able to lie for me. I might as well step up and be of some use. "My companions have been kind enough to travel with me at my own speed."

"Why haven't you seen a healer, yet?" the first one asked.

"Haven't had a chance," I replied. I could see it written all over Lockwood's face that he wanted me to *stop*, but I saw a chance to get rid of them if I spun them a pretty enough tale. "Been wandering through Unseelie territory for days before we even made it here. Ran into some avara and Unseelie ... not a lot of charity out here, let alone healers that'd be happy to see our like." I glanced back at Orianna; I didn't know when she'd done it, but she looked different ... less golden, a little more muted. I had a feeling she was trying to pass for Seelie.

The three patrol Seelie nodded to each other. "Are you all going back to friendly territory?" one of them asked.

"We are trying," Lockwood said before I could answer. His arm was outstretched toward me to prevent me from continuing. Apparently I had done enough.

"Good. It's quite dangerous out here in these lands. No place for the two lovely Seelie that you travel with." The third Seelie, with dark red wings like blood, grinned.

Lockwood's hand curled into a fist.

Something was definitely not right. Their tones were too sweet, too cheerful. Like honey covering something rotten.

"You know there's a tax for those who travel these paths," the one with the green wings said nonchalantly. The three of them fluttered down to land on the road in front of us, barring our way.

"A tax?" Lockwood asked.

The green haired faerie nodded his head, a smug expression creeping onto his features. "Not a great amount, really. A small toll. To offset the troubles of patrolling here, extending the Seelie dominions to these ... barbaric lands."

"That seems awfully convenient ..." I said, my brow furrowing. *For them,* I didn't say.

Lockwood shot me a warning look.

"Where does this tax come from?" Lockwood asked. "The court?"

The fairy with the pale purple wings sneered. "No ... it's a little more local than that ..."

"Let's say ... from your purse ... to ours," the second said, his green wings trembling with delight.

Oh. They came all the way down here to give us a shake down.

Lockwood straightened his shoulders. He was taller than all three of them, and looked rather formidable as he stared down at them. But even still ... it was only him against three.

"No," Lockwood said flatly. "Nice try. But the court will be hearing of this as soon as I—"

"What the court doesn't know won't hurt them," the purple faerie said.

"They really couldn't care less what happens to you," the green faerie said. "As long as they are getting their land and their power, they will let us do ... whatever it takes ... to keep things ... quiet out here."

"You are despicable," Lockwood said. "A disgrace to that armor you wear."

"And you would know that how?" the red faerie replied, arching his brow. "You are talking big words for such a small fool."

"Lockwood ..." I muttered under my breath in warning. I could see him rubbing the tips of his fingers together. If he were to snap them and ... who knew what ... "Maybe let's not do anything hasty."

"You should listen to your little injured friend, there," purple wings said. "Hey, maybe I'll take her along as payment, too. Not like she can get away if she tried—"

Lockwood snapped. Suddenly there was a great cacophony of metal striking metal as little blue lights appeared over our heads. As I stared at them in awe, I realized that they were hundreds of razor-sharp arrows, just floating there above us. The air around them throbbed with power, and I gaped at Lockwood. He had made these … appear …

… Out of nothing.

"Leave." The air around Lockwood was swirling like a tornado, his hair whipping around his face, which was creased with dark concentration. "Now."

The three patrol Seelie grinned in spite of their peril. Pointed teeth stuck from between their lips like miniature vampire canines, and magic swirled in their hands as they all conjured weapons of various shapes and sizes. I saw axes and polearms and swords aplenty as they stood there, the arrows hovering over them.

They stared at us. We stared back at them.

Lockwood wasn't backing down an inch.

"You really want to do this?" Red wings said. "Attacking Summer troops is a capital offense."

"You threatened first," Lockwood said coolly.

The arrows above spun slowly, still pointed at the patrol. I swallowed hard. I really didn't want to see them hit their target.

"You declined to pay the toll," the green Seelie said, casually examining his weapon. "I suppose we'll just have to claim it from your purse after you are dead—"

They all leapt toward us as one, each of them picking a target. They moved like Lockwood, speeding at us in a blur—

I flinched, covering my head with my hands.

The whoosh of arrows flying sounded like a brief rain. The sickening thud of them all hitting their targets prompted me to open my eyes even as I took a knee in a vain attempt to dodge whatever was coming my way.

But nothing was coming my way.

The patrol was dead, smote by a half a hundred magical arrows. They glowed as they stuck out of the Seelie bodies, laid out on the perfect white road, silver blood leaking across the flawless stones.

Lockwood had killed them. With such little effort, all three of those Seelie were …

"Come on, we need to go before these three are found," Lockwood said quietly.

"Lockwood … you killed them," I whispered.

"They aren't dead," he said.

It took me a second to process what he was saying.

"They … what?"

"They're still alive," Lockwood said. "Barely. It's better than they deserve."

Relief washed over me like warm water on a cold day.

"What did you use?" I looked over my shoulder. Orianna was still there, staring at the grotesque scene before us.

"Pinpointed harpy poison," Lockwood said.

Orianna nodded approvingly. "Nice choice." She snickered. "Well, they'll feel that for days, won't they?"

I could only stare at their bodies. How could they live with that many wounds?

Magic, is what I assumed Lockwood would say. Magic, and that would be the only explanation I would get.

"Thanks for the help, by the way," Lockwood said, snapping his fingers. I watched as the bodies were lifted into the air by some invisible force, and floated easily over to the side of the road. He let them down gently just behind a group of dense trees.

Orianna shrugged. "Not like you needed it. Besides, now I know what you're really capable of." She giggled, and her eyes flashed dangerously.

Lockwood rolled his eyes. Another snap of his fingers and the patrol's blood was gone.

My chest hurt from how fast my heart was beating.

Orianna crossed her arms over her chest. "You know, I wasn't going to say anything because you're so upset, but I think that's exactly the reason why I am going to say something."

Lockwood glared at her. "What do you mean?"

"I told you so," she said. "That the roads were too dangerous."

I looked at the patrol as leafy vegetation seemed to swallow them up magically, between the waist-high leaves of a blue fern. It waved and swooshed as the Seelie disappeared beneath them, there to wait until they recovered from the poison, presumably, or someone found them.

Either way, it seemed Orianna was right. I could tell because Lockwood said nothing, just looked at her hard, and led us off the white road into the wilderness once more.

Chapter 15

We followed the road but stuck to the tree line alongside it, the white stones like a glowing river on our left as we walked through the magical countryside of Faerie. A few minutes after our encounter with a patrol we saw a flight of faeries of indeterminate origin, wings the shade of pale blue silk, flapping lightly as they went by, using the road as their guide. Minutes after that, another group came through, then another after. The farther we walked, the more we saw, going in either direction. None of them saw us.

"We would probably be safe to walk on the road," Lockwood said as a patrol passed, in their distinct armor. The others we'd seen most recently had seemed to be civilians just traveling. These were obvious, though. "I doubt every patrol tries the same shakedown tactics."

"It's a lot more common than you think," Orianna said. She kept low with every pass of wings over the road. Her eyes darted around, suspicious, but she said no more.

After a time, the forest melted away once more, we left the flawless white road behind as the forest gave way to low rising hills, the treeline pushed back to make way for a small town in the distance, nestled between two green hills.

The closer we got, we realized it was not, in fact a town, something stone and dignified on the order of Stormbreak.

It was really more like a camp.

There were tents of all sizes and colors, and a large wall of what looked like ice surrounding it, almost entirely see through. Long rows of men in white armor, the same as the patrol that had attacked us, were marching in such a way that I knew they were practicing drills, streaming across the fields in slow formations.

At the center of it all stood a large, white tent that reminded me of one I'd see at a wedding.

"This is a Seelie outpost," Lockwood said after studying the central tent. "We should try and stay here for the night. If they allow it."

Orianna gave me a pointed look. "You ambushed one of their patrols just hours ago, and now you want to try and rely on the charity of Summer?" She laughed. "Certainly. Fine. Hopefully your ward won't have another tantrum … assuming we don't get found out for what you've done." Her eyes glowed a little brighter. "Or you don't get found out for … whatever you're avoiding Seelie soldiers for."

Lockwood looked at me with concern. "The tyls raises valid points, especially in regards to our actions." He shot Orianna a pointed look. "This being less an army camp than an outpost, a steady flow of civilians through will be normal. They won't be checking too seriously for identification, but," he made a wave of his hand and my wrist tickled, "just in case."

We started up one of the hills toward the camp once more.

"You aren't afraid?" I asked, looking over at Orianna.

She shook her head, and I thought I heard a sound like jingle bells. "No. As your friend said, they won't be looking closely for Unseelie. They don't think an Unseelie would be stupid enough to enter one of their camps." She smiled. "For the most part, they're right." Her eyes shimmered. "Besides, there's little an Unseelie could even do in one of these places."

I frowned, wondering what she meant by that.

Lockwood steered us through into the camp, past the walls of ice. He led the way, and knew all of the right words to say, apparently, because they let us right in. I wondered how they would have reacted if they knew what he had done, or who he really was. Another thing that itched at the back of my head, another little secret. Was it common knowledge that he had been exiled? No one asked him, and he certainly wasn't going to tell. He just marched us right through as though we belonged.

It was obvious this camp had been there for some time. Fire pits had been dug in the ground, and there were personal touches to every tent, like flowers or gemstones, and faeries milled around like they would in a town. Many called to one another happily, and children laughed and played like we were in a normal town.

"Who are all of these faeries?" I asked Lockwood as we walked through a long row of tents. It felt like some sort of music festival or camping event.

It was peaceful.

It felt … safe.

"Refugees, likely," Lockwood said, following behind an orange-winged faerie he'd asked about supplies. "Those who have been outed from their homes because of the conflict."

I jumped out of the way as a group of teenage boys came flying by, tossing what looked like a color-changing turtle back and forth between one another, laughing all the while.

"They certainly don't seem upset about being displaced," I said, watching as a mother cradled her new baby cooing in her arms, its tiny white wings flapping feebly.

"Looks can be deceiving," Orianna muttered under her breath, staring skeptically around.

We wandered up a hill toward the large white tent. I could hear more voices, and there was a pleasant, gentle breeze in the air that cleared the remaining fear from my mind, lulling me with the peaceful aura of the camp.

"We should definitely stay here," I told Lockwood. "I like it here."

There were fountains bubbling merrily on either side of the tent entrance, which was also being guarded by Seelie in white armor. They smiled at us as we approached. People that passed in and out of the tent all wore white tunics and robes, all with relaxed expressions. It was hard to believe there was some sort of war happening anywhere near here, or that any of these people had lost homes or … anything, really. It felt more like a resort than a refugee camp.

"Pleasant day," Lockwood said as we neared the guards.

"Hail," one of the guards said. "How can we help you?"

"I am taking them to see Lady Albus," the orange-winged faerie who was leading us said, inclining his head.

"Wonderful," the guard said, smiling, pulling back the flap. "Please go on in. She is likely seeing to her patients' afternoon treatments."

Patients? This was a … hospital?

I followed Lockwood's lead and inclined my head, smiling at the guards as we passed inside. Little lies, to belong.

The inside of the tent was magnificent. Greenery was everywhere. The air was heavy with humidity, reminding me of home, and an earthy, rich smell of soil swirled around, filling the space overhead with large blossoms that glittered and chimed. Some of them even cast a dim glow, making the whole space blend with the relaxing feel of the whole camp.

I sighed. Now *this* is what I hoped Faerie would be like. No pig monsters, no Seelie versus Unseelie war. Just greenery and pleasantness.

Lockwood seemed more at ease, too. I guess the Seelie were the safer group to be with. His shoulders looked like they'd lost most of their tension.

Orianna, on the other hand, seemed less enthused. Her eyes darted around and her mouth was set in a thin line. I wondered what might happen to her if she was caught … and if I would come to her aid or not. Probably wouldn't have been very smart for me to, given that I was a human, which was potentially worse than being a Winter fae.

We followed the path underneath another archway into what must have been the main part of the hospital. It looked like a concentric series of domes, and we were moving into the smaller ones in the center of the structure. White light shone over the greenery that draped from arches all over, given the place an almost heavenly feel.

It was like a luxury spa. Light streamed in from the windows that covered almost every inch of the walls, even though I was pretty sure there were no windows on the outside. There were people walking up and down the vast hall, all in the same white tunics, smiling and laughing together. The sound was musical, and it smelled like lavender.

There was a long row of beds that looked like massage tables, where faeries were tending to other faeries who were lying there, also in tunics. Some were having lotions rubbed on their bare skin. Others were drinking colorful drinks out of intricately carved crystal. Still others were answering questions from other faeries with red ribbons on the hem of their tunics. They must have been the nurses or healers.

"Wow …" I breathed. We had been roughing it compared to here, the Ritz Carlton of Faerie.

A short faerie with wild black hair stepped away from one of the beds, her pink eyes wide and alert. Her pink wings, narrow but long, fluttered anxiously.

"Lady Albus?" our guide asked. "We have some visitors who wished to trade with you."

"Oh, of course," she said, her face splitting into a smile, her black hair springing in all directions like wild ebony weeds. "I'd be happy to trade with you … if you would be willing to sit with some patients as your payment."

Lockwood looked around at the faeries resting on their beds peacefully. "Trade only, then?"

"We have no shortage of currency," Lady Albus said. "But we lack carers. What are you looking for? I have a supply of ointments and tonics, not to mention some salves for those pesky injuries. Perhaps we can strike a bargain."

"She's got an injured wing," Orianna said, pointing at me.

Lady Albus's large eyes swung in my direction.

"I'm fine," I said, feeling sweat start to bead on my forehead. "Really. I've got all the treatment I need."

"What are you taking?" Lady Albus asked. "Perhaps I can replenish your stocks. Or you could have a soak in one of our mineral baths—"

"Lady Albus, is it possible that we could find a place to stay for the night?" Lockwood asked, dragging Lady Albus's attention away from me.

I exhaled with relief. *Thank you, Lockwood.* Saved again. My lies about faerie injuries were bound to be flimsy. I'd taken Anatomy and Physiology in tenth grade, but that covered humans, not fae, and I hadn't been all that good a student anyway.

Lady Albus nodded her head. "Of course. We have some spare tents that you are welcome to use. If you know any sort of healing charms, that would be a great help, too."

"I might know of some things that could help," Lockwood said.

Lady Albus beamed. "Then I believe we have a deal." And she thrust her hand out like she wanted to arm wrestle. Lockwood brought his own up in the same manner, almost touched his palm to hers, and a flash of sparking magic made me wonder if they'd tried to light some brush on fire. A moment later, it seemed to be done, whatever pact they were making sealed with a spell.

Orianna rolled her eyes, but she followed after us as Lady Albus wandered back over toward the beds.

I wished I had been in a hospital like this when I broke my leg back in fifth grade. It was quiet, the wards filled with drowsing, peaceful patients. In the next section, I could see waterfalls rolling from the ceiling above, sunlight glinting off them and making faint rainbows in the mist. The sound of the tinkling water tempted me, but I stayed with Lockwood. I wondered if I could have a shower under them later. I hoped I would have a chance to wander around a little, get a good look at the whole place.

"Here we are," Lady Albus said. "This faerie was caught in the crossfire of one of the Unseelie attacks just a few leagues outside the camp. She was looking for refuge, and the Unseelie wasted no time doing their best to 'weaken our numbers' ..." She shook her head in disgust. "I will be overjoyed when the peace talks are finished, and we can all go home."

"If they ever finish ..." Orianna mumbled.

Lady Albus sighed heavily. "You're quite right. I don't even know if they have picked them back up."

"The last I heard, they abandoned them all together," Orianna said, shrugging. But there was a strain in her eyes as she stared at the ground.

"That is not good if that's what is happening," Lady Albus

said. "We need those talks to continue. The Unseelie can have this accursed territory all to themselves for all I care. This is hardly in our borders, after all." Lady Albus seemed to lose herself in considering this future, scratching at her wild hair. "With the war over, my hospital wouldn't be used for any more than minor injuries. And it wouldn't have to be in a tent anymore, either."

I looked down at the faerie who had been attacked. She was lying on her back, hands folded over her chest as if she were practicing some breathing exercises. But she wasn't moving at all.

I reached out and put my hand on hers, just to let her know that someone was there, and someone cared about what happened to her.

Then I shrieked, jumping away from her.

The whole room had gone dark, the light dying around me as though the sun had been snuffed out. The tent shrank, the walls turned from glass to cloth and flapped madly as if caught in a terrible wind storm. The girl on the bed was sprawled, limbs at odd angles, a long gash across her throat spewing silver blood, her eyes, open and blank, staring into the abyss.

My heart thundered in my ears, blood pumping furiously, painfully through my veins. I wheeled around.

The golden light had gone. Only dim light remained, like lit candles in the night, where I could just see cots filled with moaning, screeching, crying faeries. Nurses hurried between the beds, casting spells or charms over them, trying to do anything to ease the suffering all around.

I watched as another pair of faeries dragged a gurney in through the now-narrow flap of the tent, carrying the lifeless form of a child. The little boy's arm was hanging limp over the side, shining, silver blood dripping from the tips of his fingers. It hung there, unmoving—

Then the golden light had returned in a bright flash, as though it had never left. I was back in the vast, open space of the hospital, not in a shrunken tent, caught in a storm.

The quiet had returned.

No one looked at me. Apparently my shriek had not been

heard by any of those in the room.

My skin crawled as I pulled my hand from the sleeping faerie. Her skin was cold, like ice cubes right out of the freezer.

She was dead.

"Lockwood?" I asked.

He turned to look at me. Lady Albus looked past him at me, curious at my interruption while Orianna fluttered to the side, watching.

Lockwood's eyebrow raised in slight surprise as I grabbed him by the arm and pulled him toward the archway, back toward the door. There was no child on a gurney, no hint of death in this shining, golden place.

"We need to talk," I said, pulling him along, away from the others. He did not resist, and neither Orianna nor Lady Albus followed as I led him out of the tent.

I needed answers.

Chapter 16

"Cassandra—"

Yeah, I wasn't giving him the chance to protest.

I dragged him away from Lady Albus, back out of the tent, section by section. How was it so immense now, where in the moment that it had flashed, it had seemed smaller? Wouldn't we bump into a wall any second now?

I grimaced. I really didn't like magic very much, and the fact that it could warp my sense of reality made it even less palatable.

Like I was in the middle of the biggest lie I'd ever run across. And it wasn't even one of mine.

There were large, wide pillars that reached up into the vaulted ceiling of the hospital, plenty wide for the both of us to stand behind. When I was confident that Lady Albus couldn't see us and knew that we wouldn't be overheard, I let go of Lockwood, and we stood there, staring at each other, in an open space some thirty feet from the nearest cot. Its occupant was a male fae with blue hair who looked to be sleeping.

"What is the matter?" Lockwood asked, his eyes narrowed in concern.

"I had another … flicker," I told him, thinking it was crazy even as I said it. It wasn't possible. It couldn't be.

But I'd seen it. With my waking eyes, I'd seen it.

"What did you see this time?" he asked.

He would never understand how grateful I was that he

didn't challenge me about it or question me. A liar like me who'd been caught enough times gets used to being challenged. It was one the things that drove me the most nuts about being home with my parents lately, the constant challenges over stupid stuff.

Lockwood, though … he just believed me and skipped ten unnecessary steps.

"Everyone here …" I said, the bile rising in my throat. "They're all sick, Lockwood. Dying. Diseases, gruesome wounds … the girl that I was standing beside, the one who looked like she was sleeping? Yeah. Slit throat. Blood everywhere—"

He put his hands on my shoulder as I began to tremble.

I had never seen a dead body before. Vampires didn't count. They were already dead, and they turned to black mush when you killed them. But that girl I had touched …

She looked no older than I was. More innocent, even. She couldn't lie. And she'd seemed … alive.

But wasn't anymore. That was the truth I'd seen in the flicker.

"What I saw," I said, "it's like … I was seeing this place for what it really is, right now, instead of … some golden version of what happened in the past."

"What do you mean, in the past?" Lockwood asked.

"Remember how the faerie at the farm said that the Seelie forces had been through there weeks ago? In my flicker there, I saw the soldiers walking toward Stormbreak. And they were wearing the same armor that the Seelie here are wearing. As though I could somehow see … the past. The terrible, crop-razing event he talked about." I brushed my hair back behind my ear. "I wondered how they could have regrown all those crops so fast. It was like … an illusion or something. Just … weird."

Lockwood pursed his lips, his jaw tightening.

"Why am I the only one who can see it?"

"I really don't know, Cassandra," Lockwood replied in a low voice, his grip strengthening. "I don't understand it. I've never heard of anything like it. It's almost as if …" His gaze became distant, and he shook his head in disbelief.

"What?" I asked, not much liking the look on his face. "What, Lockwood?"

"It's almost as if you can see through glamours …" His voice was a whisper. He looked around the room, gaze hardening. "As if they are layering glamours here to keep up appearances."

"What would be the benefit of putting a glamour up?" I asked. "Wouldn't it be detected?"

"Not necessarily," he said. "Orianna doesn't know you are glamoured. And they haven't discovered hers."

"So you do all lie to one another," I said quietly. "But it's in more of an underhanded way. It's everywhere but out of your mouths."

Lockwood didn't reply. He looked pained and confused.

"So what's real?" I asked. "What I'm seeing right now?" I gestured around. "Or what I see when the whole world flickers black?"

"Both, in a sense," he said.

"Don't give me your cryptic answers," I snapped. "I am so not in the mood."

He swallowed, staring over my head.

I prodded him in the chest with one of my fingers. "What is going on here, Lockwood? Why do I keep seeing these scenes of horror and death?"

"It's the war," he said.

"What are you talking about?"

He didn't reply.

"You know," I said. "You know what's happening to me."

"I do," he said at last.

"Lockwood, tell me," I said. "I deserve to know why I keep seeing these awful things. Is this something that's happened before? Something that's about to happen? I mean, if it's a glamour, then … is it how things are now?"

"I agree, you do deserve to understand," Lockwood said, craning his neck to stare past me. He seemed desperate to not have this conversation right now. And I wasn't even sure if he could answer my questions. The anxiety emanating from him was making that pretty clear. "And I promise you that I will help you understand what is happening. But for right now—"

He grabbed onto my wrist and yanked me around the corner of the pillar. The warm, golden sunlight pouring in through the great, tall windows beside us washed over us both. I squinted against the sudden brightness.

"What the—"

"We need to hide," Lockwood said. "Someone just walked in that could ruin everything for us if he were to see me."

"Who is it?" I asked, my heart sinking.

"He's …" Lockwood said.

I carefully peered around the corner of the pillar, and saw a group of faeries standing beside the foyer stuffed with greenery, and it was obvious who Lockwood was talking about. Standing there was a tall faerie with deep green wings, dark hair, and a pointed, narrow face. His wide grin showed off perfect, pearly white teeth. He was incredibly handsome, in a dark, mysterious sort of way, but was dressed oddly, in a black jacket with tails that stretched all the way to the floor. His tunic and trousers resembled the Seelie guards' armor, though it was made of far more luxurious material.

Nurses in their red-trimmed tunics and some of the ambulatory patients were gathered around him as if he were a celebrity. He seemed to take little note of the clamor, focusing on one person at a time and giving them all his attention.

"Who is he?" I asked.

Lockwood had not looked around the pillar with me. His back was against the pillar, flat, and he was looking in the exact opposite direction, stone-faced. "He's a member of the Seelie court."

"Like … one of the people who run things in Summer?" I asked, peering up at Lockwood, withdrawing my head from around the pillar.

"Yes," Lockwood said. "That he is."

"What's he doing all the way out here?"

"I really am not—"

But then a ringing voice pierced through the dull murmurs.

"No, no, that's quite all right," the voice said, with a warm laugh. "I appreciate the offer, but I can't stay very long. We are moving on to the eastern side of the territory, evaluating the situation there."

"But Master Calvor," came a higher voice, probably one of the nurses, "surely you will stay for something to eat? It must have been a long journey, and you are welcome to rest for a spell."

There was a sound of scuffling feet, and I peered around the corner once more to see a few more nurses appear with trays in their hands, all laden with teapots, cups, bowls overflowing with fruits and sparkling treats. It was a lavish display, fit for a king.

Master Calvor waved his hands and laughed. "No, please. I wished to serve on my visit here, not be served."

"But you have done so very much for us," came the voice of Lady Albus. She had appeared within the gathering crowd, and made her way to the front to speak to Master Calvor. "Those healing here have much to thank you for."

The image of the dying patients flashed across my mind. I shook the thought away.

"I hope that bringing some fresh snowbells is a worthy offering?" Master Calvor said. He lifted a small, silk satchel from the pocket of his tunic and passed it to Lady Albus. "I ensured they were picked fresh, right before my departure."

"You are far too kind, Master Calvor," Lady Albus said, bowing deeply.

"Ah, Master Calvor. I am glad you are here."

Yet another faerie appeared, this time an elegant woman who looked more like my idea of an elf than a faerie. She had long, pointed ears that were adorned with glimmering jewels, wore a long white shapeless dress with pointed shoulders, and her eyes were slanted and heavy lidded. Her wings were nearly transparent, as white as fresh snow.

"Mistress Sana. What a pleasure it is."

The others who were gathered around Master Calvor parted like a zipper, and Mistress Sana approached him.

"I take it she's part of the court, too?" I hissed over my shoulder at Lockwood.

He glanced away, looking like he would rather be anywhere than here. He nodded his head all the same.

"I was hoping that I might catch you," she said. "Come. Let us speak in private."

And then they were heading right for us.

"Of course," I hissed under my breath. I leaned back around the pillar. "They're coming this way."

Lockwood rolled his eyes and nodded his head in a resigned, *I expected nothing less* sort of way.

The two faeries moved toward the windows where we were standing, and Lockwood and I appeared to be of the same mind as we continued to move around the pillar, ensuring we were always out of their sight. So far, neither of them seemed to suspect we were there. I kept a watchful eye for the entourage that had so recently crowded around Master Calvor, but they had seemed to already dissolve back to their duties, and none were looking in our direction.

"Just … act naturally," Lockwood said, leaning against the pillar in an unconvincing display of nonchalance.

"Right, because you're so cool," I said.

But he was right. It was best to not draw any unwanted attention to ourselves.

The other two faeries stopped on the other side of the pillar. When I peered around it, I could see their reflections in the tall windows.

"I apologize for all of the attention," Mistress Sana said in her low, breathy sort of voice. She had folded her hands in front of herself, and was peering up into Master Calvor's face.

"There is no need," Master Calvor said, inclining his head. "I am always happy to see those Seelie who are fighting for the cause. The hospital seems to be doing well." He looked around, and I ducked back behind the pillar. "Everything seems to be … holding up."

"For now," Mistress Sana said slowly. "I am sorry, Luther … I haven't had a chance to really convey my sympathies since this all happened. How have you been holding up? How is Celestia?"

Since what happened? I leaned a little closer, my ears straining to catch the words.

"Thank you," Master Calvor said. "It has been a most …

trying time. The boy's mother has been a wreck, and little aside from a mounting death toll of Unseelie will soothe her."

My heart skipped a beat. Mounting death toll sounded … rather ominous. And the outright hostility … with both of them being so open about it?

"Completely understandable," Mistress Sana said. "I would feel the same if I were in your shoes."

Master Calvor made a noise of assent. "Ensuring justice is all that matters now. Once that has been enacted, everything will be as it should be. Those filthy mongrels can go back to their open deceit and trickery, but they will always know that order shall triumph."

I chanced another look. Mistress Sana was peering out of the windows into the open fields beyond, children chasing each other back and forth among the tall grasses.

"I heard the peace talks have broken down," she murmured. "That isn't good."

"No," Master Calvor said, dipping his head. Clearly he didn't want the conversation to move that way. "There have been too many innocent Seelie slain at the hands of those … heathens. They have pushed and forced us out. Did you hear what happened at Stormbreak?"

Mistress Sana nodded. "The city itself was nearly captured. I wish it had been. We could have prevented the destruction of more homes belonging to the fae in the area. We have done all we could to provide them a place of shelter and rest. But even they have begun to suspect that things are …graver than they know."

"If that Unseelie girl had just—"

Mistress Sana held up her hand to silence him. "There is no changing the past. I apologize for re-opening old wounds. I should not keep you from your duties, and I have responsibilities of my own to return to."

Master Calvor smoothed the front of his lapel and exhaled heavily through his nose. "You are correct. Thank you, Mistress Sana, for your hospitality. The court shall be glad to hear of your success here."

"Tell them I send my regards," she said. "That I give them

my permission to use my hand in whatever vote they need to. I trust that you will do the best for the court."

"The best for the court … yes." Calvor started to pace away, his eyes fixed in a thousand-yard stare.

"Oh, and Master Calvor?" Mistress Sana said.

"Yes?" His head rose, and he blinked at her a few times.

"Do be careful."

"And you, Mistress." His face crinkled about the eyes, as he smiled as he walked off.

I lurched back around to stand beside Lockwood, whose face had paled.

"What's the matter?" I asked under my breath.

He didn't answer; he was too busy watching Master Calvor walk away.

"Lockwood … are you okay?"

He looked back at me, utterly ashen. "What?"

"What they said … did it upset you that much?" I asked.

He licked his lips and stared at his feet. "It is … not good."

"Well, I figured that much out," I said. Mistress Sana had wandered down another extension of the tent, and Master Calvor had left the tent all together, a group of guards in tow.

I leaned back against the pillar. "He was talking about a son … did something happen to a little boy?"

Lockwood shook his head. "No, not a child. The boy was an adult by any definition."

My eyes widened. "What happened?"

Lockwood stared at me, his jaw working. "He was Calvor's son, and he was killed."

I blanched. "Wow. No wonder he sounded so bitter. But …" I looked around. "… Did his son's death have something to do with the war?"

Lockwood nodded. "He was the son of one of the highest ranking Seelie in the court … and he was murdered. What is it they say on Earth? 'You do the math.'"

"Murdered?" I asked. "By who?"

Lockwood crossed his arms over his chest and stared at his feet again.

"Oh." I understood what his silence meant. "An Unseelie,

wasn't it?"

Lockwood nodded.

"Well, no wonder the Seelie are angry," I said. The aroma of rosemary was suddenly strong around me as a nurse walked by with a bowl of liquid. "I'd be mad if someone I'd been fighting for territory with just showed up and killed my son. Unless they caught him … did they know who did it?"

Lockwood closed his eyes. "Cassandra, you don't understand the circumstances. These things are never cut and dried … especially with faeries."

"What do you mean?" I asked.

"That man that you saw. Master Calvor. Tell me. What was your impression of him?"

I blinked. "Um … I don't know. I felt like they need to mop up some puddles over there where everyone was drooling over him. Powerful, obviously. He seems like he wants justice for his son."

"Anything else?" Lockwood asked.

I furrowed my brow.

"Come now, Cassandra. You're a bright girl. Really look at him. What sort of man is he?"

I shrugged my shoulders. "I don't know. He was vague? He didn't really say anything straight—"

"Exactly," Lockwood said. "Exactly! A classic sign of a politician, yes? But as a faerie, who cannot lie … he's mastered the art of the half truth, the omission of the important facts. He's dangerous, Cassandra. And his son … deserved to die." His green eyes were bright, so alive—such a contrast to the dark thing he'd just said.

I stared up at Lockwood with a fresh fear. "You … you don't actually mean that …"

"I do," Lockwood said. "I do mean it. Calvor is a wicked man, and his son was the same. He …" He took a deep breath, exhaling slowly, to steady himself. "The things those two had done, Cassandra … they were despicable."

He turned and looked at me right in the eye. "I will tell you a difficult truth, one you may not know as yet, but …" He looked around, slowly, carefully. "The people here … the Seelie … the faeries of Summer … in spite of how you may perceive them, of their beauty and seemingly fair appearance … they are like any other group. Not all of them—not nearly all—are good. And some …" His eyes were dark, muted, and a flash of anger ran across his face. "… some are simply … evil."

Chapter 17

So. Not all Seelie were the good guys, hmm?

I wished it could have been a simple black-and-white, good-guys-versus-bad-guys situation. But no. It had to be shades of grey and ambiguity. Yuck.

At least with vampires you knew where you stood. Unless they didn't try to bite your face off, they were evil.

"My deepest apologies," said Lady Albus, appearing next to us from behind the pillar. Orianna trailed after, her wide eyes staring at me curiously. "I did not realize just how strained you all were. It was unfair of me to ask you to help the patients when you, yourselves need rest."

"Lady Albus, it is quite all right," Lockwood said, though if any of us were showing the strain, it was him. "We appreciate your kindness. I would be happy to sit with some of the patients. But perhaps my companions might find a quiet place to rest?"

Orianna and I glanced at each other.

"Of course," Lady Albus said, inclining her head. "There is a small garden out back that we had erected for patients to relax. Please feel free to soak your wings in the spring. The water will help soothe your weariness." She inclined her head toward me.

"Thank you very much," I said, also nodding my head. "My wings are very, uh … weary. Why, I practically can't even feel them, they're so weary." The best lies stay close to the truth, but I probably wove a little too close on that one.

Orianna was beside me in an instant, her arm laced through my own, leading me toward the back of the tent. I glanced over my shoulder at Lockwood, who was watching us leave with a look of apprehension.

I waved at him, smiling. He didn't need to worry.

At least, I hoped he didn't.

The garden was a wonder to behold. Like a Japanese spa, steam rose from the crystal clear pond in the middle of the ground, irregularly shaped. A strong smell of sulfur was in the air, clearing my sinuses and working its way into the back of my throat. "This is like one of those hot springs on Earth," I muttered.

Orianna gave me a funny look. "How would you know?"

"I dunno," I said. "Just ... heard about them, I guess."

Her gaze sharpened. "Hm... but we should go in. Like Lady Albus said it should help your wing."

There were quite a few faeries in the garden with us. Some were seated on intricately carved wooden benches, inset with glowing crystals. Others were in the pond, enjoying the steam. I watched as one faerie, clothed in her white hospital tunic, rose from the water, not a drop of water on her.

"She's totally dry," I marveled.

"It wouldn't do them much good to be all nice and warm and then freeze as soon as they get out, would it?" Orianna stared at me as though I were a fool. "Besides, who really wants to stay wet?"

I thought of my pool back home, and how on the few occasions I'd used it, I'd stepped out of the seventy degree water and felt my teeth chatter. Maybe magic wasn't so bad after all.

Orianna wasted no time scampering over to the edge of the pond and walking right down the narrow steps inside, the steam obscuring her features.

I hesitated, then decided to dangle my feet in ... just to feel it. It didn't seem to affect Orianna's glamour, so I assumed I was safe. I lowered myself down onto the edge of the pool, not far from another faerie with pale, rose-colored wings and long, braided hair.

The water was not quite blistering, but it was definitely hot enough to make me wince. That didn't last long, though. The heat seeped into my aching calf muscles, relaxing them to the point that they felt like someone had kneaded the aches and knots out of them. I sighed with contentment, swirling my feet around. Under the glamour, I was still wearing my sneakers, but somehow I didn't even need to take them off to enjoy it.

"Feels wonderful, doesn't it?" the pale-rose winged faerie to my right said.

"It does," I said, a hum of happiness in my throat. "I can't remember the last time I was this relaxed."

The faerie had piercing blue eyes, the same color as a forget-me-not flower. But they were gentle, and wide. She was holding a small baby in her arms, its little wings wrapped around itself like a blanket.

"Oh, your little one …" I murmured, leaning a little closer. "So adorable!"

The faerie smiled. "Yes. He's only six weeks old. Can't even fly yet."

"Neither can she." Orianna had appeared, resting her arms on the side of the pool and staring up at the pink faerie and me. She gave me a mischievous look.

"Did you damage your wing?" the pink faerie asked.

I looked away. "I did, yeah."

"Well, you've come to the right place," the faerie said, adjusting the little one in her arms. He yawned and rolled more closely to her body. "This place has been our salvation. Ever since the Unseelie came to our village, we've had no place to go. My husband, he—"

The faerie's eyes filled with large, sparkling tears, and she wiped them away hastily.

"My husband was trying to get them to leave, before the tension grew anymore. There had never been any hostility before then, never. But the Winter fae were livid, saying something about how they wanted the head of one of the court members who kept a home in the town."

She shook her head. "But they were entirely mistaken. Court members hardly ever keep homes outside of the Golden City. I think it was just an excuse to burn our village

130

to the ground."

My heart clenched within me, and I wanted to reach out and touch her arm, show her that she wasn't alone. But my fear of the flickering glamour or whatever it was prevented me.

"We were nearly defenseless," the pink faerie went on, bouncing the little faerie, who was growing fussy. "It wasn't as if we had a great garrison of soldiers to protect us. My husband was one of three soldiers in the whole village." The tears returned. "We lived in peace there for centuries. Why this war all of the sudden? Why must we suffer because of some ridiculous political scandal?"

Orianna had ducked her head into the water, and was blowing bubbles just below the surface like a child. It would have been funny if I hadn't realized she was doing it because she was incredibly uncomfortable. Her eyes weren't going anywhere near the pink faerie.

I could relate, though.

"I'm sorry," the faerie said, smiling through her tears. "I know we all have our own burdens to bear. It isn't kind of me to lay this upon you when you likely have tales of your own."

"It's fine," I said. "Really. I hadn't realized that things were this bad."

"I was chased out of my town, too," Orianna said unexpectedly, emerging from the water. "Said they were turning it into an outpost of some sort, headquarters, I don't know. They killed everyone but me …" her eyes took on a vacant expression. "Told me I was the messenger, that I was the lucky one. I had to go and tell the nearest town to prepare for …" her voice drifted.

She submerged her shoulders again, drawing rippling circles on the surface with the tip of her finger. "I didn't even live in that town. I was just passing through."

I swallowed hard, the tiny hairs on my neck standing up, a small shiver racing down my spine. Orianna was Unseelie. She couldn't lie, but she was far less likely to give the whole truth. Or so Lockwood said.

I closed my eyes and took a deep breath. It never was cut

and dried, just like Lockwood said.

The pink faerie reached out and patted Orianna on the top of her head gently, smiling down at her. "You are a very brave girl. I hope that you can find peace now, moving past what you saw."

I looked between them. If this fae's tale was true, things were messier than Lockwood knew. Or maybe he already did know, and that was why he was so antsy all the time.

"I have experienced … something a little bit different than either of you," I told them slowly. It didn't feel right not saying anything. I wanted to encourage them, remind them that not everything was as awful as it looked. That faerie with her baby—she needed some hope.

I looked at both of them in turn. "I discovered a secret that was better left as a secret, and now that I have, I am in danger, constantly. I have made enemies of people in very high places, and it has cost me dearly …"

I thought about Jacquelyn, my friend from school in New York, and how my involvement with vampires had cost her her life … literally. Not to mention the respect and understanding of my parents.

"But, somehow, I've made it through. I have some very good friends who have protected me even when I didn't deserve it, and I have held onto the fact that I am not at fault for what has happened. I'm doing what I can to fix things … to make things safe for me again."

The other two were staring at me like I might be able to give them the answer to their problems … but I knew I couldn't. Even Orianna had a very transparent, desperate sort of expression.

But my own words were resonating with me. Mill … Iona … Lockwood. Those three were my strength in the world of the vampires. And Xandra. She was my strength in my personal life where the vampires and Lockwood could not tread. I was protected on all sides.

"I am very lucky to have people who really care about me … like I said, I don't deserve it." I smiled a small smile. "But I am grateful for them, nonetheless."

"Cassandra?"

I looked over my shoulder and saw Lockwood standing near the flap into the tent.

"Guess it's time for us to go," I told the pink faerie.

Orianna groaned in protest, submerging her head once more before pushing herself toward the stairs.

I reached out and put my hand on top of the pink faerie's. To my relief, the world remained as it was, and her baby wiggled in her arms, making a cooing sound. "I wish you and your little one all the best," I said. "I hope that you both find peace and comfort."

She smiled. "I hope so, too."

I withdrew my feet from the water, aware that all of my aches and pains from all over my body had gone, and walked with Orianna over to where Lockwood was standing.

"They've found a place for us to put our tent up for the night," Lockwood said, "and Lady Albus has prepared a meal for us. I thought you might be hungry."

"Starving," Orianna said.

"Did you get any rest, Cassandra?" he asked, ignoring Orianna.

I nodded. "I did. And met a really nice Seelie girl who lost her husband in an Unseelie raid."

Lockwood's face fell. "Well … I am hoping our time at the court will help turn all of this around."

That sounded funny to me. "You really think us meeting with the court is going to have any effect on this war?"

He nodded. "If I have anything to say about it, then yes. Come." And I followed him out, the feeling of temporary peace coming with me as I left the hot springs behind.

Chapter 18

That morning in Faerie was everything I wanted a morning on Earth to be. I woke up feeling refreshed, and found a large breakfast of fruits and breads waiting for me. I had the most glorious tea, a steaming cup brimming with flower petals and what looked little flakes of copper swirling around inside. It was sweet, delicate, and energizing. I made a note to ask Lockwood to keep me stocked up on the stuff.

Lady Albus had provided Lockwood with a fresh supply of food. She asked me again about my wings, which I had already forgotten about. I lied smoothly and said that the fountain had done wonders, though I still would need some time to rest them. Orianna gave me a sideways look, knowing full well that I hadn't actually fully submerged myself, but still … I did feel infinitely better than I had the day before.

We left the hospital early, just before the first sun had risen above the horizon. I had never been a morning person, but seeing the beauty all around, dawn lighting the lands in golden glow, made me want to be. I wanted to appreciate everything around me more, use my time more wisely …

I guess that was easier to think about when there wasn't a constant threat of vampires appearing at my window or killing my family.

Lady Albus seemed reluctant to see Lockwood go, insisting that he would be doing the Seelie a great service by remaining there and using his talents to help patients.

"Thank you," Lockwood said, "but I'm afraid I'm needed elsewhere."

"Should you ever change your mind, we will be here," Lady Albus said with a deep bow.

It didn't surprise me that Lockwood was good at healing. How often had I struggled with injuries and he had magically (literally) known the way to help? Salves, tonics … he even knew how to take care of the vampires.

Our farewells made, we set out upon the road, the morning breeze like a pleasant balm on my skin. The sun was warm but not hot, and it seemed to make the road glow before us.

"We are only a day or so from the Seelie border," Lockwood said, trudging along. "We will stop somewhere tonight, and in the morning, we will behold the lands of Summer." His expression hinted at both nervousness and excitement, though I supposed that those two emotions were just opposite sides of the same coin.

"That's not far," I said. My feet felt infinitely better, and I figured I could walk another day or two before they started to hurt again. Or at least I hoped so.

"Indeed it is not, Lady Cassandra," Lockwood said with a muted smile. He turned his gaze ahead, setting the pace as Orianna and I followed behind at a slower pace.

I had been looking at Orianna in a different light since the talk with her at the hot spring. She hadn't been lying … she couldn't have. But it seemed obvious she had been omitting something important. It wasn't like I hadn't during my tale, either, because I hadn't mentioned the word *vampire* once while talking, but to be the only person who had survived a massacre like that … and at the hands of her own people …

"So …" Orianna said, "Why do you let him call you Cassandra?" She kept her voice low enough that I wasn't sure Lockwood even heard her.

I looked at her, frowning. The sunlight was bright overhead, and the green, glowing haze of the forest remained in the distance. The trees were dense along the road, and the only patch of sky that could be seen was directly overhead, like a winding river in the sky.

"Why does it matter?" I asked. "I like Cassie."

"You avoided my question," Orianna said. "You let him call you Cassandra." She pointed at Lockwood's back.

Lockwood glanced over his shoulder, smirking. I guess he had heard.

"I … don't know …" I said. "He just used it once, and I never corrected him. Besides, he caught me off guard with it. He also used *Lady,* and I was more concerned about that. And … I don't know …" My cheeks turned pink. "I guess it's special when he uses it. He doesn't use it like my parents did, which was when I was in trouble. It's like … your grandfather calling you by your middle name, and he's the only one who does it."

Orianna arched an eyebrow at me, but Lockwood's smirk grew, and there was a new brightness in his eyes.

I shrugged. "It's just different with him."

"Is he your lover?" she asked. "He is, isn't he? I'm not an idiot, you know."

"All evidence to the contrary," I said. "No, I have a … partner," I said. Did faeries have boyfriends? "His name is Mill."

"Mill?" Orianna said, tapping her chin. "What an odd name."

"He's a bit old fashioned," I said.

"Yeah, but it's not a faerie name," Orianna said. "Like … at all."

"It's short for something else," Lockwood said. "He doesn't like talking about his full name either."

"Makes sense," Orianna said. "You're too good for this one anyways, Cassie."

"Hey!" I said, pointing a finger at her. "Lockwood is amazing. But he's more like a brother to me than anything else. Tells me when I'm being an idiot and protects me at the same time. I'm the one who wouldn't deserve him."

Lockwood laughed. "Brother, eh? Sometimes I feel more like your father."

Sometimes I wished he actually was my father.

But only sometimes.

Orianna shrugged again. "Strange. I just don't understand you Summer fae."

We walked in silence for a little while, and I couldn't help think about what she had said. She didn't understand Seelie? Of course she wouldn't. She was Unseelie. But how could she understand Winter fae any better? Judging by her story, they'd shown no compassion to her, and she was in exile just like Lockwood was. The two of them were outcasts, and carried all the attendant baggage that brought. Lockwood bore his well enough, I thought, looking at his gaze, anchored straight ahead. But Orianna … to think your own people betrayed you …

No wonder she felt so unsafe all the time.

"Orianna …" I said, looking over at her.

She was floating just over the ground with her hands behind her head, her face turned toward the sun. "Hmm?"

"Were you … exiled because of what happened in that village?"

She stopped floating, as if some unknown force had stopped her.

I stopped too, and Lockwood soon after. He looked back at me curiously.

"Why do you ask?" she asked.

I gave a shrug of my own. "I was just thinking about what you told me yesterday …"

Her eyes narrowed. "Yeah, well, I would have told any story to stop that faerie from sobbing all over herself anymore." But there was a pout to her lips that made me question her words.

"Because you felt pity for her," I said. "And so did I. It was a sad story, but … so was yours."

Orianna huffed and resumed her hovering down the road.

"Come on, we have to get to the Seelie court," she said.

Lockwood gave me a questioning look, but I chased after her.

"Wait, Orianna, I'm sorry," I said. "I didn't know you didn't want to talk about it."

She had folded her arms across her chest, and was staring straight ahead of her down the pristine, white road. "Yeah, well … ." Orianna said, her jaw clenched. "You started the conversation with her, and I felt like I had to say …

something. I wish it was that easy for me to feel better about things like that, because she certainly got over it easily."

Lockwood had fallen into step beside me, observing the situation.

"I overheard a part of the conversation yesterday," he said. "You were at the massacre of Howl, weren't you?"

Orianna's mouth fell open, but she quickly snapped it shut. "So what if I was?"

"I … am sorry," Lockwood replied. "That was a terrible thing the Unseelie did. The Summer Court was infuriated by the way the Unseelie treated their own people."

Orianna stared at him, her lips pressed tightly together as if she was fighting not to say something she'd regret. Finally, she huffed out a breath of air and turned away.

"Yeah, well, welcome to the real world," she said darkly. "There have been very few times where the Unseelie have welcomed me in. And believe it or not, one of the only times I can think of was when I met with Queen Pruina herself."

Lockwood blanched. "You've met the Winter Queen?"

She nodded. "I have. And she wasn't nearly as bad as the tales would suggest."

"From what I have heard, you are lucky that you lived to talk about it," Lockwood said.

Orianna waved a hand dismissively. "Exaggerations. She was very kind to me."

"Really?" Lockwood asked.

"Absolutely," Orianna said. "She was the only reason why I found any sort of home after my parents were killed."

Dead parents? Geez. This poor girl …

"I'm so sorry about your parents," I said.

Orianna shrugged. "It was a long time ago."

"What happened? If you don't mind me asking?"

"They were traitors, in some shape or form," she said, surprisingly cool, as though she were simply talking about the weather forecast. "I don't really know the whole story. I was young, and Winter fae aren't known for being very forthcoming." She pressed a finger to her cheek. "Something about passing information to Seelie scouts, or something like that. Anyway, they were executed in the middle of the

Autumn Court for all to see."

My brain spun. I thought the Winter Court was the Unseelie court? Where did this talk of an Autumn Court come from?

"Anyway, I was probably four or five, came home one afternoon to find soldiers waiting. They took me away to the court." She dropped her voice conspiratorially. "Apparently I was to be tried as well. Queen Pruina was to give me my sentence, you see. I had no idea at the time, but by the ancient laws, being the child of traitors is grounds for execution. Fruit of a poisonous tree or somesuch, and the masters of Autumn made clear that they were quite fine with that outcome. Said they feared I would turn out just like my parents, and that was too great a risk."

She shook her head, her long golden hair swirling about her as if she were in water.

"The court was … magnificent. Those golden hues and reds, the four great thrones. I was scared, so it didn't make much of an impact on me aside from, wow, these people killed my parents. But when I saw Queen Pruina, I …"

Lockwood's face was hard, and he was watching his feet as we walked. I could see from the strain near his eyes that he was listening. Intently.

"I just broke down. I was a child, what did I know, other than Mother and Father weren't coming home again? I was afraid … and there she was, all silver and blue, her hair as dark as night itself, eyes like frostbite. I was just standing there in that grand throne room on the dais made of cut crystal, trembling, tears dripping down my face. I had no hope left. I thought that something horrible was going to happen to me. But I don't know, a child doesn't understand death, right? I just expected pain."

"What happened?" I asked.

"She embraced me," Orianna said in a tone that said she hardly believed it even now. "She got down off her great throne, left her icicle scepter on the floor, and knelt before me, pulling me into her arms."

Lockwood just stared at her. I did, too.

"She told me that she was sorry that my parents were gone

now, but that she would do all she could to protect me. She said that my parents had made some terrible choices, and that she hoped that I would be able to take what had happened and grow stronger from it. Then she placed her hand on my head and told me that I was to be one of her wards. She presented me with a small, golden pin in the shape of a snowflake …"

"That is a great honor to be recognized by the queen in such a way." Lockwood was staring at her, his pace slowed.

"I found out later that she called all of the orphans in the Winter territory her wards, but I don't know how many of them actually met her. I haven't spoken to her since, though I have heard … stories of her actions." She shivered. "Like Winter itself … she can be ruthless."

"Well, I suppose even the Winter Queen wouldn't be so heartless as to harm an innocent child," Lockwood murmured.

Orianna sighed, shaking herself as if to rid herself of the gloom that had settled over her. "Well, regardless, that's my take on her. I try not to dwell on what she's done since. I get that she's hardened and lives up to her title of being the Queen of Cold, but still … there's more to her than that."

I chewed on the inside of my lip.

There was more to Orianna than her flippant attitude and moods that could change on a dime. She actually had a heart, and there seemed to be things in her past that had made her so uncaring on the outside.

"You've been through a lot," I said.

Orianna gave me a sideways glance, and a mischievous grin spread over her face. "I have. But so have you, by the sounds of it."

Throwing the spotlight on me to avoid talking about herself. A clever way to divert the conversation away from herself when things were hitting a little too close to home.

This, I understood.

"You don't even know the half of it," I said, letting her throw the attention back on me and off her past. If I had been through what she had, I would have taken every opportunity to try and forget it.

Even though my parents drove me insane, and there was very little about my life that I could be honest with them about, I was suddenly immensely grateful that I *had* parents to go home to. And they had been there all my life. They had loved me, raised me, cared for me.

Orianna had nothing but the brief embrace of a queen. Two minutes of glory and attention since she was four years old. Whatever had happened to her after that ... well, it seemed a sure bet she hadn't grown up in a loving home with people who cared deeply about her.

I sighed. "You want to hear a story?" Maybe this would take her mind off her troubles.

Orianna's eyes seemed to flutter before settling on me. "Yes."

"All right," I said. "There was this one time when Lockwood and I faced off against a vicious enemy who called himself 'The Butcher' ..."

Orianna's eyes lit with curiosity, and I could see Lockwood watching me carefully to ensure that I was keeping our secrets secret, but Orianna was more than happy to listen. Maybe faeries were always vague with one another, because telling the unvarnished truth was just too difficult.

I knew a little something about that.

Take it from a reforming liar—telling the truth can be the hardest thing in the world.

Chapter 19

"We are nearly there," Lockwood said, coming to a stop just outside of a large archway made from intertwining branches and flowers. "This is one of the cities on the outskirts of the Seelie court's territory. We will rest here for a short time and be at the court by late tomorrow."

"Why not just keep going?" I asked. "There's plenty of daylight left."

"Nope," Orianna said, shaking her head. "I'm with Grumpy, here. It's wiser to stop and rest for the night. I really would not like to walk along in the darkness. Even these borders are not safe."

I sighed. "The longer we delay …" I said to Lockwood, glaring at him to convey my anxiety about getting home.

"I know," he said. "It will all work out."

I sighed. "Fine. I could eat something anyways. That bread from this morning feels like it was forever ago."

"That's because it practically was," Orianna said. She was staring up at the archway, her hands curled into fists.

"Well, what are we waiting for?" I asked, realizing we weren't actually moving toward the village.

"I'm just …" Lockwood was standing in the middle of the road, unmoving.

It took me a second of watching him scanning ahead to realize he was worried he was going to run into someone he knew. It was like the prospect of running into an ex. It's horrible and awkward and makes you want to turn around and take off in the other direction.

Except his ex was actually the law, and I wasn't sure, but I was pretty sure that we were in danger if they caught him.

But he was the one who had dragged me here, and I was going to help him.

After seeing all of these faeries, Seelie and Unseelie, who had been affected by this war, I understood why this was so important for Lockwood to right it all. Even though I still had no idea how he was connected, or what he had done to get himself exiled.

"Should you glamour yourself?" I asked him.

"No. I should return home as myself." He shook his head. "Come, let us go and try and find some accommodations."

He started off down the narrower path paved with the same white stones as the main road. Orianna and I followed, Orianna even more hesitant about it than I was.

The whole situation was ridiculous. Lockwood was going to get in trouble if he was discovered by the wrong people. Orianna was a Winter fae in Summer territory. And I was a human posing as a faerie.

What a merry group we made.

The town itself was beautiful. There were little houses along the path, all tucked away among the gently rolling hills and trees. Most of them were up in the branches above our heads, like little bird houses.

There were shrubs and flowers everywhere, and everything looked inviting. A floral scent hung in the air, and an unfamiliar bird sang high in the branches of the trees among the homes. The branches overhead intertwined, casting cool shadows onto the paths below, like many bridges and pathways in the sky.

Lockwood was looking all around. In every direction, into every face, as if anticipating discovery at every second.

There had to be some better way to do this. Some way where he could conceal himself and still be able to get to the court.

"Lockwood ..." I said, coming up to his shoulder. "Can't we—"

"I'm all right," he said. "Truly, I am. I am going to be

discovered here one way or another. I would just rather arrive at the court on my terms, not as a prisoner."

A prisoner? He was joking, right?

Oh, right. Faerie. Can't lie.

Great.

We crested a low hill and found ourselves in the town center. It was quaint, with a bubbling fountain in the center, the figurehead a pair of faeries standing face to face with their hands interlocked, their backs arched, and their lips nearly touching. Their wings were outstretched behind themselves, carved in such a way that the play between the water and the sunlight made them appear opaque. Maybe they actually were.

The fountain's quiet rushing was like a peaceful reminder of the hospital's springs. The sun shone down, gentle kisses on my skin beneath the glamour that protected me from curious eyes.

A few larger buildings surrounded the fountain and the park that encircled it. Faeries of all ages were gathered there, either lying in the grass watching little ones play, or flying in and out of the shops in the trees or on the forest floor. A white-washed building with a thatched roof directly behind the fountain must have been the inn, and smoke poured from its large chimney.

But the front door wasn't on the ground. It was way up on the fourth floor.

The sweet floral smell was denser here, as vines intertwined between the buildings like Christmas lights, adorning every window and roof. There was a gentle breeze that carried the pleasant murmur of the voices of the faeries as they went about their daily lives.

It was as if the war being waged just outside in the forest beyond didn't exist.

"Come," Lockwood said, and we made our way along the outside of the road, away from the park and the fountain, heading in the direction of the inn.

Orianna hovered close to me, shooting me nervous smiles whenever I caught her eye.

When we were within a block or so of the inn, Lockwood

scooped me up into his arms, and my stomach lurched as he took off into the air, the door above us drawing ever closer as we flew.

He landed lightly on the small porch out front and set me down gently.

My knees trembled, the adrenaline kicking in. I willed the whole world around me not to spin. Grabbing onto Lockwood's arm helped.

"What, did you forget what it was like to fly?" Orianna sneered.

"Yes. I've forgotten what it's like to fly." I kept my face utterly straight, and noticed a waver in hers, a little horror slipping in at the thought of being so encumbered, then I pushed through into the inn after Lockwood.

It was warm inside, with a friendly fire crackling in the large stone hearth, though definitely odd because the flames were green and purple. Every surface inside was wood or stone, and I felt like I was in a child's picture book. My skin tingled as I realized how surreal my life had been over the last few days.

"Good afternoon," the woman behind the counter said. She was a very striking faerie, with long, flowing curls of fluorescent magenta, with tiny braids tied all around her head, each secured with a tiny blue stone. "You three be needing rooms?"

"Yes," Lockwood said, dipping into his pockets for his change purse. "Two, please."

"I'm sorry, but we only have one room left, with one bed."

Lockwood sighed. "All right, that's fine. We will take it."

The faerie looked at him closely. "Do I know you?"

Oh, crap. My stomach did a nasty flip.

"I'm sure you don't," Lockwood said. "I haven't lived around here for quite some time—"

"I do remember you," the faerie said, her eyes narrowing. "You were that paladin who passed through here with your men. You tore up my tavern!"

I chanced a glance at Lockwood.

His face had gone pale, and his jaw was tight. "I'm afraid that there has been a misunderstanding—"

The faerie behind the counter was growing flushed. "No, it was you. And all you did was drag them out of here. You didn't even pay for your drinks!"

"I sent payment along through the guilds," Lockwood said. "Here, let me pay for it again now. I surely have enough here to cover—"

The faerie stepped away as if the payment he offered was poisonous. With a furious look back, she dashed to the window overlooking the park and rang a tiny silver bell hanging just outside.

Horror came over Lockwood's expression.

Welp. This was not good.

"Guards!" the woman called, ringing the bell feverishly. "Guards! A man is here to steal from me!"

"I am doing no such thing!" Lockwood was bright red. He whirled around, looking at Orianna and me. "Come. We can't be caught here." He grabbed onto my wrist and we dashed out of the door.

I didn't know anything about Faerie law, but running from the guards really didn't seem like the wisest idea when he was already in exile.

"No, wait!" I said as he ran, and then flew, yanking me into the open air after him. I would have fallen like a sack of potatoes if he hadn't swooped underneath me and caught me just before we touched the ground.

He wasted no time being gentle now, though, and we flew off between shop buildings, the cries of other faeries witnessing our mad dash following after us on the wind.

Orianna was there, pacing us, fluttering over our heads.

"Where are we going to hide?" she asked, her voice anxious. Who knew if they would check her for a glamour when they caught us?

"We aren't going to hide," Lockwood said. "We are going to blend."

"How are we going to do that?" Orianna asked.

"We are going to use this," he said, and he pulled a small, glowing green stone out of the bag of charms he had purchased in Stormbreak. It pulsed in his hands like a beating heart.

"Is that an Evanescent?" Orianna asked, her eyes growing wide.

He nodded. "It should render us virtually invisible."

"For how long?" I asked.

"Hopefully long enough to get out of the village," he said, wings beating furiously.

"Couldn't we just use it again if it wears off?" I asked

"No, that would kill us," he said.

"What?" I asked, not really liking the sound of that.

"We don't have time to discuss this." He held it up in front of him as we flew. "Everyone touch it on three. One—two—"

And all three of us reached out and touched it.

A sharp shock ran up my arm, down my back, and up to my scalp, stealing the breath from my lungs. It was over in less than a heartbeat. I shivered, and looked down at myself.

I couldn't see my own hand.

Lockwood and Orianna had disappeared, too.

"Okay, the best thing is for us to land and retrace our steps back out of town so we don't get separated," Lockwood's voice said from … somewhere.

This was trippier than trippy.

"Can't we just hold onto each other?" I asked. "I really don't want to get lost."

"Fine," Lockwood said, and I felt his fingers graze against my shoulder. "Grab onto the back of my shirt. Orianna, you grab onto Cassandra."

"If I can find her …"

"Come on, we are running out of time!" he whispered.

I felt the fabric of my shirt crumple and had to stifle a gasp. If she could feel the softness of my sweatshirt and not my dress, would she know that I was glamoured?

At least I was invisible, so she couldn't see the difference in the fabrics.

Lockwood's wings flittered and he brought us down in an alley, the soft impression of footsteps miraculously appearing in the dirt as we landed. He began to walk, and I tightened my grip on his tunic, following. Orianna's grip on my clothing grew tighter, and I could feel her close behind me.

It was incredibly bizarre to feel everything I felt but not to see any of it; Lockwood's soft tunic, the ground scraping beneath my feet, Orianna's hand knotted in the back of my sweatshirt. I kept tripping over my own feet because I couldn't see them.

I clamped my lips shut as we stepped back out into the town square. Faeries were everywhere.

I chanced a glance up at the porch leading inside the inn, and sure enough, there were guards dressed in white armor speaking to the innkeeper, who was gesticulating wildly and apparently giving them quite the piece of her mind.

I wondered if Lockwood noticed them. Hell, he'd probably seen them before I did.

Carefully and slowly, we made our way back toward the main gate into the town. After what felt like hours of slow-walking through the crowds, we were out of sight of the fountain.

Questions rushed through my mind, unanswerable while we were surrounded by people: How long would this charm last? Would we make it out in time?

What did Lockwood mean that the Evanescent could kill us?

That last one kinda weighed on me the most.

The path leading out of the village was in sight, but a cluster of guards was stationed there. Had they been there before when we passed through? Or were they there to head us off?

I couldn't be sure, but with each step, I hoped that the Evanescent's power would hold and that we'd be able to walk right out under their noses undetected.

Every breath, every step, felt like it was slower than a molasses race in upstate New York in January. My lungs felt like they hurt from continuously catching myself holding my breath out of fear that someone would hear me. The road out of town was a wide path, and that cluster of guards all stood to one side.

My fingers were sweating on Lockwood's tunic, and I hoped he wouldn't notice. I couldn't hear him or Orianna, but every breath I let out sounded like a horse neighing to my ears. I watched the guards as they chatted to each other, keeping no more than a casual eye on the road, looking for us, presumably, but mostly chatting to each other.

Something flickered in front of me, and for just a second, I thought I was about to be treated to another of my visions of a more horrific world.

And, as it turned out, it was horrific. But for a different reason.

My finger was hanging there in midair, by itself, but only for a second.

Then it was joined by Lockwood's tunic. Then the rest of Lockwood. And my arm.

We were visible.

The guards were staring at us, those who had their backs turned, looking around to see us frozen in the middle of the road, me clutching Lockwood, Orianna with a hand on my back. A little procession of people stumbling out of town clinging to each other. It must have been quite the sight.

Crap.

Fear gripped my heart, squeezing it painfully, my breathing coming faster and harder as I looked around at the guards. Their cold stares told me that there was little chance we were getting out of this without a fight.

"Stand down," came a deep voice from behind the group of guards. "Allow me to handle this."

The guards closest to him looked and then parted, allowing the faerie who spoke through.

The man who spoke stepped out in front of us on the path, blocking our escape. He was the same height as Lockwood, and his white armor gleamed in the afternoon light. He had wings and hair the color of freshly cut straw, and eyes as bright blue as Lockwood's were green.

"I wouldn't have believed it if I weren't seeing it with my own eyes," he said in a low, deep voice. A voice that sounded like he had great authority.

His boots brushed along the stone path beneath his feet, the only sound around us. All the soldiers were silent as they watched the unfolding exchange.

Lockwood's shoulders tensed.

"It's been a long time …" the faerie said, "… Lockwood."

My hand began to tremble as Lockwood stared at the man blocking our path.

This was it.

We were caught.

Chapter 20

For a few moments, the only thing I could hear was the sound of my own heartbeat in my ears. It thudded dully while the world around me was frozen in time.

My knees were locked and shaking. I couldn't have moved if I had wanted to. Fear had drawn the blood from my face, my hands, my feet ... I found myself cold. Terribly cold. All of the hair on my arms and the back of my neck was standing up.

The man standing before Lockwood suddenly broke into a grin. "No need for worry, Paladin Lockwood. Do you not recognize me?"

He seemed older than Lockwood, but it may have been his beard that made it appear that way. There were no lines in his smooth face, but there was an ancient look in his eyes, like he had lived longer than seven generations of my family.

Lockwood, for his part, stood stock still. Yeah, he definitely recognized this guy.

Orianna was trembling behind me, her tiny fists knotted in my sweatshirt. I could feel little jerks of motion as she wheeled her head around. I wondered if she was considering fleeing. I wouldn't blame her if she wanted to, but the soldiers around us held ethereal weapons that looked like they could do some nasty damage, and I hoped that she would use her sense and stay put.

"Sir Roseus ..." Lockwood said through gritted teeth.

"Ah, so I am not forgotten," Roseus said, smiling wide.

"Though it's General Roseus now. I was afraid your time in exile might have had faded all memory of me." He gave a brief wave to his guards, and they lowered their weapons. "Let us give them some room to breathe, shall we? Return to your posts, hmm?"

"But, sir," one of the soldiers said, "they are wanted for theft at the inn."

"Nonsense," Roseus said. "This man was a paladin of the court. Any charges left outstanding by my friend shall be covered by me."

Friend?

I didn't relinquish my hold on the back of Lockwood's tunic.

Roseus stared at the soldiers who were not moving, annoyance puckering his brow. "Go on. You are not needed here any longer." The guards departed, one of them giving us a long look before walking off along the road with his fellows.

General Roseus clapped his hands together, all trace of disquiet erased from his face. "Well, now, Lockwood. Why all of the fuss?"

"With all due respect, Roseus," Lockwood said, shoulders tight. "I don't owe you anything, least of all an explanation."

"Well, surely you owe me a little something, seeing as I have taken care of the innkeeper for you." Roseus's smile did not fade in the slightest. "What was her trouble with you?"

Lockwood didn't answer, just stared at Roseus.

Roseus stared back, puzzling as he looked at Lockwood. "Let me guess. You stopped here some time ago leading a patrol, you drank all her spirits and then made a wreck of the place?"

"I paid for the damages," Lockwood said darkly. "I sent the funds along after I dragged my men out of there."

"Admirable, and I believe you," Roseus said. "I know that you are a man of your word." He took a step closer to Lockwood, his yellow wings becoming lost in the sunbeams leaking through the treetops overhead. He dropped his voice. "… just as I believed what you claimed about Calvor's son."

Now it was my brow's turn to furrow. What did Lockwood

claim about Calvor's son? Based on his behavior at the hospital, I knew they were connected somehow. Lockwood had said that Calvor's son had deserved what happened to him …

"And who are these charming young ladies traveling with you?" Roseus asked, peering around Lockwood's shoulder at Orianna and me. "You haven't taken a wife finally, have you?"

"No," Lockwood said, knowing full well that I would have protested if he hadn't. "I have been tasked with bringing these ladies to the court."

"I see …" Roseus said. He arched an eyebrow as he scanned over my face, and then lingered over Orianna's. "An interesting task to be assigned to an exile." His gaze was piercing, as if he could see right through my glamour. But that wasn't possible, right?

"These are interesting times," Lockwood said.

"Truly, they are," Roseus said. "You know, you should really be more careful here. There are many who would have you slain in the streets if they were to discover your return."

"I am aware of this," Lockwood said. "Which is why I am wondering why you haven't given that order."

"Oh, I have," Roseus said. "Many times."

I blanched, my stomach doing summersaults.

"It came from on high," he went on, with a wink at me. "I had no choice but to pass it along. But to see it done? Alas … you must have slipped my sight, Lockwood, and I cannot have you killed if I have not seen you, yes?"

Lockwood stared at him evenly. "I suppose not. But will your soldiers forget me as easily as you have?"

"They are loyal to me," Roseus ran fingers through his hair. "It will be no bother. Let me be honest, Lockwood … I am glad to see you safe and well. It was fortunate that it was I who found you, not one of Calvor's men." He clapped Lockwood on the shoulder.

Lockwood gave me a sidelong look. Was he worried that Roseus was going to let too much slip about the reason why he was being hunted? I couldn't tell by looking at him; Lockwood, even after all this time, and all he'd done, was such a mystery to me.

Why was he so adamant that I didn't know?

"What are your intentions?" Lockwood asked, crossing his arms over his chest.

"I was about to ask you the very same thing," Roseus said. "You're escorting these women to the court? Truly?"

Lockwood's face flushed. "I am."

Roseus brightened. "Truly? You intend to face the controversy head on?"

Lockwood stood his ground. "I do."

"This is wonderful, my friend," Roseus said. "Surely you will be able to set everything right with your return."

Lockwood glared. "That is a very optimistic view when you and I both know that half the court wants my head on a pike."

Roseus waved his hand dismissively. "The king and queen would both happily give you a second chance, especially given recent events. The tensions between Winter and Summer have grown exponentially, and if no resolution comes to ameliorate the injuries that prompted this chain of events, war is certain."

Roseus was searching Lockwood's face. Lockwood was inscrutable to me, but Roseus must have seen something there that I missed. Maybe he really was an old friend of his. Lockwood said nothing.

"Lockwood," Roseus said, "my time with you as a paladin showed me that you were incapable of the deception you were accused of. Calvor's son ... well, anyone who knew him knew the sort of man he was. He never should have been—"

"You do not know of which you speak," Lockwood said. He was reddening again, his jaw tightening after he finished speaking.

"My apologies." Roseus offered a slight bow. "I speak out of turn. I know that I have not been much help, and for that I am sorry. I have done my best in your absence to help keep the peace."

Lockwood's jaw clenched. "With a promotion, I see," he said, somewhat bitterly.

Roseus glanced down at the medal adorning his breast.

"This? Is nothing. A show of good will from the queen after you left. I think she would have sided with you too, had Calvor not been so …" he trailed off once more. "Perchance … if you let me, I could get you back to the court so you may plead your case once more. If we were to go together, no one would stop you, not even Calvor's men. I would be able to get you an audience at the court."

"What of my friends?" Lockwood asked, gesturing to Orianna and me.

"They would be welcome, of course," Roseus said. "I will arrange everything, never you worry."

Lockwood stared at him, eyes slightly narrowed. "Why are you so eager to help me now? When I was exiled, you stood by with the others and did nothing."

"Lockwood, surely you know why," Roseus said. "You defied the court, and I was but a paladin. I had no power to influence the course of events. But I believe you. I truly do. And now I am a general, and my influence waxes. I can add my voice to yours, and together, your truth will reach the ears of the court."

Lockwood searched Roseus's face, his eyes narrowed.

"We have been long acquainted," Roseus said. "We have trained together, fought together … defended Summer together." He reached out a hand, palm up. "Come. Let us be brethren once more, in this cause. I give my pledge—I will see you safely to the court so your truth may be heard."

Lockwood looked down at that, his eyes tight. "You speak, and your truths sound good. Get us to the court safely. But know why I am hesitant, Roseus. I want to trust you, I truly do. But everything as pertains to the court seems to have gone awry, and not in my favor. See me safely there, though, with my companions …" Lockwood licked his lips. "And perhaps that will change."

"I will see it done," Roseus said. "No harm will come to you—any of you—in our journey. You will be borne to the court and have your words heard by all."

Lockwood looked at Roseus once more. The two men stared at each other, each sizing the other one up, a mix of emotions in their eyes. Roseus looked the more earnest, his hand extended for Lockwood to take, like he was reaching out for a high five and Lockwood had just left him hanging.

Faeries couldn't lie, so Roseus was telling the truth about escorting us safely. What was going on in Lockwood's head, though? He seemed to be having a hard time trusting anyone … even me, I realized. He hadn't been forthcoming about the events that led to his exile, all the while relying on me to dig him out of whatever trouble he was in. If that wasn't a sign that he was blocking everyone out, I didn't know what was.

I had a sudden pang of fear that this pride, this reluctance to trust might be what got him killed. Him … and me, of course.

"Lockwood …" I said gently. "Not everyone is your enemy."

He held my gaze for a moment, too, the bright verdant green narrowed just slightly with suspicion as he pondered my words, and Roseus's offer.

"I mean, in my own life I've seen it," I said. "I couldn't have gotten through everything I have without Xandra, for example. She was the only one who believed in me when everything went south, remember?" I cast a look at Roseus, who still stood with his hand extended. "Wouldn't it be better to just trust your friend here?" I asked.

I hoped he knew that I was talking about myself as much as Roseus.

Lockwood stared at me for a moment, and then reached out, placing his palm against Roseus's. They clasped hands in some weird, sideways faerie version of a handshake.

"Welcome back to the lands of Summer, my friend," Roseus said, his smile triumphant. "Long have they missed your presence and steadfast defense."

"Thank you, Roseus," Lockwood said. Some of the tension left his shoulders, but there was still some reservation in his face.

"If we were to leave now, we could get to the court before nightfall," Roseus said.

"One of our number is unable to fly," Lockwood said, indicating me.

Roseus's face fell. "Oh, my. What happened?"

"My wing," I said, looking over my shoulder at the thing I couldn't see but was claiming hurt. "Those damned Unseelie, you know."

Roseus nodded. "Indeed I do. All my difficulties these days are Unseelie difficulties."

"Yes." Orianna's voice was stiff. "Very, uhm … troublesome people, those Unseelie."

"We ran into some avara, as well," Lockwood said. "Shortly before we met our friend here, trying to get back to safe lands."

Roseus smiled at Orianna and me. "I welcome you home as well, ladies. It is good to have Summer folk back in Seelie territory. Your troubles are now over, and we will have your injuries tended to in time. For now, though," he looked at Lockwood, "she could ride one of the pegasuses."

I wanted to blurt out my excitement, but Lockwood's stare squelched it before I even had the chance.

"Your kindness is appreciated," Lockwood said, and we started on our way, following behind Roseus. He led us around the tower structure where the soldiers had stood their guard. On the other side stood a small stable, open air and covered with a thatched roof. Within waited a pegasus that stood taller than any of the faeries. He was a glorious creature, white bodied and maned, with feathery white wings that lay back from his wide shoulders. He had a golden saddle on his back, and he stared unthreateningly at us as we approached.

"Glorious, isn't he?" Roseus asked, walking me over to the pegasus.

"Indeed," I said, a little muted as I tried to keep from spraining something in my excitement or embarrassing myself in front of Lockwood. "Very nice." A ridiculous understatement, but they thought I was fae, so it probably didn't matter too much. I was dancing like mad on the inside.

"Have you ever ridden a pegasus before?" Roseus asked me as I approached.

"Never," I said.

"She's too young," Orianna said from beside me. She was giving the pegasus a jaded once-over, like maybe she rode them all the time. "Hasn't done much, really."

I shot her a quelling look. "Speaking of not doing much, how about you do that—right now?"

"It's very simple," Roseus said, ignoring my clap back at Orianna. "He will understand whatever you say to him. And he knows where we are going."

"I certainly do," the pegasus said.

"Whuuuuuut?" My eyes nearly bulged from my head. "And he speaks?"

"Of course I can, dear girl," the pegasus said. "I am no ordinary beast."

"See?" Orianna told Roseus, a little smirk of triumph draped across her lips. "Lived under a rock for her whole life so far."

"What a grand experience this will be for you, then," Roseus said. He steadied me as I slung a foot into the stirrup and climbed up into the saddle. Once I was settled, I realized it was actually comfortable, unlike most saddles on Earth. It was made from supple leather, with a blanket wrapped snuggly beneath it to provide comfort to the pegasus, but it felt like I was sitting on my couch.

"What is your name?" the pegasus asked, craning his neck to look at me.

Still dumbfounded, I just stared into the pegasus's large, black eye. "Cass—Cassandra," I managed to get out. Part of me still wanting to squeal, though that part was muted by the fact that the winged horse was talking to me.

"Cassandra …" the pegasus replied. "Wonderful to meet you, child. I am Orion."

"Like the hunter," I said, and then really wished I could go back in time to take that back.

"You know of the Earth myth?" Orion blinked once.

"Just a little bit," I said, trying to cover. "My, uh, father, told me about it." Actually true.

"How curiously rare you are," Orion said, then stamped his feet. "I am ready."

"Make sure that you hold onto the reins," Roseus said,

patting Orion's side. "We don't need you falling out of your saddle if you can't catch yourself by flying. Take good care of her now, Orion."

"I shall indeed."

"Are we ready?" Roseus called to the others.

Lockwood nodded his head. Orianna had shuffled up next to me, and grinned nervously up at me.

"Then let us go," Roseus said, and he leapt up into the air, wings fluttering as he rose. Lockwood and Orianna joined him, the beat of their wings like the loudest cicadas I'd ever heard.

Orion didn't wait long to follow, taking three great strides forward from beneath the thatched awning. His gallops were great, lurching steps, and then his wings unfolded and with a beat that blew my hair back, he rose into the air with a great sweep. My stomach plummeted as we flew, leaving the ground behind, the twisting locks of my hair swirling all around my face. Orion's chest heaved as he drew in great breaths, and I could feel the flex of his muscles against my legs as his wings rose and fell.

I clutched onto the saddle desperately, but …

There was no fear. My hands were steady on the reigns, the wind blowing furiously against my face like I was sticking my head out the window on the freeway. Lockwood, Roseus and Orianna were ahead, fluttering furiously as I rode atop Orion, his great wings beating us aloft with slow power and confidence.

And all I could feel was just …

Pure elation.

My eyes were streaming, and it was hard to catch my breath against the wind pounding my face as we flew, but I had never felt anything quite like this before. The car ride with the head out the window didn't quite cover it, because the ground was hundreds of feet below. It was nothing like an airplane ride, either, with the wind blowing hard against my face.

Everything was a rush of color and smells as we flew. Orion's great wings whooshed as the air passed over them and rushed in my ears.

Orianna lagged back, coming alongside, watching me as I grinned like an idiot. I thought I might burst into tears from the excitement of it all. She just shook her head and sped up, leaving me behind to rejoin the other two.

This was the most wonderful feeling in the world. Better than getting sucked into a movie. Better than any game. Better than a song that hit you right in the feels.

Flying was better than all of that. I was completely addicted.

We swooped over the pointed tree tops, the beating of Orion's wings sending them swaying as we passed. We climbed as we wove our way around some mountains, peaks of snow high above us and yet still, from my perch atop the pegasus, seemingly within reach. Low hanging clouds parted as we rushed through them, Orion following in the wake of Roseus, Lockwood, and Orianna as we sailed the sky.

It was exhilarating. My heart pounded in my chest. I couldn't remember the last time I had felt this alive, this free …

"Do you think the queen is going to see you?" Orianna asked Lockwood. I could barely hear her voice over the sound of Orion's wings. We burst out of the cloud bank, and a green valley lay spread out before us, multi-colored smoke coming from the dots of faerie settlements.

"Perhaps," Lockwood said. "The Spring Court is now in retrograde, moving toward Summer. If it has not happened already, they are sure to hand off very soon."

I didn't quite understand that.

Orianna rolled her eyes. "Seelie politics."

"You dislike our ways?" Roseus asked, turning his head just slightly so I could hear him over the rushing winds.

"I don't much care," Orianna said, shrugging. "Though I have heard that the Queen of Winter and her king are very much on the same page. Unlike here, where they have entirely mismatched agendas." She squinted in thought. "What is that called … a marriage of convenience?"

Lockwood shot her a glaring look. It probably wasn't safe to talk about these things in the open. And it definitely wasn't safe for her to imply that she knew too much about the Unseelie.

"Hold on a second …" I said, cutting him off before we drew any attention from the others. "Forgive me, for I've been in the, uh, outlands for quite a while." Roseus gave me a strange look, then nodded in a *go on* kind of way. "There's more than one court?"

"Summer and Winter each have a subcourt," Roseus said. "Autumn for Winter, Spring for Summer. They take up the reins in their respective season, subject to the oversight of their mother court."

"Like … literal seasons?" I asked. Because back on Earth, it was definitely late spring, leading into summer, which dovetailed nicely with what Lockwood had said.

Lockwood met my eyes, and I suspected his answer was veiled to carry additional meaning that only I would catch. "Close enough. Though the seasons do not change within their own respective kingdoms, as it were—Winter remains in winter, for the most part, and Summer … well, you get the idea. The neutral lands, however—"

"Are currently warmed by the gentle sunshine of spring," Orion finished for him. Still not used to my flying horse talking. "Soon they will be beat upon the strong heat of summer, and the crops will grow stronger."

"I did notice that as we passed through," I said, taking it all in. If I understood Lockwood's implications correctly …

The change of court power here seemed to coincide with the seasons on Earth. That was … interesting.

"The orderly transition of that power has been the hallmark of our world for centuries," Lockwood said.

Orianna snorted. "Orderly. That's a good one."

Lockwood sent her a searing look. "You would prefer the chaos of seasons gone awry? One day of crippling snow in the neutral territories followed by the next a searing heat?"

"Hardly," Orianna said, looking right back at him without flinching. "I merely suggest that it's not as ordered as you imply." She looked at me. "There is bickering and ill feelings between the Summer and Winter factions. Squabbling, I suppose you could say."

"Nothing as complex as this comes easily or without flaw," Lockwood replied. "It is a measure of how we have advanced ourselves that there is no war every time the transition comes. That territories have generally remained constant—"

"Till now, anyway." Orianna's face was scarlet, and she flew around to the other side of Orion to be away from Lockwood.

He shrugged. "Life is change."

"So there's a king in charge of the Spring Court?" I asked. "And that is who we're meeting?"

"If the Spring remains in charge, then yes," Lockwood said, lagging back to come alongside me and Orion. "I would probably do better to plead my case in front of Queen Pruina of Summer, but I have no control over which court is in session."

"That's … really confusing," I said, keeping my voice low and hoping only the pegasus could hear me. And not read too much into my ignorance of their ways. Hey, I was just a poor faerie girl from way outside their civilized territories. Or something. I still wasn't entirely clear on how this world worked, but from what I'd inferred and the reactions of Roseus and Orianna to me, I had guessed that this was not an entirely unheard of thing. "You know that, right?"

Lockwood sighed. "Yes. I do."

"Do you think we can trust Roseus?" I asked in a low voice. "Because you looked like you were really struggling with it back there."

Lockwood stared at the back of Roseus's head, considering my words. "I think we can," he said slowly. "It was fortuitous that we ran into him and not another paladin. Perhaps, with his aid, we will make it out of this yet."

"Oh, good," I said. Nice to know that our hopes of survival had been so stellar from the beginning. Not.

"Are you feeling all right?" he asked, flittering in a little closer to me, wings flashing in the sunlight.

"Yeah," I said, hands solid on the reins. The wind blew across my face and I closed my eyes for just a second. "Amazing, actually."

"Good," he said, a look of relief passing over his face. "Mill would never forgive me if anything happened to you."

Mill. Everything in faerie had engulfed me so fully that I'd hardly had a moment to think of Mill.

Man. He was totally going to be jealous that I got to ride on the back of a pegasus.

We fell into silence, and I just enjoyed the rhythmic rise and fall of Orion's wings, the passing of the green scenery around us. We passed over an enchanted lake that was as red as rubies and smelled sweetly even a hundred feet up.

"What's that?" I asked, staring into its crimson depths.

"The Lake of Croamar," Orion said, turning his head to look at me. His black eye reflected the red of the lake below, the refraction of the sun off its surface giving his flawless coat a pink hue. "Should you drink from it, you will fall into an enchanted slumber filled with peaceful dreams."

"That sounds … magical," I said, as we passed back over land and the most verdant trees filled the ground to the horizon. There was a new warmth to the air as we flew, and it smelled fresh and spicy, almost like a sweet cinnamon, or cloves.

"It is," Orion said.

Something glittered in the distance, and I stared. It was like a rainbow come to life, a disco ball of light erupting at the edge of the sky like some sort of prismatic volcano.

I let out a gasp as I realized … it was a city. Vast, colorful, and magnificent. And at its center … a great castle atop a mighty hill. It was taller than it was wide, with many turrets of all sizes reaching into the sky above, each sending up its own rainbow of light.

"Do you like it?" Orion asked as the others fluttered ahead, his words jarring me out of my stunned state.

"I … It's magnificent," I breathed as we swooped closer. It was enormous now, like a dozen skyscrapers from New York City knitted together in one glorious, prismatic fortress.

"Welcome to the city of Starvale, young Seelie," Orion called over his shoulder as we drew nearer to the stronghold of the Summer Court in all its shimmering glory. "Welcome home."

Chapter 21

Starvale was unlike anything I had ever seen before. *Enchanting* wasn't strong enough of a world, and *other worldly* seemed too mundane. *Movie-style CGI* wouldn't have done it justice, either. The best way I could think of to explain it was to cross a rainbow with an anime scene that Xandra had tried to show me.

The gate to the city was a large bridge made of bright purple crystal, so clear that I could see everything through it, including that the city itself was on a floating hunk of rock large enough that I was sure that all of Manhattan island could have fit on it comfortably. Beneath the rock was a pool of glowing blue … something. Liquid? Gas? I wasn't sure. It sparkled and swirled, but moved like water.

Seelie guards stood in white armor along the arching bridge that was as wide as a three-lane highway. They bowed to General Roseus as he strode across it. We had landed just shy of the bridge, and Orion was now carrying me across on his back as I took in the scenery, wide-eyed.

The city gates were wide open to all who wished to enter, but with every step, apprehension swelled in my chest. My time in Seelie thus far had made me wary that there was something here beyond the bright lights and big city. Something here that I couldn't see.

Almost as if on cue, my vision flickered, and I stared up at a huge metal door, steel grey and forbidding, larger than a cathedral, with a thousand locks scattered over the surface.

I blinked, and the image cleared from my eyes.

A glamour? Was that what I was seeing in the rainbows and the glory of Starvale? A giant glamour meant to make it look amazing while the reality beneath was cold and forbidding?

Because if so, that suggested everything I'd seen—dead unicorns, the horrors of the hospital—it was all some sort of massive display of magic meant to … what?

Make everything seem more awesome than it was?

"Lockwood …" I mumbled, and he adjusted his pace to come alongside me. Once he was, I leaned down to whisper in his ear. "I just saw a door here."

"Your sight flickered again?" he asked.

"Yeah, but I don't know … it sort of happened when I wanted it to this time. And it hasn't really happened since we entered Seelie territory—"

"Come, friends," Roseus said from the front of our little procession. He beckoned Orion toward a stable, where fresh straw sparkled like gold.

I patted Orion on the neck as he dutifully clip-clopped over and then knelt to allow me to dismount easily. I slung a leg over him and touched ground, then ran a hand along his mane as he rose again.

"Thank you, Orion," I said. "You were amazing."

Orion nuzzled his nose against my cheek. "It was a great pleasure, little one. I hope to see you again soon."

I hoped so, too, but kept it to myself as I fell in behind Roseus and the others, into the bustling streets of Starvale. With a look back, I saw the gates still seemed to be wide over the purple bridge.

So … why did I get the feeling that they'd shut behind us? No flicker greeted me this time to confirm it, though, and I turned back to following Roseus along the wide, impressive avenue through the city.

Houses of all shapes and sizes, colors, and materials lined each side of the street. The long, white-stoned avenue provided a neutral center, leading all the way to the castle up on the hill, but everything around it was such a hodge-podge of colors that I could hardly understand which way was up.

"This is very unlike a human city …" Lockwood whispered to me. "Faerie order is less about having things neat and tidy, and more about having things the way they we want them."

That much was obvious. Some houses were floating, others were tucked up in trees like they had been in the first Seelie town. Some were tall and skinny, with a door at the roof, and others were round like orbs, with no apparent entrance at all.

Even in the chaos of the surroundings, it was beautiful.

Voices rang out over the street, somewhere between a chorus and crowd noise, and very unlike a human street. Faeries flew overhead in every direction. Some in pairs, some singly, others with their families, their little faerie children swinging between them, their small wings inadequate to the task of holding them aloft yet.

I smelled roses and lavender, vanilla and coffee. I caught notes of sea water and cotton and lemons …

It was all a little overwhelming.

"Come," Roseus said. "Lockwood, why don't you carry your injured friend to speed us along? She won't mind, will she?"

Lockwood looked at me for an answer.

"Of course not," I said. I trusted Lockwood to carry me, and smiled to show him that.

Much more gently this time, he lifted me into his arms as if I weighed no more than a doll. We lifted off after Roseus and Orianna, heading toward the glimmering castle of shifting colors.

"It looks like crystal …" I murmured, staring into its depths. Even as clear as it was, I could see nothing through it.

"The Court of Summer is the oldest building in the Seelie territory," Lockwood said. "It was the very first thing ever built here. Its sister castle is in the Unseelie territory."

"They have the same castle?" I asked. Though I appreciated his effort, I missed being carried by Orion.

"It's … similar," Lockwood said. "Also made of solidified magic. Though I believe it differs in appearance from ours."

We came in for a landing on the outskirts of a grand garden, filled with flowers, fountains, and shrubbery. It was quiet up on the hill, away from the hustle and bustle of the city. Two guards in white armor more elaborate than I had yet seen, greeted us.

"Good evening," Roseus said, giving the same signal with his hands that Lockwood had back at the farm. "I bring a Seelie to speak before the court."

"It shall have to wait until the morning," the soldier replied through his mask. "They are in recess."

"Of course," Roseus said, then beckoned to us. "Come this way. We'll find you quarters for the evening."

"Lockwood?" I asked, voice low, looking at the faeries strolling through the garden around us. "Doesn't anyone recognize you?"

"If they do, no one will say anything while we are with the general," he replied quietly.

The doors into the castle were large and crystalline as well, and I gaped as they opened, revealing a vast world beyond, surely far larger than the castle that held it.

We crossed the threshold into a tropical paradise.

A crystal blue lake filled the center of the room, perfectly round, yet still appearing oddly natural. I could barely see the shore on the other side. Water washed lazily against the shore, glowing an unearthly cyan from within.

The ceiling overhead stretched far out of reach, but I could see faeries flying up there among glowing crystals of all different colors, glowing and shimmering just like the rest of Starvale. Another purple crystal walkway stretched across the lake, and hovering in its middle was another chunk of rock just like the city rested upon.

"Lockwood ... is that a miniature replica of the city?" I asked, pointing to the floating mass.

"It is," Lockwood said. "It is a magical map, allowing the court to observe anything that goes on within Seelie borders. Inside of Starvale, specifically, but if the need arose, they could change the map to show any city belonging to the Seelie."

"Whoa ..." I stared at the floating Starvale. A male faerie with flowing blonde hair and periwinkle wings fluttered down over the map, and indicated something to another faerie close behind. The map flared, and the portion of the city he pointed to grew larger, as if the map was zooming as it might on a smartphone.

"Come," Roseus called, waving us farther inside.

We followed him through a wide passageway with large windows on either side. Each looked out onto a different landscape, every one utterly different from the environs outside. One was covered in delicate, pure snow, another a desert of bright yellow sand. I saw one that looked just like the forest that Lockwood and I had been in when we first arrived in Faerie, but I couldn't be sure it was the same.

I had hundreds of questions, but I tried to act like I was a Seelie and that all of this wasn't as fascinating to me as it really was. I was kinda torn, because in my role as recent outcast, I maybe could have gotten away with asking some questions, but … if I slipped up, no good would have come of it, so I shut my mouth and walked on.

Orianna had appeared beside me, reaching out and taking my hand in her own, squeezing it tightly. I stared at it for a moment, eyeing her. She'd run kind of hot and cold on me since we'd opted to take her in, and half the time I couldn't even remember why I'd agreed to that.

Oh, right. Pity.

I smiled reassuringly at her. My commitment stood; I wasn't going to let anything happen to her. I may not have known her motives yet, or what she wanted, but I was starting think she was harmless enough, if a little annoying. Her flippant attitude was just to hide the sensitivity underneath.

I guess she was at least a little like me. Whatever she was feeling, though, she evinced only awe as she looked around, taking the castle in as we moved on down the corridor.

I could understand why she would be nervous with so many Seelie around. Not to mention the guards, who appeared almost as frequent as the civilian faeries, many of whom wore elegant dresses, the men in tunics and wearing belts of shining metal.

"I wonder why everyone is so dressed up," I whispered to her.

"These are nobles," she said. "Those with influence and power. They always dress like that."

"How many of them do you think are glamoured?" I asked.

"Oh, all of them," she said. "Their hair, their faces, their gowns. All of it glamoured." A flicker of expression ran across her face just as surely as if I were seeing through her own facade, but there was nothing magical about the contempt it revealed. "For a supposedly truthful people, the Seelie have their own special brand of lying."

"Why not just change those things?" I asked, as I tried to consider what she might have meant with that jab at the Summer fae.

"Glamours can be changed any time," she said. "These women could have a different dress for each meal of the day."

I could see the appeal in that. How nice it would be to be able to wear sweatpants and baggie T-shirts to school, but look like I was wearing something super cute, or as if I actually cared about doing my hair?

I could wake up and never do my hair or makeup again. I wondered if glamours worked on Earth …

A grand staircase appeared, wide enough for four or five people to be able to walk up it, but there was a large opening in the middle as it spiraled overhead, and I quickly understood why.

Faeries fluttered up and down that wide vertical pass, some hand in hand with other fae, others zipping up as if to deliver a message to someone higher up in the castle, still others reading or examining something in their hands.

"This whole place is just … amazing," I said, staring up at the staircase. Even with their wings, there were almost as many faeries taking the stairs, walking elegantly up and down. They had a sort of grace to them that the flying fae lacked, even the ones who seemed to be taking their time doing so.

"If you will remain here, I shall go and speak to an attendant, and get you squared away in guest quarters, yes?" Roseus beamed at the three of us.

"Of course," Lockwood said, inclining his head.

Roseus started off down another wide passageway, this one lined with dark wood, with glowing buds hanging from vines that grew out of the ceiling.

"All right," Lockwood said in a low voice, turning to Orianna and me. "Let's agree that I am the one that is here to see the court. You two are here with me, and nothing more. I don't want you to be subjected to additional scrutiny."

"But I thought that I was going into the court with you," I said.

"You will speak when we are presented to the court, but they need not know that yet," he said quietly. "We need to get through this night with as little interest from others as is possible, then tomorrow we can present our case before the court. We will just keep our heads down. Especially you."

I realized he was staring at me, and not the Unseelie. "What do you mean, *me*?" I asked.

"You are notorious for trouble finding you, and we cannot afford for trouble to find us here."

"All right, here we are," Roseus said, stepping back out of the dark hall. "These three will be taking you to your rooms."

My eyes widened as I stared at three little … pixies? They were no bigger than my hand, hovering in the air, little stones dangling from their necks glowing brightly. They looked only marginally bigger than the ones I'd been attacked by in the limo just … two days before? Was that all it had been?

The pixie on the far right with bright red wings and beady blue eyes like a cat's flew over right over to me, hovering in front of my nose. "Happy, happy, little Seelie. I am Nino, and I shall take you to your room." His voice was high pitched, squeaky, almost like what I imagined a mouse would sound like. Every time Nino moved, there was a soft tinkling sound, like miniature wind chimes.

Orianna's little pixie was yanking on her hair, which was making Orianna frown and glare. "Stop! Stop!" Orianna was saying as the pixie pulled her along a side corridor of glowing emerald stone.

"Come along, little Seelie," Nino said, tugging at my hand.

"We must go up the stairs. General Roseus tells me that you hurt your wing?"

"I did, yes," I said, and I felt bad for lying to such a tiny creature. He was warm against my fingers, like a flashlight bulb.

Nino buzzed with exuberance as he pulled at me. "Come along, come along!" he chittered.

I looked around, expecting Lockwood, at least, to follow me. But he was being led back the way we'd come.

"Wait, where are they going?" I asked.

"Being taken to their rooms, of course," Nino said, voice a squeak. "Just as I take you to yours."

"But I thought we would have had rooms together, or at least near one another …"

Nino did not respond to this, just kept pulling me. I probably could have resisted, but he seemed so determined to get me where I was going that I didn't fight back. Fear flickered inside me as I watched Lockwood and Orianna flying away from me in opposite directions. I watched as Lockwood turned to look at me, and he nodded. I took it to mean he thought it was safe, and just went along with Nino.

"How did little Seelie hurt her wing?" Nino asked as we started to ascend the stairs.

"I was in the neutral territory for a little while," I said. I wasn't entirely sure at this point what the going lie was, and without Lockwood to back me up, I stayed vague.

"Oh," Nino said. "Too dangerous for little Seelie. Little Seelie must take care not to hurt herself."

"Stellar advice," I said. "I will definitely be trying not to hurt myself going forward."

"Good, good," Nino said. "Little Seelie will have a much easier life if so."

I opened my mouth to respond, but I had nothing but snark to offer, and Nino was being sincere, my irony flying over his little head. Of course I hadn't set out to hurt myself—and I wasn't actually hurt—but whatever, it was decent advice if I had gotten injured. Just don't get hurt anymore. Perfect. Yeah.

We made it to the top of the stairs, and I wasn't trying very hard to hide the fact that I was out of breath. I didn't particularly like cardio, and it was catching up to me now. Walking ten thousand miles over the last few days had already tired me out, and walking up a never-ending, ornate stairwell was the icing on the exhaustion cake.

"Little Seelie must miss flying," Nino said, watching me huff and puff.

"I really do," I said, thinking of the wind rushing over my face as I flew on Orion's back. I sighed.

But my exhaustion quickly melted away as Nino led me down a long hall lined with different colored doors. They were all very close to one another, and made from different materials.

"Here we are," Nino said, coming to a stop in front of a door made from a pale, grey wood. The door appeared unfinished, rough and splintery. It was a strangely out of place note in an otherwise flawlessly charming castle, and I stared at it.

"Do I just … go in?" I asked.

Nino nodded his tiny head, his cat eyes fixed on me.

There was no handle, so I just pushed the door inward with a little thrill of worry. Was this a trap?

All of my fears passed away as I stepped into the most peaceful meadow that I had ever seen.

The floor was all grass, filled with fragrant flowers and sunlight shone down from overhead. I looked up and squinted in the great blue expanse.

It was the sky. It had to be.

There was even a gentle breeze, fluttering the flowers at my feet and the trees in the far distance. Butterflies of every color slowly made their way from flower to flower, their wings like brilliant jewels in the light. I felt like I should be singing and twirling like Julie Andrews in *The Sound of Music*.

"This is my room?" I asked, trying to take it all in. It was … a lot, since there were no walls.

Nino zoomed in front of me, giggling. "It is, it is. Do you like it?"

I looked around. The door had totally disappeared. "Uhm … problem. How do I get out?"

"When not needed, the door disappears," Nino said. "Look for it, and it shall be there."

I thought about leaving, wheeled around, and there it was, standing once more among the tall grasses. And then I blinked, and it was gone.

"Okay, that's magical," I said. "Now … what about a bed? Or a bath?"

Just as I mentioned them, I noticed a bed made from twisted roots out of a nearby tree, forming a four poster. White, sheer fabric hung from the canopy and rustled gently in the breeze. A bathtub, deep and made from green, shining stone, appeared beside it.

"Wow …" I gawked.

Nino laughed. "Is little Seelie pleased?"

"I've … never stayed in a room quite like this …" I said. "So … yeah. I am pleased."

"Wonderful," Nino said. "Is there anything else needed?"

"I can't think of anything."

"Most fabulous," Nino chittered. "Your servants will be along soon to help you prepare for the ball."

My stomach lurched as I stared at the little pixie creature. "Wait—there's a ball?"

Nino nodded. "Tonight, indeed. Long-planned. General Roseus has invited you and your party to attend with him."

"Uh … and me without a thing to wear," I said.

Nino squeaked. "It will all be attended to. Your servants will be here in half an hour. Feel free to bathe yourself or rest until they arrive and they will bathe you. If you need anything, just call."

And with a snap of his tiny fingers, Nino was gone.

"What—no one needs to bathe me," I said, looking around. "I am fully capable of bathing myself, okay? Nino?"

But he didn't answer. I was alone in this bizarre, beautiful space.

"Great," I murmured. "A ball. I've never even been to prom, and now I'm attending a ball in the land of Faerie. Because the pressure to wear the right thing for Homecoming wasn't intense enough."

I looked down at myself, wearing a blah sweatshirt and

some faded jeans. It wasn't what I looked like to anyone else, but it was how I was—bland, modern human, and utterly out of place in the magic of Faerie.

Butterflies fluttered slowly around my ankles in the meadow grass and flowers, and I wondered if I had accidentally swallowed any of them, the way that my stomach was feeling.

Balls meant dresses, which meant that I was going to have to put one on. And given what I'd seen so far in this land … it was going to be stunning, spectacular, and completely out of place on mundane, little old me.

Chapter 22

It didn't take me long to figure out what Nino had been telling me about being able to message Lockwood and Orianna. All I had to do was think about talking to someone, and a small pool of water formed in the ground just as the door had appeared before.

A fountain shot straight out of it, and as the water cascaded down, the shape of a faerie woman emerged, composed entirely of water.

"To whom do you wish to call upon?" Her voice echoed as if she were in a cave.

"Lockwood," I said. "I'm not sure what room he is in—"

But the faerie disappeared, and a moment later, there was Lockwood, or rather his silhouette, made from water, standing there on the surface of the little pond in the meadow's grass.

"Uh ... hi," I said, looking at him curiously. "Is this live?"

Lockwood chuckled, his voice echoing as well. "Yes, it is. How are you liking your accommodations?"

I gazed around. "It's ... breathtaking. Can you see it?"

He shook his head. "No. I can only see your silhouette in my own two-way looking glass."

"But you're a fountain of water to me."

Lockwood grinned. "Interesting. What sort of room are you in?"

"It's like a meadow."

He nodded. "A nature room. How very pleasant."

"What sort of room are you in?" I asked.

He looked around himself. "It's ... like an old study on Earth. Lots of books, lots of wood. There's a great window looking out over Starvale." He turned to look at me once more. "I assume you needed something?"

"This ball ..." I said. "They are coming to bring me dresses, right? Because won't the glamour I'm wearing hide whatever they bring me?"

Lockwood nodded his head. "A very good point. All right. It should be easy for me to rework your glamour to just your wrist, wings, and your hair. One moment ..."

"Yeah, no problem, I'll hold," I said. "So long as you don't put on elevator music."

Lockwood seemed to freeze, and then just as I was starting to worry that he had gone, I watched his watery silhouette snap, flicking water onto the front of my shirt.

"There. It's done. Just be aware of anyone touching your hair."

"Got it," I said, running my fingers over my wrist. "And the Seelie sign?"

"Should be in place," he said.

"I wish I could see it."

"Ask your room for a mirror. You'll be able to check."

"Great," I said, and imagined asking. Another pond appeared a few steps away. "Thanks, Lockwood."

He nodded. "I will see you for the ball, all right? Remember what I said. Keep your head down."

I nodded. "I will."

A trace of a smile appeared on his lips. "Now ... please hold." And he hummed a few bars of something melodic and peppy before his silhouette collapsed back into the tiny pond, which then was swallowed up by the dirt around it. Which was good, because I was about to throw something at him. Playfully, of course.

Once he was gone, I checked my reflection. He was right; the sign was in place on my wrist, my wings looked fine, and everything else seemed in order.

"Well, okay, then," I said under my breath, looking around. No faerie servants had made themselves evident yet, but it was just a matter of time, according to Nino. If I waited … it sounded like they'd try and bathe me. Being neither a dog nor a child, I decided to get that out of the way before they arrived.

The tub filled magically, the water swirling with little blossoms. The water was fragrant too, flower-scented oils floating on the surface. Small glass bottles rested on the side of the tub.

I poured something that looked like coconut milk into the tub, along with some tiny pink crystals that popped when they struck the water. I upended frothy foam from a jar into it. Mom hated it when I filled my own bath with bath salts and the like. She always complained about how it made the bottom of the tub slippery.

I sank into the water, exhaling with relief. There were few things in my life that I appreciated more than a hot bath. I scrubbed at my tired skin, and watched as dirt and other debris fell away into the bottom of the tub.

I kept my eyes on the edges of the meadow, half expecting pixies to come bursting in at any time. Was it standard service to send a whole entourage of people to help some lowly girl get ready for a ball that she'd been invited to on a whim?

I didn't linger long, not wanting the faeries who were coming to help me to see me in this state, so I hopped out, the water draining from the tub immediately. All that was left were the little flower petals that had been floating on the surface.

"I'll be back for you later tonight …" I told the tub, running my fingers along the edge. I definitely wanted to enjoy another a hot soak like this while I could.

Only a short time later there was a knock from … somewhere. "Miss Cassandra?" a small voice echoed in the meadow. "Are you in there?"

"I am," I said, standing up from the tree bed where I had been sitting.

The door appeared across from me, and in came six faeries, each of them carrying dresses in all colors and shapes. They were led by a green-haired faerie with purple eyes and purple wings. He wore a long sleeved white tunic with a blue vest overtop, a gold cord tied around his waist. His tunic fell all the way to his knees, and he wore black boots and golden trousers beneath.

"Good evening, Miss Cassandra," the faerie said, bowing his head. "My name is Felix, and I am your personal designer for the ball this evening."

The other five faeries in the room arranged their burdens so that they could clap enthusiastically, beaming at Felix.

"Thank you, thank you," Felix said, bowing at each and grinning at his plaudits.

"Um ... hi," I said. Having had no experience with personal designers, I wasn't sure what the protocol here was.

"Mmmm, you are quite the pretty thing," Felix said, strolling through the tall grass to stand in front of me. He was about a head taller than me, peering down into my face. "Crisp features. Though ... your clothes," he said, pulling at the sleeve of my sweatshirt. He gave me a curious expression. "I have never seen ... such a thing."

My stomach twisted uncomfortably, and my heart rate sped up, thudding in my ears.

"Oh, this? These are just what we wear in the hinterlands," I said, nodding my head, trying to look confident. "They're very, uh ... fashion backward outside Summer, you know."

Felix laughed. "But of course they are. How silly of me to expect anything else." He clapped his hands, and three of the faeries stepped forward. "See these? I have made these myself and they are the very height of Starvale fashion. Whatever dress you would like, whatever your imagination can construct ... We shall create the perfect look, just for you."

"What about one of these?" I asked, staring around at the other faeries. One held a dress made of what looked like liquid moonlight. Another had one made from shimmering leaves that changed and morphed even as you looked at them.

"Ah, did one of these catch your eye?" Felix said happily. He snapped his fingers and a large full-length mirror appeared in midair, like a perfectly still river floating a few inches above the ground.

He pulled me in front of the mirror and I got a good look at myself. I could see that the glamour was holding around my hair. I lifted my arm to pretend to scratch behind my ear, and saw the silvery star tattoo there where it should be.

Good. Lockwood's long-distance magic had done its job.

"Which of these did you like?" he asked. I could see all of the dresses in the reflection of the mirror. The ones with the leaves kept catching my eyes, a beautiful changing hue of blue and green, light passing over it like water.

I pointed at it. "That one."

He clapped his hands and the dress was thrust into his hands by the faerie holding it. "Here we are," and he took my hand in his.

My stomach dropped like I had missed a step. Was he going to undress me right then and there? "Uh, wait, I—"

Before I could finish, he twirled me around a few times, and when I came to a stop, I was wearing the dress.

It looked lovely with my pretend blue-green hair, and it echoed the ivy knotted in the braids Lockwood had given me. The dress draped over one shoulder, and was surprisingly modest, given all of the sheer fabric.

"This is beautiful, but ... it doesn't feel like you," Felix said, shaking his head.

I looked in the mirror. "You're not wrong."

Felix tapped his chin, and then his eyes lit up. "Yes, I know just the thing."

He took the moonlighty dress and hung it up on a peg that had suddenly appeared out of nowhere, hanging in thin air. As he touched the fabric, it moved and changed, growing where he pulled gently, and retracting where he pushed. As he waved his hand over parts, the colors changed from white to grey.

We did the twirl thing again, and now I was wearing the moonlight dress.

I wrinkled my nose. I didn't care for how wide it made my hips look. I worried if I'd be able to actually get out of the door. "Uh ..."

"No?" Felix asked, brushing fingers against his chin.

179

"You're right. No. No."

The dresses were all so marvelous to look at, but I just wanted something that wouldn't make me feel entirely unlike myself to wear it. These were so … elaborate. "Do you have anything simpler?" I asked hesitantly.

Felix looked into my face, as if trying to find the very essence of my soul.

"Simpler? Hmm … yes … I can do simpler."

He clapped his hands and the other dresses disappeared, and he pulled a thin wooden stick from his pocket, and began to wave it around.

I watched in awe as a pale golden thread burst from the tip and started to weave itself together right before my very eyes. It twisted and turned in the air, glimmering in the warm sunlight overhead. The other faeries watched just as closely as I did.

Soon the threads had formed a fabric that appeared to be lighter than air itself. The fabric grew and began to join to itself, and soon the shape of a dress formed. A narrow dress, with no frills or extras, just a slender pale gold sheath, sleeveless and long. He waved the stick in his hands once more, and silver thread flew out to join the golden, and a small, narrow braided band attached itself right at the waist, giving the gown a simple elegance.

The dress slowly drifted toward Felix, who picked it up and ran his hands over it. The fabric began to shimmer like a diamond as he stroked it.

"There," he said, grinning. "Perhaps this is better?"

I looked at it, eyes wide with awe.

It was the most beautiful dress I had ever seen.

"It's … perfect," I said. I felt ridiculous getting emotional over a dress, but this one was just too amazing. I had literally watched it come together in front of me. With magic.

"Let's try it on." Felix smiled, holding it draped over his hands.

He spun me once more, and when I looked at myself in the mirror, I gasped.

I was not sure that I had ever looked quite so much like a woman before. The dress hugged my frame in all of the right places, yet was not tasteless in any way. It was comfortable, incredibly soft.

I wiped at my eyes.

I really wished that Mill was here to see this …

"There now, I'd say we've done it," Felix said. "You are happy?"

"You have no idea," I said, looking at myself in the mirror. Leaving aside the blue-green hair … I didn't even recognize myself, but … it was me. No lie. Just an impressively crafted magical gown. "No dress has ever made me feel like this before."

Felix grinned. "Good. Good. I must leave you now. I have others to attend to, but these five will remain and help you finish getting ready."

I looked at the other five, and the gowns they had carried before had vanished, replaced with a variety of jewels in small boxes, as well as different shoes and shawls.

"Felix …" I said as he fluttered toward the door, which had reappeared a few feet away. "Thank you."

He bowed once more, smiling. "My pleasure. And so nice to be asked for something … simple, for once." His eyelids fluttered, purple flashing, and then he was gone.

"So …" I said, the five faerie attendants staring at me expectantly like I knew what in the world I was supposed to be doing. "What now?"

They fluttered closer, two of them bearing their offerings of jewelry first. I chose a simple necklace and tiny crystal earrings. I took a shawl from the third, deciding it might be wise in case the ball was cold.

Magic, seriously … I could get used to this.

The servants moved about me, clasping the jewels around my neck, others stepping up to help me choose the shoes I wanted to wear. As I watched them flitter, it made me wonder about them, who they were. "So, do you all live here in the castle?" I asked.

"Yes, miss." A little pink faerie polished the earrings I was to wear before she handed them to me.

"That must be very … interesting," I said.

"Indeed, miss, it is," she said.

I looked up at her. "You must meet all sorts of people, don't you?"

The faerie's face paled, and she stared at me with wild horror, transfixed for a moment. The other four faeries were glaring at her as though she'd let a mighty belch or something.

"Y-yes, miss, we do meet interesting sorts," she managed to reply. "But it is a servant's job to hear but not listen, see but not understand."

"I see," I said, feeling a little guilty about how nervous I was making her.

I looked at the young faerie boy who was insisting that he put my shoes on my feet instead of me doing it. "And what about the ball? Who can I expect to meet there?"

The boy faerie looked at me with the same terrified expression, as though sure he was going to say something out of turn and get walloped by someone for it.

The faerie beside him shook his head. "We don't know, miss. We just know that you will have a very nice time." He grinned up at me, but man was it fake.

"Will the King and Queen of Summer be there?" I asked. "I'm supposed to meet them in court tomorrow morning, but I'd like to see what they look like before I get there." I was trying to use my best casual voice, but it was very evident that these five did not want to talk.

"They will be there," the pink faerie answered, nodding her head. She appeared relieved that I had asked an easy question.

Well, time for another hard one.

"What about Master Calvor?" I asked. "Will he be there?"

This time, all of the faeries froze, but only for the briefest second.

"We don't know which members of the court attend any particular gathering," the faerie who had helped the young boy replied, getting to his feet, my shoes now on and looking perfect with my gown.

I stared around at them, trying not to show even a hint of what I was thinking. They all seemed frightened, but why? Being Seelie, what did they have to fear here in the Court of

Summer?

Or, conversely … what were they trying to hide?

"What do you know of the war?" I asked. "I was at one of the field hospitals, and it doesn't look good out there."

The faeries around me all sucked in breath nervously, almost as one. "We should not be discussing such matters," the young boy faerie said. "We are not supposed to—"

One of the others jabbed him in the gut with his elbow.

"Will that be all, miss?" The faerie was looking at me with an expression of intense distaste. His tone was even, though it carried a hint of a challenge.

"Yes …" I said, looking at myself in the floating refraction of water. "Yes, that's fine. Thank you all, for your help and your care."

They all bowed, and left the room in one rigid line, considerably stiffer on their way out than when they had flitted in. As the closed the door behind himself, I sagged onto the bed.

That hadn't gone well. And it wasn't a great sign that the servants in this place seemed stiff and worried about discussing … well, anything, it seemed.

There was a knock at the door, and I leapt off the bed, my heart stopping for a second before doubling its tempo. "Yes?" I called once I'd steadied myself.

The door swung inward, and tiny little Nino reappeared. "Oh, my! Little Seelie looks ravishing!"

I smiled. "Thank you, Nino."

"Is little Seelie ready to go see her friends?"

My heart jumped again. "Yes," I said, twirling once, looking in the mirror one final time. This … was as good as I'd ever looked. Which meant I wasn't likely to improve by just standing here.

"Then follow Nino. I shall escort you to the ball."

I smiled, giving myself one last look as I followed him from the room. Nino certainly liked to play follow the leader.

As I walked down the hall, other faeries that passed me stopped to look. With each passing glance, the color in my cheeks deepened. I wondered if it was the plainness of my dress that was catching their attention? Looking around at some of the other attendees making their way through the corridors, mine certainly lacked the ornateness of their gowns.

Nino took off down the stairs ahead of me, but I knew my limits in shoes with any kind of heel, so I took hold of the railing, slowly making my way down.

I felt like a princess in a castle, my prince waiting for me at the bottom of the stairs. Chalk it up to every little girl's bucket list; be a princess for a day. Wear a pretty dress. Dance until midnight at the ball. Make it home before your carriage turns back into a pumpkin and your gown into rags. My shoes, fortunately, weren't made of glass; in fact, they were very comfortable.

Orianna and Lockwood at the bottom of the endless staircase. There were a great number of faeries milling around them, all of whom were dressed in strange and incredible outfits.

Lockwood wore a bottle-green suit, handsome as ever. Orianna's hair and wings were still grey, but she wore a golden dress, more elaborate than my own by miles. Still, it felt very much like her. I was glad she was allowing some of herself to show through.

Lockwood looked up at me then, and his eyes nearly popped. Orianna followed his gaze, and she, too, stared.

"Knock it off, you two," I said, hurrying down the last few stairs to level ground. "You're going to give me a complex." I darted a look around. "I know, I know. Too simple a look for here, but—I couldn't help it."

"You look lovely," Lockwood said. "Mill will be very unhappy that he missed seeing you in this."

I smiled at him. Well, that wasn't nothing.

"That dress …" Orianna said, "it's so …"

"Yeah, I know, underdone—"

"Flawless," Orianna breathed. She oozed sincerity, unable to take her eyes off me. "It's perfectly understated. I wish I had worn one like it instead of … this." She fiddled with a ruffle on her train.

"Thanks, guys," I sighed with relief.

"Shall we?" Lockwood asked, offering his arm to me.

"We shall," I said, taking it and feeling happier than I had been in a long time.

And we strolled down the hall, following the others toward what felt very much like a dream.

Chapter 23

It was sort of like being in a movie, but with faeries. There were handsome men and exceptionally gorgeous women, people dancing and laughing together. The colors were so bright I felt like my sight might be forever dulled after this.

The ballroom itself was easily as large as a football field, with vaulted ceilings overhead that were higher than a cathedral, tall windows all along the far wall made of stained glass, and large golden chandeliers hanging from above.

The floor was entirely see through, as if it didn't exist at all. Far below in what must have been the hunk of floating rock itself, was a cavernous ravine, filled with mushrooms that glowed, pulsing and emitting falling sparkles like stars.

"Is this glass?" I asked, my heart skipping a beat as I allowed Lockwood to pull me out onto the floor.

"No, it's magic," Lockwood said.

I liked the idea of magic better. Glass wouldn't hold several hundred faeries in a room as vast as this was.

Music came from instruments against the wall of windows, carrying through the room as if projected through speakers, though there were none in sight. Who needed technology when there was magic?

The room smelled of flowers and perfume, intoxicating in its sweetness. Shimmering lights danced overhead, and I realized with a jolt of fear and wonder that they were pixies, just like Nino.

Large balconies waited on opposite ends of the room,

immense wooden doors allowing entry to each. Stars carved upon them, the same shape as the Seelie tattoos.

"So this is the Seelie court …" I murmured.

Lockwood nodded, watching everything around us with mingled apprehension and curiosity. "The location, at least. If you were here during a court session, you would experience something entirely different. Chairs along the outer wall, a great dais in the middle made of crystal where the royal presently in charge has their pronouncements made for them—or does it themselves. Usually there is a rather large throne with—"

"It's nice and all …" Orianna butted in. "But the Unseelie court is better. More mysterious—"

Lockwood shot her a dangerous look. "Watch your tongue when you are here, Unseelie." I couldn't tell if he said it was self-defense or to protect her.

As we walked farther into the room, I noticed groups of faeries standing together, their heads bent toward one another, their hands over their mouths barely concealing wide grins. There were an awful lot of giggles, some gasping, scoffing … it reminded me a little of every clique of high school girls I'd ever seen.

"Aren't you worried someone will recognize us here?" I asked Lockwood.

Lockwood didn't reply for a moment. Only when I looked up at him did he say, "I am, but there are so many people here that I am likely to go unrecognized by most. And if we were brought here underneath Roseus's protection, then …" he trailed off. "I expect we are safe. For now."

For now. I sighed.

"What do we do?" I asked, looking around, suddenly feeling foolish as I stood there. Yes, the dress I wore was perfect, but … "I don't know how to dance."

"Ah, there you are," came Roseus's voice, as if Lockwood speaking his name had summoned him. I wondered for a second if it had. "You all look … wonderful." Did I imagine it or did his eyes linger on me a little longer than on Orianna?

"Thank you," I said. Orianna mumbled something similar.

"Would you care to join me at my table?" Roseus asked.

"Have something to eat? Perhaps meet some of the other guests?"

Lockwood's arm stiffened beneath mine. "I was just about to ask Cassandra to dance."

"Plenty of time for that later," Roseus said with a laugh. "Come, relax. You're here now. You'll have your chance to plead your case before the court in the morn."

I looked up at Lockwood's face. It was blank, but he was listening intently to Roseus.

"Lockwood, no one is going to harm you while I am behind you," Roseus said. "No one would dare."

"You truly have ascended, haven't you, friend?" Lockwood asked. I wished I could hear what he was thinking, but his tone was so neutral. Eventually, he sighed. "Very well. We will come with you."

"Wonderful," Roseus said, and he turned, making his way around the circle of dancers spinning in time to the music.

"I can watch the room with Roseus as well as I can from here," Lockwood said. "Besides, it is best to remain close to any allies we might have here. If others support Roseus, they will support us."

"That's a relief," I said. "It's nice to know not everyone is our enemy here."

"Not everyone," Lockwood said, and again I felt he was trying to tell me something. "Come on."

We walked around the outside of the dancers, and I marveled at all of the faeries. There were some hovering above the floor, others near the ceiling, spinning as if their feet had never left the floor. I imagined it would be hard to dance in the air, but with wings, who knew what was possible for them?

Roseus made his way to a table that looked to be made from cut sapphires, like water and as clear as the Gulf of Mexico. It was draped with a sheer cloth, and bowls and plates of all sizes covered the surface, along with bizarre curving carafes that looked strangely like the head and neck of a giraffe in size and shape. They were filled with brightly colored liquid. I saw some of the tea that I had at the hospital, with the floating specks of coppery metal, and my mouth watered.

Other faeries stood around the table, some wearing masks over their faces, others with crowns or glittering tiaras. Even from a distance, it was obvious that these people had more power than others here at the ball.

"How is your wing?" Roseus asked, and it took me a second to realize he was talking to me. "No improvement yet?"

I shook my head. "The doctors at the hospital at the camp we visited gave me some treatment and told me to take it easy until it healed."

"That's very unfortunate," Roseus said.

"You hurt your wing?" called one of the faerie girls beside the table.

"You poor dear," another said, her bottom lip sticking out. It vanished and was replaced with a wicked grin almost immediately. "Must be torture to have to walk everywhere."

"It's not so bad," I said airily. Like I knew anything different. Other than riding Orion, which, if that was a hint of what I was missing by not being able to fly … yeah, I was a poor dear. All humans were.

"Come, Lockwood—starfruit," Roseus said, gesturing to a dish of fruits that looked like tiny pomegranates, except they were green and covered in a red syrupy sauce. "I asked the chef to make this especially for you."

Lockwood stared, then blinked. He seemed … touched. "Thank you, Roseus. That was very thoughtful."

The fruit was soft and gently sweet, incredibly tart and … my eyes flew open. I had never tasted anything quite like them before. It was tart, yet it wasn't sour, sweet without being cloying. The syrup was light and delicate, a perfect compliment to the juicy fruit.

"We were just discussing Mistress Laurel's recent engagement," Roseus said.

"She's engaged now?" Lockwood asked.

Roseus shook his head. "I apologize. It's been so long since you've been here. Of course, yes. She was engaged just a month ago. To Master Levem."

"Of course, I think she could have done much better," said

one of the faeries just on the other side of the table, wrinkling her nose. Her eyes were so dark that it was almost impossible to see her irises. Her wings were just as dark. "She should have taken Master Calvor as her husband."

"I thought Master Calvor had a wife …" I said quietly.

The other female faeries giggled together like a bunch of high school girls.

"All right, ladies," Roseus said, though he was smiling, too. "That's enough of the latest gossip. Surely our guests don't want to hear about all of the drama in the court."

They laughed again, a pretty, tinkling sound. Then the conversation shifted to some other topic, a woman whose glamours were not what was expected, then to another whose gown was far out of fashion, then to yet another who—

It occurred to me what I was watching.

Mean girls. The fae version of mean girls.

"This would be the opposite back home," Orianna muttered under her breath to me. "When the Unseelie don't like each other, they're openly hostile. None of this whispering behind one another's backs nonsense …"

The sound of horns blared, and everyone turned to look toward either end of the room.

I froze at the sound. What was going on?

The wooden doors on both balconies swung outward, and as I looked between them, two faeries stepped out. One was male, the other female. They were more beautiful than any humans I had ever seen. She was as radiant as a summer's day, with hair as gold as sunlight itself, flowing almost all the way to the floor, adorned with tiny little braids and a crown of flowers upon her head. Her wings were the palest blue, like the sky and clouds overhead. She was dripping with elegance and grace.

He was dark haired and lean, with a strong jaw, a broad smile, and the face of a knight in shining armor. Even I blushed a little as I looked at him, with his green wings the color of new leaves, the way he held his chin high, and the power he radiated.

There was no doubt about it. They were the king and

queen of the Summer Court.

"Did you know that this is the first time that they have been seen together in almost six weeks?" one of the fae in our circle whispered.

"I'm surprised it was that recent," the green haired faerie said under her breath.

My, these faeries were snarky. I could see why Lockwood didn't mind staying on Earth. This was like being forever in high school.

Still, it was hard to be too annoyed with them when there was majesty and beauty everywhere I looked.

"Citizens of Seelie," came the voice of the king. "Welcome to our court."

Chapter 24

The whole room around us had gone silent, hanging on the king's words. It was obvious just how much power these two held; they were just as terrifying and awe inspiring as Lockwood and Orianna had made them out to be.

Lockwood glanced down at me and gave a subtle shake of his head, but he needn't have worried: I had no intention of saying anything. I was so overawed, I wasn't sure I could have anyway.

I stared up at the king, then just as it had at the hospital, just as it had at the farm, the whole world around me flickered.

The king and queen remained as they were, standing above the crowd on their balconies, but everything around them was washed in shadows, the faces of the faeries around me veiled as if they were wearing masks of darkness. They stood at rapt attention, nothing moving, no one speaking.

It was a dark sort of beauty, with thorns encircling the ceiling and glass shards littering the floor. The vision kept shifting between the pleasant reality of the ball and this strange, flickering image of shadow and horror. It was as if all the world was fighting, trying to keep me from seeing what was behind the veil …

"Friends … colleagues … people of Seelie," the king continued in his booming, clear voice, "our hearts are gladdened by your presence, and we are eager to begin the night's festivities."

A woman's voice spoke in clear, ringing tones, and I turned to study Queen Ignes. "We are eagerly anticipating the coming Summer Court. Our victory assured, we press forward to a new dawn—one which will see the Seelie rule over all of Faerie!"

The fae around us broke out in applause. Lockwood applauded as well, though far less enthusiastically than the others. Orianna remained entirely still. She was staring up at the queen with a look of barely veiled disgust.

The king held up his hands. Either they were really good at giving each other a chance to talk, or they rehearsed this so much that it was second nature. "We hope that you will feast and be joyful, filling your cups with wine and your hearts with joy."

"Thank you all, once again, for your loyalty and your service," the queen said.

More clapping. I joined in to be polite, that time.

I noticed Lockwood was looking over his shoulder, his brow furrowed. I followed his gaze and realized that Roseus had disappeared. "Where did the general go?" Lockwood asked. The fae next to him shrugged.

I looked back. The king and the queen were now standing in front of incredibly intricate thrones, which had appeared in the few seconds that my back had been turned.

The king's was made of a large tree, one continuous piece of wood that had been carved down and shaped until smooth. Tiny buds were popping all over it along the branches, and the seat itself was furnished with a luxurious red silk cushion.

The queen's appeared to be made from water, and it shimmered and wavered in the light of the flickering candles behind and above it. It appeared to hold a great depth, and I could have sworn tiny fish-like creatures swam around inside of it, as if it were a giant aquarium.

This place would probably never stop being weird.

"Cassandra, would you like to dance?" Lockwood asked me. He had an *I have to talk to you* sort of look on his face.

"Yeah, sure," I said.

Orianna gave me a forlorn look. *Don't leave me here!* she

mouthed.

I shrugged as Lockwood pulled me away from the group.

"Hey, little faerie! I thought you couldn't fly!" called one of the drama faeries after me.

I didn't reply. Why would I? I couldn't fly.

"She has a point there, Lockwood," I said under my breath as we started a sort of waltz. "And I'm not really much of a dancer."

"Not to worry," Lockwood said, taking one of my hands in his, and placing his hand on my waist. Instinctively, or because I had seen so many princess-y sort of movies, I placed my hand on his shoulder.

Man, this was just getting weird and cooler all at the same time.

He lifted me in the air, very gently, and I found my feet on top of his shoes.

Soon we were spinning along with the dancers around us, moving quickly enough to keep up with the music, me like a little girl on her daddy's feet. Which felt … a little awkward, given Lockwood was definitely not my father. There was so much about him I just didn't know. To think, at one point not that long ago, he had been nothing more than a limo driver to me.

But not now. Lockwood was a magical paladin of Seelie, and a ballroom dancing master. He was an exile of the court, and yet here he was, standing inside their walls, right beneath their noses.

He was scanning the room around us.

"What?" I asked.

"Something isn't right," he said, still looking around.

"Well, no duh, nothing has been right since we came to Faerie in the first place." I looked down at my feet, still atop his. "Sorry. I sound like those snotty faerie noblewomen."

Lockwood smirked ever so slightly. "No, you are very unlike them. But … this is not what I expected."

"What were you expecting?" I asked.

"More a struggle to get into the court," Lockwood said, smoothly gliding with me across the air over the ball. "A frostier reception at the gate. More … lies, I think." He looked at me and smiled. "I did bring you for a reason, after all."

"Yeah," I said, coming back to earth metaphorically even as I continued to float in Lockwood's arms. "And it's not the way I wear this dress." I wanted to sag in his arms, or just drift back down.

"I didn't mean to ... diminish you in any way by saying that," Lockwood said, looking me in the eyes, his green ones flaring in the multicolored light of the ballroom. "You are a very special young lady, Cassandra."

"Sorry, I didn't mean to drag you down there," I said, looking past him as another couple waltzed by in a slow twirl. "I guess I was feeling a little sorry for myself. Ever since I came to Florida, it just ... feels like lying is the only thing I'm good for, you know? I had to lie to save myself from Byron, to stop those Instaphoto vamps, to dodge the Butcher ..." I shook my head. "I lie to my parents, all the time. Again. As if completely burning my bridges in New York didn't ..." I lowered my head and closed my eyes. "Damn."

"What is it?"

"I just ... swore that things were going to be different when we moved to Florida," I said, opening my eyes again to find Lockwood's rimmed with concern. "I wasn't going to lie any more, and yet ... here I am in an entirely new world, and what am I doing? Lying. About who I am, about ... everything. Because this is what you brought me here for."

"Lying is not ... always bad," Lockwood said, but he was pretty half-hearted about it.

"Oh?" I gave him a smirk of amusement. "Give me an example where it's good."

It only took him a second. "Try to picture how things would go with your parents if you attempted to explain your relationship with Mr. Mill using only bracing honesty."

I did imagine it, and ... "Yeah, okay, you have a point there," I said.

Hey Mom and Dad, I'm dating a vampire. Sure, he looks like a teenager, but he's older than both of you combined, I think. Been kinda scared to ask. Also, yeah ... vampires are real.

195

Yep. That'd go super well.

"I apologize for putting you in this position," Lockwood said with a great sigh. "We are here now, though. And perhaps you are right. Perhaps … the truth will have its day here as well." He blinked, once. "It would be nice if I were able to just … speak honestly rather than put you in the position of having to spin an untruth to save my sullied honor."

"Well, if I'm going to employ my considerable lying talents," I said, my gown rippling around me, "at least here I'll be doing it for the good of someone else, and not just to spare myself some uncomfortable questions or for the thrill of it."

The song slowed, and Lockwood and I slowly stopped revolving, too. A small round of applause echoed through the room as we came to a stop.

The room continued to spin, though. In the distance, still standing beside the long sapphire table was Orianna, her arms crossed over herself, staring at Lockwood and I with a vacant expression, the other faeries nearby completely ignoring her.

Ah, it was like I'd never left high school.

Lockwood pursed his lips, looking up at the queen on her aquarium-esque throne. She appeared entirely at ease, sitting there with a clear goblet filled to the brim with electric blue liquid. She took a small sip as a servant beside her whispered in her ear. She nodded, and returned her attention to the dancers.

Lockwood's eyes did not leave her, narrowing. "I'm sorry to say it, but … something appears greatly amiss here."

The music started again, and he picked me up, resuming our waltz, but more slowly this time. I wondered if I had left my stomach back where we had stopped. Wherever it was, it churned uncomfortably. "Why?"

He was quiet for a few moments that felt like an eternity, his bright green eyes still scanning the room. "I know my people. I know how we act, how we flaunt and tease and carry on." He smiled insincerely—man, there was a lot of that around here. "We have learned how to say everything and nothing at the same time. To lie without speaking a single untruth, and yet being false all the same."

His face had grown hard.

"I was trained in it. It was I who trained him," Lockwood said, seemingly forgetting that I was there. "Doesn't he remember that I was the one who negotiated for the territory south of Elderwood? I who made Mistress Valen think that it was her choice to leave the court?"

"You lost me," I said. My heart was starting to beat faster. Here was another side of Lockwood that I didn't understand. The going-crazy side.

He paused in midair, looking me in the eye. "Cassandra, I'm afraid that we have made a terrible mistake."

My heart sunk right to my shiny shoes. "… What do you mean by that?"

Lockwood looked down at me. "You saw that Roseus left during the speech?"

I glanced over my shoulder, and regretted it almost immediately. Now we were spinning so fast that it felt like my head suddenly weighed a hundred pounds, and the blood was roaring in my ears. Nausea crept up my throat, and I closed my eyes, willing it to go away.

"I noticed you notice it," I said, wondering when our little dance had become a tilt-a-whirl ride. "But Lockwood, I think you're being a little paranoid. Roseus seems to think the world of you. He was so eager to help us back at the village, and he's gone to great lengths to keep us safe here. He promised us his protection, didn't he?"

Lockwood's face was still dark. "Of a sort."

I blinked. "… Of a sort?"

"He promised us safe passage here," Lockwood said.

I thought about that for a second. "Uh … just here?"

"Yes," Lockwood said, with a knowing look. "Very specifically. Which is what worries me."

"Why?" I asked, suspecting I already knew the answer. Half-truths … well, they used to be one of my favorite lies.

"It's … a subtle art that I am well acquainted with," Lockwood said. "I understand when someone is not saying what they really mean, or leaving important things out in order to cover their tail."

"So, you always know when I'm lying?" I asked.

He spared me a fleeting look. "Nearly."

The music suddenly cut out, and the room fell silent. All of the dancing ceased, both in the air and on the ground.

"What's happening?" I asked.

Lockwood held my wrist. "Stay close to me."

"Why? What—"

Orianna was suddenly beside us, her eyes wide and staring past us at the far end of the room. Lockwood was, too, though his were narrower.

I turned slowly to see what they were staring at, and my mouth fell open.

The queen was standing on her balcony, hands gripping the white railing in front of her. Standing before her on the floor were at least three dozen Seelie guards, their white armor shining bright even in the well-lit room. The queen looked anything but beautiful now. Her lips were curled into a wicked smile.

At us.

But that wasn't what had stunned me.

General Roseus stood beside the queen, the same sort of wicked grin on his face as he stared right down at Lockwood and me.

"Lockwood, we—"

He shooshed me, his eyes narrowing.

The queen stared around at the hundreds of faeries gathered there, her icy gaze sweeping over us all. I stood frozen to the spot, Lockwood's grip around my wrist cutting off my circulation, the tips of my fingers starting to go numb.

She appeared to be enjoying the tension. Her grin grew wider.

I tried to swallow past the lump that was forming in my throat. I couldn't remember the last time that I blinked.

We had no weapons.

No defenders.

We were trapped.

Her voice rang out, echoing off the far walls and the vast

ceiling, triumphant. "My fair subjects … this is a most auspicious night … one in which we celebrate the return …" Her smile widened, Cheshire-like, far too large for her face, "… of a traitor."

Chapter 25

I stood in the midst of a lava flow, surrounded on all sides by hot magma. It was the Summer fae's idea of a dungeon, and a pretty good one, at that. Like a sauna, but far, far worse, heat pressed in against me from all sides, making me cough and wheeze. Every breath made me feel like I was being slowly roasted from the inside.

Wide, snaking rivers of flowing magma separated me from Orianna, whose glamour had been stripped from her as unceremoniously as my own, guards pressing in on us and draping charm necklaces over us with rough hands.

The gasps when they'd found out I was human? Pretty impressive. Almost as shocked as when my parents had found out I was a giant liar.

The rivers of lava popped and gurgled, sluggishly winding their way down to the lip of the hill and out of sight. Each time a hiss of steam emerged, more heat filled the air.

Sweat started to form above my lip and on my back.

Dragons the size of mastiffs crouched on rocks outside the lava rivers. Black and reptilian, their wings were folded against their sides, their teeth bared, each staring at us with one wide, yellow eye.

I hadn't seen Lockwood since Orianna and I had been paraded out of the ballroom, our glamours stripped.

The last time I'd seen him …

I drew a deep, sulphuric breath and felt it burn my throat, my eyes.

The last time I'd seen Lockwood … he was being beaten by a circle of angry guards as the entire ball cheered.

I let out another breath, and it burned when I drew my next. The air was so hot, my eyes were stinging. Was this real? Or just another glamour?

And my ball gown … the beautiful, shimmering fabric …

It was nothing more than a dirty cloth now. I was as good as Cinderella.

"Well, this is great," Orianna said, sinking down to the ground below her. She folded her arms and legs, staring pitifully into the lava.

Her dress had burned too. Her shoulders were bare, and there was a large hole over her thigh. A tear in the side made it look as if she had been struck by a sharp object. No blood was in evidence, though, which made me think maybe she'd just been dragged or something. I could just make out the edge of the silvery snowflake tattoo on the underside of her wrist.

"Are those … real?" I asked her, pointing at the dragons still snarling at us from across the lava.

She sighed. "Most likely. They're here so I can't fly away." When she caught my questioning look, she made a fist and then a noise that I took to be a fireball, smacking her own wing. "Get it?"

My stomach lurched. A faerie without wings … that would be a hell of a punishment.

"The lava could be real, too," she said. "I definitely don't want to take my chances that it isn't."

"How could they …" I asked

"You've been here for a while, and every time you ask, the answer is always the same. Do I really need to spell it out for you again?" she asked.

"Magic," I whispered.

"Exactly," she said, gingerly gathering the remains of her gown and bunching up underneath her before sitting on a rock. "In Faerie, it's always magic."

"Got it," I whispered."

"Finally, I see the grace of the Summer Court," Orianna said, laying her head on her knees. "My only consolation right now is that … at least I'm not Lockwood."

My skin crawled. "What do you mean?"

She looked up at me, giving me a look as if she couldn't believe the stupidity. "Did you not see what they were doing to him? Because that's a warm up for what comes next."

"Torture?" I asked, blanching. "No, they wouldn't …"

Orianna looked up at me, hatred twisting her pretty face. "Maybe they do things differently on Earth, but here in Faerie, torture is very common. Especially for those who sit on the court."

"Yes, things are different on Earth," I said, looking all around for some means of escape that didn't end in me being burned to death in lava. "At least … it is where I come from. We try our criminals, we don't … whatever you do here."

Orianna made a noise of disgust. "Unbelievable …" she muttered, looking away from me.

"What?" I asked. "What's unbelievable?"

"You!" she snapped, whipping her head back around to glare at me. She crawled to her feet and pointed a thin, golden-tipped finger at me, the lava making the snowflake tattoo appear to be glowing. "You are a liar."

"Yeah," I said. I'd been called a liar by a lot worse than Orianna. "And … ?"

"You've been a human all this time," she said.

"All my life, actually."

"And you didn't tell me." She shook her head with disappointment.

"Do you blame me?" I asked. "I'm in Faerie as a human. Why wouldn't I hide my identity when I had no idea how anyone would react?"

"But you didn't tell me," she said, sounding … actually very insulted. "You knew the truth about me. And all along, I thought that I knew the truth about you, too." She put her head back down on her knees. "Liar."

There was that word again. It was my trademark, wasn't it? It was all that anyone was ever going to know me as.

The greatest liar there ever was.

"I didn't know if you could be trusted," I said coldly. "And you know what? I still don't."

I watched her jaw work as she contemplated what to say in response to me. "Lockwood knew, didn't he?" Then she rolled her eyes. "Of course he did."

"Uh, yeah," I said. "I came here to help him."

"Is anything that ever came out of your mouth the truth?" Orianna asked, peering at me, her head still sideways on her knees.

I paced calmly back to the lava on the farthest side from her, looking for … anything. A way out, really. "My name, I guess. Maybe some of my stories. I dunno."

"Well, your wing being broken was a lie," she said, listing them off on her fingers. "You being a Seelie was a lie. Though I guess that explains why you knew nothing about being a faerie."

"I guess you've got me all figured out," I said, staring at the dragon leering at me from above.

"What about at the hospital, huh?" Her voice was climbing. "You said all of those pretty things to that woman with the baby? The one whose husband had died? You told her a sob story to get her to help you, didn't you?"

"That … wasn't a lie," I said.

"I don't believe you." She folded her arms across her chest, her gaze icy.

"I don't care." Fatigue was setting in. Anxiety was nibbling at me.

I was trapped in a mystical dungeon, stuck in the middle of a lava flow with someone who hated me.

And Lockwood …

Lockwood was captured. About to be tortured.

Maybe as good as dead.

"How in the hell did it come to this?" I muttered to myself, staring up at the dragon. A week ago, if you'd told me I was going to see the magical land of Faerie, was going to be standing in a place like this, looking up at a dragon …

I would have been excited to go. Maybe not if I'd known that it was going to be in a prison, but … overall the scenario, minus some of the finer details? Sounded kinda cool. Lava mountains and rivers, and a dragon. Nifty.

Except now I was stuck here, imprisoned. And Lockwood was …

Gone.

What did that mean for me, then? How was I going to get back to Earth?

Would I even get back?

My skin vibrated, every nerve on fire, burning with worry and small little hints of rage, buried underneath the concern.

Here I was, stuck beside a faerie who I thought once to be a sort-of friend, who apparently hated my guts now. The feeling was definitely getting toward mutual.

And Lockwood … the one I came to help and protect was possibly dead … all because I had come with him to Faerie in the first place.

"What? Truth finally starting to settle in on you?" Orianna sneered.

"Shut up …" I said, but I had lost all of my steam.

I was just tired now. My whole body was so heavy.

Nothing mattered anymore. Why shouldn't I just curl up here on this floor and sleep until it was all over?

"Hey," Orianna said. "Hey, don't think you've won this, human. Don't sit there all smug, thinking that you got the better of me. You didn't."

"Whatever." Pure teenager. I really didn't care anymore. How had I cared so much in the first place?

Lockwood …

My heart clenched.

Mill …

The dragons on the other side of the river suddenly perked up, their heads turning to look at something coming up the side of the cliff.

"What was that?" Orianna asked.

I didn't have a chance to answer her, because suddenly the stifling heat was gone and I was on the shore of a vast beach, with vibrant blue-green waves gently lapping up against a shore that stretched all the way to the horizon.

Chapter 26

The beach seemed to go on forever, the sand soft and warm beneath my fingers. A pleasant breeze blew the sweaty curls from my face. There was a scent of salt water in the air, though I was definitely alone. Orianna was nowhere to be seen.

A large island lay in the distance, the sun was setting just behind it, painting the sky in bright oranges, deep pinks. Behind me, the first stars were starting to wink into existence.

I swallowed, a big ol' nervous gulp.

How did I get here?

For a second, I wondered if I had somehow been transported back to Earth. It felt like Earth. There was only one sun. The water was the same color of our oceans on Earth, the color that never shows up quite right in a photo.

I looked over my shoulder and scrambled to my feet as I saw Roseus standing there.

He was wearing a pair of trousers rolled up to the knees, and a pastel blue button-down shirt, short sleeve. The sort of thing my dad would wear on vacation. He had sunglasses resting in his windswept straw-colored hair.

If I hadn't hated his guts, I might have thought he was rather good looking.

"Well, Cassandra … what do you think?" he asked, sweeping his hands out around him.

I didn't say anything.

"I know Lockwood was hiding where there were beaches like this. You must have been from around there. Does it feel like home?"

I noticed a flash of pink out of the corner of my eye and looked down. I was wearing a pink summer dress with tiny white flowers that was flowing in the breeze with a white cardigan over it.

Not exactly the exact outfit I would have chosen for myself for the beach, but hey, props for trying, Roseus. "Next time, I'd rather wear blue," I said with a smirk I didn't entirely feel, given the circumstances. I gritted my teeth as the fabric changed to a lovely powder blue with the blink of an eye.

I turned around and started walking away up the beach.

"Now, hold on a second," Roseus said, hurrying to catch up. "I just want to talk, okay?"

I rounded on him. "You tricked us," I said. "You played Lockwood's friend and then you sold us out." A little spittle flew from my lips as I pointed my finger at him.

Roseus didn't even try to deny it. He sunk his hands into the pockets of his khakis and stared at me like we were some couple having a squabble on a date.

"I thought you were his friend …" I said, as the water washed over my bare feet. I noticed my toenails were adorned with little Seelie stars.

"Lockwood and I have a long history," Roseus said gently, walking up beside me. "Sometimes friends go through rough patches, right? Unfortunately for us, this … is a rough patch."

"Getting him thrown in jail for torture and execution? Yeah, that's pretty rough," I said, turning to walk further along the shore. My feet were leaving footprints along the wet sand, which were quickly washed away as the tide rolled in.

He fell easily into step beside me.

"Are you all right?" Roseus asked in a very convincing tone. "The guards didn't hurt you at all, did they?"

I didn't answer him. No, they didn't hurt me at all. But why did he care? Really?

"Cassandra … it's Cassandra, right?" he asked.

206

"It's Cassie," I snapped.

"Ah, yes, my apologies," Roseus said. "Cassie, I want you to know that I know you were caught up in all of this by mistake. Lockwood dragged you into it without telling you the whole truth, didn't he?"

The water sloshed against my ankles. It was warm and pleasant, warmer than the beaches around Tampa right now.

Yeah … he hadn't told me the whole truth. In fact, he'd told me less than ten percent of it before we actually got to Faerie. And it had redlined me into some frustrating territory, being kept in the dark.

"I trust Lockwood implicitly," I said. I wasn't sure why I felt the need to justify myself in front of him. "See, that's what friends do for each other."

"After all that you still trust him," Roseus said, staring at me. "That's interesting. I just want you to know that I am going to do whatever I can to help you, all right?"

"Oh, yeah?" I asked, glaring up at him. "Why would you do that for me?"

"Because you are innocent in all of this," he said. "I know that it was Lockwood who told you that you had to wear a glamour and pretend to be something you aren't. You didn't choose to get caught up in all of this nonsense happening between Seelie and Unseelie. He brought you here during a very dangerous time. He should have been more concerned about your safety."

My cheeks turned pink, but I was staring at the ground below me as I walked aimlessly. Safety had been an afterthought for me these last few months, hadn't it? If Lockwood had endangered me, it had been because I'd gotten myself in a hell of a mess through all my lies first. Given all the vampire stuff I'd been through since leaving New York, this Faerie adventure didn't seem all that bad. A little scary, sure, but … I was dealing with a lot of that lately.

"Look, Cassie," Roseus said, "there is a way that I can help you, but it might be … difficult."

My stomach turned over. What did he mean difficult? What could be any more difficult than what I was dealing with right now? I stared at him, waiting for him to go on.

"The Crown only has leniency with those who are openly honest," Roseus said. "I know that as a human, that will be hard for us to verify. While we don't ever lie, we have certain means to tell when others are."

I still didn't answer him. Might as well make some good on my word.

"Clemency is offered to those who answer our questions, provided they are innocent of any crimes," he said. "If I ask you some questions, can I have your word that you will tell me the truth? I know that a human's word is binding to them."

I glanced up at him. What a nice world he lived in, thinking humans didn't break their word. When was the last time he spent any time on Earth? The Revolutionary War? Because this was certainly opening a door for me.

"If I tell you the truth, you will get me out of here?" I asked, slowly.

"I am going to do what I can." He nodded his head. "You know how these things are. I must take responses to those above me, and then those will be passed to the Crown for evaluation." He stared with piercing eyes at me. "I know that you are innocent, Cassie. You have done nothing wrong while here in Faerie. The testimonies of those who have interacted with you would be able to prove that."

The Crown had leniency for those who were openly honest?

And they had means to know, according to him. They had figured out that both Orianna and I were glamoured, after all.

I thought of Lockwood, on his knees, head hanging. It pained me too much to think of him suffering, so I just tried to ignore it.

"What about Lockwood?" I asked.

"Hmm?" Roseus said. He had been staring up into the darkening sky overhead.

"Lockwood," I said. "What's going to happen to him?"

Roseus's face fell, and he scratched the back of his head nervously. "I am not at liberty to say—"

"Is he still alive?" I asked, my heart beating faster.

"Of course," Roseus said. "We wouldn't kill him. What would be the point?"

Immense relief washed over me, much like the waves pulling the sand from my feet. The sickening knot in my chest loosened. Not entirely, but enough to let me breathe a little more.

"If I give you the answers you want, will you let me see him?" I asked.

"Bargaining, I see," Roseus said. He sighed. "Well … I don't want to make any promises I can't keep."

I sighed.

"However … it will likely help your chances."

A chance was better than nothing. What were my other options? Sit in faerie jail with Orianna, staring at the lava dragons with no semblance of a plan? At least if I got to Lockwood, I could talk about some sort of plan for busting out of here, getting back to Earth.

Getting back home.

It may have been the longest shot in the history of long shots, but I had no other choice, did I?

"All right," I said. "Ask your questions."

"Very good," Roseus said.

He came to a stop, so I turned to face him.

"My first question is … why would Lockwood come back to Faerie after all this time?"

Hmm. Tell him that Lockwood had come to lie to the court about whatever had gotten him exiled? That didn't sound like a winning strategy. The best lies built on the framework of the truth, and while I didn't know if I was going to need to lie just yet, I knew I didn't want to tell the whole truth. I started at the beginning.

"He was attacked," I said. "And I was with him. I saw the whole thing. Pixies came out of nowhere and started bombarding his car." I left out details, like the fact that Mill was with us, and that Lockwood had just picked me up from school. "They destroyed it. They came after me, and he managed to chase them off …"

Roseus was watching me closely. I hadn't lied yet, so it was even easier to hold his gaze.

"He thought that someone here in Faerie had it out for him, and so he came back to see what was going on."

Okay, that part was kind of a lie. But it wasn't far from the truth, being the gist of what he had told me in the beginning. It just left out the crux of what he was doing.

"All right," Roseus said. "Next question. What was his plan?"

"Simple," I said. "Try to figure out exactly why he had been attacked. Those pixies weren't there to play. They meant to hurt him, if not kill him. They could have killed me, too."

"Yes, but what was his motive?" Roseus asked.

"To settle the matter. Because Lockwood is honest and straightforward," I said. "Unlike that Master Calvor or whatever his name is."

"You know about Master Calvor?" he asked, and his face … changed. Got grimmer. "How much do you know?"

"Only that he has a lot of power in the court," I said quickly. I'd stumbled on something here, and I wasn't sure I wanted to linger on the subject. Learning more would have been nice, but I felt like I could also get entangled in the topic given Roseus's somewhat dark look. "And that he doesn't have the greatest reputation." Enough honesty to satisfy the desire most people had for gossip, but vague enough he hopefully wouldn't think I knew more.

Roseus chuckled, and I felt a little relief. "Yes, well … that is what Lockwood would think of him, isn't it?" He scratched his chin. "All right, Cassie … one more question. Lockwood brought you along. Why?"

This was a question that I genuinely did not know how to answer. The way that he was staring at me, it was as if he already knew the true reason why, and he just wanted to hear me say it out loud as confirmation.

But I was not going to give him that satisfaction.

"It wasn't to destroy your precious court or whatever," I answered, crossing my arms over my chest. "The way everyone reacted in that ballroom … you'd think I'd pulled a gun on them and threatened to start unloading."

Roseus arched an eyebrow—apparently the reference had

gone over his head—and sighed heavily.

"You were an uninvited guest to the Seelie court," Roseus said, as if this was something I should know. "We prize our hospitality, and would welcome a human to our lands— provided that we could prepare for their coming. What would we have done had you brought some of that dreaded metal of yours here, hmm?" He cocked an eyebrow at me. "We could have had Summer fae dying by the dozens if you had but a little iron and a little anger, hmm?"

Good to know. I made a mental note to start wearing exclusively iron jewelry when I got home. It would have been nice to have something to swing around during the pixie attack.

I blinked. I'd assumed I was going to get home just then.

That feeling … warm and certain, in my stomach, solidified.

I *was* going to get home. It was no *if*.

"Think of a lion, or a wolf entering your home unannounced," Roseus said. "Surely you would be frightened that it would kill you, yes? But with the proper preparations, it would be no harm at all, right?"

Was that all I was to them? Some wild animal that needed to be kept down? "What, like a cage?" I asked. "A weapon, pointed at it the entire time?"

Roseus let out a low chuckle. "Not exactly. But you might want to, ahh … cork its fangs. We have a name for your kind … 'Iron Bearer.'" His humor dried up. "It is not a polite term."

He took my silence as agreement. He was right, but I still hated it.

"Well, Cassie, I wish that you had more to tell us. All of this business with Lockwood has been very nasty, and the court … well, we would all just like to put it behind us."

"Yeah, so would we who are not of the court but caught up in your business," I said. "So, are you going to let me see Lockwood?"

"I don't know …" Roseus said. "As I said, these decisions rest with those higher up than me." He sighed heavily. "But they are so very busy trying to … talk to Lockwood right now that I don't think they will even be able to hear your request at the moment … if I were to pass it along."

If … *if* he were to pass it along?

That hollow, sinking feeling returned to my gut. "… You really have no intention no letting me out of here, do you?"

He hesitated. "Ah … no," he said, kicking some sand with the toe of his sandal. "It isn't that I don't think you are innocent, because believe me, I do." He shrugged. "It's just that you ended up being at the wrong place at the wrong time. Does that make sense?"

It made too much sense. So much sense that I couldn't believe I didn't see this coming from the beginning.

I hadn't told him very much, but they knew about the attack now, and that Lockwood had told me about Master Calvor. He would naturally assume that I knew about his son being offed by an Unseelie, too.

That mere knowledge likely made me a liability now.

"Well, thank you for your company, Cassie," Roseus said, executing a little bow. "It has been a pleasure."

"Maybe for you," I said. And then he was gone, as if he had never been there.

As if I had imagined him.

I stared out into the sunset, realizing that it hadn't actually moved in the sky at all.

The only sound was the waves lapping against the shore, and the wind in my ears, taunting me about home. A place that I might never see again. That certainty I'd felt only moments before was gone, like a sandcastle when the tide came in.

My lip trembled.

No. I wasn't going to cry. Not here. Not alone where no one would hear me or see me. I held it in, pushed it down, but it felt like a strangled, burning feeling in my heart.

There was no way we were getting out of here.

And it was all my fault.

Chapter 27

The ocean rolled by, salt breeze filling the air. My hair stirred around my shoulders, the cotton dress soft against my skin. Acid burned the back of my throat, combining with the salt to produce a strange, tangy taste in the back of my mouth that reminded me of times when I'd been sick.

And I definitely felt sick right now.

I had experienced situations like this before. Ones where it felt like there was no way out, no way to fix it.

Byron was one of those experiences. I'd been helpless, at his mercy. I would have died if I hadn't managed to get a lucky hit on him.

Or when that vampire gang of Hollywood wannabes found out I was human and nearly killed Mill and Iona and was moments away from dragging me by my hair up to Lord Draven's penthouse as a peace offering.

And of course I couldn't forget that time that vampires set my house on fire *while I was still in it*, trying to murder me and my team when we fled.

I'd been in situations that looked pretty grim, where death was definitely on the menu and hope was pretty thin.

But all three of those situations had one thing in common:

I had been on Earth.

Now I was Cassie the pretend faerie, locked in some sort of spell or alternate dimension or magical cell type thing, with no way of getting out, and no way of getting home.

At least in all of those other times I had the hope of

daylight, or a wooden stake, or holy water.

Here? I had nothing.

I sat in the water, staring out at the ocean, hoping to sear the image of the scenery's beauty onto my brain. Was that why Roseus had brought me here? Was this my own form of torture?

Seeing home, or something like it … but not being able to actually be there?

I cradled my head in my hands, squeezing against my temple.

This whole thing could not have gone any worse.

"Where did you go?"

I looked up.

The volcano had returned. The heat washed over me, pulling the breath from my mouth and filling my lungs once more with the hot, sulphuric air. The rivers of lava still chugged along, the dragons above still stood watch.

"What … what happened?" I asked.

The beach, the water, the summer clothes … they all were gone.

I was back in the Seelie prison, and Orianna was peering through heat of the shimmering air at me with her wide, golden eyes.

"That General Roseus guy stepped over the lava into your little area there, and as soon as he did, both of you just disappeared.

I looked around. "We … were actually gone?"

"More likely he just glamoured you to make me think you were gone," she said. "Whatever the case, I didn't hear a thing."

A dull, throbbing headache started behind my eyes. All of this magic was just too much to deal with on top of the imprisonment and uncertainty of our peril.

"I'd like to learn some tricks like that," Orianna said.

"It was weird," I said. "I was at this infinite beach. It was beautiful, peaceful. We were just walking along, talking …" I frowned. "I think he tried to make me more at ease by putting me in a more familiar place."

I shook my head. Joke was on him. He should have

plopped me in the middle of a forest if he wanted me to be comfortable. Spent way more time around those in my life. Florida was too recent and too dangerous for me to feel entirely comfortable in its environs.

"So?" she asked, her wings fluttering. "What was it all about?"

Had I been gone so long that she forgot her anger toward me? Had I already forgotten mine toward her?

As I thought of it, it came rushing back, and I glared at her. "Why do you care?"

She rolled her eyes. "For the same reason you want to tell me," she said. Her eyes flashed. "Because maybe it holds a seed of something we can use to get out of here."

"Yeah, well, that's not going to happen," I said, sitting down on the black rock. "Roseus made *that* pretty clear."

She pouted her bottom lip. "What do you mean?"

"Just that," I said. "He told me how he knew I was innocent and that I did nothing wrong. Spouted off something about the Seelie court showing lenience to those who speak with open honesty, or something like that."

"Okay?" Orianna said. "And?"

"And … he asked me questions about Lockwood," I said. "He told me answering would help my chances—"

Orianna cackled, clapping her hand over her mouth to stifle the sound. Her eyes were bright and dancing.

"What?" I snapped. "Why is that funny?"

"Because he told you that he wasn't going to let you out right then," she said.

I arched an eyebrow.

"'Help' your chances? Vague terms, wouldn't you say? Nothing solid? No specifics?"

I was an idiot.

"So what all did you tell him?" Orianna asked, smiling wide in spite of our imprisonment, obviously way more interested in harassing me at this point than anything else. "You told him everything, didn't you?"

"No, I didn't," I said. "I hardly told him anything. As you said, I'm a liar."

"Yeah, but Seelie are really good at wording things to get

the right information out of you, even if you didn't want to say it. They'll even make you think it was your idea." She snickered again. "Well, that's what you get for trusting a Seelie," she said.

"Hate on the Summer fae all you want but I still trust Lockwood," I said, wondering again if he was all right. "Nothing that anyone tells me here will make me stop trusting him. I actually know who he is—unlike the rest of you people."

Now she arched her brow. "Do you really?"

I hesitated. "He … he's saved my life," I said. "More than once."

"Someone can save your life without telling you a single thing about themselves," Orianna said quietly. "Besides, I wasn't talking about Lockwood. I meant that was what you got for trusting that Roseus would actually let you out."

"Well, I thought it was a better chance than just sitting here, twiddling my thumbs," I snapped. Orianna seemed unperturbed. I changed my approach. "Besides … I thought the Unseelie were the tricksters and liars?"

Orianna flicked her hair, though it didn't really change much; it still hovered around her as if she were suspended in water. "Nope. The Seelie are just as bad as us. The Unseelie are just more open about their deceit." She tossed her head back and laughed. "You might say the Unseelie are the actual honest court, because we don't hide behind veiled threats and minced words."

"I don't understand," I said. "Everything that Lockwood told me—"

"Was probably a lie," Orianna said.

"I refuse to believe that." I shook my head.

"Deny it all you want. That doesn't change the fact that it's probably true," she said. "That's how the Seelie are, human. They don't lie outright. None of the fae do. We can't. But you'd be a fool to think that we haven't learned how to do it in other ways."

"Lying isn't always about saying the opposite of the truth," I said. "I'm really good at the full spectrum of deception, thank you."

"All right." Her wings fluttered, catching the attention of the dragons, and she settled them right down, watching warily. "Since you're the resident liar here, why don't you tell me? How else can someone lie besides speaking falsely?"

"They can tell half-truths," I said. I was pretty good at those. As long as I was doing what Mom wanted me to do, what was the harm if I left some stuff out that she didn't need to know? Like hanging out with Mill or Iona. Or staying out all night hunting vampires.

"Uh huh," she said, nodding her head. "And?"

"Lies of omission, totally leaving out an entire story. Changing the subject, or drawing the attention back around to the other person," I said, ticking them off on my fingers as I went through my toolkit.

Her eyes flashed dangerously. "You really would make a good Seelie. Still, that is just the beginning. Faerie has existed for centuries upon centuries … you don't think that creatures who can live that long haven't mastered the art?"

"Lockwood isn't like that," I said, a little too quickly. I wasn't sure if I was saying that for her benefit or my own.

"See, we Winter fae will pull your hair, make poorly worded deals with you humans, or even snatch your children … but we don't hide behind masks or pretty words to make our real intentions known." Her eyes glittered with darkness.

"Like that's any better," I said.

"Tell me … which is more dangerous?" Orianna stepped toward me, golden eyes flashing. "The enemy who stabs you in the front? Or the friend who stabs you from behind?"

I didn't know how to answer that. I'd experienced that very thing far too recently. And I had done my fair share of dosing it out, too.

But Lockwood would never do that to me. I trusted him. He had never given me a reason to not trust him, not ever. And he had countless opportunities to harm me instead of help me, if that had been his intention.

I swallowed, but my throat was dry and cracking. I needed water. I felt like I would die of heat exhaustion in this awful place before the guards ever came back.

"The Seelie avoid the truth whenever possible," Orianna

said. "They dance around it, with their flowery language or leave out important parts by papering over them with clever deceptions."

I stared around. Flowery language wouldn't do us any good where we were.

"Haven't you noticed how they focus entirely on the positive, and ignore the negative?" Orianna smiled. "Instead of 'Oh, you're going to bleed out from that wound,' it's 'How can I make you more comfortable?'"

"They can't all be like that," I said.

"Of course not," she said. "Look at me. The difference between Lockwood and me is that I don't try to deny who I am, or where I came from."

"Lockwood has never once denied that he was Summer fae," I said. "Lockwood truly believes that Seelie are on the side of right, in spite of his problems with them, with the court. He believes they stand for justice and order."

She let out a bitter snort of laughter. "He probably does believe that. But that doesn't make it so." She cocked her head at me, smiling—but it wasn't a nice smile at all. "You remember us talking about the massacre of Howl? How everyone was killed except me, who was left alive to tell the world about the horrible Unseelie and what they'd done?"

I nodded. "I didn't understand why they'd kill their own people—"

She rolled her eyes. "They didn't. It was the Seelie who destroyed that town, who killed old people and children—" She stopped, unable to speak for a moment, then her voice dropped to a whisper. "They were just glamoured to look like Unseelie."

"What?" I said, hardly able to absorb her words. "Why would they do that?"

She gave me a look that implied that I was profoundly stupid. "Seelie have a twisted sense of justice. And they probably wouldn't mind the chance to grab some Unseelie territory while they were at it."

I swallowed. "But ... Lockwood would never do anything like that. What about his time in the paladins?" I asked. "I may not know very much about them, but it sounded like they were meant to be peace keepers who took the side of truth."

"Again, skewed like everything in Seelie," Orianna said, her big eyes glued to me. "What you see as truth and what others see as truth are two very different things. I mean, why do you think he was tossed out into exile?"

"Scheming," I said.

She rolled her eyes. "Well, yes, since this is the Summer Court we're talking about. But also, probably because he thought something was the truth, and the king or queen thought differently."

"Truth is truth, no matter what," I said.

"Funny thing for a liar to admit to," Orianna said.

"I know when I don't tell the truth," I said.

She frowned. "You may be one of the few, then. I honestly believe the Seelie don't even see it anymore. They truly don't realize how blinkered they are. Their lies have become a truth to them." She shook her head. "Doesn't matter anyway. You, me, Lockwood—we're all exiles for different reasons ... but they all seem to revolve around the truths we told."

"What are you talking about?" I asked. "I'm not an exile."

Her big eyes found mine, and she smiled, smugly. "No, liar? You're well thought of in your own land? Everything going smoothly for you?"

Ouch. Not gonna lie, that stung. I ignored it, though, trying to keep a straight face. "Why did you get kicked out of Winter?"

"Told you," she said. "Because of the truth." She kicked at the rocky earth.

I stared at her. Her situation was starting to sound an awful lot more like Lockwood's.

"It's not like it matters ..." she said, turning around and staring off into the distant, red clouds overhead. "Being of Winter, I'll likely rot down here before they even remember they've got me. If they don't execute me first."

"You don't think they're just going to leave us down here, do you?" I asked, a nasty flood of fear rushing up my arms and down my legs.

She shrugged. "Who knows? I don't see what use they have for us now. You probably told them what they wanted, or at least enough to get Lockwood to spill his guts, figuratively. And if he doesn't …" She shrugged. "They may do it for him, literally.

I quivered a little. "Roseus said that Lockwood was still alive."

"He may have been when Roseus last saw him," Orianna said. "Remember what I said? Dancing around the answer."

The relief that had been so welcome was gone again, replaced with nagging anxiety again as I wondered if Lockwood was all right.

"When you were talking to Roseus, I don't suppose you tried to ask for my freedom too, did you?" Orianna asked. There was a tinge of sadness in her voice. The question hung unanswered a moment too long. "Yeah … I didn't think so. Why would you? It's not like we were friends or anything …"

And then she sat with her back to me, staring into one of the lava rivers. The dragon across the other side of the lava slashed his tail through the air as I made eye contact with him, as if daring me to try and flee.

I wondered how much it would hurt to get eaten by a dragon … or if they were actually real or not.

Part of me hoped I could get my vision to flicker again, that it might show me the truth of where we were, or what was happening.

But it was useless. I couldn't will the flicker into happening. Or maybe there was nothing to see.

I stared up at the roiling clouds overhead, thinking just how much they looked like the state of my soul.

Lockwood …

Somehow, in the hands of the Summer Court …

I had a feeling he wouldn't even last the day.

Chapter 28

It got very quiet in that prison cell. The passage of time seemed to slow under the heavy, sulphuric air, nothing to mark its passage except the sweat that trickled slowly down my back. There was no movement of a sun, or a moon, or stars; only black, smoky sky overhead.

I'd sat there for so long, unsure what to do, unsure what to think, that my legs were cramping beneath me. No matter how hard I tried, I couldn't think of anything. I didn't know how to get to Lockwood. I didn't know how to deal with this faerie magic on my own terms.

I had nothing, and no one.

There was hardly any sound, aside from my own breathing, in and out, and the soft, ominous roar of the lava as it rolled past. Thunder rumbled occasionally overhead, but I lived in Florida, the lightning capital of the world. I was familiar with thunderstorms.

Well … at least I *had* lived in Florida.

I wondered what everyone back home was doing. Was Mom in hysterics yet, because I hadn't come down for dinner? Was Dad already threatening to call the police to send out a search party for me?

What about Xandra? She probably wouldn't know I was gone until the next day, and by that point, hundreds of years could have passed here in Faerie. I'd be bones and dust by then.

And what about Iona? Would she know that I had gotten

myself mixed up in something with Lockwood? Would she mourn me?

And

Mill …

When would Mill find out? *How* would he find out? One of his friends and his girlfriend vanishing in one fell swoop? Even for a man who'd lived as long as he had, that probably wouldn't be easy to bear.

I bit down on my lip to stop myself from crying. Physical pain was easier to focus on than the heartache that was worming its way through my chest and in my guts.

I glanced over at Orianna. She hadn't moved in hours. She still had her back to me, and she was refusing to look in my direction.

I didn't bother calling out to her. What would I even say? *Sorry for getting you trapped, even though it's not really my fault.*

I didn't want to believe her about Lockwood being tortured. What reason would the Seelie have for torturing him? Why not just send him back to Earth, prevent him from coming back somehow? After seeing the state of things in Faerie, I wouldn't blame him for being like, *Yeah, fine, whatever. I'm out, suckers. Peace.*

At least, that's what I would have done.

I struggled with a small worm of betrayal that had wriggled its way into my heart, too.

Even after all of this, I still didn't understand Lockwood's part in this fae drama. What had he done? Why hadn't he told me? Why wouldn't he let me in?

Roseus's face on the beach flashed across my mind, and I suddenly understood.

If anyone was ever going to question me, I could say *truthfully* that I didn't know anything.

I swallowed hard, trying to remove the lump of worry in my throat. The feeling of anxiety was so intense now that I thought I might retch right into the lava. What a pretty sight that would have been for Orianna. I wouldn't be able to sleep, not here. Not only was the heat heavy and the smell repugnant, but how could I possible rest when I didn't know if Lockwood was all right … or if I would even wake up?

I wanted to voice these questions, but the only other person here was Orianna. I didn't have anything left to say to her, and she certainly had nothing to say to me.

I had no idea how much time passed, maybe a couple of hours, maybe a full day, when suddenly, a bright spot of white appeared across the lava river from us, beside the dragons, which had never once lowered their guard. It was one of the soldiers, dressed in gleaming armor. He leapt easily over the superhot river to stand in the little black square of rock that Orianna was sitting on.

Orianna got to her feet and rose into the air, her wings fluttering furiously. "What are you doing?"

The guard followed her a step into the air, and reached out. She was slow, and he caught her arm, yanking her toward him. He pulled what looked like manacles from out of sheer nothingness, clanking them closed on her wrist. They were glowing white hot, like metal freshly out of a forge. Orianna screamed.

"Don't try and get away, you filthy Unseelie deceiver," the guard said. "If I had it my way, these would be real Earth iron." He pulled on the manacles and dragged her over the lava river toward the dragons.

"Wait!" I called, scrambling clumsily to my feet. "Where are you taking her?"

The guard did not reply.

"Where are you taking me?!" Orianna struggled as much as she could against the burning handcuffs, yelping in pain. I could just hear the sizzling of the metal against her flesh. Tears glittered on her cheeks.

But even as I watched, they both disappeared as if they had been engulfed in a shadow, and I was left with silence.

My heart was beating rapidly, my breathing coming in quick bursts as if I had run a mile.

They had taken Orianna. Where?

They weren't going to torture her … were they?

Stay calm, Cassie. Losing my head right now would do nothing for me. I needed to fight the heat and just … chill. But it wasn't easy. I was sweating what felt like gallons and hadn't had a drink in forever. I mopped my brow with a sodden sleeve and sat down again to wait.

Just as my breathing was starting to return to normal, another guard appeared from the light and fluttered over to the lava rock where I sat.

"Iron Bearer," he said coldly, "come with me."

"I'm leaving the prison?" Slowly I pulled myself to my feet, dizzy from the heat.

"I am going to have to bind your hands," the guard said, and I heard a distinct tremble in his words. "For your protection."

For my protection, my ass. I lifted my chin into the air ever so slightly.

There was one thing in this world that I was better at than all of these faeries … one thing that I could do that they outright could not.

Lie.

So I shrugged and held out my hands to him. "It's not like I need them, anyway."

Perfect.

The guard's eyes grew just a fraction wider, and he hesitated for just a second before he put the magic cuffs around my wrist. They were a pale, icy blue, and for a moment I wondered if they'd be painfully cold, the opposite of Orianna's, but they just felt like ordinary metal. Perhaps they didn't consider me that much of a threat after all.

The guard didn't seem convinced, though. He stared at me, stiff and uncomfortable. "Would you prefer I carry you out? Or would you like to walk?"

"I'd rather walk, thanks," I said. I didn't want any faerie flying me anywhere. I was going to leave on my own two feet. "Where are you taking me?"

"Sorry," the guard said. "I am not at liberty to say."

Well, at least he was honest about it. "But you know?"

The guard hesitated again. He really did seem genuinely nervous about being near a human.

"Yes," he said.

Awesome. Maybe this could work.

"Fine. *Vamonos*," I said.

He stared at me blankly.

"It means, 'Let's go,'" I said.

"Right." He nodded curtly and waved his hand. A chunk of rock emerged as a stepping stone over the lava, then another.

I stared down at them, white-hot lava flow running around the tiny little rocks in a stream of desperate heat. "Uh, yeah … Phys ed is kinda my worst subject because my coordination is not great."

The guard stared at me in plain confusion.

"You better make it a bridge if you don't want me to fall in."

"Ah." He twirled his hand, and more rocks emerged from the lava, forming a bridge about two feet wide with no rail. It arced over the center of the river, rising enough that it didn't even touch the bottom of the stones in the middle.

"Thanks," I said and started over it. He followed a step behind, watching me as I walked.

This begged an interesting question: How much more could I get him to do? Could I get him to … trust me?

Fear me?

I had to get Lockwood back. And Orianna, if I could.

I hadn't given up yet. I was still in this game.

As I got to the other side of the bridge, the scenery changed abruptly, and I was standing outside of the cell in the dank, dark hallway where I'd originally entered.

Dungeon, really. Let's call it what it was.

"If you would follow me, please," the guard said, just barely touching my arm to steer me the way.

I glared at him, and he withdrew his hand as if I had burned him.

I was a human, and that made them wary of me.

It wasn't much, but it was better than nothing … and I'd find a way to make it work.

Chapter 29

The guards—of whom there were *seven;* another one seemed to join us every few steps—walked me out of the dungeons and back into the castle proper. Their metal boots rang on stone floors, a steady cadence that made me think of gunfire. It was a disquieting contrast to the normal whisper of wings that one heard in this land.

On that note, it was much quieter; fewer faeries floated overhead, and most of them were no longer in fancy ball attire. Though it was hard to tell; Faerie fashion was far different from Earth fashion.

Maybe the faeries thought so too, because I got a lot of strange looks as I was marched down the long corridor with the windows that looked out onto different landscapes. Every faerie we passed fell silent and many scurried to get away from me as fast as they could.

It was as if I were a plague victim, and they were all afraid they were going to catch something horrible from me. I swallowed hard. That couldn't be good news for me.

The guards walked me toward a large group of guards, who were piling bundles wrapped in what looked like cloth or leather into a golden carriage pulled by two pegasuses.

I kept trying to look over the guards on my tiptoes for any sign of Orianna or Lockwood, but I didn't see them anywhere.

"Care for something to eat?" I wheeled around, stomach plummeting, and saw Roseus standing there, munching on a bright red apple. He chewed it happily, some of the juice dribbling onto his chin. "This is an Earth fruit, right?" He took another bite. "They're rather good, though not very sweet, are they?" He didn't even finish chewing before he had taken another chunk of it between his teeth. "I imagine you must be starving, being in that dungeon all night long."

I figured out his game pretty quickly. Of course he wanted something. "I already told you I don't know anything."

Roseus smirked. "Oh, that much is obvious."

I glared at him. "Where are you taking me?"

"I'm not taking you anywhere." He took another bite. "No, little human, this was not my decision to make. As I said, these sorts of decisions are left to my higher ups."

If what he had been saying earlier was true, then he was already pretty highly ranked within the court. There couldn't be all that many people above him.

Did that mean … the queen had made some sort of decision?

"Where's Lockwood?" I asked, taking a step toward him.

Two of the guards immediately stepped between us, blocking my path to him.

"Uh, uh, uh," Roseus said, wagging a finger like a metronome. "I'm not at liberty to tell you."

I grimaced. Is that all that these faeries were going to say to me?

Roseus's smirk widened. "You aren't going to ask me about your little Unseelie friend? What a pity. I'm sure she will be delighted to know that you have already forgotten about her …"

I balled my hands into fists. I'd have given almost anything to have my dad's cast iron skillet with me right now. I could clock him upside the head and … what happened to fae when they were exposed to iron? Did they puddle into slag like a vampire? Because I was getting used to dealing with that by now.

But I didn't have any iron. I released the tension in my fists and smoothly stepped back into my circle of guards. "You just wait …" I murmured. "You have no idea what I'm capable of."

Roseus laughed. "Oh, yes. I'm positively quaking."

And with that, he walked off toward the front of the procession.

A clank of manacles surprised me, and I looked down to see one of my guards locking a pair of the icy-looking bonds to my wrist. The other end was already latched to the guard, a tall fellow with red hair and wings.

"What the hell?" I asked.

"Since you can't fly …" the red guard said, "we will have to suspend you between us."

"Excuse much?" My stomach lurched. "Like, you're gonna dangle me over open air … ?"

The guards didn't even look at me. They just concentrated on attaching their manacles to my wrists and ankles.

"Whoa, whoa!" I said. "What about giving me another pegasus to ride on? Why not one of those?" I pointed to the two standing near the doors with the carriage. "Or how about Orion? He knows me; I rode on him when we were coming to the court."

They said nothing. My throat grew tight as my guards spread out, circling me, the chains strung evenly between them. "Uh, guys—I think I've seen this before in medieval history books. It's called drawing and quartering. You guys are gonna get spooked, and I'm going to end up in pieces—"

A trumpet blew, and before I even had a chance to prepare myself, I was yanked into the air, feet-first, the ground below me slipping away as if it were being sucked down a drain. Everything I thought I loved about flying from before was gone in an instant, ripped away like the ground.

I was being pulled by my legs, the double attachment of manacles to each ankle providing the primary force dragging me forward. One of the guards had wrapped a chain around my waist like a belt, and was holding me aloft while the others pulled. The wrist manacles were being held by two guards who brought up the rear. They flew almost directly behind me, keeping close but not too close.

Any second, I could drop to the still receding earth below—and *splat*. That would be the gruesome end of Cassie Howell. My inner ear was having fits, and I kept looking around, writhing as best I could, trying to get a view of what was happening. Other than flying. Flying was definitely happening, and it was nowhere near as fun and calming as my flight with Orion.

This flight was disorienting and panic-inducing, being dragged by the legs through the air while someone held me up just enough to keep me from feeling like I was falling. That vertigo sensation was ever present, wind whipping past my face. I tasted bile in the back of my throat as my stomach did its own flight, on a very different vector than the one I was on. I swallowed, barely keeping it down.

What was better? Getting eaten by vampires, or dying from falling from a great height in Faerie?

I couldn't take it anymore.

My stomach lost its battle with the vertigo, and everything I'd eaten for the last day or twelve went flying. The two faeries bound to my wrists executed a stunning dodge, barely avoiding my gastrointestinal explosion with sneers of disgust, raising their altitude to avoid the mess that fell back down toward the city of Starvale below. I felt sincerely bad for whatever tradesperson might be standing outside below, about to get a random shower of unspeakable bile, but … well, they'd probably just have it glamoured away or something.

Me, though, I was left feeling wretched. I couldn't even wipe my mouth off.

I lifted my head weakly, wondering when my spine was going to pop from the chain wrapped around my waist, and I realized that Orianna was suspended between two guards not that far ahead of me.

I meant to call out to her, but as soon as I opened my mouth, I snapped it shut. Would she get in trouble if I tried to talk to her? Would I?

Also … the nausea had not passed, even if every single thing I'd eaten for the last week had.

Besides, Orianna was hanging between her captors even more limply than I was. Her wings didn't so much as twitch, and she swung slightly between the two chains as I watched.

What had they done to her? They hadn't exactly been kind

when they yanked her out of her cell.

From where I was dangling, I couldn't see any marks on her, no silvery faerie blood. Did tyls have silver blood? Or was it gold, like the rest of her? If it was, then it could have been all over her, or her dress, or in her hair, and I'd never see it.

Why did I have to be so completely helpless?

Having to stay in a world where I was completely at a disadvantage certainly didn't help. I had none of the charms nor the sword that Lockwood had, nor a single drop of magical blood in my body.

Yet ... the guards all were frightened of me. Iron Bearer, they called me, even though I literally had nothing with me or on me that was made of iron. Still, they treated me like I was a bomb about to go off.

How could I use that to my advantage? Was there any way that I could somehow use my human-ness to win this?

Because right now, from where I was hanging, it looked like I was losing. Big time.

By the time we started to descend, my arms had gone completely numb from guards' post-vomit position shift. As soon as the blood started pumping back through them, they were going to hurt. "Are we here?" I asked.

"No, we're stopping for a rest," the red-winged guard said without looking at me. Hey, finally a response.

They gently lowered me to the ground, my legs collapsing from underneath me as soon as I put any weight on them. I fell to my knees, and if I had hoped that they would let me off my leash for a few minutes, I was sorely mistaken.

They had lowered Orianna, unconscious, to the ground, too, manacles clanking. Her head lolled against her chest.

We had landed in a clearing, an eerie green haze blurring the trees that surrounded us. A small stone cabin surrounded by empty fire pits and large logs split into benches sat in the circle of grassy space separating us from the forest.

As the blood ran back down into my arms and fingers, my nerves prickled and stung as if I was being stuck with long, thin needles. I shook my arms out, willing them to wake up.

"Would you care for some water?" one of the guards

asked, gesturing toward me with a leather water skin.

"Yes, please!" I wasn't too proud to beg. Between the lava dungeon and throwing up, I was now desperately dehydrated.

He had to pour it into my mouth, my hands being bound and all. The first attempt ended with water sloshed all down my front, and me breathing in more than I actually drank. I sputtered and coughed, spitting water onto the grassy ground.

"Apologies," the faerie said nervously.

I looked up at him, cold water droplets clinging to my chin. "Just … don't pour it as quickly." He took it a little slower, and soon I was gulping it hungrily.

I guess it isn't until you haven't had water for a long time that you really, truly appreciate it. I kept drinking until I drained the whole water skin.

The faerie looked and frowned. "I'm sorry. I don't have any more."

I shook my head, already feeling better. "That's fine. Thank you for that. I really needed it." Then I realized that I probably shouldn't have said anything. I didn't need them to think that I was dependent on them for anything.

The guards pulled food from their packs, starfruit, some meats I didn't recognize, and purple bread. They gradually started to move toward one another, beginning a friendly banter not unlike long-suffering co-workers griping about their shared experience.

"How much longer is it from here?" one asked.

"I don't know," another, a guy with green wings and yellow hair said. "We just follow, you know." That prompted a round of laughter that I didn't quite understand, at least not totally, though it did remind of that old joke about how if you weren't the lead dog in a sled team, the scenery never changed.

I wondered how long we were going to linger here, but I knew this might be the best, and last, chance for me to figure out what the heck was actually happening here. Or where we were going.

"Take this," said a different guard, one with green hair and wings. He thrust a small bowl into my hands and I barely had time to clench them before he walked off to join the circle of guards that were chatting and eating. A couple of them kept a wary eye on me, but they must have thought I couldn't get up to much with two bindings each per leg and one on each arm. At least the guys who'd manacled themselves to my arms weren't pulling them tight. Right now, anyway.

"Thanks," I said, and I looked through the bowl. It was fruit that looked reasonably all right. Not as impressive as the stuff at the ball, but not bad. Or at least glamoured to not look bad.

I shuffled over to one of the benches and sat down, almost at the limit of my chains. The guards watched, but nobody yanked me back, and there I started to pick through my food, trying a little. It tasted fine.

The pegasus horses landed nearby, the carriage between them laden with poles and multicolored fabric. Some faeries peered over the side, moving the poles around, as if checking to ensure that whatever was beneath them was still there.

I popped a starfruit in my mouth, bowl resting in my lap, my legs crossed. The juice burst on my tongue, sweet and succulent. My mouth watered as I chewed and I listened to the chatter around me. Some of the guards were discussing the trip, flapping their wings slowly like a human stretching their legs after driving for a long time. Others were talking about their personal lives.

Another group of guards, who were standing off to the side somewhere behind me, caught my attention when they said the words "front lines." I turned my head slowly to look at them and saw only a half-circle of guards standing around, not looking my way at all.

"… I thought he was trying to be clever, act like he's more important than he is," said one of the guards, his voice deep and rumbling. "But when they summoned us to the garrison, well … I couldn't believe what I was hearing."

"I know," said the other, with a raspier sort of voice. "I didn't understand, either. Apparently, something happened at that ball last night?"

"You didn't hear?" the first asked. "The court was

infiltrated."

"What, by these two?" the other guard asked, tossing a look over his shoulder at me, then Orianna. I turned away before he saw me looking. "I wondered what they did that we had to haul them along with us … So an Unseelie and …" He dropped his voice. "That's really a human?"

The other must have nodded, because I didn't hear anything.

"I've never seen one before," the raspier voice said. "Weird looking, aren't they?"

What. An. Ass.

"I also heard Paladin Lockwood was the one who brought them to the court. You know. The exile."

"What? No …"

"Indeed. General Roseus brought him in and turned him in at the ball, in front of everyone. The queen was quite pleased, apparently. It gave her a chance to provide a satisfying show for the whole court."

"Pleased? I heard she was furious because he was traveling with a human and an Unseelie spy." The speaker said both of those things with contempt, but if possible he seemed slightly more repulsed by Orianna.

"So this is why we're going to the front lines," the scratchy voice said. "It's about time, though. I've been waiting to slay some Unseelie tricksters."

"I can't believe that the queen has allowed negotiations to go on this long. We all knew that war was inevitable. We should strike now, pummel them, while Spring is ascendant."

"It's all for appearances," the other guard said. "Mark my words, all this skirmishing will end and we'll start the war in earnest tonight, despite whatever else happens today."

"Woods! Raven!"

One of the other guards was calling to the ones talking, and I watched out of the corner of my eye as they wandered toward the other side of the camp.

The starfruit tasted like ash in my mouth all of the sudden, as the realization of what was going on settled in around me. My chest burned with anxiety, my heart fluttering nervously.

The whole time I had been in Faerie, the word *war* had

been thrown around, but it was always discussing the *chance*, the *possibility*. The tensions had obviously been high on both sides, but the way the soldiers were talking, it was as if something had changed last night.

Something *had* changed: we'd been discovered.

How could Lockwood's return to Faerie tip the scales toward war? Did they really think that Orianna was a spy?

Better question: *was* Orianna a spy?

She may have been annoying, and a trickster, but hearing her story about the Queen of Winter, and about her upbringing, the village she watched getting slaughtered …

No. Orianna wasn't a spy. She couldn't be.

Regardless of what I thought, or how I felt, the Summer Court had apparently decided to go to war. And if my visions showed the truth of what had happened so far, a real war was bound to be horrific.

Was that where we were going?

If we were going to the front lines, then it meant we were likely going back toward neutral territory, back toward Stormbreak.

It was torture, being completely helpless. Like being Byron's victim again, pushed around, useless in the face of his overpowering strength. Here, it was magic and an army of fae that overwhelmed me, but the feeling …

The feeling was the same. Helplessness.

Orianna was unconscious.

Lockwood was nowhere to be seen—if he was even still alive.

This war between the Unseelie and Seelie was coming—tonight, by the sounds of it—and there was nothing I could do to stop it.

Chapter 30

We didn't stay in the clearing for much longer. I didn't argue when the guard with the red wings returned, taking the bowl and checking my manacles. The other guards packed up their things and were ready to leave within minutes. The efficiency of the military, I guessed.

My arms were still not fully recovered, so I gritted my teeth as we prepared to launch up into the air.

My mind buzzed as if thousands of tiny flies were zooming around inside. I couldn't process any of it. How could all of this have gone so wrong? This was supposed to be a simple trip with Lockwood. Go to a magical land, do my lying best to make them think he hadn't done ... whatever he'd done, and boom, back home to safety and goodness and Xandra and Mill and—

Yeah, okay. I always knew my lying luck would run out eventually but why here, in Faerie? Why now, when we were right underneath the nose of the king and queen, who had a serious grudge against my traveling companion? Of all the times for things to go sideways ...

The faerie guards took off and I was launched into the air again, yanked up by my feet and waist, my arms above my head, ears knocking against my inner arm when they pulled me to the left or to the right.

Faerie had been such a wonderful place to see. It was more beautiful than I could have imagined. The forests were lush and filled with mysteries, ones that I would have loved to explore. There were castles, and healing waters, and foods unlike anything I had ever tasted, making everything I had on Earth seem mundane in comparison. The things that Lockwood had told me when we first arrived had seemed so impossible, and yet, the longer I was here, the less and less I was surprised by it all.

Magic was the answer to every question here—and it also was the root of every question I had.

What had Lockwood done that had made him need to leave? Why did the queen and Roseus hate him as much as they did? What did Master Calvor and his son have to do with it? How had the court figured out who and what Orianna and I were?

Why was *I* being punished, when I knew almost nothing?

What I couldn't understand was why such a large group of soldiers was needed to escort Orianna and me, helpless as we were. If they were needed at the front lines, why were they not there already? Why did we have to travel with them?

And why was Lockwood not here with me to help me figure this all out?

I breathed in heavily through my nose, trying to get oxygen to my brain, forcing myself to remain calm. I could not afford to lose my head when I was heading into a situation that I knew nothing about.

I couldn't think about Lockwood. I couldn't think about Orianna. I couldn't think about Mill. My mind fixated on the mystery before me. How did all this fit together? I needed to figure it out if I were to have any hope of coming out of it alive.

I scanned the horizon, attempting to locate some sort of landmark that could give me a clue where we were. A small voice in the back of my head mocked me, telling me that if Lockwood could get lost so easily when we were wandering through Faerie, then I had absolutely no hope of finding my way. I shoved the voice aside, and looked anyway.

The forest all looked the same from overhead, just one great, big sea of different colored leaves. There were no discerning markers, no buildings. There weren't even any bodies of water.

Just how big was Faerie, anyway?

I remembered Lockwood saying something about the trees, and how they would lead you astray. Was that why I couldn't see anything?

Before long, the faerie guards had begun their descent, but I couldn't see anything below us that told me where we'd arrived. My heartbeat started to quicken, and the hairs on the back of my neck stood up as we came closer and closer to the tops of the trees.

Just as I was afraid that we were going to slam into these branches, the trees shimmered and disappeared, and the long, wide white road we'd traveled on before appeared beneath me like a landing strip.

So the trees here were a glamour. Was that how this whole forest was?

Fae waited on the road, too, as far as my eye could see below the glamour. If I thought the squadron that we were traveling with was large, it was nothing compared to what I saw here.

The road stretched through tall trees and came to a stop at a bridge very similar to the one that Lockwood, Orianna and I had crossed when we fled from Stormbreak. It spanned a great river that rushed between the trees, sending spray up into the air.

We were headed just beyond the bridge, over the border into neutral territory.

The guards gave me a moment of slack in the chains to shake out my arms. I tried not to wince at the uncomfortable pins-and-needles sensation, not wanting them to see the discomfort I was in.

But they didn't give me long. Soon they were pulling me up the road, following the caravans of soldiers that were landing along the road from above, others crossing the bridge and into whatever lay beyond the green haze. It was a slow march under the glamour, and it took me a minute to realize what was happening.

We were marching under the cover of the glamour to hide the movements of the Summer army.

We approached the bridge, the roar of the river growing

louder with every step. When we stepped onto the bridge, the bonds around my wrists vanished, and I gasped. The guards had anticipated this, however, and grabbed my wrists, clenching tightly.

"What happened?" I asked.

"The spellbreak on the border. Magic needs to be reestablished on this side of the neutral territory," the guard said, in a falsely confident tone. "A minor inconvenience."

Minor inconvenience, yeah, okay.

Interesting. Not all magic worked in the neutral territory? Or it just dropped away at the border? Was that why the hospital and the camp surrounding it had been so well fortified?

It was as if I'd stepped into a huge football stadium, but instead of a glass or steel dome overhead, it was leaves and branches, stretching up from trees that were hundreds of feet tall. The ground in front of us was clear, aside from the soldiers who were working to construct something.

On the opposite end of this huge canopied clearing, there was another bridge just like the one we had crossed, and another white road stretching through the trees, until the green haze beyond consumed it. It was dark, almost as if it were twilight, but a number of tiny pixies were carrying glowing rocks overhead, creating a peaceful, ambient light, soft and comforting.

I didn't have much of a chance to figure out what the faeries were constructing, because I was dragged off to the side.

There I saw a perfectly square box that looked as if it were made from pale blue glass atop a marble plinth. It was obvious that whatever was inside was meant to be displayed, like a trophy.

Or, I realized with horror … *whoever* was inside.

Because as I stared up at it, my eyes fixed on something gold slumped in the corner. Gold hair, gold dress.

Orianna.

The guards hoisted me up the stairs that ran up the back of the thick marble slab. With a touch of one their fingers, part of the glass wall vanished, and they pushed me inside.

As soon as I whipped around, the glass was back in place, and the guards were walking back down the narrow marble steps.

"Welcome to the cage, *little Seelie,*" Orianna said.

I didn't even care that she was trying to be scathing.

I flopped down on the bottom of the glass box beside her, staring at her with wide eyes. She wasn't slumped on the floor like I'd initially thought. Instead, she was curled up, forehead on her knees, arms wrapped around her legs, hugging them close.

"Orianna, you're okay," I said, crawling up to her. My relief that she was all right kind of surprised me, especially given her nasty tone.

She shifted her head so one gold eye could glare at me from beneath her flowing hair. "That's relative." Her voice was slightly muffled by her own legs. She hid her eye once more.

"I thought … something terrible must have happened," I said. "When I saw you hanging between those guard faeries."

"Yeah, well, they're going to have to do more than throw me around to break me." This she mumbled.

"They … actually did that?" I asked. I hadn't seen it, but it had probably happened before our flight.

"You really don't know anything, do you?" Orianna said, lifting her head so I could feel the full heat of her stare. Then her face slipped into a malicious smile, her eyes darkening.

I sat back. So she still wanted to be that way, huh?

"I'm glad you are all right," I said. Because I was.

"Oh?" Orianna rolled her large golden eyes and rested her forehead back on her knees. "I'm supposed to take the word of a human who's been lying to me from the very beginning?"

I really didn't have the strength, or desire, to get into a debate with her about all of that again. Nor did I think it was important, given our circumstances.

"No," I said. "See, trust is something that you *choose* to give to a person. I realize that you and I haven't built much of that … .that I haven't earned yours, but I do think you should know that I never meant to hurt you in any of this." I sighed heavily. "I just wanted to help my friend."

Orianna remained silent. I took that as a good sign, since she wasn't lashing out at me in rage.

"If you hadn't come with us, this never would have happened to you, so … I'm sorry," I said. Apologizing was always hard for me, but especially when I knew I needed to and really didn't want to.

It really was because of Lockwood and me that Orianna had ended up in this situation. It wasn't fair to her, and she didn't deserve to be treated the way that she had been just because she had gotten caught up with us.

Guilt by association, right? It could have happened to anyone who had crossed our paths, though it had probably hit her all the harder because she was of Winter. I hoped that the farmer and that the shopkeeper in Stormbreak wouldn't suffer for the small roles they'd played.

"Yeah, well …" Orianna said. "It probably would have happened to me either way. Since I'm trapped between two kingdoms where they hate me. Really, nowhere in Faerie is safe for me …" Her voice trailed off.

A strange lurch came from my heart, and I wondered if Lockwood would consider taking Orianna back to Earth with us, if he could somehow find a way to do it.

I had to keep thinking positively, because if I didn't, I was likely to lose my mind.

I couldn't get stuck here. I had to get out. I had to get home.

We sat in silence for a little while, each of us absorbed in our own thoughts. Guards passed by, staring up into the glass cell like we were animals in a zoo. I gingerly touched the outer wall, and it gave a little bit, like sinking my hand into a memory foam mattress. It worked on the front wall, too.

"It's solidified magic," Orianna said, watching me without much interest.

"Like the Seelie court castle?"

"Lockwood told you that, did he?" Orianna sighed. "Yes, it's like the castle. It prevents me from using any magic because any sort of counter charm is built in already." She smirked. "Too bad you don't have any iron on you. We'd be able to break out of here in a second."

A faerie wanting iron?

Maybe she had given up all hope.

"So …" I tried again, sitting down and crossing my legs. "What exactly are they doing over there?" I asked, looking in the direction of all the faeries pounding large, thick wooden pillars into the ground.

"Constructing the meeting site," Orianna said.

"Meeting site?" I asked. "For what?"

She shrugged her shoulders. "For whatever is happening."

I arched an eyebrow. "O … kay?"

She rolled her eyes and huffed. "They're building one of those tents like the hospital. It's like a temporary meeting place, warded and everything. Lots of magic in place around it, and in it."

"But why didn't we just stay at the castle?" I asked. "What's the point of coming all the way into neutral territory?" I shuddered as I remembered the guards' conversation from back at the checkpoint. "Some guard said that the war was probably going to start tonight. That can't be true, right? I thought the Seelies would do everything they could to keep the peace."

Orianna snorted. "There's been a *war* going on for months now. Sure, now they'll formalize it, and it'll be even more horrific, but it's nothing new. After everything I've told you … after everything *Lockwood* has … how can you still think the Seelie are the good guys?"

Well, I didn't, really. "But wouldn't they want to save face? You know, try to keep up the illusion that all is well?"

"Did you not see that ball last night?" Orianna asked. "All of the glitz and beauty … to them, everything is always fine. Their illusion will hold, no matter how horrific it gets out here. The Summer lands, the Seelie beyond the border? They won't even know anything is going on."

That hit me a little strangely, thinking that there'd be a vicious, total war happening here while the Seelie back in their country basically had no idea it was even going on. But, I supposed, that wasn't exactly unheard of in my world, either. "I still don't understand why we are all here," I said, trying to drag my mind off that unhappy topic and onward. "I don't get why this is turning into some huge processional. It doesn't make any sense." I pushed against the flexing magical glass. "Well … at least we're safe from the war."

"Safe?" she said, golden eyebrow arching. "Wait … you're not serious, are you?"

"What?" I asked. "Of course I'm serious."

"We're anything but safe here," Orianna said. "Isn't it obvious?" Her voice was soft and distant as she watched the faeries start to erect the white canvas-like material of the tent, pulling it over the top of the pegs.

"Isn't what obvious?"

She looked up at me with sad eyes that reminded me way too much of Iona.

"… We're going to be executed."

I thought of all I knew of Orianna. Her flittering, her silliness, her slightly histrionic tendencies …

This wasn't a lie. It wasn't a trick. She fully believed the words that were coming out of her mouth.

And I suddenly found myself all the more afraid because of it.

"Wait, no—" I said, sweat starting to bead up on my forehead. "They wouldn't actually do that … would they? We haven't done anything!"

She ran a finger over the magical glass on her side of the cage. "Well, they're definitely going to execute *me*. I'm an Unseelie who infiltrated their castle. Their inner sanctum. I was as good as dead when I set foot in there. It's possible they could let you go, after you watch me get executed," she said as if she were talking about the weather. "But more likely you'll be right there with me."

My heart hammered in my ears, my head spun.

No. No, no, *no*.

Executed?

My voice caught in my throat as I caught a glimpse of slate-blue hair and recognized a figure being dragged between two Seelie guards.

Lockwood.

I leapt forward, pressing my hands against the wavering glass.

They dragged him closer, and my eyes stung with tears as I saw that he wasn't conscious. His feet were splayed out behind him, his wings limp. They carried him as if he were already dead …

"Well, that's good news, I guess," Orianna said. "If they brought him here, they might mean to kill him with us." She pasted a slightly vicious smile across her face. "We can all die together. Yay."

Tears spilling onto my cheeks. "He isn't already dead?"

"Well, he isn't far from it, it looks like," she said.

She wasn't wrong.

The Seelie guards tossed him onto the ground and walked away, as if leaving trash behind.

Another guard stepped up. A shimmering halo appeared above Lockwood, and then the halo shot out beams of light that arched the ground below, locking him in a bright cage.

Silvery blood painted his cheeks and his neck, and a large hole in the side of his shirt showed that he had been wounded there, too.

"Somebody put him through the ringer …" Orianna muttered. "If you can actually *see* blood … it's bad."

I could only stare at him, at a loss for words.

He wasn't dead, but he wasn't in much better shape than that.

"He wouldn't be able to hear me if I called for him … could he?" I murmured.

Orianna shook her head. "Afraid not."

I swallowed nervously, willing Lockwood to wake, willing him to give me a nod of encouragement.

I needed him right now.

I needed a friend.

Chapter 31

I watched Lockwood for a long time while the faeries constructed the rest of the tent. It took them some time, even with as many of them as there were. I stopped caring about what exactly this whole thing was for, the soldiers and the tent and the neutral territory.

What did any of it matter if I was going to be dead in a short time, anyways?

Lockwood lay motionless within the magical cage. I imagined that the cage would do something to his magic, preventing him from doing anything to set himself free even if he woke up. Orianna appeared to be done with our conversation. Having just curled herself into a small ball, she just sat there, as still as a statue.

I had found myself in a lot of sticky situations in the past, but this one ... trapped in the land of Faerie, slated for execution ... yeah, this one seemed to take the cake. All I'd done was wander into this; it wasn't like I'd taken a piece of iron and gone full Cassie and started staking Summer fae with it.

But the Seelie were ruthless. I had seen as much.

Not only that, but they seemed to be on the verge of starting a war and invading their neighbors, and somehow, Lockwood and I happened to be at the center of it. Whatever Lockwood's secret was, it was the core of this whole thing going on.

And time had run out for us to fix it all.

I was impossibly far from home, with no way to even leave Mill or my parents a note about what had happened. They would just waltz into my room eventually, and see that I was gone. Maybe they would think I'd been kidnapped. Or that I ran away … uh, again, since I'd taken off to New York just weeks earlier.

They would never know where I ended up. My face would show up on the side of milk cartons. I would forever be seventeen, and they would spend the rest of their lives wondering what had happened to me.

Mill would never know, either, but might put the two and two together if he found Lockwood missing, as well. Maybe Lockwood had sense to leave something behind for him to find. Maybe Mill would deduce that Lockwood's disappearance had something to do with the attack of the pixies.

I hoped that he'd find some way to tell my parents that I was gone, and that I was likely never coming back, either. Give them closure.

My hands trembled as I contemplated all this, sitting in the corner of the glass cube.

And the icing on the cake was that the last person I would ever get to speak to was Orianna. She still had her head on her knees, staring out the cage with the back of her golden head to me.

I still didn't feel like I had a very good read on Orianna. One minute she'd be silly, the next angry. Mercurial, that was the word.

In spite of her more irritating qualities, I found myself growing warily fond of her. But was still super annoyed with her a pretty good portion of the time.

I wondered idly if this what having a sibling was like.

A couple of guards appeared and held their hands out in the direction of our little prison, and I tried desperately to hold on as the glass cube rose into the air.

"What's happening?" I asked.

Orianna paled.

The magic cube moved toward the giant tent they'd spent all that time erecting, then floated, a little less than gently, through the front flap. My fingers pressed against the magical bottom of the cage, the pressure turning them white.

The tent was enormous and reminded me a little of the Seelie court where the ball had been held. Long, tall, and oval in shape, there were four thrones, two on either end of the room. A wading pond, perfectly round, lay in the very center of the room, no more than a foot or two deep.

But it didn't appear finished. Pixies were still zooming overhead, suspending glowing crystals in the air like little multicolored stars. Other faeries were arranging seats; there appeared to be enough room for a thousand or more inside.

There was no ceiling, either. A bright sunlight sky shone overhead, with clouds of pink and orange, as if it were nearing sunset.

They set our magical glass cube down on the other side of the pond, back on its marble plinth, which had floated in behind us. From here, raised above the ground, I could see the entire room.

But, I realized, my stomach clenching, the whole room would be able to see us, as well. Bad time for my fear of public speaking to rear its ugly head. You'd think it would have taken a back seat to being executed, but the way my stomach was churning, apparently my body was too stupid to prioritize.

This whole place was beautiful, just as the hospital had been, a meadow surrounded by trees in late spring. Flowers littered the grass, and there was a gentle breeze rustling through them. "This feels like an odd place to put us," I said.

Orianna was staring around, too, though far more skeptically than I was. "Yes … odd," she murmured, too distracted by our impending executions to be all that interested in our precise location.

My heart skipped a beat as I watched them float Lockwood in next, hovering him next to where Orianna and I were placed. Another marble plinth was settled in place, and they settled Lockwood's cage upon it. Lockwood, his face mashed lifelessly against the glass, did not stir.

He was only feet away now, so close I could see his eyelids flutter. They were taunting me, I knew it. Why else would they bring him so close to me?

I pressed against the wall of the glass, feeling it warp and bend beneath my weight, but it wouldn't give, no matter how hard I pressed.

So close … and yet infinitely far. I stepped back into the center of my magical cage.

Without warning, the whole world shook, slanted, and then my vision flickered.

I fell to my knees, and I could see faeries beginning to file into the tent at the far entrance, but the beautiful interior of the tent had disappeared. Sure, I could see some pretty crystals, some nice chairs, but the pond had vanished, as well as the sun overhead.

The faeries who entered were not like they had been at the hospital, all stark horror, but they didn't look all glorious and sweeping and supermodel-y like they had at the ball, either.

It was as if someone had wiped away their beauty, like a photo in a magazine before the airbrushing effects had been applied.

I stared around at the female faeries who had been wearing such lovely dresses. They were so … plain, ordinary. A woman with a huge zit on her nose walked past our cages and cast me a dirty look. The guards who looked so strong only a moment ago were no more commanding or soldierly than Gregory, my friend from school. And he was a skinny guy who could squeeze into hipster jeans without even trying that hard.

The entire Summer Court suddenly looked like Cinderella at the ball. Or at least how she looked when the clock had struck midnight. Everything had turned back into a pumpkin.

I closed my eyes and shook my head.

"What's the matter with you?" Orianna asked.

I opened them again. The beautiful meadow had returned, along with the cotton-candy clouds, and all the faeries filing into their seats now looked as lovely and as ethereal as ever.

I didn't know what to say. Lockwood knew about the flicker, but … would Orianna even believe me? Would it be wise to tell her? By instinct alone, I knew that Lockwood would probably tell me to keep my mouth shut, that she didn't need to know any extra information. And normally, I would have gone along with that.

But … the situation we were in … slated for execution …

Did it really matter anymore?

"I … don't really know what it is," I said finally, turning to look at her. "It's this weird thing that's been happening to me ever since I came to Faerie. The first time I looked at Stormbreak, my vision sort of … I don't know … it flickers … like I can see two sides of the same coin at the same time. I saw Stormbreak, all pretty and snowy, and then in the next second, I saw it shrouded in shadow, dark and eerie."

Orianna was staring at me, one eyebrow cocked curiously.

"And it wasn't just there. Remember when I saw the unicorn at the farm? Yeah. I saw the farm in ruins, dead unicorns everywhere."

Orianna pursed her lips. "No wonder you freaked out."

"Yeah, no wonder …" I said. "Then at the hospital, I saw all of the patients lying there, dead or dying. It was like a sick and twisted version of what we were seeing. I … I just don't understand." I sighed, staring around. "It's like someone is pulling back a curtain, letting me to peek inside to something secret."

Orianna snorted.

"What?" I asked.

"Let me guess, you just saw something here, too?" she asked.

"Yeah," I said. "It was like … everything is pretty now, right? The sun, the sky, the little flowers. But when my sight flickered, it just … Everything went ugly. It's like everything is … fake."

Orianna tossed her hair and laughed. "Well, that's the Seelie for you."

"What do you mean by that?" I asked. "You keep saying that the Seelie are all about the façade and whatever. Aren't the Unseelie even worse?"

She shook her head. "The Unseelie, particularly those in the Winter Court, do all of this," she waved her finger around, "… to some extent. I mean, it's magic, of course we use it to look better, but the Summer Court fae take lying to the next level."

"So, what …" I asked. "Am I like … seeing through their glamours?"

"You just might be," Orianna said. "There's no way to know if a Seelie is telling you the complete truth. They bathe lies with lies, they layer them on top of themselves, like pretty bows or sparkly jewels."

"But I didn't think they could lie."

"It's not about lying outright," Orianna said. "You should know this. It's using their words to circumnavigate the truth. It's always in little ways, subtle ways. Like changing the color of their eyes. It's harmless, yes … but aren't they lying?"

I considered her words.

"So, what's the truth?" I asked. "Obviously we are inside of a tent. The sky overhead, the trees, the lighting … it's all an illusion."

"Or, in other words, a lie," Orianna said. She grinned mischievously. "Somehow, Cassie, you see past the veil of illusion that the Summer Court wears like perfume."

"What about stuff like the farm?" I asked. "There weren't really a bunch of dead unicorns there, right?"

Orianna shrugged. "Probably, if an army marched through like he said." She leaned a little closer to me. "You have to understand that for faeries, almost everything is about looks. It's what's on the outside that counts, what it *appears* like to others."

"Doesn't everyone know they are just fooling themselves?" I asked.

"It's part of the mystery," Orianna said, leaning closer. "Never knowing what's truth, what's a glamour or a half truth. Those with power have been able to master the art. Like some sort of great game."

That sounded a lot like court intrigue on Earth from medieval times. Information could be more valuable than gold.

But if it was a game … then maybe …

There had to be a way to win, right?

"Orianna," I said, "this flicker thing I have … you think it shows me the truth?"

"It shows you *some* truth," Orianna said. "Why?"

I looked over at Lockwood, eyes stinging again. I clenched my hands into fists, anger replacing the fear. Anger was easier to deal with, anyway. "Maybe we could use this to help us."

Orianna perked up at once, her eyes wide. "How?"

"I don't know yet," I said. "But if I can see through their lies, and if they don't know that I can do it, then maybe we can find an advantage somehow."

Orianna raised an eyebrow. "Maybe, but I don't see how. You can't control it, right?"

"No, but ..." I said. "It's all I've got."

Her shoulders shook with a small laugh. "Most people, faced with execution ... they give up. You ... you're plotting how to use your ability to see through cosmetic glamours to somehow beat the Summer Court. Interesting."

Before I could rebut that, a great clatter in echoed through the air. A huge rumbling like thunder started just after, and it took me a few seconds to realize that they sounded like huge drums, deep and booming.

Orianna drooped, wrapping her arms around her knees once more, pulling them in close to herself.

"What is it?" I asked. "Orianna, what is it?"

She shook her head, face tight, pale, golden hair swirling. "It's—"

Her words were cut off by another resounding *BOOM BOOM BOOM!*

The faeries in the tent were starting to look around. The circular pond rippled with the sound of each *boom*. Lockwood remained unmoving, stretched out in the bottom of his glowing cage.

"What, is it ... a dragon?" I asked, thinking about what could possibly be making that noise, shaking the ground. The booming could be footsteps, after all.

Orianna shook her head.

"Okay ... a giant?" I was watching her to see if she reacted. Again, she shook her head.

"Would it be something that I wouldn't know because I'm

from Earth?"

She nodded.

Wait.

Another sound now—still the booming, but also a sharp *rap rap rap* as well, like a snare drum.

It sounded like steps in a procession. A military march.

My mouth went dry.

We'd left Seelie territory with a whole army. The Seelie had built a tent, and—I cast a look around. Half of it wasn't occupied or filled with … anything. The meadow stopped in what looked like a shroud of darkness that hadn't been there a moment earlier, as though something was chewing at the edges of the magical illusion here.

The steady cadence continued, unending, and with it came … understanding.

Understanding of what was going on. Of the ceremony.

Of the danger that I was in.

Orianna's eyes darted like a mouse that realizes the cat had cornered her, and who had nowhere to run. "The Winter Court approaches."

Chapter 32

The thundering sound of an army's footsteps was like a steadier version of my heart's now-usual hammering. "Wait a second," I said, an odd pressure in my head, sunlight streaming down through our magical cage, "I thought the Unseelie and the Seelie hated each other."

"Oh, they do," Orianna said, staring into the void of darkness where the sunny meadow came to an abrupt end. "That's why this is bad."

I stared in the direction of the dark end of the illusion that filled the tent. "What ... does this mean, then?"

"Whatever it is ..." Orianna said. "It's nothing good."

"Oh, wonderful," I said. "Because we've had just way too much good news lately. Why, I don't know if I could even handle any more good news right now." I nudged Orianna, getting her to look away from the magical void. "Is this the beginning of the war? The Winter fae marching on us here?"

"Look," Orianna said, her thin, golden-tipped finger rising to point behind me.

I turned in time to see the king and queen of the Summer Court walking along the far side of the circular pond toward two golden thrones that rose out of a platform shrouded in white silk. The queen's long hair was braided all the way to the floor below, and she wore a green dress that trailed along behind her, the exact color of the grass at her feet. He was wearing a deep black robe, with a high-pointed crown on his forehead. She held her chin high; he looked straight ahead.

They both had a golden glow that seemed to radiate from their skin.

More tricks. More illusions.

The tension among the fae grew as silence fell, and they took their seats.

I glanced at the other end of the room, and two more thrones had appeared in the haze, but they appeared to be made of silver, or platinum, shining in the cooler way of those metals.

Orianna was right. Both courts were going to be in this room at the same time.

"Are we safe here?" I asked her.

"They won't attack each other outright, if that's what you mean," Orianna said. "But I don't know the last time that anything like this has ever happened."

"Are they here to discuss the war?" I asked. "Like try to come to some sort of peace agreement? Before it starts?"

"It's … possible?" Orianna said. Then she frowned. "More likely they're here to charge Lockwood with treason, and allow the Unseelie a chance to punish him in their own way, if he somehow offended them as well."

I looked over at Lockwood. I sighed, thinking how much easier this would be if only he'd trusted me with the truth. Sure, I would have probably been more vulnerable to the fae, I might have had to lie, might have been in more danger, but …

Dragging me into this without giving me the truth? Hot resentment rolled around inside me, bringing a flush to my cheeks. I felt like I'd been used, trapped, dragged into this unknowing. The unknowing was maybe the worst part, surprising as that sounds, given I was staring down execution.

I mean, I'd faced down vampires. I'd gotten myself fully involved in vampire dealings, put myself in peril with the threat of having every drop of my blood drunk dry. No part of that had been easy for me, but I'd been willing to do it because I'd known the stakes (sorry, bad pun). Byron was threatening my family. The Instaphoto gang was going to kill my neighbor. The Butcher was attacking my family and friends in New York.

But when Lockwood had taken me to Faerie, it had been with the vaguest of stories to back it—"I'm in danger. Something happened back home that was bad. Help me with your power of lies."

And here my dumb self was, and how much use was I?

Not useful at all. I didn't even know what to lie about, I was so thoroughly in the dark.

Everything about the situation made me feel sick, just sick. It was like spinning in total blackness, unable to see the hand in front of your face, you're so thoroughly in the dark.

"Well, I guess I understand why we are in the neutral territory," I said, sinking back down onto the bottom of the glass cube. The pressure of the solidified magic against my shoulders carried no reassurance. Up was down, down was up, nothing made sense right now. The world was completely off its axis. Hell, I wasn't even in my world.

This was worse than when I'd found out that vampires were real and one was stalking me. More confusing, more infuriating. I felt so …

Helpless.

Orianna was still rigid.

The void at the far end of the tent was changing now, beyond just the thrones sitting in the darkness. A little chill seemed to move through the crowd of fae before us, and they shivered. The meadow grass closest to the void seemed to be frosting, white crawling up the green stems.

The drumbeat and tapping gave rise to soldiers appearing out of the darkness, steady and true, marching out of the void. They were stern and stoic, reminding me of the guards outside Buckingham Palace who never smile. Their armor was a gunmetal grey - dark, shiny and futuristic. Their helmets only revealed their eyes, masking and protecting the rest of their faces. Their wings lacked the bright hues of the Summer fae, favoring midnight blues and forest greens.

As if reading my thoughts, a cold wind whipped through the walls of our cage, bringing with it a smell like winter in New York, and a hint of pine. I shuddered and wrapped my arms around myself, wishing I had my sweatshirt back instead of the ruins of the once-beautiful dress I'd been wearing at the ball.

A neigh so loud it overcame the booming march rang out, and the Summer fae let out cries of awe. Behind the soldiers came a carriage, all chic style and sharp lines. It rattled to a stop before the thrones, and the door was thrown open.

The king, because he obviously was the king, had red-orange hair so bright it looked as if it were actually on fire. He wore a bright red cloak lined in black silk, and a very simple black robe beneath, trimmed in silver. He was handsome, and had a smirk on his face that made me think of someone who takes pleasure in knowing things that others around them do not. His wings were the color of copper, and they unfurled as he stepped down first, then offered his hand up back into the carriage.

The queen was dangerously beautiful. Raven-colored hair fell in wide, loose curls down her back, and she wore a sleek dress, simply cut but stunningly elegant, in a pale grey that matched her feathery wings. She didn't appear to know how to smile.

Truly, she was the Winter Queen.

Orianna's face was a mask of awe and terror.

They were probably less than fifty feet from us, a few ranks of soldiers all that separated them from our cube. The Winter Queen's gaze roamed over us, mildly curious. One of her perfect eyebrows was arched in question.

Her eyes, which were icy blue, made contact with mine, and I felt as if I had been struck in the gut with a frosty punch. She moved her attention past me to Orianna, and I saw a flicker of recognition pass over her flawless face. It was brief, but it was there.

"You okay?" I whispered to Orianna.

Orianna did not reply.

The magic void was disappearing, replaced by a meadow in winter, snow and frost creeping out to meet in the middle of the tent. The pond had frozen halfway through, and I stared down at the ice, which ceased at the halfway mark as though by ... uh, magic.

Half the tent was Winter.

Half the tent was Summer.

"No Autumn or Spring," I muttered.

"They're the subject courts, and they have no place in this power struggle," Orianna said under her breath.

I looked to the Winter Court as the king and queen took their seats. The queen's electric blue gaze had had an almost physical effect on me … and I didn't like it, but …

There was something about it that worked on my preconceptions of how things were in Faerie. I'd come here thinking Summer were the good guys, Winter were the bad guys.

Then the Seelie had gone had gone and put me in a cage, and now part of me wanted desperately to believe that in spite of their cold look, maybe the Unseelie were the good guys.

But I was thinking like a child, in terms of good guys and bad guys, black hats and white. Standing where I was, a prisoner in a magic cage, sitting between the two sides. I knew I couldn't count on either of them for support.

We were all alone in this.

Looking back to the Summer side, I recognized Master Calvor standing not far from the Summer dais, a nasty sneer twisting his lips as he glanced across the pond at Lockwood's cage. He wore a crown of white metal, as intricate as lace, on his dark hair.

I grimaced. What was he so happy about?

Roseus was there too, in his military best, his armor gleaming and pristine. He gave me a wry smile, and glanced at Lockwood for the briefest of moments. No hint of regret there.

A faerie with purple wings fluttered out to the middle of the pond, his wings whipping around him. He waved his hand out in front of him, and a scroll appeared in the air with a *pop* and a flash of bright light. He took it scroll from the air, unsealed it, and rolled it open. Adjusting his glasses on his nose, he gazed at the scroll before his voice rose to fill the meadow.

"Hear ye, hear ye! Let the proceedings of the royal courts begin!"

Chapter 33

My eyes seemed to be playing tricks on me as I watched blossoms blow in a nonexistent breeze in the Summer Court's side of the divide. Snow nestled so softly in the branches of the tree in the Winter Court's section of the tent.

Caught between the two, I felt the chill from Winter, the hot breeze from Summer. I stood under a sky split between overcast and grey over Unseelie territory and sunny and blue over the Seelie. There was a smell of fresh flowers out of the summery meadow, and the chilly aroma of snow and pine needles from the frigid snowfield.

And here I was, smack in the middle of this study in contrasts … and what looked like the start of a war. I just hoped it didn't begin here, over me and my companions, though it certainly seemed it was destined to.

A rustle of movement out of the corner of my eye made me turn, and my heart did a flip as I saw Lockwood stir. He moved his head first, then his arms, ever so slowly, raising up into a sitting position. He touched his head and grimaced, as if it were screaming in pain.

I finally chanced a small look in his direction, the purple-bearded faerie still calling out names, and found that he was looking up at me.

My eyes grew wide.

His narrowed.

"Are you okay?" I said aloud, though I had no idea if he could hear me.

He nodded as the grandiose announcements of the court proceeded around us, but he cradled his head gingerly; even the slight motion of the nod seemed to bring him pain.

"Shhh," Orianna whispered, finger across her lips. "This lot does not take kindly to being interrupted."

I clamped my lips together to prevent myself from saying anything else. I didn't doubt her.

"Since the Summer Court has called this meeting," called the announcer faerie, some of pomp and circumstance done, "they will speak first." He bowed to Summer.

The Queen of Summer smoothed her skirts as she stood, a kind smile on her face, but a nasty glint in her eye.

"My fellow fae—" she barely got out before the Winter Queen stood up across the gap between them. The Summer Queen's expression darkened, her face twisting as her opposite number flapped her wings and rose a few feet above the Unseelie platform. "Yes, Queen Pruina?"

"I have no stomach for Seelie dissembling today, Ignes," the Winter Queen said. There was not a trace of amusement to be found anywhere on her face, and she stared, impatience clear, at her Summer counterpart. "Let us speak plainly for once."

"I see no reason why protocol cannot be observed—" the Summer Queen said.

"Because you have invaded our borders," Pruina said. "Because you have slaughtered our people, burned their homesteads, seized our lands—need I go on?"

"Your provocations forced our hand," Ignes said, the Summer Queen's shoulders moving up in a light shrug. She was smiling now, though faintly. "We can hardly be expected to stand by while you—"

"We have done nothing to you!" Pruina said, rising higher on the flap of her wings. There was a cold blue magic radiating out from her now, a corona of cyan energy that reminded me of her eyes.

"Oh, yes, Winter is always innocent of any wrongdoing," Ignes said with a little giggle. "I forgot."

"Winter is always guilty of being murderous wretches," came a voice from below the Summer dais. I recognized it, though I hadn't heard it since the hospital.

Calvor.

Master Calvor had shoved his way to stand beside the dais, and now he rose to just a foot or so lower than the Summer royals. He nodded at Ignes, and she deigned to acknowledge him with a nod in return, as though giving him leave to speak. He turned his attention back to the Winter Court, and his eyes were glowing with a hot rage of his own.

"No one here knows better than I what Winter stands for." Calvor drew every word out, a little dribble of rage-drool slipping down out of the corner of his mouth. "Lies. Dishonesty. You stand here in the presence of our great and gracious queen and spit in the face of her offered hand—"

"Only one person here is spitting, man, and I don't think it's Pruina," I said under my breath. Orianna shushed me.

"How do you spit in the face of a hand?" Queen Pruina asked, as a ripple laughter ran through the Winter Court. "Does a hand have a face? Do you draw it on, perhaps, like a child treating their fingers as puppets?"

Calvor flushed tomato red. "You do us great dishonor, Queen of Winter—"

"You do yourself plenty of dishonor all on your own, Calvor," Pruina said. "When your son isn't doing it for you."

That one landed like a lightning bolt in the middle of the assemblage. Everyone shut up in a hot second, even the queens, though Ignes turned a furious shade of red.

She was the first to break the silence. "We will find nothing but insults here," the Summer Queen said, rising higher on her beating wings, as though she were trying to match Pruina in flying height, even across the pond. "Our satisfaction will come elsewhere, on a different field, I think."

Lockwood beat upon the flexing, magical glass. "My queen, I beg your leave to speak—"

"Silence, liar!" she said. I could have sworn she sent a hot gust our way, one that I felt even through the magic of the glass around us. "I will not suffer to hear your insult added upon that already tasted this day."

"How do you taste insult?" I asked. "I thought kids my age spoke funny, with all the 'literally,' but you guys screw with the English language in ways that would drive my teachers bananas." This time, Orianna did not bother telling me to be quiet. The court was already erupted into a steady rumble that spread about the meadow.

Lockwood slumped back down in his cube, and I wondered what the hell was wrong with him. If he had something to say, this seemed like the time to say it.

Unless … maybe he knew that what he had to say was only going to make things worse. Though it was hard to see how that was even possible, at least from where I sat in the middle of what looked like an argument that was heading toward war.

"We have not even addressed the tyls problem," the Summer Queen said, and a halo of sunlight shone down on my cage, forcing me to squint.

"I don't have a tyls problem," Pruina said, fluttering just a touch higher. What kind of a contest was this between them?

"You sent a spy into my court," Ignes said, and I felt every eye in the place turn to me. Well, us, since I was in the cage with Orianna.

"This is awkward," I said, as a rage erupted on the Summer side, fae showering our cage with thrown stuff. I counted a few starfruit and a sparkly shoe, all of which bounced off the magical sides of our enclosure. Thankfully. The shoe had a heckuva a heel and looked like it would have hurt.

"I've dealt with worse," Orianna said. She was holding her head high … uh, literally. Damn, even I was not immune to the ways of my people.

Something heavy smacked against the magical glass and slid down. I peered at it as it rolled off and rolled into the pond. "Is that a codpiece? Because I'm not sure how you can deal with worse than having a crowd of angry fae throwing a codpiece at you."

"We have a saying in Faerie," Orianna said, apparently undisturbed by the codpiece chucker. "'The truth lies in the dark.'"

"What does that even mean?" I asked, as the Summer crowd continued to rage, though they had stopped throwing stuff.

She shrugged. "Well, it's a pun, I think, with the 'lies' part."

"Lame."

"Other than that," she said, "I guess it means that it's really hard to see the truth in this place."

I looked at Lockwood, who was slumped down in his cage, his back turned to the Summer Queen, his head down. He was studying his knees with great intensity. I thought about all the illusions, the talking around the point, the casual misdirections. Mine, in this case, but every single one of them applied to the fae I'd met since I got here. "Well, that seems pretty spot on."

She nodded as a howl went up from Winter, the soldiers banging their weapons against each other in some sort of display designed to match the ferocity that had risen from Summer only moments ago. I'd never been in the middle of a war rally before, but it kind of struck me that it was aptly named in that it was a little like a pep rally, with less pep and more, uh … war.

My vision flickered, just as it had before, and again … I saw something way different than what was in front of me.

The sound of thunder rang, as though the Winter army had gone from hooting and jeering into becoming a living lightning storm, raging around me with skies of black-grey hanging overhead. Gone were the colorful uniforms and wings, and in their place were endless ranks of soldiers in armor—one side bright and the other side dull. No hint of camouflage like you'd see from Earth armies; these were like some garish throwback to medieval times.

But that wasn't the worse part, the armored ranks. The worst part was that there seemed to be hundreds of thousands of them. They stayed in close ranks, their magical weapons clenched tightly in their hands, staring across the field between them, and I realized …

This was what actually lay around us. Not a court, not a pretty meadow or a frozen one. There was no sign of the queens and kings in my flicker—just two armies squaring off, with us stuck in the middle.

Everything else was just magical illusion that allowed these two opposing sides to yell at each other with the illusion of closeness. Who knew how far apart the royals actually were?

My breath came fast and heavy as I looked all around, and found my answer. In the distance, far removed from the field of battle, were the thrones of the Seelie court. Whipping around, I saw the same was true of the Unseelie court. They seemed about a mile apart, but Lockwood, Orianna and I …

We were actually on the battlefield. On the verge of war.

I blinked a few times, and I was back in the glass cage, sweating profusely.

No one seemed to notice my freaking out apart from Orianna, who was looking at me with mild alarm. "What?"

"I just figured out where we actually stand in all this."

She raised an eyebrow. "It's bad, isn't it?"

"Well, it's certainly not good …"

Somewhere in the middle of my vision, the Summer Queen had started shouting, partially drowned out by the hubbub of the armies and the fae.

"Enough," Ignes said. "For too long we have let this drag on. No solutions are forthcoming."

"What solution do you seek?" Pruina called back. Her voice seemed magnified, which it probably was, since she was a mile away from us. "Short of Winter ceding our entire territory to you, what would you have from us, Ignes?"

The room fell silent.

"The truth at last," Calvor said, when the Summer Queen looked at him. "All these insults, all these provocations … they are an orchard that grew from one singular seed." He inflated himself, and rose just a little higher. "One of your little tramps … murdered my son."

"Is that so?" Pruina asked.

"It is so," Calvor said. Ignes nodded along, apparently content to let him do the talking on this one.

"How do you know this?" Pruina asked.

The silence fell again. Calvor blinked a few times. Apparently, this was not the question he'd expected.

"What …" He shook his head, as though trying to clear out a particularly hazy thought. "What do you mean? How do we know? Because we *know*, of course—"

"How?" Pruina asked again.

"You insult us again," Ignes said, cheeks reddening.

"No," Pruina said. "I am very carefully avoiding giving insult. I am asking a question in earnest—by what means did you come to this suspicion?" She flittered down, just a touch, and I wondered if she was trying to diffuse some of the anger. "And against whom do you levy your charge?"

"Against one of your subjects," Calvor said, and he rose, along with his voice, suggesting some sort of aggression or anger coming with his movement. "Some little forest trash—"

"A name?" Pruina asked. "You have one, I presume, since you accuse?"

"Gretha, I believe it was," Calvor said, reddening just a little more. "A forest nymph of some sort."

"Now, this is interesting," Pruina said. "For I have spoken to this Gretha … and she does suggest murder." The Queen of Winter's eyes flashed an icy blue. "She suggests … she defended herself against assault by the Master's son—"

The Summer side erupted again, and this time a volley of stuff that seemed way worse than fruit and a shoe (but not as bad as a codpiece) showered down on the Winter troops. It was a curious thing, that Summer had brought what amounted to an angry mob in their glamour, while Winter had brought soldiers. I'd seen to the heart of it, and they were both obviously troops, but that they portrayed them so differently …

Well, it was curious.

The Summer Queen raised her hands and the mob of disguised troops settled. "More Winter lies. The word of a murderer held up as truth? I should not be surprised at this, coming from your court—and I am not." Her eyes glowed with malice, lips a thin line of distaste.

"If by your odd, Summer reckoning you mean 'truth,' I should not be surprised, were I you," Queen Pruina said. "The truth, so long excluded from the hearing of the Summer Court, must have the strangest ring to it when it does find its way in. But yes, we only have the testimony of the girl who committed the act …" Pruina smiled slowly, thinly, "… and your paladin who witnessed it."

Another shock of silence rocked the would-be battlefield.

That was how Lockwood was involved.

That was why he had avoided Calvor like he had at the hospital.

But why would witnessing an event like that cause them to send him into exile? Something didn't add up.

"There will be no resolution here, my Queen," Master Calvor said, looking to Ignes. "There is nothing to be gained by parlaying with those who would insult us, would lie to our faces, would impugn—"

"I'm not impugning anything," Pruina said, "merely suggesting you could listen to your own loyal paladin—"

"You speak true, Master Calvor," Queen Ignes said, floating a little higher. Her wings shone with a subtle silver gleam as they fluttered in the summer sun. "Our satisfaction will be gained not through talk ..." Her face hardened, eyes flashing a dark angry color. "... But through action alone." She straightened up. "Let us commence."

"Oh, no," I muttered under my breath. I hadn't seen a flicker, but somehow I knew what was going on beneath all the illusions right now.

The battlefield ... the one we were standing right in the middle of ... the one that had been at relative peace only a moment earlier ...

Was about to become the center of a war.

Chapter 34

The charge of the armies against each other should have been louder, I would have thought, after the sounds of thunder that had rocked me before we'd even begun. The Summer army surged over the pond, and it rippled out of existence, replaced by ground where a thousand boots tread as the mob of spectators turned into a colorful, angry army of Seelie. I still couldn't see the armor that I'd noted in the flicker, but they were moving forward in a disciplined movement now, all the chairs cast aside as though they'd never even been there, and more of them swelling from beyond the trees that surrounded the meadow.

"Uh oh," Orianna muttered as the Summer army swarmed past. Winter had girded itself, its soldiers planting themselves in place. The snows appeared to melt as the Seelie moved forth, as though the scenery were the most dramatic pronouncement of how the battle was unfolding. Snow giving way to grass was like a visual cue for what was happening around us, the front line of the Summer armies colliding with the Unseelie defenders in a magnificent clash.

I couldn't see all that well, but there was no missing the flashes of silver blood that appeared as army met army. My earlier question about whether Orianna would bleed gold was put to rest; it was all silver, everywhere, on all of the fae, regardless of their court of allegiance.

We were well behind the front rank of the battle now, the Summer army pushing Winter back as the meadow grew and the snowfield shrank. The clangor and chaos was scary as hell for me, the shouts and screams of battle like nothing I'd ever seen before, but the line of Unseelie held, rising up three and four ranks high as Summer soldiers took wing and started to try and fly over. They met in a great clash of sides, and soon enough I couldn't see the front of the battle.

A bright blast of green streaked over my cage, and the fae of Summer swept out of the way in a circle without even seeing it. It passed through their front, striking Winter soldiers in a blast that forced me to look away from the brightness. It was so intense, but when I looked back, the ranks had closed again, and I could not tell if anyone had been killed by it.

I couldn't be sure, but it looked like it had come from where the Summer Queen floated, glaring at the battle ahead. But … she was a mile away, wasn't she? Had she really just thrown a spell from that far back?

"I wish I could say it's been nice knowing you," Orianna said, watching the ebb of Summer soldiers moving around us, "but … I think we both know I can't lie." She flashed a look at me.

"Oh, I don't think I do know that," I said, looking her right in the eye. "You've been a spy all along, haven't you?"

Orianna broke into a slow smile, then shrugged. "I have my loyalties, just like your friend Lockwood. But I was supposed to see you home safely in hopes that he could avert … this …" She cast a slow look around the Summer army moving around and past us. "Clearly," her face fell, "that didn't happen."

"Clearly," I said, doing a little looking of my own. A squad of Seelie buzzed past in light armor that reminded me of insect carapaces, their wings the only part of them that was uncovered. Just as soon as I thought that, something like a lance sailed out of the Unseelie lines and pierced one of them right through the undefended wing. He came crashing down somewhere in the crowd, which did not produce so much as a ripple in the endless movement of soldiers. "What's the truth that Lockwood knows?"

"Maybe you should ask him," Orianna said, fingers

brushing the magical glass. It didn't even ripple. "It's not really my story to tell."

"Maybe he should have told me," I said. "But he didn't. Probably because he didn't want to put me at risk of torture."

"You're being too kind," Orianna said. "Like I told you— Seelie lie. Not directly, but it's what they do."

I got up in her face. "Not Lockwood. He's different. He's gone out of his way to avoid lying."

"Well, he's gone out of his way to avoid telling the truth, too," Orianna said. "Otherwise, why accept exile and go to Earth? It's not like there aren't territories here that wouldn't have been favorable to him. But going to the land of iron and Iron Bearers?" She shook her head. "That's a level of madness I wouldn't care to contemplate."

"It's not so bad," I said, wishing like hell I was in Tampa right now instead watching fae battle each other in some sort of bloody grudge match. A spell flashed red in front of me, and three fae just disappeared. No flicker hinted at their fate, but I had a feeling they were dead. "He seems to be doing well enough. I mean, if you avoid the carpentry and metalwork industries, you'd probably be okay there."

"I prefer not to take any chances, thanks," she said, then grimaced as she remembered where we were. "Okay. Well. Usually I prefer to avoid them. Today I might be willing to take a chance."

"Spies don't always live a long life here, I'm guessing," I said.

Orianna fluttered her wings. "Is that what it's like on Earth?" I nodded. "Well, maybe that's one way our worlds are alike, then."

I caught different-colored movement out of the corner of my eye, and realized there were a phalanx of lighter-armored fae moving past us, so many soldiers heading into this battle … I looked back; the queen and the court were gone, now, their dais out of sight behind the swarms of fae moving forth to fight.

Hmmm.

"Orianna?" I asked, and she tore her gaze off the battle for a second to look at me. "Promise you won't be mad."

"About wh—" she started to ask, but I slugged her, hard, in the mouth before she could finish. She bounced off the side of the cage and hit the ground.

"Owww," I groaned, shaking out my hand. Mill had warned me not to punch with a closed fist, but I'd gone and done it anyway. I'd had to.

Orianna was laid out on the floor of the cell, dripping blood from her mouth. I looked around to see if anyone had noticed. They hadn't. Everyone was way too focused on the battle to care about little old us. Rolling to her side, she moaned, stirring only a little. "Stay still," I said under my breath, and then smeared my hand with the silver blood from her lip.

I turned to the nearest fae soldier, one of those lightly-armored ones that seemed to be moving up. "Help!" I called. "Help me!" I waved a silvery hand in front of my face.

He paused, last of his line, and they moved on without him, toward the front. "What?" he asked. I couldn't hear him, but I could see his lips move.

I held my hand out. "The prisoner. She passed out. She's bleeding from the mouth. I think she's dying."

The soldier did something completely predictable. He looked around for some authority to appeal to. This was the delicate part. If he could call out to the queen from here, my plan was finished before it started.

After a few seconds, he realized that there was no authority to appeal to. "I'll see if I can find someone to help you—" he started to say.

I was ready for this. "What's your name?" I asked.

He was a soldier, caught up in the flow of battle. "Irise."

"Hey, Irise," I said, "how do you think your queen is going to react if this prisoner dies before she can be executed? Because I'm guessing bad—"

"I'll go find someone—"

"There's no time," I said, putting an arm under Orianna's face and tilting it toward Irise. She was drooling silver blood and it looked horrible. If she wasn't unconscious, she was playing her role magnificently. If she was … uh … I might have punched her too hard.

Well, I'd be sorry for that later.

"Stand back," Irise said and drifted closer to our cage. He put out a hand, running it along the front of the magical glass. He kept his weapon clenched tight in the other.

"I can only go so far back," I said, putting Orianna's arm under mine and trying to haul her to her feet. She was heavy and I wasn't that strong, so it didn't go so well. "Ohmigosh. She's like a ton."

"A … what?" he asked. The door was open, and he flittered closer.

"Hard to explain," I said. "Here, help me lift her. We can get her to a—what do you call doctors around here?"

"Doctors," Irise answered, lowering his weapon and taking a step forward. "Is that not what you call them?"

Oh, good. He had a natural curiosity.

"No, no, it is," I said as he lifted Orianna up. His weapon fell to his side, out of easy position to stab me. "I thought maybe it was something different for you, because—it's funny how we speak the same language, that's all." He looked at me across Orianna's drooling face. "You know, being from different worlds. Kinda weird. Feels like you should be speaking Martian or something, you know?"

"No," Irise said, frowning through his helmet's facial slit. I had a feeling he was starting to develop a suspicion that he'd been had.

"Oh, well," I said, "all right, let's get help. Where do we take her?"

He moved to point at the rear of the battle, where the Summer Court was probably waiting, though I couldn't see them. "The relief will be found in the rear of—"

His eyes went wide, and there was a slight flash as his helm flew a couple inches up, and he toppled forward under the stampede of the Summer army. No one even noticed. Bad luck, Irise. Hopefully his armor would help him survive the trample.

"Thank goodness you did that," I said, looking at Orianna as she rubbed her jaw, looking at me just a little irefully. "I mean, I had a plan for getting this far, but I wasn't sure what

I was going to do from here."

"Feels like you should have figured that out before you hit me," she said, popping her jaw. The army was still stampeding past, though they'd slowed somewhat. No one was paying any attention to us, what with a war going on not a hundred feet away, and all them blindly charging into it.

"Oh, quit your whining, we're out of the cage," I said, and nodded at Lockwood, who was watching us, wordlessly, from inside his own, on his feet. "Let's get him out and—"

"Do something even more foolish?" came a too-familiar voice from behind me. "That would be hard to imagine."

I turned, slowly, to find Roseus standing there, grinning—again—a few soldiers at his back with weapons in hand. The world seemed to be shifting around me, the soldiers moving away, allowing Roseus's men to move freely in a circle to hem us in. Their weapons glowed, poised and ready to strike. Even though they seemed to be at a distance, I had a feeling that once again, Faerie was not telling me the truth. They were ready to strike us down.

A flicker showed my fears to be true, a flash showing a spear just an inch from my throat, before it snapped back to the "real" world, and it seemed to be feet away.

They had us.

Chapter 35

I wish I could fight.

As I was being led away, a pointed spear in my back courtesy of the nearest fae soldier, that was the thought that kept coming to me. I wanted to be one of those lady badasses from movies and TV, who could bust out a fighting move spin, yank the spear out of this guy's hand, and shove it up his nose.

My fighting experience was pretty limited, down to what Mill had taught me. Against vampires, I was getting … well, okay. Against a big guy in a dark alley, I could probably inflict some damage.

Against a faerie with a weapon pointed at my back? Yeah … it wasn't going to work out like the movies. My version of the Hollywood ending would finish with me getting stabbed mid-spin trying to disarm the soldier who had me at his mercy.

They were bringing Lockwood along, too, and Orianna. We were being marched in a procession through a split in the line of fae that were still rallying forward toward the battle. Every once in a while a blast of magic would shoot by from the court, though I couldn't see them now that I wasn't high up on the plinth in my cage anymore. The aura of a glowing surge of blue or green was a pretty solid cue that magical craziness was afoot, though.

"The queen has ordered your executions to commence immediately," Roseus said, a certain smug satisfaction layered on his face. He was walking alongside, between me and Lockwood.

Poor Lockwood. He had five spears pointed at him, a couple of which were resting a few centimeters into his flesh. They were taking no chances with him, and silver blood was welling in small beads at the site of the wounds.

"Come to Faerie, they say," I muttered, feeling the not-so-gentle poke of the spear in my back, "see the magical world, they say. Well, let me tell you something—no wonder there's no Earth-to-Faerie tourism industry, because your hospitality here sucks. Figures you'd execute me just for showing up and doing … basically nothing."

"Now, now, you didn't do nothing," Roseus said, still smirking. "Give yourself at least a little credit. You helped deliver this traitor to us." He waved a hand at Lockwood.

"I was an honored paladin of Summer," Lockwood said, his teeth gritted in pain. He was holding up pretty well. I'd taken a little pain lately, upped my threshold, but I was pretty sure if I was being frog marched with spears piercing my flesh, I'd be crying at least a little. "I chose exile rather than to allow our kingdom to suffer under the burden of my knowledge. But I have always been loyal in my heart."

"It is an inconvenient truth of rule," came a voice from out of the lines of armies to our right, "that knowledge is indeed a terrible burden." Master Calvor stepped out from between two ranks of soldiers, as though he'd been inspecting them and decided to just meander over and join us. His eyes were flashing with amusement, but his mouth was a hard line, devoid of any joy. "You should have born yours quietly."

"I did," Lockwood said, pausing just long enough that one of his guards sank his spear tip into the meat of Lockwood's shoulder. I cringed, but Lockwood did not move, staring down Calvor. "I kept my quiet. Accepted exile as the price for keeping our kingdom whole and unharmed. But that wasn't good enough for you, was it?"

Calvor cracked a little smile. "No. Another truth of ruling—if you're going move forward, sometimes people will get in your way. This leaves you with limited options. Go around them, if they let you. Decide not to move forward.

Or …" And he made a vague wave at Lockwood.

"Crush them?" I asked.

Calvor smiled. "Indeed. I don't care much for reversing course or going around."

"Yeah, you don't strike me as the kind who'd detour an inch around an orphan," I said. "You'd just roll right over them."

"In fairness," Calvor said, casting a subtle eye over the battlefield, "there are so many orphans, especially after today. Yet only one me."

"I'd like to see the number of both greatly reduced," I said.

Calvor turned back to me and smiled. "I imagine you would, 'Iron Bearer. But I care not what you think—what matters is my people and my legacy." He shrugged. "Anything else is hardly worth concerning yourself about."

"I suppose it's unfortunate then that your legacy is somewhat curtailed with the death of your son," Lockwood said.

I blinked at him. That was probably the nastiest thing I had ever heard Lockwood say, just savage AF, and the worst part was that it was delivered so dryly, like one of those old timey British insults, but man, did it land like he'd sledgehammered it home.

Calvor reddened, looking like he might lurch forward and attack, but he got control of himself swiftly. "My legacy will just have to be what I deliver to my people, since you … you saw to it that my son did not survive."

"Your son brought about his own death," Lockwood said. They were staring hard at each other. "I had nothing to do with it."

"But you could have saved him," Calvor said. "Just as I could save you now." He leaned in, close to Lockwood. "And I will take great pleasure in doing you the same courtesy you did him—none." He waved a hand, and looked to Roseus. "See it done."

"I will bring them to the executioner myself," Roseus said, and nodded at his guards. Our little stay of execution was over, and now we were on the march again. Calvor disappeared into the ranks of the soldiers, and we were marched over the vivid green grass toward the back of the lines. The soldiers were fewer here, and it seemed the bulk of the army had moved forward now, into the battle at the front line.

"You don't have do this," I said, inadvertently parroting the single stupidest line that every person in every TV show and movie said whenever they were in a dire bind like this.

"Of course he does," Orianna said. "His patron just ordered him to kill us. How do you think this turns out for him if he fails?"

The soldier walking me gave me a not-subtle jab with a spear, and I jerked my shoulders forward at the sting. "Gah!" A little drop of blood ran down my spine. I tried to reach the wound, but it was right at the spine between my shoulder blades where I couldn't reach it. "I hope it turns out he gets locked in a cage with a bunch of angry, hungry avara, honestly."

Roseus smiled. "That's not bad. I'll talk to the executioner, maybe we can add that as an option in the future. For now, though … we're a simple people, probably unlike you Iron Bearers and your complexities. I hear you have wagons that move as if by magic, but without any actual magic?"

"They're called cars," I said. "I'd love to show you one. Especially if it was made of iron. And traveling eighty miles an hour at your face."

"I regret that you shan't get the chance," Roseus said. "But as I said—we're a simple people. Your methods are complex, but ours … have a certain elegance in their simplicity." He nodded at a dais ahead, where a faerie was waiting, one so huge he looked like a pro wrestler who'd been juicing hard for a long time. He wore a feral grin, stretching almost ear to ear, and had one of those black masks that wouldn't have been out of place in a medieval movie.

And he swung a giant axe up to rest on his shoulder.

"Up you go," Roseus said, bringing us to the edge of the platform and beckoning us to climb up. "Now, now, don't be shy. If you don't climb up on your own, then we'll be forced to—"

"Kill us?" I almost rolled my eyes. "Oh, no."

Roseus smiled. "The headsman will be swift. If you force us to … we will not be. Your blood will flow slowly, and your life's leaving will be a great, seemingly eternal pain."

"I know which I pick," Orianna said, fluttering up to the platform under the watchful eye of her guards. They remained down on the ground, though watchful.

Lockwood, too, climbed up without a word. His guards gave him one last poke, too, a little silver blood washing out from the new wound inflicted on his calf. Lockwood, for his part, only grimaced, but remained upright, now upon the dais.

I looked at Roseus, who seemed to be waiting for me to do his bidding. "Iron Bearer? Are you going to make this easy on us both? Or will I be forced to look at your strange, dark, non-magical blood as it runs over the green fields of Faerie?"

Something about that caused a tingle across my scalp.

"I just want to go on record saying," and I prepared myself to take a step up to the dais with the other two, "you're a giant jerkface. You're all liars here, every last one of you. Believe me, because it takes one to know one and you—you people are liars. You live in lies, you bathe in them, you wear them every day of your life like high fashion."

Roseus did not look impressed. "Your words carry some small sting. Not as much as the headsman's axe, I imagine, but still—they find their mark. Fare thee poorly, my dear." And he gave me a little shove as I tried to step up onto the platform, but his push made me topple and hit my knee.

"Ow," I said, pulling back my ragged dress material to see my leg. Skinned it, a little scrape showing red where I'd landed. I snapped a look back at Roseus. "You'll pay for that."

He snorted. "I greatly doubt it, though it amuses me that even in parting, on your way to death, you find time to lie with these idle threats of your own."

I ran my finger over the welling blood, and the tips came away red, the liquid running between the whorls of my prints. "Yeah … that wasn't a lie."

Roseus didn't even bother to restrain his smile. "It's going to be quite fun to watch you—"

"General Roseus!" someone shouted, fluttering down from above the crowd. It was a soldier in full armor, silver blood glazing his armor in a few spots. "They are coming at us from the upper flank, trying to get around it. Colonel Halware requires your assistance immediately to hold, sir."

Roseus sighed, then looked at me, Orianna and Lockwood all in turn. "This is the trouble with being so very important to your kingdom—someone always needs you." He nodded at the soldier. "I will be along directly." He glanced back at us. "Such misfortune, to not be able to see your ends with my own eyes. But I'll look forward to examining your lifeless eyes when the battle is won and I return." He sketched a rough salute at Lockwood. "I can't thank you enough. If not for your honor and nobility and utterly foolish idealism, why … I might still be stuck under you, rather than climbing to the heights of general." He smiled. "And if not for you, Iron Bearer, and your spy friend? Why, my star might not be rising in the court. I might be forever stuck in the lower ranks rather than ascending to my proper place. I can't thank you enough." He waved. "But, alas … the headsman's axe will have to convey my regards. Do take care to make it as painless as possible, my good man. Unless they force you to do otherwise, in which case … swing badly. I won't mind."

And with a last nod at the executioner, he was gone in a flutter of wings, taking his soldiers with him.

Chapter 36

"Well, this is a fine kettle of fish, as they say on Earth," Lockwood said as the three of us stood on the executioner's platform, looking at the leering fae in the black mask who watched us with his axe slung over his shoulder. I couldn't imagine a much scarier looking guy this side of a vampire with blood running down his face, honestly—he was frighteningly large, and the axe had a curve to it that suggested it was pretty good at taking the heads off people.

"What's a fish?" Orianna asked, nose curling at the bridge.

"What's a kettle?" the executioner asked, slinging his axe back down to catch it with his other hand just below the neck. "Never mind. Who wants to go first?"

I looked at the heavy block sitting in the middle of the platform. It looked nice and clean, metallic, like an anvil. No discolorations to suggest use, but I had a feeling they'd have a glamour over it. You know, to keep those waiting in line a little calm. I stole a look around; there weren't any soldiers immediately nearby.

The executioner was suddenly up in my face, breathing a sweet, surprisingly floral breath right into my eyes. "Don't even think about it. You won't make it a step."

"Can't blame a girl for trying," I said, looking him in his pale-silver eyes. Gulp.

"I think you just volunteered to be first," he said, taking hold of my manacles and steering me toward the block.

"That is a pretty loose definition of volunteering," I said, putting a little effort into slowing our forward momentum. I twisted my head around to look at him. "I mean, by that definition, I volunteered Bobby Anders in eighth grade, just because I was looking at the wart on the side of his nose. Which I totally felt bad about, but—"

A shock of brightness caused me to lurch back, the flicker taking over again like a fork of lightning landing in front of my face. I gasped, arching my back and causing my fresh stab wound there to scream at me from the movement. I staggered and fell, hitting sideways and accidentally rolling to my back like a coin that landed on its side.

The world around me took a turn for the much worse; the tent that had been above earlier shredded, hanging limply in rags from poles. It looked like the fae had just sliced their way through when the war began, leaving me with a clear view to a stormy sky racked with lightning. I looked sideways and there were dead trees as far as I could see, chopped down, the fires of war spanning out in the opposite direction of the troops. Screams came from the front, and I started to look that way—

But the executioner swam into my view first. And he … did not look at all as I remembered him before the flicker.

Gone was the black-masked specter with the evil grin. In his place was a thin fae with drooping wings to match his face. The corners of his mouth turned down, even as he peered at me, and his eyes held a deep sadness of the sort you only see in people who have suffered something terrible.

"Are you all right?" he asked, and even his voice was different. It sounded …

Quiet. Genuine. And as I blinked at him, he recoiled slightly, puffing up. "I mean … get up," he said, and here he sounded a touch harsher.

"I … I see you now," I said, a little chill running down my scalp, down my spine.

His thin brow furrowed heavily. "I … what?"

"I see you," I said, staring at him. "You're not … not what they want you to be. Underneath it all, I mean. You're not what they're trying to make you be."

His eyebrows arched, and he straightened just a little. "I—I don't know what you mean."

"What have they done to you?" I asked, peering at him. "You didn't want this job, did you?"

He looked torn between a terrible response, but it passed, and he swallowed visibly. "No," he whispered. "I hate it. I wanted to be … anything else."

"I am so sorry," I said softly, with utter sincerity. "What's your name?"

"Tanner," he said, eyelids fluttering. "My name is Tanner."

"Tanner," I said, catching stray, bewildered looks from Lockwood and Orianna, hovering behind Tanner, "I want to end this war. I want to stop it. Do you understand?"

He looked away. "I … I'm supposed to—"

"I know what you're supposed to do," I said, and he looked back at me, his eyes full. "And I know you don't want to. I don't blame you. Having to pretend to be somebody you're not …" I swallowed heavily. "Well, let's just say I understand it, and … it sucks."

Tanner blinked. "Sucks … what?"

"Like a pig?" Orianna asked. "A suckling pig?"

"You've got pigs but no fish?" I asked. "Really?" I turned back to Tanner. "Never mind. It's a terrible feeling. That's what I meant. It's a terrible feeling, having to hide who you are. Pretend to be somebody you're not. To do something that … wrenches your very soul." I swallowed again, trying to keep down emotion. "Did you want this war?"

Tanner shuffled his foot, and put the haft of the axe down against the platform, keeping the blade up. In a very small voice he said, "No."

"I want to end it," I said. "And I think I can end it—we can, anyway. But not if you do what you're planning to do with … that." I nodded at the axe.

"You don't understand," he said, blinking, a glittering light flashing in his eyes as little diamond-like tears spilled out. "This is what I have to do."

"No, you don't," I said, getting to my feet but no move toward him. "It's what you think you have to do. But every time you execute someone … you feel a little less like yourself." It was like me, every time I told a lie. I could almost see the girl I was, before all the compulsive lies. She was lost, somewhere way, way back along the path. "You keep telling yourself that if you just keep going, it'll get better. But it won't. You'll feel more and more lost as time goes by. And one day, you'll look in the mirror … and you won't even recognize yourself."

Tanner stared at me. "How … how did you know?" he whispered.

"I've been there," I said, looking him in the eyes. "Tell them we escaped, if they ask. You've done a good job for long enough. Tortured your own soul trying to be what they want you to be. You don't have to do it anymore. Not if you don't want to."

Tanner smacked his lips together and flexed his fingers once, then twice.

Then he let go of the axe, and it dropped, ringing out as it hit the platform. He looked up at me, tears still in his eyes. "Go," he said, and turned away, as though to keep from looking at us.

"Come on," I said, snagging hold of Lockwood's manacles as I walked toward the far end of the platform. Neither he nor Orianna said anything, and all that I could hear other than our footsteps were the sobs of Tanner as he stood there, contemplating where things had gone terribly, terribly wrong in his life.

Chapter 37

"That … was really quite something, Cassandra," Lockwood said as we hurried across the churned up field, a flicker showing me the horror that had been done here by an encamped army. They must have been here for days before we showed up, just waiting for the right time to invade Winter.

Well, now they had it. The battle was raging in the distance; I could hear it in both the "real" world and when there was a flicker showing me the one beneath. That meant either way … it was close.

"I had a little bit of a revelation back there," I said, hurrying along. I paused a second, stretching up. The flicker disappeared, and sunny skies shone down on me from overhead. But they felt cold now, lacking any of the warmth this beautiful glamour had cast when I'd first gotten here.

"Do tell," Orianna said, fluttering a few steps behind me.

"See, nobody here is exactly what they seem to be," I said. "Like you said, Orianna—it's all lies, all the way down."

She nodded. "That's the Seelie for you." Lockwood shot her a glare, and she shrugged. "I don't make them lie, all right? They're your people."

"Everybody lies at some point," I said. "But what people lie about tells you a lot about them." Like a teenage girl lying about stupid stuff? That tells you she's petty, small, and self-involved.

And that was a stinging revelation to come to, let me tell

you.

"A society so obsessed with appearances that they have to lie about them in every way, though?" I caught a glimpse of my ultimate target, far up ahead on the dais of the royals. "That is a person—or a people—who are deeply insecure about … well, everything, probably."

Lockwood was limping along behind me, bleeding from the dozen shallow stab wounds the guards had inflicted on him during the march to the executioner. "And what would you know about this, Cassandra?"

I flashed him a smile. "Lockwood, I'm a teenager. I understand insecurity. Trust me."

"That's funny," Orianna said, "because you're confidently leading us into absolute insanity. Or am I wrong about the direction you're taking us?"

"You're not wrong about either," I said under my breath. The field was clear ahead, the army having moved on to engage with the Winter forces. No one was even looking in this direction, not even the Summer Queen's guards. Of which there were only a handful. Probably because the queen seemed capable of defending herself, sending a blast of green magic forth, hurtling toward the front, all her attention focused on the battle.

Which was good, because I was aiming to make this a surprise.

"I would caution you here, Cassandra," Lockwood said as we drew to within a few hundred feet of the dais. We had yet to be seen, the guards watching forward for attacks, the occasional large bolt of magic swirling in from the front lines like some kind of artillery. "The reception you are going to receive once you get the attention of the queen and her guards is bound to be … frosty."

"Oh, hilarious, because she's the Summer Queen," Orianna said, a little snippily. "I would have gone with 'fiery.'"

"You will only have one chance at this," Lockwood said. "So I would caution you, whatever you do—get it right." He gave me a fatherly, reassuring squeeze of the shoulder.

"Okay," I said, and the world flickered around me. The queen flickered too, turning from a lovely, golden-haired creature into a dark-haired, angry crone with a furious scowl and a much less … shapely figure than in the glamour. Seriously, she was at least three bra sizes smaller.

The glamour snapped back into place, and it hurt a little to go from seeing her as an angry middle-aged lady with all the requisite wrinkles and iron-grey hair … to this vision of beauty.

But it gave me an idea.

"Hey, Queen Ignes!" I shouted. "Does anyone know that you're totally a bottle blond? Like, magical bottle blond? Or is it just me?"

It felt like the entire battle halted at that exact moment. Every guard left around the queen pivoted, turning their attention to me and, by extension, Orianna and Lockwood.

"Well," Lockwood said, and there was a hint of restrained terror underneath his dry delivery, "that certainly seems to have … gotten some attention."

"Yeah," Orianna said, and she sounded even more strained than he. "So … what now?"

That was a great question. And as I stared at the Queen of Summer, the answer escaped me for a moment, and her entire army turned its attention on us.

Chapter 38

It was pretty clear that the Seelie queen was pissed, bright flames sprouting from her shoulders as she seethed. I could feel the heat, even at this distance, and she flamed brighter, fire burning out of her like some 80's shoulder pads I'd seen in pictures of my mom when she was younger. The flames crackled, and the warmth felt like I'd stepped outside to Florida sunshine, sweat beading on my forehead as I stared at the Queen of Summer.

"Uh oh," I said, thinking maybe, just maybe, I'd taken my insult a little too far—

"Fiend!" A guard leapt at me, and a timely flicker was the only thing that warned me he was not twenty feet away, as I had expected, but in fact less than five as reality bent around me, and I dodged in the way Mill had taught me.

Lockwood leapt forth and turned aside his spear thrust, catching it in the crook of his elbow and dealing a palm-fist to the fae's nose that drew silver blood and rattled his armor. He strained, sweeping the spear out of the man's grasp and knocking his feet from beneath him.

"Thanks," I said as Lockwood kicked him, sending him flying sideways through the air. I blinked in surprise at the force of the blow, and I snapped back into the glamour as the guard shot away from us as though launched from a cannon. "Uh … wow. This place just does not like physics, does it?"

"Magic and science are ever at odds with each other,"

Lockwood said, tucking the haft of his stolen spear under his arm and assuming a defensive stance between me and the queen. He held up a hand that crackled magic, and some of Ignes's remaining guards stepped forward, forming a defensive half-moon between us and her.

"Wait," I said, "I didn't mean to start a fight."

"When you insult a woman's hair color, how can you expect anything else?" Orianna asked under her breath.

"You have stepped into a war, Iron Bearer," the queen said, and she seemed to swell in size, becoming a taller, more frightening figure, golden hair blowing all around her as if caught by a fan mounted beneath her feet. "Are you so naïve as to fail to recognize what happens in war?"

"The only thing I fail to do here," I said, "is see any truth. Not from you, not from your soldiers, and definitely not from the men feeding you lies and pushing this fight."

The queen's eyes burned. "Coming from one with as a poisonous a tongue as yours, that means … nearly nothing." She raised a hand, snapping her fingers. "Dispatch them."

The guards swarmed at us, and Lockwood immediately caught three of them, engaging with his spear, moving blurry fast in spite of his injuries. Silver blood dripped and splashed, and within seconds it was not just his I was seeing. He struck quick and true, and the guards he crossed blades with did not seem well-prepared to deal with him.

"Okay, this is bad," Orianna said, fluttering her wings without any actual lift taking place. She held up her hands, taking a step back and putting a hand on my arm to drag me back with her. "Gentlemen … there's no need to get rough. We're unarmed, we're—"

One of the guards reached for her, putting aside his spear just long enough to swipe forward at Orianna's exposed arm. As he did so she grabbed him by the wrist and pulled him, yanking him off balance. As he came down she raised a knee and caught him in the jaw. He let out a grunt of pain and she grabbed his spear, twisting it out of his grasp in the same way Mill had taught me—pull toward the thumb, where the grip was weakest.

That done, she brought it around and dinged him on the

helmet, knocking it off. Then she raised up the butt of the spear and clubbed him in the back of the head before bringing the tip around at the remaining guard.

"I don't know what your plan is here," she said, keeping her eyes completely fixed on him, "or if you even really have one. But you better do something fast, because I'm not sure I can take this guard one on one, and Lockwood seems … a little busy at present." She nodded her head at the queen without taking her eyes off her foe. "Also, I think Ignes might have some words for you. Magic words, ones that will disintegrate your body and soul."

"I should never have left New York," I said. "I should never have told my first lie. I—oh, to hell with it." I gathered up the shredded remains of the train of my dress, looking at the bare remnants of what had been so pretty only a day or so ago. "All right, Queen Ignes—I think we need to have a conversation." And I started toward the dais, where she waited, blazing at me and little else.

"I am a Queen of Faerie," Ignes said, growing even taller, a giant to my Lilliputian self. "What needs to be said between us two? What could possibly be spoken but lies from you and righteous fury from me?"

A flicker showed me something horrifying, just for a second. Ignes was pouring green energy forward at me, magic blasting at little old me, burning toward me like green, verdant flames—

And something was stopping it just a couple feet from my face. A barrier of blue that bled off her spell magic, swirling and raging like a river rapid.

"I don't need to say anything to you, really." I took a step up onto the dais. "I don't know anything about Faerie except you people use an awful lot of magic. And you seem to be about to kill each other in great numbers. Which is not wonderful. But I do know someone who has something to say to you … someone not like me. See, I am a liar. Been doing so for as long as I can remember. Deception has been like a second skin to me, really. My parents don't even trust me anymore." I shook my head. "So … I don't think you should believe a word that comes out of my mouth, because

… why would you? You don't even know me. But …"

I felt like I was inches away from her now, and I hoped whatever was keeping her from annihilating me could hold out just a little longer. "… But," I said, "I know someone who you should listen to. Someone who can't lie—like you." Boy, did I bite my tongue on that one, because holy smokes had the Seelie showed me a thousand more ways to lie without actually speaking a full blown lie. "Someone who you once trusted."

I turned, and Lockwood stood there, his three guards vanquished, along with Orianna's. He seemed to have picked up a couple more wounds, with the silvery sheen of the blood dripping down his arms, and yet …

He was strong. Commanding. And he stood before his former queen with his head held high.

"This man was a paladin of your kingdom," I said. "And regardless of how angry you are with him … don't you at least owe him a chance to explain what happened?" I looked the Queen of Summer in the eyes. "Don't you owe him a chance to speak the truth to you, knowing that—unlike me—he can't lie?"

Queen Ignes stared at me, and her shoulders relaxed, her head coming back. She pointed her chin down at me, and seemed to shrink, just slightly. "Even in the forest of your lies, there may stand a truth or two."

"Gee, thanks," I said.

A flash of darkness crossed her irises, and she looked at Lockwood. "You served me well for many years, Lockwood. What say you? Does this Iron Bearer speak true? Do you have something to tell me?"

Lockwood just looked at her, his eyes glazed. After a moment, though, he stirred, and swallowed.

And he opened his mouth to speak.

Chapter 39

Lockwood

I have served you, my queen, for all my life.

In the days of my youth, I waxed rhapsodic about your grace. When I was elevated to paladin, I felt the tremors of true satisfaction. It was an impossible goal, one you know is achieved by so very, very few.

I fought so many, many wars in your name. Golgara Frontiers. Skypeace Hamlet. The Firesand Valley Campaign.

I invaded foreign lands, subdued angry revolts, brought sword and shield and your light to many corners of Faerie. I faced Winter in my turn, over and over, proving out my courage and bringing your rule to the borders.

And then ... I went to Veritas.

A village on the edge of the frontier, bordering Winter, it was the last true step in neutral territory before reaching the holds of the Unseelie. I went with my squad, all lesser knights, all dispatched as ordered by you, by your throne—or so I thought.

We were sent, in reality, by Master Calvor.

I did not learn this immediately, of course. No, it was only as I sat in the inn where we sheltered on the second night that I learned the truth of the matter. My orders had come on parchment, in a simple hand, and I did not question them because they bore your seal, my queen. That was good enough for me, in my youth.

"A peculiar assignment, yes, Lockwood?" asked Vexo, one of my lieutenants, a fresh-faced young man straight out of academy. Vexo had been something of a disciplinary problem, often drunk and once starting a brawl in an inn in Starvale. Foolishly, perhaps, I wrote it up to his youth and assumed that experience would make him more disciplined.

We sat by the fire, and it crackled a bright purple, magic burning in the hearth as I stared, my armchair overstuffed and my cup overfilled, the heavy bouquet of the wine filling my nose. I looked up at Vexo, who watched me for a response. "An assignment from the queen is never peculiar. It is our duty to carry out her will, whatever it is, wherever it takes us."

"Of course, of course," Vexo said, nodding along as he took a sip from his cup. "But do you not find it peculiar that this is where she sends us? The arse-end of nowhere?"

To this I smiled. "I have been to the arse-end of nowhere more times than I can count. And so shall you be sent— should you be fortunate enough to serve as long as I." With that, I bade him good eve, leaving the rest of my wine and retiring to my quarters.

The nights in Veritas were long and cold, Winter having exerted its hold in its turn on this section of the borders. She was in full bloom, and I watched the frost form on the window as I awoke after a brief sleep. I could not tell the hour; no stars were visible under the blanket of clouds.

It was noise that jarred me from my bed.

A scream.

I rose and donned my armor, hurrying downstairs and out into the snowy streets of the village. Everyone seemed to be sleeping, or at least their curtains were drawn save for perhaps a crack here and there, a face staring out into the snowy oblivion, flakes falling around.

The scream came a second time as I trod through the ankle-high snow on the cobbled streets. I gripped my weapon tight as I rounded a corner into an alley to find—

Vexo. He had a local maiden by the throat, choking her with one hand while holding her tightly with the other.

Her own hands were empty as she struggled against him.

"Come on," he said, and even from twenty paces I could smell the stink of wine on his breath. "Don't feign modesty—you're just a local girl, surely a harlot by trade in that outfit—"

My opinion of the events had already formed in my mind, of course. Here was a local girl, weaponless, in the grip of a soldier who'd been on a ride for a week, that angry edge in his eyes before he took his alcohol. I'd seen this before, and I never found it acceptable.

I shouted my outrage and went to draw my sword—

But she beat me to it. She pulled his own blade as Vexo drunkenly squeezed at her—

And she buried it up to the hilt in his guts in utter panic.

I could see it in her eyes. The girl was terrified, and she had every right to be. I don't know that he meant to kill her, but he certainly meant her no good.

Vexo gasped his last, and I stood there as she turned the sword on me.

"Hold," I said, putting up one hand while I sheathed my sword. "I mean you no ill. You did what was called for."

She let out a gasping breath, back against the alley wall, not relinquishing the sword. "He … was one of yours?"

I looked at Vexo. He was still, the snow falling on his armor. "He was. But you'll find no complaint from me for your conduct here. It was righteous, and he was much in the wrong. I'll not defend him, nor prosecute you."

She was watching me carefully, her eyes a darker blue, like still waters at night. "You'll let me go, then? And you commanded this man?"

"I was his commander," I said, looking upon his body, "but I hardly commanded him, especially in this act." I kept my distance. "You should go. Get out of town, if possible. I can speak only for myself in this. I will tell the truth of what happened here, and I believe no danger will come your way, but this is neutral territory. No one here will come to your aid against the might of Summer."

She said something else, though I did not hear it. It might have been a curse. I doubt it was thanks, for her life as it was died in that moment, in that alley. She turned and ran, taking

Vexo's sword with her—as a guard in case I decided to change my mind, I suppose.

But I did not. I went back to my room in the inn and rousted my fellow soldiers. I led them outside, and spoke the truth of what had happened to their ears. That done, I composed a letter to command, and sent it in the care of one of my soldiers back to Starvale.

That task complete, I set out to do what my orders commanded, now short two men.

Within a week, you might guess who arrived in town to speak with me.

It was, of course, your trusted Calvor.

He came on a day of bitter cold and biting wind. All of Veritas was tucked quietly away. Not a whisper had been heard of the girl in question since I'd seen her in that alleyway. In truth, I was certain that she'd taken my good advice and fled. A wise fae takes wise counsel, and here she'd done what I'd suggested. Fear might have made her listen, but it was clever indeed of her not to chance my sincerity.

Calvor stepped into the inn, his dark eyes sliding over the patrons who were huddled around the fires, trying to keep whatever warmth at hand that they could. His entry let in a cold wind, and I felt the drink in my hand chill as I stared at his silhouette, framed in the entry, for a moment longer than it took me to realize it was him.

"Master Calvor," I said, rising. My men rose as well, upon recognition. How could we not, knowing who he was? The shock was seeing him this far out, so distant from your court. Calvor was hardly a man known for leaving the corridors of power and walking in the hinterlands such as these, especially given the wintry disposition of the neutral territory. No true servant of Summer could have found comfort in Veritas that day.

And I certainly did not.

"Outside. Now," Calvor commanded with clipped disinterest, holding the door wide. The patrons of the inn continued to shake as the cold seemed to invade the inn like Winter's own army, battling back any offensive mounted by the hearth fires. "Only you," he said, pointing at me as two of my trusted lieutenants made to follow.

I looked to my men, granting reassurance with a glance. "I shall return shortly."

And I followed Calvor out into the snow.

"Show me where it happened," he said, his head lacking any armor against the freezing cold. His boots crunched in the snow and mine seemed to pick up a chill the moment I stepped outside. Without word, I led him around the corner to the alley where it had happened and nodded at the place where the body had lain. There was hardly a spot to mark it, now, a small indentation in the snow was all that remained after the passage of a week and a modest snowfall.

"It was here," I said, but he was already past me and looking at the spot where the body had come to rest.

"Tell me what happened," he said, staring at the place where it had happened.

I did not protest. "I heard a scream. Came out to find Vexo clashing with a local girl—"

"A whore," Calvor said, not looking up.

"I don't believe so, no," I said. "She was dressed modestly enough, and did not seem interested remotely in his overtures, for money or any other compensation."

Calvor stood with his back to me like a shadow, then turned, his gaze hard. "You must accept that she was a harlot. One who wronged Lieutenant Vexo, entrancing him with her wiles, and that done, turning upon him to cause his death."

I froze, and it had nothing to do with the weather. "That … is not what I believe I witnessed."

Calvor let out a small snort. "You 'believe'?" He took a step toward me, eyes colder than the wind from across the border. "Let me tell you what I believe. I believe that you must be mistaken. That what you think you saw cannot be what you actually saw." He stepped closer, and a thin smile appeared on his lips. "Lieutenant Vexo, you see, comes from an honorable family. My family. He is—was—my son. My only son."

I straightened. "I … did not know that."

"No one was to know," Calvor said, eyes slitting as he

stared at me. "Vexo wished it so. He wanted to be … how do you say it? 'One of the boys.' Wanted to make his own way in the world, in the army, to advance on his merit, not his name. Foolish, I told him. 'Tis not what you know, but who. He listened not at all, of course, but … I kept the rough hand out of his affairs, and used a silken touch. A whispered word here, a delicate mention there. This was to be a plum assignment—high profile, low risk. Winter hasn't moved against us in years, after all, especially not on these borders." His jaw quivered. "He was to be safe here." His eyes flicked to the spot in the snow where his son had rested.

"I … am sorry, Master Calvor," I said. Truly, of course.

"Let me tell you how this must go, Paladin Lockwood," Calvor said. "I do not give a feather nor a wing for how you must twist your words, but this story you have told?" He produced my parchment letter from beneath his coat. "It will not be allowed to stand. Do you hear me?" He leaned in closer to my face, hot, stinking breath carrying a hint of alcohol. "You will not smear the memory of my only child, my only son, with this."

"I … I cannot lie," I said.

How utterly naïve I was.

"I am not asking you to lie," Calvor said, grinding each word out from between gritted teeth. "I am asking you to realize the truth. The girl was a Winter agent, a probable whore. She likely crossed the border to gather information about your mission here. When Vexo saw through—"

I was shaking my head. "There was no deceit in her, only fear—"

"I will not have my legacy ruined by some jumped-up tramp in a fleaspeck village!" Calvor was shouting now and his voice echoed in the alley. He lowered it. "My son may have died, but you will not dishonor his name and mine, paladin." He was looking me right in the eye now. "There are alternate explanations for what has happened. You will acquaint yourself with them, and you will write one—subject to my approval to replace …" He lifted my letter in his hand. "*This.*"

With a snap of his fingers, my letter burst into flames.

"Stay out here for as long as it takes you to open your mind to the possibilities I have mentioned," Calvor said, sweeping past me, his coat tails drifting along behind him. "You will not return to court until you've accepted what really happened here …" He did not look back. "… Even if it means staying until your blood freezes and your bones crack with cold."

And with that, he left me to dwell on my thoughts. Which I did, for almost a minute.

That done, I left the village of Veritas and went into exile, knowing that so long as Master Calvor was in your service … I could not be.

Chapter 40

I listened to Lockwood finish his tale, wide-eyed, watching the Queen of Summer as she seemed to take it all in. It was hard to tell if she was listening intently; her shoulders were still on fire, and she was still as large as a giant. There was a smell of rose petals on the wind that blew gently from behind her, and the feeling of the sun shining above in glamour was radiating off my exposed arms and making my hair feel just a touch hot.

"Wow," I said, "that's a heck of a story. It has everything, really. Court intrigue. Attempted lies—"

"There is only one liar here," came a voice to my right, appearing out of a rank of soldiers that had seemingly materialized out of nowhere, "and it is you, Iron Bearer."

Damn. Roseus. And he'd brought a good portion of the army with him.

"This from the guy who confessed that he was glad Lockwood went into exile," I said as Roseus stepped forward, a few soldiers behind him fanning out to surround us in a half moon, their weapons held up. "Or do you not recall talking about how thrilled you were about your promotions in his absence?"

Roseus's gaze flitted to the queen for just a second, as though testing her reaction. "My queen, I will see this matter dealt with for you. I apologize it was not done before." He grimaced. "It would appear that if you want your orders carried you, you have to do it yourself."

I blinked. "Yeah, on Earth we just say, 'You can't hire good help these days.'"

I took a step back as Lockwood came forward. He raised his spear. "You have dishonored us both with your ambitions, Roseus," he said.

"You did neither of us any favors with your lack thereof," Roseus said, and with the motion of his weapon, his solders sprang into action, striking.

Lockwood moved as best he could, clashing with two of them, then directing his offensive onto Roseus himself, who met it with a grunt, just barely blocking Lockwood's attack.

Another soldier, this one with red eyes, came at me sideways. He would not miss, I realized a little too late.

A spear blocked his attack, and Orianna's wings flittered in front of me. "If you could just … try and finish this out satisfactorily?" she asked, straining to hold back the soldier and failing, forced to give way and come at him again sideways out of a spin. "That would be a lot more helpful than just standing around making us defend you."

"Maybe if I had a weapon, I could do something," I said as Orianna drew off the red-eyed soldier's attack to my right and Lockwood tied up Roseus and four of his soldiers to my left. There was a mighty clash of weapons, and here I stood, in the middle of it all, feeling about as helpless as when Byron was tormenting me.

I looked to the one source of hope I could see—

"Queen of Summer," I said, looking into her pensive eyes, "please. You have heard the truth now. Surely—"

"I have heard the words of a paladin disgraced," the queen said, her eyes hardly moving, but sliding off of me nonetheless. "Now … I think I wish to see the truth of his actions."

"Uh … what does that mean?" I asked, as Orianna continued to strain under the withering assault of the red-eyed soldier and Lockwood fell back amid the onslaught from Roseus and his lackeys. "You're just gonna … sit back and see who wins?"

The Queen of Summer said nothing, but she raised her head so that all I could see was her chin.

She wasn't even watching anymore.

"Oh, for crying out—" I started to say, but someone slammed into me from behind.

I landed face-first on the ground. It was hard and rocky and split my lip. The sting didn't even have a moment to fade before someone laid rough hands on my shoulder, yanking me up and around, my dazed eyes staring into furious ones that looked past me—

Calvor.

"Your hope is finished, Paladin Lockwood," Calvor said, dragging me by the remnants of my dress's neckline. "You see what you have wrought here, by your intransigence? Nothing. Justice will still be settled, as it should have been that day in Veritas. You could have ended it by staying in that alley, keeping your mouth shut, letting Winter claim a victim."

"The only victim it would have claimed," Lockwood said, ceasing his attack against Roseus and his guards, "would have been the truth."

"The truth is a matter of perspective," Calvor said, smiling thinly. He knew he had Lockwood, because he had me.

My face ached, my lips hurt, split open. Blood dribbled down my chin. I could see Orianna, also stopped in her fight, holding her weapon out defensively, the red-eyed soldier opposite her, waiting for Calvor's command.

And he was waiting with me in his grip, ready to strike a killing blow if either of them resisted.

"The truth …" I said, staring up at him, utterly defeated, blood hot and tangy in my mouth, "… lies in the dark."

Calvor cocked his head, looking down at me. "What did you say?"

"I said …" and tasted my own blood, "… the truth … lies …" on my lips, so warm and metallic …

Metallic?

"… in …"

Right. Because in science class, they taught you that human blood had …

"… the …"

Iron.

"… dark."

I was an Iron Bearer.

Calvor opened his mouth to say something, but I didn't wait to hear what it was. I summoned up the vision of every pro baseball game I'd ever seen my dad watch, and spat a very unladylike glob of blood right in Master Calvor's face.

It caught him in the eyes, and he blinked in surprise. "What do—"

That was all he got out before the iron in my blood started to work on him.

Human blood couldn't have had much iron content to it, but apparently faeries were incredibly sensitive to it, because steam started to pour from his face a second later, and he screamed to the heavens a moment after that.

Calvor stumbled away from me, dropping his sword, which I snatched up. He screamed and screamed, and finally hit his knees, writhing in agony. When he lifted his fingers up from his face …

I almost threw up.

It was … horrible.

Lockwood swept aside the weapons of three of the guards, planting his spear into Roseus's chest. Roseus stared at him, silver oozing out between the general's fingers, eyes wide and planted on Lockwood. "It would appear your ambitions have led you far astray, Roseus."

Roseus clenched his hand over the wound as Lockwood pulled the weapon out. The soldiers who had been guarding him a moment earlier made no move to stop him, still riveted in horror by what I'd done to Calvor. Their eyes were wide with fear, frozen in place.

Calvor's screams died a moment later, with him, and silence fell. I listened and realized that the noise of the battlefield, too, had faded.

I looked to my right, and where the armies had stood a moment before, the dais of the Winter Queen and King now lay, as though they'd emerged from some deep fog to simply appear. I stared at them, saw a flicker—

The Queen of Winter's hands glowed blue …

Like the shield that had protected me from Ignes's magical

attacks.

Had they been there all along, listening? Watching?

Helping me?

"Is this matter settled to your satisfaction now, Queen of Summer?" Pruina asked. She truly did have a cold majesty to her, radiating off her like a chill. Something about it was far more reassuring to me at the moment than the glamour of the sunny skies overhead.

The Queen of Summer deigned to look down, her eyes still full and dark. "It is done. If not to my satisfaction, it has at least reached some end which will settle." The scene flashed, and I caught a glimpse again of the dark-haired crone beneath her illusions. "Do not imagine me weak for this, Pruina—"

"Then do not act weak now," the King of Summer said, loud enough to be heard by all present.

She quelled him with a look, then turned her attention back to the Queen of Winter. "Do we have an understanding? Or shall we continue?"

Pruina waited only a moment, long enough to convince me she was trying not to leap all over the offer the Summer Queen had made her. "For my part, I am quite done," Pruina said, adjusting her crown.

"Then we are finished here," the Queen of Summer said.

And with that, she stood, and the illusion of tall trees and greenery and the meadow seemed to fade as she receded into the distance, as though she—and the war—had never been here at all.

Chapter 41

The slow fade of Summer's grip left me feeling a slight chill, but that, too, disappeared in a few seconds, and with the next flicker, I saw that the blue magic that had been coming off Queen Pruina's hands had faded. She seemed closer to us, now, lingering at a short distance, her hands now at her sides, and one being held by her king.

"Well, that was an ordeal," Orianna said, throwing down her spear and letting out a slow breath now that the Summer soldiers had disappeared. She ran a hand over the ruin of her own dress, then looked at mine, and I could almost see her deciding hers was in better shape, as though that was some sort of accomplishment.

"Yeah," I said, dabbing at my still-bleeding lip. "I gotta be honest—this has not been my favorite vacation ever. This barely rises above that time I got a stomach flu in the Poconos, actually."

"You're hurt," Lockwood said, coming over to me, all concern now that the threat was removed.

"Whoa," I said, holding up a hand to keep him away, careful not to touch him. "I've got a real anti-faerie biohazard going on here, Lockwood. You don't want to be too close to me right now. One good sneeze and you'll end up like …" I waved a hand at the corpse of Calvor, which looked … I shuddered. Revolting was not a strong enough word for it. He'd lost his entire face, and there wasn't a glamour in Faerie that could make *that* look right.

"Thank you," Lockwood said, keeping a careful distance. "But your worries are unnecessary. Here." He waved his hand, and a warm wash of liquid ran down my face like a summer rain. It made me blink a few times, and when it was finished …

I looked down. The grass was dead, and my blood was kind of … eating into the ground.

"Uh … guys?" I asked.

"I'll take care of it," Lockwood said, staring at it in mild concern. Another flourish of his fingers and there was a flash, and the ground stopped steaming and hissing at my feet.

"Did you actually take care of it?" I asked. "Or did you use a glamour to paper over it?" I set my hands on my hips. "Is that going to eat through the ground to Faerie China, surprising the hell out of some innocent farmer when his rice paddy turns violently acidic?"

"No," Lockwood said. "I magicked your blood out of existence. It will not eat into the ground." He shuffled his feet. "And there is no 'Faerie China' beneath us. This world is flat."

"There's a whole society on Earth who would be so jazzed to hear more about that," I said. "Me? I've had about enough of Faerie, flat or otherwise."

"I am sorry to hear this, Cassandra," Queen Pruina said, making her way over to us with a flutter of her wings. The king and the court remained behind, circled around her dais under the grey sky. "You are the first human to come to our world in quite some time. I should like to have shown you our hospitality and the beauty of our world rather than having you become embroiled in seeing the worst of us."

"I'm a teenager, so I'm not a big stranger to being introduced to the worst aspects of stuff," I said. "I mean, mine is the Beanboozled generation, so …" I shrugged. "A magical war of fae involving treachery and near death? I'm getting used to this crazy stuff going on around me." I looked down at my dress. "Besides, for like a minute there, it was almost fun."

The queen seemed to get what I was saying, a little smile

popping up on her lips. She waved her fingers—

And my dress was whole once more, with silvery highlights like she'd threaded winter snows into the fabric.

"Well, gosh, that kinda turns the disappointment around a little," I said, admiring my dress. "Nice shoes, too." I looked down at my heels. Perfectly comfortable.

"I believe they might even last the transition back to your world," the queen said, looking me over appraisingly. "It is … the least I can do, given what you have done for us."

"Well, it wouldn't have been possible if you hadn't sent Orianna along to help," I said.

Orianna grimaced. "You weren't ever supposed to know that I was anything other than a ditzy tag-along."

"You've done a marvelous job of playing ditzy and tagging along," I said. "But let's face it—under pressure, the truth was bound to come out. And we … definitely experienced some pressure, between the whole pilgrimage to Starvale, the craziness along the way, and … y'know prison and imminent execution. That tends to powder keg the truth of things right out." I mimed an explosion.

The queen shook her head. "It would have been a shame if a war were to begin for no reason, and the only Seelie witness that knew and could speak the truth had been killed before he had the chance to bring it before his people."

"I'm a little fuzzy on how you knew that, though," I said, staring at her.

She raised an eyebrow at me. "Paladin Lockwood was hardly the only one who knew what happened in that alleyway on that eve. That Master Calvor took his bitterness and rage for his son's own acts and turned them against my kingdom? Hardly surprising … if you knew Calvor."

"I did not know Calvor," Lockwood said quietly. "Not truly. Perhaps if I had confronted him, in the court, about this, after it happened—"

"You would have died on the way," Pruina said, looking at him with absolute conviction. "He would not have allowed you to speak that truth, and you would not have seen your end coming. Indeed … there was no way, nor any reason for it to come out until now. Things between Winter and

Summer have been unsteady, true—but until war was on its way—"

"Ohhhh," I said, slapping my hand on my forehead. "It was you, wasn't it?"

Pruina smiled slightly, though it was somewhere between a grimace and a smile.

"What?" Lockwood asked, his neck straight. "What was—?"

"The pixies," I said, "the ones that attacked the car. You were the one who sent them."

The queen's eyes grew a little sad. "Yes. I regret any harm that might have befallen you, but … there was a war. People were dying. The truth needed to be told, and it could come from no one else."

Lockwood nodded, though there was a weariness about him. "You forced me out of exile."

"And sent help to make sure—as best I could—that you made it to your appointment with the Summer Court," she said. "I am sorry I could not provide more, but … we were trying to ready for a war that looked all but impossible to stop."

Lockwood let out a low sigh. "I have found, of late … that when one wants the impossible done, Lady Cassandra is the person to call."

"I—what?" I turned on Lockwood. "I—did not do this. At least not most of it. This was you, Lockwood. I just … cleared a little bit of space for you to speak up."

"And speak you did. You have made enemies in the Summer Court on this day," Queen Pruina pointed out. "Though they will not say so."

"It was the dyed hair comment, wasn't it?" I asked. "That was probably a little over the top, I'll admit."

The queen's stern face softened ever so slightly, and I could see the hint of laughter in her eyes for just a second, and then it disappeared. "You told the truth that they did not want to hear, and that is enough for them to hate you." She reached out a hand across the feet between us, and I felt her cool fingers brush my cheek, just briefly. "You have done this land a great service, Cassandra. It will not be forgotten."

With a subtle nod to Lockwood, she receded, just as the

Summer Queen had, drifting away as Winter frost seemed to follow along behind her.

"I did not expect that from her," Lockwood said softly, watching her go. "Not after … all these years."

"Because you always hated Winter?" I asked.

"They taught me to," Lockwood said. "Taught me they were nothing but liars. Perhaps …" And here he turned to look at Orianna. "Perhaps … I have learned wrongly."

"Let's not push this any further than it needs to go," Orianna said, rolling her eyes. "You're Seelie, I'm Unseelie, but let's be honest—we wouldn't like each other even if we were the same. Because you're a giant dullard, Lockwood, and so serious."

I snickered under my breath.

"And you are entirely flippant and irritating," he said, with a hint of a smile. "I shan't miss you."

"Nor I, you," Orianna said brightly. "Fare thee well, paladin of Summer."

"You as well, spy of Winter," Lockwood said.

Orianna turned to me. "You, though … I might miss. Just a little."

I raised an eyebrow at her. "Really?"

"Yes, really," she said. "Are you done bleeding? Because I don't want to die horribly."

"I think so," I said, feeling my face. "I mean, it seems like—"

She shot forward on flittering wings, wrapping her arms around my neck. "I didn't know what to think of you at first, you know? I didn't know you were human, because I couldn't believe that Lockwood would be mad enough to bring someone over from Earth, but …" She raised up to look at me, taking her head off my shoulder. "Now I'm glad he was out of his head. Because otherwise I wouldn't have been able to watch the villain's face melt off, and if there was anyone who deserved that, it was scheming Calvor."

"Uh … thanks, I guess." I didn't know what else to say to that.

Orianna laughed, and it sounded a little wicked. "Take care of yourself, little …" her eyes moved around as she reconsidered, "… human."

"You too, Orianna," I said, and she brushed my hand with hers as she pulled away.

And with a flutter of her wings, and the tiniest of winks, she, too, was gone, like the queen.

Chapter 42

The war was over. The truth was told. I'd insulted a queen's natural hair color.

"Heck of a trip," I muttered, just me and Lockwood left standing where there'd once been a tent, once been a battlefield, once been the courts of two opposing kingdoms. Now it just looked like a beaten-up meadow, all the glamour—in both senses of the word—gone out of it. It looked more like a campground after a festival back on earth than any of the magical scenery I'd come to expect from Faerie.

And honestly … that made it the best place I'd been since I'd gotten here.

"What are you thinking?" Lockwood asked. He did not meet my eyes.

"I think you just heard it," I said, taking a breath of air, smelling the dirt lingering in it from all the fae who'd presumably flown through and disturbed it.

"That's all?" Now Lockwood looked me in the eye. "After all this, the only thing you come up with is 'Heck of a trip'?" He looked away again. "Nothing about … me, the one who drew you into this, who nearly got you killed, who …" He performed a very thorough examination of his muddied boots, "… Who didn't trust you with the truth."

"I'm kinda the last person who should be bagging on anyone for withholding the truth," I said, easing over to him and plopping a hand on his shoulder. I tried to make it really casual.

He snapped his head up in surprise anyway. "Truly? You don't think … less of me?"

"Lockwood, you've saved my life more times than I can count," I said, "and up until now, you've never put it in peril. As long as you don't make a habit of this … yeah, I don't think any less of you. And even if I did, my opinion of you is so high that even you fae couldn't reach it if you flapped your wings as hard as you could." I winked.

He let out a long, slow breath, and I recognized his relief. "That is … very kind of you."

"Well, I've learned a lot while I've been here," I said. "And the things I learned … I saw a lot of myself in the Court of Summer, and not in a good way." I frowned. "I've been lying my whole life, and I thought Florida was my chance to start fresh with my parents. When the whole paranormal world came busting in on me, I used it as an excuse not to tell the truth to my parents because … well, I figured there was no way they'd believe me. Now, I don't know what was going on in your head during this trip, but I suspect it was something similar—"

"It was," Lockwood said. "My walking away from the truth in that alley felt like a grand departure from courage. It felt like cowardice, masked under the excuse that …" He bowed his head. "'No one would believe me'."

"So very familiar," I said. "I would have believed you. I do … believe you."

"I know you would," he said. "I suppose I was trying to protect you. And also … that after keeping a secret for so very, very long … it becomes a bit difficult to part with it. The words do not come easily."

"Well, I'm glad they showed up when they did," I said, rubbing his shoulder. "Because I don't think the queen was going to show us any mercy or even let us fight it out for ourselves until she heard what you said."

"I expect not," he said.

"So … what now?" I asked, looking around.

"Now … I should take you home," Lockwood said, beckoning me forward. "This way, about thirty steps."

I frowned, but followed. "Why thirty steps?"

"Earth does not seamlessly connect with Faerie," he said. "There are certain areas where I simply cannot cross us back. The magic here is strong from the war, but a little farther." He reached a spot of empty field, and seemed to brighten. "Ah, yes. Here."

"Wait," I said, looking around. "What are you going to do … after you take me home?"

He blinked, and a little grey sadness crept in around his eyes. "I will return to my house, of course, because …" He forced a smile. "I cannot return to Seelie, even after … all this."

"Why not?" I asked. "Didn't the truth … set you free?"

"Free, yes," he said, still smiling sadly, "but … it did not free me of the consequences of my actions. As the Queen of Winter said … now we have enemies here. But it's all right." He stepped a little closer. "I rather enjoy Earth, all things considered." And his smile grew a little wider as he scooped me up into his arms. There was a great rush of color and light around us, and then the magical world of Faerie faded away.

Chapter 43

Before I'd left my room, it would have seemed to me that the mundane world of the humans could not possibly compare to the glamour and magic in Faerie.

Wrong.

I couldn't have been happier to be back on Earth.

I snapped back in as though I'd never left, into my familiar room that smelled of lavender and vanilla. I took a deep breath as Lockwood set me down.

Everything was just as I left it. My bed was a crumpled mess of blankets. The tea that I'd made was still steaming on my bedside table, probably way over steeped now. There was a pile of clothes on the floor of my closet from changing three times before school that morning.

"Holy cow … we made it back." I whispered to him, looking around.

My eyes fell on the little ceramic unicorn on my dresser, and it made me smile. I crossed over to it and picked it up, turning it over in my hands. "I wish I could have seen a unicorn properly … without that weird flickering vision power thing."

Lockwood gave me a sympathetic smile. "Next time, perhaps?" He paused. "On that note...I think I may have an explanation for your ability to see beyond the glamours of Faerie – if you'd like to hear it.

"Sure." The room dipped slightly and I hastened back to the bed to sit down again. "Whoa. Feeling a bit dizzy."

"It's those return symptoms I mentioned." Lockwood looked apologetic. "It shouldn't last very long."

I blinked. "I think it's already a little better." I nodded at him reassuringly. It didn't matter if I was dizzy or caught a cold or whatever. It only mattered that I was back where I belonged.

"Right, well...you recall the avara, yes?" Lockwood asked, eyes focused on mine as I gave him a nod of concurrence. "They were men who, through the magic Faerie, became reflective of their true nature after time spent in the world. I believe your ability to see beyond was a similar manifestation of the world's magic working upon you-"

"Because I am – I was – a liar," I said, feeling a little chill wash over me.

He gave a subtle nod. "Exactly."

My mouth felt a little dry. "What...what would I have become if I'd stayed in Faerie? As a liar, I mean?"

Lockwood stiffened uncomfortably, and looked away. "I don't know. But..." He looked right at me, for a second, green eyes dampened in their enthusiasm by what he was telling me. "I expect it would not have been good."

"Cassandra!" Mom's voice pierced the air before I had a chance to answer, and my stomach plummeted. Hard to tell which caused it to dive worse; Mom's yell or the knowledge that if I'd stayed in Faerie...

I would have become something else entirely. Some monster on the order of the avara.

And all because of who I was.

Because of the choices I made...to lie.

Lockwood's eyes grew wide at my mother's shout, but he placed a finger to his lips. With a wink, he flew out the window.

I ran after him, both hands smacking the sill as I peered out into the night.

But he was gone.

"Tricky Seelie," I whispered into the humid night air. It felt so … heavy, so real after the magical lightness of Faerie.

It was so good to be back.

"Cassandra!"

I turned my back on the window, hurrying over to the door and pulling it open. "Yeah, Mom?"

She said something too quiet for me to hear. Obviously not to me. Presumably to Dad.

I sighed. Probably complaining about my lack of a response. "Yes, Mom?" I asked, a little louder.

"Get down here." Her voice carrying up the stairs. Her tone meant business.

Wait, was I wrong? Had we been gone longer than I thought?

What was I walking into?

I rubbed my hands over my face, tiredness of the last few days like a shroud blanketing itself over me. I looked at my newly-spruced up gown and shrugged, sliding it off in a hurry. I grabbed a sweatshirt and slid into it, kicking off my beautiful shoes of faerie magic. I caught a glimpse of myself in the mirror.

Back to normal, I thought, as I tossed aside the gown in favor of a pair of jeans. I headed for the stairs, buttoning them as I went, not eager to make her wait any longer.

As I descended, I tried to refresh my memory. What had been going on the night that Lockwood and I left? Had Mom been angry with me?

Oh, yeah ... I'd been late coming home from school because of the car accident. I'd caught hell, and was now exiled to my room. Where I'd totally been for like ... minutes before the Faerie excursion. Definitely living up to the terms of my parentally imposed punishment.

Except ... I really hadn't. Not that they'd know, but ... a little feeling gnawed in my belly. I'd been gone for days, absolutely violating the "Stay in your room" doctrine. There wasn't anything much I could do about that, though ...

Right?

I wondered if the sudden exhaustion that was making my eyelids feel like they were made of lead was because I was fae-lagged ... Lockwood had sort of warned me that it would happen. I had been awake for at least a whole day by now. When had I slept last? When we were camping before we even reached Seelie territory?

I saw Mom standing in the kitchen as I reached the bottom stair. She didn't look as angry as she sounded. As I padded across the hardwood floor toward the kitchen, she turned to look at me, and gave me the most Mom look that she could.

It wasn't because she was angry, but she was definitely annoyed. I had done something wrong, obviously. It couldn't have been the Faerie trip, could it? How would she have known …?

I came around the corner and saw Dad sitting in one of the barstools in front of the kitchen island, turned and looking into the living room. Maybe the television was on? But I couldn't hear it.

Maybe something awful had happened on the news. Tampa was pretty safe, but that didn't mean that it didn't have its fair share of murders and other crimes. Maybe it had something to do with one of Mom's cases at her firm, or one of Dad's patients from the hospital.

Maybe my school was blown up. Maybe dinner had blown up. I mean, it smelled fine, but there was no telling what might have happened in the minutes I'd been gone. Dad could have accidentally nuked it. He'd done it before.

But as I came around the corner into the kitchen and looked into the living room, I froze, my heart leaping into my throat.

Mill was standing there.

In my house.

In front of my parents.

I stared at him, and he stared at me, and suddenly …

I understood what was happening.

He had been talking to my parents. And I didn't have to think very hard to know about what. Why else would he reveal himself like this?

The blood was rushing in my ears, so loud I couldn't even hear my heart beating. Though I was sure it was thundering right now. Mill could probably hear it all the way across the room.

He was staring at me with a sort of sad, sympathetic look. It's like he thought that he was doing something good that I wouldn't understand. Throwing himself on some unseen sword.

"Mill came by a little while ago," Mom said. It was *really* weird hearing her say his name. "We've been having a very pleasant talk."

I shot him a look. "Oh?" My look said something different: *Why did you come here?*

I wiped my sweaty hands on the side of my pants. "Okay …?" I asked. I gave them room to tell me. Standard practice for dealing with a lie—let the person you're talking to set the expectations. That let you lie accordingly in response.

"He came to tell us about the accident this afternoon," Dad said, his eyes turning to look at me above his glasses, like I was a patient who needed to lose weight but lived on a diet of gummy bears and Pepsi.

"He said he picked you up from school, and that the accident happened just before he dropped you off," Mom said, folding her arms across her chest and giving Mill an appreciative nod.

I looked at each of them in turn, waiting. Letting them set those expectations. I half figured they'd say something about pixies? Or that he was a vampire, but …

Obviously he wouldn't tell them that.

"Why didn't you tell us what happened?" Mom asked me. She looked so serious.

I looked down at my arms, and I couldn't see the scratches from the accident anymore. They had faded while I was in Faerie.

"I just didn't … I just—"

"Cass, Mill told us that you two have been dating for a little while," Dad said in a gentler voice.

Fear and relief both hit me at once. Fear of the wrath that was sure to follow—and relief to have it finally out in the open.

"He said he wanted to be honest about your relationship." Mom's face tightened as she spoke. "That he didn't want you to have to hide it anymore. He knew how much of a strain it was putting on you to keep it from us."

I looked over at Mill, and he was watching me, trying to gauge my reaction.

He had done something infuriating but … kind of adorable. He had somehow managed to make life simultaneously harder and better for me.

"He also brought dinner," Mom added, with a small smile. "Which we kind of need because Dad burned the chicken … again."

Dad hung his head, rubbing the back of his neck nervously. "Some day I will learn to use the oven for good and not evil … but it is not this day."

"Why don't we all sit down at the table?" Mom asked, gesturing toward the dining room.

As we walked in, the smell of garlic reached my nostrils, strong and making my mouth water. I was surprised I hadn't noticed it before, and looked at Mill in question. *Did you really bring something with garlic?*

He just shrugged and smiled. A vampire boyfriend with a giant sense of irony.

Mill was here. My parents knew we were dating.

And we were all about to sit down together and have a family dinner with my vampire boyfriend. After I'd just returned from the magical world of Faerie.

My life was really something since I'd moved to Florida.

I slid into my seat, and Mill sat down beside me. Dad took his place at the head of the table, and Mom at hers across from me. I looked at the veritable feast before us; there was pizza, salad, and steaming garlic knots. They had a delicious, greasy sort of shine in the light, and I caught Mill's cringe out of the corner of my eye from just being this close to them.

"So, Cassie," Mom started, spooning salad on her plate. She gave me a surprisingly gentle look, only a little scrutinizing. "Mill told us you've been dating for a few weeks?"

I stared at the food before me and realized … I was so not hungry. I nodded my head, trying to resist the feeling that I was going to melt into the floor. My head was spinning, but the up-down motion of the nod helped. It was easier than using my words, anyways.

"And that you met at school?"

I hesitated.

That … was a lie.

I froze, just sitting there, my parents watching, Mill silently egging me on. He brushed my elbow, and I just …

Kept.

Staring.

Because I just … I couldn't do this anymore.

After everything … after the Summer Court, the queen, Calvor and Roseus … Byron and the Instaphoto gang, and even everything that I went through when I was in New York …

All of my troubles revolved around lies that I either told myself, or that were told to me.

Lying. Lies. Half-truths. Hiding things.

Every single problem I'd faced in these last few months … had come from lies.

And I just couldn't do it anymore.

So, with everyone watching, I opened up my mouth …

To finally tell the truth.

Cassie Howell will return in

HER LYING DAYS ARE DONE

Liars and Vampires
Book 5

Coming September 18, 2018!

Author's Note

Thanks for reading! If you want to know immediately when future books become available, take sixty seconds and sign up for my NEW RELEASE EMAIL ALERTS by visiting my website. I don't sell your information and I only send out emails when I have a new book out. The reason you should sign up for this is because I don't always set release dates, and even if you're following me on Facebook (robertJcrane (Author)) or Twitter (@robertJcrane), it's easy to miss my book announcements because...well, because social media is an imprecise thing.

Come join the discussion on my website:
http://www.robertjcrane.com!

Cheers,
Robert J. Crane

ACKNOWLEDGMENTS

Editing by Sarah Barbour in her antepenultimate editing performance.

Proofing by Lillie of Lillie's Literary Service (https://lilliesls.wordpress.com) and Jo Evans of Raj of India.

Cover by Karri Klawiter (artbykarri.com).

Co-authoring by Kate Hasbrouck.

Formatting by Nick Bowman (http://www.nickbowman-editing.com)

Sanity NOT by Robert J. Crane's family. But I love them anyway.

Other Works by Robert J. Crane

The Girl in the Box *and* Out of the Box
Contemporary Urban Fantasy

World of Sanctuary
Epic Fantasy

Defender: The Sanctuary Series, Volume One
Avenger: The Sanctuary Series, Volume Two
Champion: The Sanctuary Series, Volume Three
Crusader: The Sanctuary Series, Volume Four
Sanctuary Tales, Volume One - A Short Story Collection
Thy Father's Shadow: The Sanctuary Series, Volume 4.5
Master: The Sanctuary Series, Volume Five
Fated in Darkness: The Sanctuary Series, Volume 5.5
Warlord: The Sanctuary Series, Volume Six
Heretic: The Sanctuary Series, Volume Seven
Legend: The Sanctuary Series, Volume Eight
Ghosts of Sanctuary: The Sanctuary Series, Volume Nine
Call of the Hero: The Sanctuary Series, Volume Ten* *(Coming Late 2018!)*

A Haven in Ash: Ashes of Luukessia, Volume One *(with Michael Winstone)*
A Respite From Storms: Ashes of Luukessia, Volume Two *(with Michael Winstone)*
A Home in the Hills: Ashes of Luukessia, Volume Three* *(with Michael Winstone—Coming Mid to Late 2018!)*

Southern Watch
Contemporary Urban Fantasy

Called: Southern Watch, Book 1
Depths: Southern Watch, Book 2
Corrupted: Southern Watch, Book 3
Unearthed: Southern Watch, Book 4
Legion: Southern Watch, Book 5
Starling: Southern Watch, Book 6
Forsaken: Southern Watch, Book 7
Hallowed: Southern Watch, Book 8* *(Coming Late 2018/Early 2019!)*

The Shattered Dome Series
(with Nicholas J. Ambrose)
Sci-Fi

Voiceless: The Shattered Dome, Book 1
Unspeakable: The Shattered Dome, Book 2* *(Coming 2018!)*

The Mira Brand Adventures
Contemporary Urban Fantasy

The World Beneath: The Mira Brand Adventures, Book 1
The Tide of Ages: The Mira Brand Adventures, Book 2
The City of Lies: The Mira Brand Adventures, Book 3
The King of the Skies: The Mira Brand Adventures, Book 4
The Best of Us: The Mira Brand Adventures, Book 5
We Aimless Few: The Mira Brand Adventures, Book 6* *(Coming 2018!)*

Liars and Vampires
(with Lauren Harper)
Contemporary Urban Fantasy

No One Will Believe You: Liars and Vampires, Book 1
Someone Should Save Her: Liars and Vampires, Book 2
You Can't Go Home Again: Liars and Vampires, Book 3
In The Dark: Liars and Vampires, Book 4
Her Lying Days Are Done: Liars and Vampires, Book 5* *(Coming August 2018!)*
Heir of the Dog: Liars and Vampires, Book 6* *(Coming September 2018!)*
Hit You Where You Live: Liars and Vampires, Book 7* *(Coming October 2018!)*

* Forthcoming, Subject to Change